THE BOYS FROM IRELAND

An Irish Immigrant Family's Involvement in America's Civil War

Neil W. Moloney

PublishAmerica
Baltimore

First printing

Softcover 9781627092555
PUBLISHED BY PUBLISHAMERICA, LLLP
www.publishamerica.com
Baltimore

Printed in the United States of America

ACKNOWLEDGEMENTS

Although this work is a fictional account of an Irish family's migration to the United States during the time of the American Civil War it is in part, based upon the stories about that journey as told by subsequent generations and passed on to family members. In researching this story the author wishes to acknowledge the work of some wonderful people in Rushford and Caledonia, Minnesota, New York City, and in the State of Washington and in Saskatchewan Canada who helped in collecting the historical documents used in laying the groundwork for this work. Ms. Anne Spartz, Rushford, Minnesota provided the author information from the Rushford Area Historical Society and from Saint Joseph's Catholic Church in Rushford MN. Angela Murphy in Caledonia MN provided valuable information from the archives of the Houston County Historical Society; this data helped immensely in telling the real story about the principal characters of this story.

In addition, the author wishes to thank Debra J. Richardson, Director Fillmore County History Center, & Genealogy Library at Fountain, Minnesota and Mr. David U'Ren, Administrator of Saint Joseph's Catholic church, in the City of Rushford. These folks provided additional information for this work from public archives, and Church records. Some of the public data collected for this work included information on President Lincoln's support for passage of the *Home Stead Act of 1863*, and the Canadian Government's adoption of similar legislation in the *First Dominion Lands Act of 1872.*

The Homestead Act and the Dominion Lands act led to the migration of American Civil War veterans and others to the "Northwestern" U.S. and on into the Prairie Provinces of Western Canada. Many, enticed by the abundance of newspaper stories about the availability of "Free Land," came west by the thousands, some on horseback, others by covered wagon, or canoe.

The author is also indebted to the folks in Plato, Saskatchewan who provided a copy of an official Canadian publication, *Canada One Hundred, 1867 - 1967* and a locally produced document in 1980 titled *Celebrate Saskatchewan.* These books record the real names of many of the principle characters portrayed in this work. Many of these men fought in the American Civil War and when the war ended migrated to the Northwest, (Minnesota, Michigan, Dakota Territories, etc.) and on into Western Canada to claim their portion of this "Free land."

The author must also thank Traci Ann Hollingsworth, and Major Raymond L. Carroll, ret., for correcting the many mistakes the author made in putting this work together, along with the inevitable typing, spelling, and grammatical errors discovered and corrected before this work "Went to Press."

CONTENTS

CHAPTER 1

IRELAND

"Molly, what time is the train from Dublin due in today?" Annie Murphy asked of Molly Sullivan as the two elderly widows enjoyed a cup of tea with their fellow Poorhouse lodgers this beautiful spring morning. The "Old Folks Home" as the Poorhouse was known to their neighbors, overlooked the Great Southern and Western Railway station in the village of Mala in the South of Ireland. "Annie Murphy," Molly Sullivan responded derisively, "Ye are eighty-eight years old and ye have been sitting in that chair for now going on to five years, looking out this same window and watching that train when it arrives everyday but Sunday. Ye know it arrives at noon, but it's never on time. Nevertheless, it always gets here unless the conductor and his crew get drunk or the boys from the 'Movement' blowup the track."

"Oh, it does that, I am sure," Annie Murphy, replied, "but ye have been busy with your chamber duties that the county has imposed upon us in this place and ye have not seen what's happening out there, today. Look at the crowd that is gathering. We have not seen that many people at the station since His Eminence Cardinal Cullen arrived here last year on his annual trek to Cork. What do ye suppose is going on?"

"Didn't ye silly women read the Examiner last week?" Eighty-six year old Dorothy Kennedy, sitting nearby and taking time out of her knitting obligation, interjected her words of wisdom into this discussion. The task of knitting a cap and booties for her last to arrive great great-granddaughter, Cara would have to wait. "The Galway Five boys are due to arrive today," she said. "One of them is my sister Margaret's great grandson Patrick, he's named after my husband, God rest his soul," she added, proud that her Paddy's name would be carried on by her sister's great grandson long after she left this world.

"Oh, I wouldn't be sounding so proud of a great grandson if he was mine and just getting out of the hoosegow." Alice Marlow responded smugly. Her commitment to the Cork County Poor House did nothing to improve the demeanor or attitude of this senile eighty-year old cantankerous widow. Marlow's own family convinced the local magistrate to commit her to the Poor House because they were unable, some said unwilling, to put up with her delusions of grandeur and riotous temper tantrums.

"Alice, be kind." Traci Ryan responded, patiently. "Ye are not with your family now and there is no need to disparage your fellow guests. Most of us know that what happened to those boys was another injustice committed by the Queen's men and they should not have been sent to jail over a call in a rugby game."

"Oh, there ye go again Traci, always blaming the Crown for the mistakes and crimes made by ye Catholic Irish. I wish the hell I were English and I wouldn't be here."

"No, ye wouldn't, Alice, your family would have put ye in the loony bin on the funny farm," Annie Murphy responded with a laugh.

"Now ladies, let's not do this." Traci Ryan scolded. "This is too nice a day to have your little misunderstanding spoil it. The train should be here any minute now. Let's see who gets off."

"I want to see the Malone twins," Alice Marlow said, nodding her head, "Oh if I were only sixty-years younger I would set my hat for either one of them." She smiled.

"Well, by the looks of the crowd out there ye would not have much of a chance, Alice." Molly Sullivan responded, smiling. "Look at all those young girls; they're not there to meet a long-lost relative. Every one of them would like to get their hands on any one of those young men; but if it was me I would like to visit the haystack behind the byre with the McCaffrey boy."

"That would be a splendid choice, Molly. I'd go for him too," Annie Murphy responded with a smile.

"I hear the whistle now; it will be here in a moment."

"I see it."

"Who is that pulling up in the fancy rig? He and his impressive looking horses are blocking our view." Alice Marlow exclaimed angrily. "Knock on the window and get him to move out of the way." She said.

"Calm down ladies, ye know why he is there." Traci Ryan said. "That's Sheriff Solomon Reed's calash and ye can guess who he has come for; it will be for one or all of those boys. He'll probably take each one home and warn their parents that the Crown will not put up with anymore of their shenanigans; he'll threaten to put them back in jail if they give him the slightest excuse."

"Look, he is only taking one of them," Dorothy Kennedy, yelled excitedly. "Is that Patrick?"

"No, Dorothy, calm down, that's not Patrick," Traci responded soothingly, trying to allay the fears of this frail and elderly widow. "There are four and they all look very scruffy and thin, but I think that's Jimmy McCaffrey."

"One of the Malone twins was sent home earlier," Molly Sullivan said. "They say he was at death's door; so frail and sickly looking his own mother did not even know him."

"Yes, I saw him, when the Sheriff took him home." Annie Murphy responded angrily. "What do ye suppose that bugger is going to do with that McCaffrey boy now?"

"Whatever it is, it won't be nice." Molly replied. "It is a good thing that his mother was not here to see her son being carted away again by one of the Crown's worst scoundrels. Reed is a disgrace to the Irish race."

His brothers and sister Katelyn and close friends called him Jimmy. At nineteen he was a good looking young man, tall, nearly six foot, with black curly hair and the beginnings of a dark beard and mustache that belied his age. However, to his mother Mary Katherine McCaffrey he was still James Robert, her first-born son, named after her father James Robert Kennedy. Moreover, as with all eight of her children, she and her husband John named each child after one of Christendom's most celebrated Saints.

James Robert McCaffrey was in fact quite handsome. While tending his landlord's sheep or bringing the family cow in for the evening milking the neighborhood girls always hoped that he would stop and talk to them. Even though some may have rolled down their stockings a bit when he approached or undid a button or two on the top of their blouse or tugged at their skirt to raise a hemline, James Robert paid little heed to these formidable enticements. Still whenever they encountered him, he was always polite and acknowledged each girl with a friendly wave and a smile.

However, the young man that these girls grew up with was no longer the same person they knew at an earlier age at Saint

Joseph's school. This boy lost his innocence at Kilmainham Jail in Dublin where he spent the last two years for assaulting an officer of the Queen's Army. Released just two days ago County Sheriff Solomon Reed brought him home from the train station in the nearby village of Mala.

Prison authorities had released his former cellmate, friend, and cousin Kevin Malone a month early because of illness. At that time Kevin's mother, Margaret sent word to her brother John that James was to be home today. John McCaffrey was standing in his front yard since early morning waiting for his son and the sheriff to arrive. It was past noon when he saw the officer's matching team of splendid Connemara ponies drawing the elaborately emblazoned and official looking calash approaching the farm. He went out on the road to meet them and was thrilled to see his son looking much better than when he visited the boys at Kilmainham nearly two years ago. James jumped out of the carriage and embraced his father.

"Hello Daddy," he said quietly, with both men near tears; John because he was happy that the boy was home with his family once again; and that he arrived in time to see his mother before she died. James however, was struggling to hold back the tears, for he hardly recognized his father. The man's pitiful physical appearance, left no doubt that he suffered from a critical ailment. The boy was accustomed to the ravages of death from within the walls of Kilmainham, and he assumed the croup or some other illness so common to the Irish would soon take his father.

"Ye are welcome to set a spell, Sheriff." John McCaffrey offered quietly. "I shall have the boy water the horses if you like. They are a fine looking pair. I am sure you are proud of them."

John McCaffrey tried his best to be civil, for he wanted no more trouble for him and his family with the Crown's henchman. He was resolved not to show his utter contempt for this most visible public servant of the Queen, in County Cork.

"No, they are fine, McCaffrey." The Sheriff replied gruffly. "I will take my leave, but before doing so, I came in person to warn ye that the Crown shall not look kindly to any more shenanigans by your son or that of his friends. Should they decide to continue with their devilment after coming out of prison, I should see to it personally that they return to Kilmainham jail. In addition, I need to leave a message with you and James personally. For the next six months, James McCaffrey ye are not to stray more than a day's walk from home, or ye shall suffer the consequences," Sheriff Reed warned. "We'll be watching you young man. Ye are not to associate with your former teammates and ye shall not patronize any public house in the village. Should ye disregard any of the Crown's directives, Lord Willingham shall evict ye and your parents from his lands. Do ye understand that Jimmy McCaffrey?" The sheriff asked scornfully, his tone of voice clearly expressing his contempt for John McCaffrey and his rebellious son.

"Yes, Sheriff, we understand." Jimmy's father John McCaffrey responded quietly before James had a chance to answer the question. Yet the older man struggled hard to contain the rising anger building up within him for he knew that this sheriff, a political hack, and close friend of their landlord, His Lordship Albert Willingham was fully capable of carrying out this threat against he and his family. The Irish farmer never took the ever-present possibility of eviction lightly. In spite of that, John McCaffrey knew the sheriff could only evict him and his family if directed to do so by

His Lordship. For the time being however, it was in the best interest of his landlord to keep as many of his tenants on their former farms as possible for with emigration rising again laborers were scarce and skilled farmers irreplaceable.

"Let him speak for himself, McCaffrey." Sheriff Read snarled in reply. "I want to hear him say so. I don't want any more trouble from you; is that understood Jimmy?"

"I understand you Sheriff. I will cause you no trouble." James responded quietly. "While I'm here I will tend to the animals and help my father till the land and harvest the crop. So you don't have to worry about me."

"Ye sound like ye are planning on leaving the country." He growled. "I told His Lordship that the Crown should have deported ye, when they had ye and that bunch of hooligan friends of yours in Kilmainham. Too bad they didn't do that."

John McCaffrey could see that if this conversation between his son and the sheriff continued it could only lead to further troubles for his family. Interceding he thanked the sheriff for bringing his son home, then offered to send him off with a couple of chickens and a slab of salted pork. The sheriff welcomed this; after all the troubles brought upon his office by members of the McCaffrey Clan he believed he deserved some recompense for his handiwork. Had it not been for the connivance and machinations of the Office of the County Sheriff the act of expropriating the ancestral lands of the Irish would have been much more difficult for the Crown. With the stroke of a pen, Parliament decreed that all animals and structures on the land belonged to the Crown, not to the one who built the home and labored in the barns and fields of their ancestral lands to feed their families and their nation. Since assuming office in 1852, Sheriff Reed and his men participated in forcibly evicting more than one hundred families, both relatives and nearby neighbors of the McCaffrey and Malone Clans.

Eviction for nonpayment of rent and/or tax arrears was used by the Crown to seize the most productive farms. There was no appeal. This enabled speculators and those of unquestioned loyalty and past service to the Queen such as Lord Willingham, the former military governor of India to take over whole sections of the country. Parliament set up Encumbered Tax Courts to speed up the process of eviction. To give the appearance of fair play and equitableness in the seizure of these lands, the law allowed the Irish farmer to own one cow, a horse, and domestic poultry if their total value did not exceed five pounds.

The mockery of this injustice was a boon to recruitment by the more radical elements of the Nationalists. This group of several thousand disenfranchised Irish men and women banded together with the objective of reestablishing Home Rule. They insisted upon regaining the right to govern their own. It was not long before protest groups began to make their appearance throughout all of Ireland, midnight raids and open clashes with the constabulary became almost daily occurrences.

Officials from the Crown's bureaucracy moved swiftly against those who forcefully resisted the takeover of their homes, farms, or businesses. Large numbers of these young Irish men and women who resisted this usurpation of their land and lived though what were often violent encounters with the constabulary or county sheriff faced an uncertain future. When caught, hundreds quickly found themselves in the dreaded "Deportation Yard" at Kilmainham Prison in Dublin.

However, to protect their families most farmers yielded quietly, moving their families into nearby cities, and then emigrating to North or South America or Australia. Those who stayed on the land however, became little more than a tenant farmer, or at best, a liegeman on their own land to serve the needs of the new proprietor.

In some ways however, Sheriff Reed and the rest of the Crown's Irish minions were now worse off than these former Irish landowners were. Despised by their fellow Irishmen and only tolerated by the English gentry who now controlled nearly all aspects of communal life on the island, they soon became second-class citizens themselves. Reed and his fellow sheriffs across the country, with no land of their own were beholden to the Crown's unscrupulous and often ruthless English peers who answered only to the Queen.

Turning to his eldest, John McCaffrey said, "Jimmy, will ye run over to the coop and pick out a couple of those fine looking roosters for the Sheriff and get that slab of rib hanging in the scullery." Having directed his son to fetch these *gifts* John McCaffrey could not resist this opportunity to remind the man that he too, for all his high-mindedness was regarded by the Crown as little more than a lackey; a lackey that served at the pleasure of His Lordship.

"Your family will enjoy these," John McCaffrey said, handing him the sack of roosters and a slab of salted pork. Then, never quite being able to conceal his loathing for this representative of the Crown, he added, almost derisively, "His Lordship will not need to know where these came from." The sheriff was well aware that the gifts offered were not McCaffreys' to give. Chagrinned, the man accepted his gratuities, without further comment. Yet he was clearly rankled by this farmer's ability to get the best of him on this, his first official visit to the McCaffrey home in more than two years. On his last visit, he stood by while the Army callously searched the McCaffrey home for any incriminating evidence that might support their assault case against, the Galway Ravens' star rugby player. He threw the sack into the cart and without so much as a thank you, bid farewell to John McCaffrey and his eldest boy.

By the time James turned seventeen, he had become one of Ireland's most accomplished sports figures playing fullback for the Galway Ravens. On a warm Sunday afternoon in May 1859 the Ravens, after defeating every team in the Galway/Mayo County league, accepted a challenge to play a tough young Army team from the Queen's Royal Fusiliers assigned to the Belfast Garrison. The Ravens' coach, Patrick Murphy was opposed to this match, not because he thought his boys were not up to the challenge, for they were clearly one of the best teams in all of Ireland and certainly the best he ever coached. He was worried of the potential for serious problems on the field as tempers were sure to flair should one side or the other gain the advantage. His fears were well founded, for regardless of who won the match, in the past two years riots broke out in nearly every instance where a British Army or Navy team took on an all-Irish rugby team.

Notwithstanding this potential for trouble, Galway Mayor Hugh Donaldson was determined that the team and the Galway community not back away from "This responsibility," as he called it. "The community's reputation rests largely upon our boys standing up to the Crown's challenge."

"I believe that too, Your Honor." Coach Murphy responded, speaking softly. "But defending the city's reputation by placing our boys at risk of injury is, I believe unwise. It is something I am reluctant to do."

Still, the mayor persisted, "No matter how you look at it, Patrick," he said, waving both arms in the air, hands out stretched flamboyantly, almost as if he was quieting a group of citizens pleading their cause before him. "Our boys are better than they are. Besides, Dublin, Cork, and Derry have all taken a crack at this Army team and held their ground. Are we any less capable?" He asked, clearly ignoring coach Murphy's concern for his boys.

"No sir. However, you know what happened Mayor at all three of those matches; in the riots that followed, people died." Coach Murphy replied shaking his head. "The Queen's Army is noted for misdeeds on the field. They pay no attention to the rulings of the referee and are not a bit bashful about using any tactic to win. Should there even be a hint of our people getting out of line, somebody is going to get hurt."

Yet, the mayor would have it his way. However, unlike what occurred in Dublin, Cork and Derry, the rampage at Galway occurred on the field and not on the streets of the city. After repeated infractions called against the Army for unnecessary roughness, the Fusiliers commanding officer and four members of his coaching staff stopped the game. In a heated exchange between the referees, the officers and the coaches, the Army Commander struck Coach Murphy in the face with his riding crop—a full-scale melee followed. When it was over James Robert McCaffrey, along with teammates, cousins Patrick Kennedy from Limerick, the Malone twins Kevin and Donald, and Mike Ryan from Cork, who came to their coach's defense, were arrested for assaulting an Officer of the Crown. In the trial that followed all five were convicted with the younger boys sentenced to two years hard labor in the prison at Dublin. The court ordered that Pat Kennedy and Mike Ryan, both in their twenties, to be held for "Deportation."

James and his fellow teammates were soon to lose their innocence at Kilmainham Jail.

"Ye bring in the animals for the night, Jimmy?" His father asked, a note of irritation in his voice, for he saw his oldest visiting with two of the Haggerty girls who lived across the road from the McCaffrey farm.

"Yes, Daddy, Joe is milking the cow now; we'll be in, in a minute." James smiled, for he knew that the Haggerty family expected their girls to be in their house before sunset and it was nearly dark now. However, what he did not tell his father was that the youngest girl was in the barn with his seventeen-year-old brother Joseph. Tomorrow, as usual, Mrs. Haggerty would be on her way to Mass at Saint Joseph's and undoubtedly would bring this to John McCaffrey's attention.

"With your mother down in bed, I don't need the troubles those Haggerty girls can bring into this household. Ye tell Joseph to be done with the milking and get to the house."

"Yes, Daddy," James responded, concealing a grin.Even at fifty-two years and in bed much of the time himself ailing with the croup, his father was well aware of the trysts his two middle sons Joseph and Michael carried on with the Haggerty girls over the last year or two while his eldest was in prison.

Before sitting down for dinner their father, accompanied by Katelyn the boys' ten-year-old sister took a cup of warm milk, bread and a bowl of potato and turnip soup into Mary Katherine's bedroom. Although weak and frail she lay propped up on two pillows reading her bible. She welcomed both, with a kiss for her husband and a hug for Katelyn.

"Did my Wee One milk the cow tonight?" She asked, with a wan smile.

"No, Momma, of course I didn't," responded Katelyn. "You know that's Joseph's job. Every time I ask to help, he just squirts milk in my face. I hate him," she said, showing her displeasure with her older brother. "I'm old enough to milk a cow."

"Of course ye are, but your time will come, Dear." Her mother replied, weakly. "But hopefully ye will have met a nice boy by then and he will do all the chores; ye will just manage the house and be the grand mistress of your own home."

Katelyn, with her nose turned up and lower lip and jaw jutting out, offered a response heard many times before in this household, "I hate boys. They're so stupid."

"Oh ye mustn't say that," her mother responded, quietly, "someday that will change and ye will be the happiest girl in all of Ireland."

"Enough Mother," John McCaffrey interjected quietly. "Ye eat something now. Katelyn will bring her supper in and stay with ye; the boys want to speak to me about America tonight. Ye knew that was coming and I am afraid it is time, but we will make no decision without ye. Come Katelyn, Jimmy will fix ye a plate."

At the end of supper, the two younger boys went about their daily chores without even a nod from their father. They cleared the table, washed, dried, and put away the dishes, while Joseph sprinkled and swept the dirt floor of their cottage. Their father sat at the kitchen table with James and Michael where the three brought out their tobacco and corncob pipes; these were Christmas gifts from John's youngest brother Paul in America. In 1845, when he was a young man, at the height of *The Great Hunger* Paul emigrated to the U.S. In recent years, he encouraged his brother John to bring his family to America. He wrote that he was now in a position financially to help them emigrate. He promised that upon arrival in New York, John's family would have a place to live until they could build their own home. When Paul arrived in America, he joined the New York Police Department and as a rooky patrolled many of the toughest sections of the city. In his latest letter, he mentioned that after fourteen-years on the force he rose to the rank of deputy police commissioner.

In this letter, he assured John and Mary Kate that America's War Between the States would be over by the time they arrived in New York intimating that the North had completely routed the secessionists. Nevertheless, Paul doubted that John or Mary Kate would ever leave their beloved Ireland. Although no one told him his sister-in-law was ill, the tone of John's letters suggested to he and his wife Ruth that something was amiss in his brother's household. His brother never mentioned that Mary Kate was ailing, or that their oldest son was in prison. However, Paul and many other Irish immigrants still subscribed to either the Cork Examiner or The Dublin Times and kept abreast of major news stories coming out of Ireland. Both papers headlined the troubles in Galway, which ended with the imprisonment of the "Galway Five."

In recent weeks as the sickness began to take its toll on Mary Kate's body she pleaded with her husband to go to America and leave her for she knew she was dying.

"Ye go too, Daddy," she said. "There is nothing left here for ye but trouble and sickness. Find a new place for our children where Katelyn will have a chance to recover. If she stays here she too will die before her time."

Her husband's only reply was, "We'll see." However, John McCaffrey did not intend to allow the Brits or anyone else to run him out of the country. They had taken his land, but he vowed to die where he was born and no interloping English landlord was about to run him off.

After lighting their pipes, his two eldest brought their father up to date on their plans for the trip to America.

"I talked to Captain Sinclair again yesterday, Daddy." James said. "He will sail at high tide a week from Tuesday. All we need is an additional forty-two pounds and he will take all five of us to New York. Michael, Joseph, Thomas, and I all agree that we would be ready to go by then."

"What about me!" Daniel exclaimed loudly, his response accompanied by a scornful glance at his older brother. Then turning to his father, complained, "Daddy, I'm almost fourteen; that's old enough to decide for myself. I am not sure that I even want to. But it's not fair that they didn't tell me what they were going to do."

"Ye are right of course, Daniel," his father replied kindly, patting his son on the arm. "We should not have left ye out of this, but that was my doing. I was afraid that if too many people knew ye were all going that Lord Willingham would move us off our land before ye left. He wants a tenant with young men to harvest the crop and tend his sheep. So blame me for that, not your brother's; but now ye will have a full voice in what is about to take place."

"Sorry, Daniel," Jimmy offered apologetically, "but now you know and we will respect your decision."

"I will sell the cow," his father continued. "That will give ye a few extra pounds."

"No Daddy," his eldest replied, solemnly, glancing briefly at his brothers then back to his father. "We won't accept that. Momma needs that milk."

"Okay," his father replied, "but ye haven't answered my question yet. Where are ye going to get the money before ye sail? Ye will also need money when ye arrive in America. How do ye plan to handle that?"

"It's best you not know, Daddy." Michael replied, his lips pursed and shaking his head. "If you knew the Brits might force you to tell 'em."

"What the hell ye mean by such a statement." John McCaffrey demanded angrily pounding his fist down on the dining table. "Tell them what? No Englishman is going to force me to tell them anything that I don't want them to know."

"I didn't mean that Daddy," his son Michael responded, taken aback by his father's indignant reply. "We just thought that we didn't want to trouble you and Mother with what we have planned."

"Ye are our sons. We have a God given right to know what ye are up to. Your mother and I shall decide what ye must do to achieve what ye are planning. Besides, if all five of ye be going to America, ye must take the Wee One with ye."

The older boys looked at their father in stunned silence; they could not believe what he said. James was the first to respond. "You can't mean that Daddy!" He exclaimed. "Katelyn is only a child; should something happen to us, who will look after her? Besides that, she is not well!"

The other boys chimed in with Michael adding, "Daddy, she's just a baby—surely you have heard the stories about these *Coffin Ships,*' that's what our cousins call them. There are a lot of youngsters that don't survive the *Crossing*."

"Indeed I have heard those stories;" he conceded, "and some may be true. However, most are exaggerated. They tend to keep a family of workers on the farm and the English lords love it. It gives them a built-in labor force; their tenants will stay put and the landlord need not pay wages for field hands. The Haggerty's and the O'Reilly Clans have kept their children close for fear of losing them in the *Crossing* and ye can see what it has gotten them. The men folk spend most of their time at the pub or in jail for fighting and some of the women are nothing but whores. But it's settled, the Wee One will go with ye; if she does not she will die here before another winter passes."

The boys knew that what their father said was true—short of a miracle, they suspected Katelyn would join her mother and her two older sisters in Saint Joseph's Cemetery before the end of the year. The two older girls, each taken with the consumption died in their teens.

"Who'll be going with ye?" Their father asked.

"Mike Ryan, Kevin and Donald Malone and Pat Kennedy; we talked about going while we were in Kilmainham. They and a dozen or so of their kin will join us. There will be eight or ten from Galway and several other members of the Malone clan from County Cork and Killarney, including Bobby Burke and Leo Gordon. Those two escaped from the old Derry bridewell two months ago; they are on the run now. They are in Cork and trying to get out of the country. The Brits are looking for them; they robbed the Army Paymaster in Dublin. I heard they hid the money before the Army caught up to them."

"If the Brits catch them this time Daddy," Michael offered, interjecting himself into this conversation, "they'll hang 'em for sure. Their brothers claim that after Bobby and Leo get out of the country the remaining members of the family will use that money to go to America. To ally suspicion the families will take the Belfast ferry to Scotland and train on into London and go aboard ship there."

"Sinclair wants the Queen's stallion," Jimmy continued; "the one that took the Derby in Belfast last spring. He told me he would allow four passengers of my choice free passage if I could deliver that horse to his ship before he sailed. Pat Kennedy, Kevin Malone, and I will be the only ones involved—we have it planned for next week. They board the stud with the Army's mounts at Mallow Castle. It will take us two or three days to get it to Sinclair's ship at Cork. We planned that Michael, Joseph, and Thomas would take Daniel aboard Sinclair's ship on Tuesday afternoon. Kevin, Pat, and I will come aboard with the stud after dark with Burke and Leo Gordon."

"And ye trust Sinclair?" John McCaffrey asked his oldest son.

"I do Daddy." the boy replied, confidently. "We have an arrangement."

"And just what kind of arrangement do ye think ye can make with a scoundrel like Sinclair?" His father demanded. "He's a thieving bastard with a nasty reputation. It is common knowledge that he takes his passenger's last shilling before landing in America. He robs them of whatever gold or money they have kept hidden in their packs. His crews are always on the lookout for that during the crossing—they are as crooked as he is."

"He will not do that to us, Daddy." Jimmy responded calmly quite confident that what he said would take place without a problem. "He won't be able to race the stud anywhere in Ireland, but he figures it will bring a fortune in America. Besides, you and some others will know about his scheme and if we don't arrive safely, at the fare agreed to, the Brits will find out how the animal got onboard his ship."

"What about your cousins?" Their father asked, shaking his head bewildered by his son's plans for financing their trip to America. He was well aware that his two sisters' families, who married into the Burke and Malone Clan, were poorer than *church mice*. "Their families couldn't raise a Queen's sovereign between them. Where are they going to get their money? Is there more to this story?" he demanded.

"Yes, Daddy there is more." James responded, unruffled by his father's query. "The older Malone boys raided the Queen's cattle range at Kilkenny. Right now, they are driving about twenty head of the Army's prime beef cattle to Smyth's estate at Waterford. They can only travel at night so it will be four or five days before they get there.

"Between the two ships they carry about four-hundred passengers and crew and since the Great Hunger the Navy won't allow the ships out of the harbor unless they have sufficient supplies to feed both crew and first-class passengers. There will be eight or ten First Class passengers on Captain Sinclair's ship. The Brits are fearful that the American war makes it too dangerous to travel to the U.S. so nearly all First Class passengers, there are more than a hundred, will go with Captain Smyth. He is going on into Canada; that is why he wanted the beef. By the time the Army misses their cattle, the captain's men will have it butchered and the meat loaded aboard ship. If you remember Daddy, the Queen Herself got involved. She said she was aware of the stories of passengers starving onboard these ships and she was going to put a stop to it."

"I am aware of that," John McCaffrey responded, "but she did so only after the stories begin to show-up in the French and American newspapers. She is a cruel bitch; do not ever forget that. And ye remember that except for fresh water, the folks in steerage still must fend for themselves."

Upon hearing the details of the boy's plan to acquire the funds needed for the Atlantic crossing John McCaffrey was dumbfounded. He raised both hands to his face and looking up at the thatched roof, prayed aloud. "God Almighty, help me. Please!" He thundered. "Save these young fools of mine from themselves."

Turning back to his children, shaking his head and pointing at each one of his sons he continued, "Ye don't know it, but if ye are caught, ye will be branded as thieves along with the rest of those boys. Believe me that is the least that will happen if the Brits get ye. Ye youngsters are playing a dangerous game here. They will hang ye for stealing that horse or deport ye to Australia or to some other godforsaken island on the other side of the world."

His sons, stunned by their father's charge did not respond; for like many of their generation, they too feared the British Army and were frequently the recipient of stories of the atrocities committed by the Brits against their neighbors. The reality of these stories all came home to haunt them when their brother Jimmy became a prisoner in Kilmainham Jail.

John McCaffrey was looking at his sons in complete disbelief. However, he had to admit that to spirit away the Queen's prize stud was quite original. He thought they might just get away with that since they would soon be out of the country. Notwithstanding that, to steal a herd of beef cattle and drive those animals across two counties, at night was downright reckless. They would be lucky if not discovered by a local constable or an Army patrol. However, he knew they were more likely to come upon a tenant along the route who could place these young men in harm's way. Except for his eldest, he was sure that his children were not fully aware of the danger that may come from a friend or neighbor.

Since *The Great Hunger,* the Brits had become experts in developing informers within these formerly close-nit Irish families. They were quick to learn that it was quite simple to recruit a starving man, woman, or child to betray a neighbor or even a family member.

Still staring at his eldest, his lips pursed and grim, he inquired, mockingly. "And just who in God's name came up with such a masterful plan as ye have described here today?"

"It was my idea, Daddy," James exclaimed, quite proud of his plan. "Our cousins all agreed with it. So do not worry we will make it okay and we will not have a problem with the stud. Once we deliver the livestock neither Smyth nor Sinclair can afford to pull any shenanigans on this crossing. They won't be a threat to any of us."

Getting up from the dinner table, their father walked over to the end of the room and knocked the ashes from his pipe into the now dying embers in the stone fireplace. Before responding, he turned slowly looking directly at each one of his children; his voice now hushed and clearly worrisome, said, "Your Grandfather used to warn us not to count our chickens before they hatched, so don't tell me not to worry. The Brits are not stupid. Moreover, some of my sister's kin were behind the byre door when the Almighty was dispensing common sense. Ye known what will happen to all of ye if they catch ye; so do not look upon this as some kind of youthful adventure. Ye have to be smarter than they are; Kilmainham Jail is full of young Irishmen who thought they could outwit the Brits. Ye will not be safe until ye are on board Sinclair's ship and have set sail for America, then ye face a new enemy, the Sea. Ye may find it less forgiving than the Queen's militia.

In addition, one thing ye must never forget, once at sea the Captain is the master of all those innocent souls on board his ship.

"If ye are successful in carrying this out, ye must not go aboard the same ship with Burke and the Gordon boy," He warned. "Both the Army and the Constabulary will be looking for those two. Should they find ye with them, they will arrest all of ye. Five former prisoners of Kilmainham Jail and two escapees from Derry, all cousins, on the same ship is a fool's cargo." Then repeating his earlier warning, his voice grim; he said again, "Bobby Burke and Leo Gordon must not board Sinclair's ship. Do ye understand that?" He demanded his tone of voice deadly serious.

His sons remained mute, shocked by their father's warning. Yet, much to their amazement, John McCaffrey went on with his instructions, now becoming quite precise and detailed. It was as if the man had been through this many times before. Except for his eldest, the younger boys had no inkling that their father knew anything about the difficult tasks that may lie ahead for those who chose to challenge the Queen's authority. In addition, the boys were completely ignorant of the horrific ordeal or misfortune they might encounter on board ship when crossing the Atlantic Ocean.

"Sinclair always sails with William Smyth," their father said. "Smyth is the master of the *Hampton Court*—they make the crossing together; sometimes they are accompanied by a third vessel. Should one of the ships get in trouble there will be another close-by. I will talk to Sinclair and Smyth. However, these two are both a couple of scallywags; I have known them since they were officers in the Queen's Navy. I will see to it that they will do what is required; but ye be on guard until the ship docks in New York. Do ye understand that?"

"Yes, Daddy," James answered quietly, not realizing until now just how dangerous a plan he had devised for getting his brothers and now his baby sister to America. He knew it was too late to change the plan, as others were already committed. Although Smyth and Sinclair encouraged the theft of the livestock, the plan to carry out the raid was Jimmy McCaffreys' and his alone and it was well underway by now.

Brothers Michael and Joseph sat transfixed by their father's foreboding admonishment; they turned to their older brother as if for an explanation. James merely nodded his head in agreement with his father, holding up his hand as if to say to his brothers, leave it alone Daddy knows what he is talking about. For Jimmy remembered the stories Matthew Haggerty told him years before about his father's brush with the Queen's Navy and the Royal Marines at Galway.

During the time of *The Great Hunger* John McCaffrey and his brother Paul were members of the *Young Ireland Movement,* an offshoot of Daniel O'Connell's National Repeal Association. O'Connell's group sought the repeal of the Act of Union, which among other draconian measures dissolved the Irish parliament in Dublin. When they failed in their attempt to reestablish the Irish legislative body a small group of former Nationalists, identifying themselves as the Young Ireland Movement chose to challenge the Crown's usurpation of the Irish Parliament. Like O'Connell's group, the Movement's intent was to reestablish home rule for the people of Ireland. Yet, unlike the Nationalists peaceful approach the Young Ireland leaders would strive to accomplish this objective by force if necessary. Their intent was to drive the British from Ireland by violent means if that was called for. They began the resistance with a series of attacks upon

British military supply depots including cattle rustling and the theft of weapons. Violent attacks upon the Crown's autocratic and often tyrannical property owners and members of the constabulary soon followed.

Mathew Haggerty said Jimmy's father, as a member of the Movement required him to track the British fleet whenever they approached Galway Bay. The Royal Navy's bastion at Kilronan in the Aran Islands, a short distance from Galway, was homeport for several ships in the North Atlantic fleet. A contingent of Royal Marines from Kilronan provided operational support for the constabulary in Galway, Clare, and Limerick Counties.

McCaffrey using what small funds he received from the Movement leadership bribed two junior officers of the Royal Navy and obtained schedules of naval ship movements on Galway Bay. The report prepared by naval supply officers Charles Sinclair and William Smyth also identified the amount and type of supplies the Navy would require once the ships dropped anchor in Galway Bay. The report identified each ship, the naval complement on board, including the number of Royal Marines available to support the Galway Garrison and size of the local Constabulary force in the event of trouble.

His effort to bribe these two junior naval officers was easier to accomplish than John McCaffrey ever imagined it might be. The two officers loved their Bushmill's Irish whiskey, and beer and the *girls of the evening* who satisfied their sexual appetites. All of this provided secretly by members of the Movement and brought to their hotel by a young rebel known to them only as "Johnny, the Irishman from Limerick." However, in his last two contacts with these two, John McCaffrey found them more difficult to deal with than usual. He wondered at the time if the officers' superiors suspected that they might be involved in inappropriate or illegal activities. He realized however that it was more likely their excessive use of liquor, contrary to the conduct expected of a naval officer that probably forced the Crown to intervene.

Haggerty said that one night as Jimmy's father approached the two in Galway in the back room of Mickey Ryan's bar, he found them in an ugly mood. Both men had consumed more liquor than usual and they confronted the Irishman in the presence of two local prostitutes.

"We will be doubling our fees from now on. Ye tell your boss that," Lieutenant Gordon Sinclair snarled. "You'll get nothing else from us until we hear that clang of the Queen's silver in your belt and see it here on the table."

Lieutenant Smyth echoed his fellow officer's demand. "We know what you have been up to you Irish swine." The man snarled, "If you and your traitorous gang of smugglers want to continue it will occur only if you bring something with the Queen's picture engraved on it. Is that understood?" He bellowed contemptuously, never for a moment considering the possible consequences of revealing to two common prostitutes their treasonous activities.

Lieutenant Sinclair, startled by his fellow lieutenant's blunder in disclosing their criminal ties to the Irishman from Limerick intervened by changing the subject. Looking first at his compatriot then to their Irish visitor he growled, "He's had too much to drink Irishman, but don't try to pass-off any of that rotgut whiskey you're bringing in from Dublin. We will take Bushmill's and none of that Irish poteen crap that your people peddle. You understand?"

Haggerty said Jimmy's father told him that, "It was obvious that the man was trying to cover-up his intoxicated accomplice's lack of discretion."

"Your father said he understood. The two prostitutes merely giggled apparently completely oblivious to Smyth's revelation of the serious crimes involved."

Late one evening John and Paul McCaffrey escorted two young prostitutes to the Galway navy dock while a French fishing vessel glided silently into Galway Bay. It carried five hundred weapons, both rifles and pistols and over one thousand pounds of explosives for members of the Movement. One of the Movement's leaders, Patrick Sheehan assigned the McCaffrey boys to make sure the two Royal Navy officers would not be in a position to observe the transfer of these weapons or identify any of the smugglers.

When John and Paul entered the Royal Navy warehouse, a contingent of well-armed Royal Marines hidden in the far reaches of the warehouse opened fire on the two couples. One of the girls screamed and went down; the other stood still until Paul McCaffrey dragged her down behind several crates. "Stay here," he said to her quietly, "and you'll be okay." Then turning to his brother, he pointed to the edge of the dock and made a diving motion with his hands. Both men scrambled out onto the dock and dived into the water as the marines opened fire once again. Fortunately, the bullets missed their mark; the two men quickly swam under the pier where they remained hidden for more than three hours. They escaped detection, but the cold water numbed their bodies.

The following morning the Navy seized the French fishing boat and a contingent of Royal Marines surrounded Dunguaire Castle where the smugglers were holed-up. In the short, yet violent siege that followed only six of the original twenty-one men that took refuge at Dunguaire survived. In the trial that followed the Crown prosecutor sought the death penalty for Sheehan and his number two man Thomas Flynn, but settled for deportation on the remaining men captured at the castle. Members of the Movement never discovered the informant's identity. Of the original smuggling, group everyone except John and Paul McCaffrey, who escaped the net thrown up around Dunguaire Castle, were dead, or in jail awaiting execution or deportation. In the eyes of members of the Movement, the two brothers immediately became suspect.

Coming ashore before daylight, John and Paul McCaffrey were wet and cold and Paul, shaking from the chill whispered to his brother, "Johnny, someone tipped-off the Brits; this was too well coordinated. They'll surely suspect you and me because it looks like we are the only ones that got away."

"Let them think what they will Paul," John responded, "but this thing is not over yet. We will head for home and lay low for a few days until we find out what happened to rest of the crew. Then we'll decide what to do."

Within days of their capture, the Queen's Court in Galway convicted and sentenced Patrick Sheehan and Thomas Flynn to hang. A week later, a Constabulary lieutenant accompanied by eight armed officers arrived at the jail to transport the two men to the Galway train station. Their last ride on this earth would be on board the Dublin Express en route to Kilmainham Jail. John and Paul McCaffrey accompanied by three others from the Movement, including Mathew Haggerty, assisted by a handful of irate Galway citizens blocked the narrow street leading to the station. The angry citizens, following John McCaffrey's direction arranged a simple ambush scenario by blocking the street with a dozen or more wagons. As the coach and its armed escort reached the barricade, the good citizens of Galway moved more wagons in behind the entourage cutting off the constables' escape.

John and Paul McCaffrey, Mathew Haggerty along with two others from the Movement, wearing masks, had taken up positions on the roofs of buildings on either side of the street, directly above the barricaded coach. Then showing their presence, John called out to constabulary escort. "You people are surrounded," he yelled. "Drop your weapons and we will allow you to live and you will be free to leave."

The uniformed officers were in a quandary, they were well armed, and some thought they could fight-off these Irish brigands. Yet, while two or three appeared to be ready to take flight the lieutenant cursed aloud, "You go to hell, you Irish sons of bitches." He yelled. "Shoot them." Yet his men could not see their attackers. John and Paul's group dropped out of sight waiting for the signal to respond.

"I will give you one more chance Lieutenant," John called out to the men below. "Lay down your weapons and you are free to leave on foot. Resist and we will shoot you out of your saddle."

"Fire on those bastards," the Lieutenant yelled, yet the words were barely out of his mouth when John McCaffrey shot him. He fell to the street with his startled horse galloping off. Seeing his lieutenant go down a second guard opened fire in the direction from where he heard the warning voice, yet he saw no one. When that happened all five men opened up on the guards below dropping three from their mounts. Seeing what happened the remaining officers dropped their weapons and raised their hands, at which time John McCaffrey showed himself ordering the remaining guards to dismount and release their two prisoners. "Ye are free, to walk away." He said after he made his way to the street. "Take your wounded with you."

Patrick Sheehan and Thomas Flynn fled first to France then on to America. The British never learned the identity of John McCaffrey, but his brother Paul, fearing a leak from the unknown informant following Sheehan and Flynn, escaped to France then to the U.S. Within months of the Galway incident with their leaders gone, the *Movement* collapsed.

Two years were to pass before the Royal Navy court marshaled Sinclair and Smyth on unrelated charges and kicked both of them out of the Navy. Years later, they became masters of two of the most dreadful sailing ships ever to ply the oceans of the world. The Navy never learned of the bribes the two junior officers received from John McCaffrey that allowed members of the rebel group to smuggle thousands of weapons from France to bolster the Movement's arsenal—for that, the two men owed their lives to the man they knew only as Johnny, the Irishman from Limerick.

John McCaffrey was sure that these two scallywags, as he called them would accede to his demands and protect his children until they reached America. If they did not the Queen's Navy would receive a file of documents, which would link the two former officers to the Galway incident.

"What provisions have ye gathered for such a long trip?" John McCaffrey asked of his son James, for he was fully aware that ship owners required families traveling steerage class to provide their own food while aboard ship. The crossing could take up to a month or longer depending upon the wind and ocean conditions.

"We have some dried cod and apples, Daddy," Michael said. "We have enough that we can probably get by."

"Ye will need more than that son." His father responded forcefully as if speaking from personal experience. "We'll butcher one of Lord Willingham's prized sheep and the young heifer and smoke the meat along with a dozen chickens and a few salmon and more cod. Ye will also need potatoes, turnips, and fruit for the Wee One and plenty of soap. Ye boys get at it tomorrow; your brother and I will pay a visit to Captain Sinclair and Captain Smyth. If Lord Willingham's men show up for the monthly livestock inventory while we are away, get the Haggerty girls over here; they can distract the bastards during the count. Run two of the lambs through a second time; they won't notice the difference."

His children, including young Thomas smiled, but made no comment about their father's suggested plan of action. Either one of the two oldest Haggerty girls could turn the head of even the most straight-laced English squire or that of any of his henchmen. Colleen, the eldest at eighteen had a crush on James; it would not be hard to convince her to play the part desired by his father. Yet she was no dummy; James was sure she would know that the McCaffreys were up to something besides just arranging cover for a short count of animals to fool the property owner's underlings. Her family had participated in such duplicitous activity before. However, this time James suspected the Haggerty family would surely suspect the McCaffreys were planning to leave for America. Knowing her as he did, he was certain Colleen would want to go along.

It was early evening when Colleen approached James from her father's field. "You and your brothers are going to America, aren't you?" She said, staring directly at him, her lips drawn tight with not a hint of a smile. Her words were more of a statement than a question with James quickly realizing his neighbor's oldest daughter already knew of the McCaffrey family's plan to flee the country.

The girl, with her long beautiful black curly hair hanging down, combed neatly, stood facing him from the other side of the rock-walled fence that separated the two farms. She was taunting him now with that all-knowing smile just beginning to show. She knew she had the upper hand on this, hot-blooded young Irishman who she would bed before this evening was over, even if it was to be in the hay in one of Lord Willingham's barns.

"I'll be going with you, Jimmy McCaffrey. You will not get away that easy. I can pay my own way—I have been working in the mill since I was fourteen years old and I have the money. You will take me won't you?" She crooned with a hint of merriment in her voice.

Her friend had seen that look and heard that lilting voice before; the two of them spent more than one evening together in Lord Willingham's barn prior to Jimmy going off to jail. In fact, he spent many a night while confined in that horrible institution dreaming about those times. Still he was lucky. Hanging or deportation was the usual outcome for a rebellious young offender convicted of assaulting a representative of the Queen's own. The only thing that saved him and his fellow teammates from either the whipping post or Deportation Yard at Kilmainham was their youth and the public outcry that followed the incident. Even the London papers questioned the severity of the charges leveled by the Crown against these young men. The much-publicized protestations in support of the Ravens following the Galway rugby incident and the tender age of most of the defendants undoubtedly resulted in a more lenient sentence than could be expected from the presiding magistrate.

"We'll talk about it Colleen," he responded as he walked through the gate in this solidly built rock fence built so many years before by French prisoners of war. The opening allowed access to her father's farm as she called it, for it too, by the stroke of a pen now belonged to the Crown. Lord Willingham was well on his way to becoming one of the largest land barons in the county.

"Let's walk," he said, taking hold of her hand, "and Colleen you will tell me which one of my brothers told you that we were off to America."

"No one had to tell me, you silly boy." She laughed. "I know the McCaffreys well enough that I can always tell what your family is up too. You are getting ready to bury your Mom. She is dying, and when she is gone, all of you are going to America. Your Mother told me Mom that she will not last the month out and that you boys would be off as soon as you came home. Well you are home Jimmy and your Mom is dying—God rest her soul. Now tell me I'm wrong."

As the two of them walked behind the barn, he took her by both arms and brought her up to within inches of his chest, held her tightly for a moment then set her down in the hay. He could smell her body—that same sweet wonderful fragrance he experienced so long ago when the two of them first embraced here. Taking a milk stool, he sat down facing her. He had not thought about taking any of the Haggerty's with him and his brothers. There were already too many people involved and they would be lucky if they got out of the country before the Queen's constabulary and Lord Willingham's men got wind of what was going on.

However, James had not counted on taking his ten-year old sister either, nor had he foreseen the escape of his two cousins from the Army stockade in Derry. The families of the two men were trying to spirit them out of the country. Unbeknown to him at the time, Mike Ryan's father Patrick called upon

James' father for help, as he knew that John McCaffrey still had ties to the Nationalists, the largest and most active anti-Crown organization in all of Ireland. Home Rule was still a dream to many of its members. As things stood now, he realized taking the Haggerty girls with them could work to his advantage. It was possible that Colleen and her sisters might allay suspicion by posing as a wife to one of his cousins. A husband and wife team with a small child would certainly not arouse the suspicion of the Queen's Constabulary. Besides, she and her sisters could help care for Katelyn. It might work to everyone's advantage.

"Listen to me Colleen," he said, his voice now low and intimidating, "before we go any further on this you must promise me that you will confide in no one other than your father in what I am about to tell you; not your mother and certainly not your sisters. You promise?" He demanded, again taking her by both arms and drawing her near to him. As she came close he was nigh on to once again being overcome by the sweet fragrance and beauty of her warm body. She was so close that he found it nearly impossible to fight the urge to make love to her at this very instant. Yet, he was aware that such an unrestrained desire on his part, at this moment might not be in his best interest.

Colleen Haggerty was startled by this turn of events. She had never heard her Jimmy speak so forbiddingly. Nor had she ever been alone with him when the two of them did not, at the first opportunity, explode into a hot-blooded orgy of beddable lovemaking. She fully expected that by now the two of them would be intimately involved; when that did not happen, she realized the Jimmy she knew as a child, no longer existed.

"You are right, of course," he said, then went on to explain what he and his brothers' plans were about, leaving out the

Malone brothers' cattle rustling venture. Nor did he mention his scheme to steal one of the Queen's highly prized studs to pay for their passage.

"But you must play your part well, young lady, for if Lord Willingham's men find that we have butchered one of his prime sheep, a calf, and stolen a dozen chickens, you won't be going to America, or anyplace else, you'll be in jail with the rest of us.

"Tonight when you go in, tell your father what we are about. I will not take you unless he approves and then you must do as he and my father tell you. You can take only a few clothes, for you will have to carry enough food for yourself and two others. There will be about twenty-five of us and we must take care of our own needs aboard ship. If we run into bad weather, the crossing may take four or five weeks or possibly even longer."

Colleen Haggerty was smart, beautiful and trustworthy; this young woman would follow her father's advice, and she would do what Jimmy McCaffrey thought would be necessary to distract Lord Willingham's men. When the monthly livestock count took place His Lordship's underlings would have no idea that this young beauty had hornswoggled all of them.

When they finished discussing their plans for the crossing, she was pleased to learn not only that she was invited to go along with members of the McCaffrey clan, but that her former lover had not lost his appetite for sex. It was past midnight when they returned home.

CHAPTER 2

THE ARRANGEMENT

It was still an hour before daylight when John McCaffrey and his son Jimmy arrived at the train station in the village of Mallow to catch the morning train from Limerick en route to Cork. When it arrived nearly two dozen other tenant farmers boarded with their crates, cartons or boxes of produce, ducks, chickens, piglets, smoked meat, or bales of wool destined for merchants or the woolen mills in Cork. Jimmy's father chose to take a half dozen chickens in a small wire basket for his widowed sister Margaret Malone and her family. The woman lived above the River Lee near Queen's College. Margaret, four years younger than her brother, the mother of twenty-year old twin boys Kevin and Donald worked as a scullery maid at the college.

When Jimmy questioned his father regarding the crate of chickens, the man responded, "Son if ye expect to board a ship unnoticed at the Quay in Cork, we must continue the masquerade of being a law-abiding tenant farm family. Until all of ye are aboard ship and beyond the eyes of those who would inform on ye none of ye are safe. If we run across one of Lord Willingham's men we must play the part the Queen and His Lordship would expect from a good servant; we are lawfully engaged in the pursuit of farming, nothing more, nothing less."

"Will Aunt Margaret be expecting us, Daddy?"

"No, and I'll not be going with ye. When we arrive at the station, I will continue on to the Quay. I want to talk to Captain Sinclair and Smyth if he is there. Ye go on to your

Aunt Margaret's house. If everything goes well I will meet ye there later this evening; we'll take the last train out."

"Don't you think I should go with you, Daddy?"

"No Jimmy, I have dealt with these scallywags enough that I believe I will be able to best accomplish what we want if I am alone."

"I know, Daddy," Jimmy replied with a worried look, "but I saw that you're carrying your revolver. You must be expecting trouble."

"No, Son. Don't worry." His father responded with a smile. He was trying to convince his son that he should not be concerned for his wellbeing. "The gun is just a precaution. I do not expect any problems from these men."

When they arrived in Cork John McCaffrey produced a large envelope from his coat pocket and handed it to his son. "If I am wrong about this meeting, ye give this to your Aunt Margaret. She will know what to do with it. But don't worry," he smiled, trying once again to reassure James that all would go well at his meeting with the two merchant marine captains. "I do not expect that there will be any trouble. Ye go on now to your Aunt Margaret's place, I shall see ye this evening." Yet Jimmy McCaffrey was worried, for he knew quite well what his father was capable of doing when his family was threatened.

Although the boys from the Galway Ravens escaped both the Deportation Yard and the whipping post in Kilmainham Jail all were severely beaten by the Fusiliers while en route to Dublin. The beatings continued within the jail. When John McCaffrey and his sister's brother-in-law Patrick Malone visited the boys at the jail, they found Jimmy's face bruised and bloody and his upper torso covered with open wounds.

"Who did this to you, Jimmy?" His father demanded.

His son looked first at his father then at a nearby guard before responding. "No one, Daddy, I just got into a fight and I lost. Do not worry about it. I'm okay," he offered bravely as if to assure his father that he would survive whatever difficulties he and his teammates may encounter in prison.

Later as the two men left Kilmainham Jail a guard approached Jimmy's father and quietly whispered, "It wasn't our people, McCaffrey. We have some queer ducks working here but we do not treat prisoners that way. It was the Fusilier Lieutenant and his people who brought those youngsters here from Galway."

"Why the hell should I believe ye?" John McCaffrey retorted angrily, "They are in your custody. Ye are responsible for my son's safety."

"Ye believe what ye want." The guard snapped. "I have no reason to lie to you, but your son will be out in a few months and he will tell you himself."

Patrick Malone, listening to the conversation between the guard and John McCaffrey said nothing until the two men were outside the prison.

"What the guard told ye is right, John. The boys witnessed Jimmy's beating. They said they went after him because he refused to cower to those buggers. Jimmy defied them and they wanted to send a message home to all of us."

"Well I got the message, Patrick." John McCaffrey responded grimly. "And I won't forget it. But these bastards will pay for what they did to our children."

"What can we do John?" The elder Malone asked, shaking his head. "No one in Kilmainham is going to come forward and admit that the Queen's soldiers shackled Jimmy and then used their boots and rifle butts on him. They nearly killed him, and then laughed about their handy work. The boys said he held out against all of them until he was unconscious."

"Do!" John McCaffrey exclaimed. "We shall not do a thing Patrick, as long as our boys are in that hellhole; but when they return home, I will do what is necessary. Ye stay out of this; ye have a family to look after."

"I'm no different than ye John," Malone responded angrily. "Ye forget two of those boys locked-up in there are my nephews and they have no father to look after them."

"I'll not be forgetting that, Patrick, for they are my sister's kids. Notwithstanding that, for the sake of both our families, it will be best if only one of us settles this score. Should I fail then I leave it up to ye to do whatever ye think is proper. However, understand Patrick the man responsible for this will die for what he did. I'll be-go-to-hell if the Queen thinks her henchmen can come after our children and not suffer consequences!"

When the Malone boys returned home John McCaffrey questioned the two closely regarding the Kilmainham incident. They confirmed the guard's story that one of the Army coaches, a Fusilier Lieutenant named Aaron Gray, was responsible for the brutal beating of Jimmy McCaffrey. Gray ordered his men to shackle the boy so there was no possible way he could defend himself.

Three months after the release from Kilmainham Jail of all five members of the Galway Ravens rugby team, the fusilier lieutenant was dead. Someone killed Lieutenant Gray in a crowded pub on O'Connell Street in Dublin. Although there were many witnesses, no one could or would identify the shooter, describing him only as "A middle aged man, short of statue, with a revolver."

Nevertheless, it appeared from the beginning that the police suspected John McCaffrey was the shooter for within a week Sheriff Reed, accompanied by Lord Willingham's overseer and two soldiers arrived unannounced and searched the McCaffrey residence. They found nothing, for Jimmy's father took great pains in concealing the only firearm the family possessed. He removed two large stones from the front of the fireplace leaving a space large enough for his revolver and cartridges. Then taking a tallow candle and shock of smoldering turf re-blackened the stones, once again concealing the chamber. However, the risks were great for those who chose to defy the Brits. The mere possession of a firearm by anyone other than a member of the Queen's henchmen or the army was a penitentiary offence. Notwithstanding that, this day Sheriff Solomon Reed and the Queen's soldiers would not find John McCaffrey's weapon, for once again he concealed it in *plain sight*.

It had been a long time since John McCaffrey had visited Cork. After their clash with the police in Galway, he sought to find a boat for Paul's escape to France while his brother remained hidden outside the city. Eventually, John made contact on the waterfront with a French fisherman and obtained passage for Paul on a vessel bound for Le Havre. Today, as he walked through the bleak and desolate streets of the city he saw that little had changed since the famine. Although the city appeared to have grown considerably, now over eighty-thousand inhabitants, there seemed to be fewer people on the streets than at that terrible time.

John would never forget what he encountered on that visit. Thousands of Irish families had migrated to the city at the time of The Great Hunger. Hundreds of others, driven from their own homes because they could not pay their rent sought refuge in the country's largest metropolitan areas. Many others crossed the Irish Sea and settled in London, where they sought to escape the frightful consequences of the famine. Yet, some, too weak to travel any farther were denied passage aboard ship and died on the streets or in the alleyways of Dublin, Cork, Limerick, Galway and other metropolitan cities. Some in his sister's family were among them. John McCaffrey could still hear the frightful cries for help from those soon to meet their maker, and the sight and stench of the dead was enough to dull ones senses. Yet even to this day, the Queen and Parliament in faraway London continued to ignore the plight of their Irish citizens. John McCaffrey would not forget what he saw here nor would he, like so many of his compatriots, forgive the Crown for failing to come to the aid of so many desperate souls.

Although the famine was nearly twenty years in the past, the city still exhibited a vast landscape of terrible poverty and squalor, not unlike that of the 1840's. Yet today, with Great Britain experiencing a tide of phenomenal growth and expansion, and well on its way to becoming one of the greatest-industrialized nations in the world, Ireland's major export was still its young men and women. For those who stayed behind, most lived in stark poverty in homes best described as mud huts, with many sharing accommodations with their livestock, all under the same thatched roof.

Driven from their lands, without jobs, funds or hope the Irish farmer continued to migrate to the largest cities where if arrested for stealing food, they ended up in jail, while others, if caught begging on the streets ended up in the Queen's Work House. The government conspired with the ship owners to place as many of these largely illiterate and unskilled itinerant farm families aboard the first available vessel leaving for Canada, New Zealand or to the United States. They were not concerned where this wretched cargo of humanity would go, only that they would leave their city.

It was this attitude however, of both the English and Irish public officials that proved beneficial to many escaped convicts or persons fleeing the Queen's retribution. It made it possible for many of them to immigrate if not to the country of their choice, to some place free of the British flag. This catastrophic genocidal policy of coercing law-abiding citizens from their ancestral lands resulted in untold hardship including the tragic loss of life for thousands.

Although the vestiges of that policy continued, John McCaffrey believed today that it could work to the advantage of his family. Nothing about his young family would set them apart from hundreds of others waiting to board ship. Yet he was worried for he was sure the authorities would be on the lookout for the Burke and Gordon boys. He would have to warn his children once again to avoid any contact with their cousins' families should they be present to see their sons off.

John McCaffrey noticed something else that was quite different from his last visit to Cork—the number of sailing ships tied-up on the quay totaled less than half of those docked here at the time of the Great Hunger. In addition, the ships were different; most were a combination sale and coal fired side-wheelers. He remembered reading that the newly powered steam driven ships were now setting new records crossing to New York, often in less than three weeks time. That was good news.

Most of the larger ships that set out to cross the Atlantic during the famine were three-massed frigates; they dropped anchor at Cork only long enough to take on additional passengers. The death toll aboard those ships was high. Many of the emigrants onboard, weakened by hunger and disease died within hours of setting sail from Belfast or Dublin. When that happened, the ship's passengers, at the direction of the captain disposed of their bodies into the Irish Sea. Crewmembers frequently refused to participate in this gruesome event for fear of ending up like the afflicted voyager. Yet these deaths never dissuaded the ship owners from replenishing this cargo of human souls. The ships put-in at Cork, staying only long enough to take on additional passengers bound for America.

It did not take John McCaffrey long to locate Captain Gordon Sinclair's ship the *Isle of Jersey*. Captain William Smyth's ship the *Hampton Court* was also tied-up on one of the nearby finger piers. Both were three-masted Clipper ships and each exhibited an exterior of unkemptness, uncommon for a British merchant ship of their vintage. John McCaffrey was not knowledgeable about seagoing ships, but he thought the outward appearance of these two sailing vessels would not lead a layperson to choose one for transport on the open ocean.

Approaching the ship, he hailed a man carrying a duffle bag up the gangway of the *Isle of Jersey*. He was a large man with a full head of red hair and matching beard.

"Who ye be looking for, Man?"The Seaman responded gruffly, having reached the deck and setting down his bag.

"Captain Sinclair, Sir." John McCaffrey replied respectfully.

"And what business have ye with the captain, may I ask?"

"I came to discuss the Atlantic crossing as my family is booked to travel to America with ye next week. I am also at liberty to pay the fare at this time, Sir."

"Ye don't have to address me as sir, Mister." He laughed. "I'm just the ship's First Mate. I am not in the navy, although sometimes the captain likes to pretend that he and I are still officers with Her Majesty's fleet of fine ships. However, the Captain is not here this early in the morning. At this time of day, he and Captain Smyth take breakfast at O'Leary's bar at the ferry terminal. Ye can catch him over there; his breakfast often lasts most of the day." He chuckled.

"May I have your name, Sir?" John McCaffrey asked, now smiling, "So I may tell him that I talked to you."

"Jason Winters and like I said ye can drop the sir." The man responded. He too was smiling.

"I wonder Mr. Winters, while I'm here if I could see where my family would be berthed on this voyage?"

"Ye are not accompanying the family to America?"

"No, my wife is sickly and unable to travel."

"I am sorry to hear that; sure, come aboard. What is your name?"

"John McCaffrey."

"Ye first class or steerage, Mr. McCaffrey?"

"John, please Mr. Winters. I think steerage, but I need to discuss that with the Captain."

"Too bad, sure I'll show ye both areas. We have eighteen first class compartments and only two of them are committed. With the war going on in America, no one except the poor are brave enough to emigrate to that part of the world for the fear of getting involved. Most first class travelers feel it is much safer to go on into Canada, than to the United States. The *Hampton Court*, ye see there, that is Captain Smyth's ship. They will accompany us to Newfoundland and then go on into Canada by way of the Saint Lawrence River." He continued talking as he led the way toward the first-class compartments. "Watch your step here we are renovating steerage a bit to hold a few more livestock. We try to keep them separated from steerage passengers as much as we can."

"I did not know ye carried livestock aboard ship."

"Well we will always ship livestock to and from America and Australia; but soon it won't be necessary for food purposes. A crossing to North America used to take four to six weeks and Australia up to two months, so we had to have fresh meat. We will have a few turkeys, pigs, and calves on this trip. However, the industry will cut the crossing time in half within a year or two. With the new steam-driven ships coming online, there will not be a need for a chef to substitute as a butcher. That's progress I guess." He laughed. "And next week we will be taking a stud and a few brood mares. The Captain fancies himself as an expert in horseflesh. He will sell them in New York or Baltimore. We always hire a half dozen steerage passengers to care for them; they get a little extra food for their families as we only provide limited meal services to steerage class passengers; they get oatmeal in the morning and soup and bread at night."

John McCaffrey thought that the first class compartments looked terribly small, particularly when Mr. Winters explained the shipping company designed them to accommodate a family of five. Each contained two stools bolted to the deck, and three fold-down bunk beds with sleeping mats and two hammocks. Steerage was quite another story. Entering the nearly dark chamber, the First Mate explained, "These two decks house our steerage class passengers, each deck will accommodate one-hundred or so people. Here," he said, taking his visitor amidship and down a stairwell into the dark recesses of the hull, "as you can see, there are wooden bunks that line the bulkheads on both sides of the ship. We also have two water toilets here; each has the latest hand operated pump. They flush seawater just with a pump of the handle. They also provide water as needed for bathing and cleaning purposes. And we can sleep additional people if necessary on these tables," he added pointing to the two long tables that served the dual purpose of preparing meals during the day or for sleeping space at night.

John McCaffrey grimaced as he took this all in, for to escape the vengefulness of the tyrant who ruled his country, his family would have to cope with these grim and wretched accommodations for the next month. This angered him; he thought it inconceivable that in a civilized society, the ruling class of Englishmen would visit such torment and affliction upon the Irish people. His family, was not only being torn apart by the brutal behavior of the cruelest of all tyrants in the English speaking world, but now they were about to experience the horrors of being cooped-up for days if not weeks in an inhospitable cubicle to escape her tyranny.

For a sovereign to stand by and allow such barbaric behavior to take place and not lift a hand to protect eight million of her citizens was an iniquitous circumstance of the times. John McCaffrey, concerned for the health of his children during the voyage was sure there would be no doctors or nurses aboard should there be a need for one such was the case during the exodus of the 1840s. In those crossings, typhus and the dreaded cholera killed thousands before they ever reached their destination. He knew it could spread like wildfire in steerage-class passenger compartments. Crews fearing for their own lives often locked-down escape hatches to minimize contact with sick passengers, allowing no one out until the ship arrived at its port of call. These thoughts raced across John McCaffrey's mind as he walked back down the gangplank of the *Isle of Jersey* and headed for O'Leary's pub.

O'Leary's was not unlike most pubs in the largest Irish cities, except that it was located on a pier near the city's ferry terminal. Today, it was nearly vacant except one table in a back corner, occupied by two men dressed in clothing that had all the earmarks of the British naval service. John McCaffrey recognized both men almost immediately, yet physically the ageing process had not been kind to either man. Twenty years earlier these two young, robust and active naval lieutenants were well on their way to becoming career officers with England's finest. Both graduated from the Queen's Naval Academy and fought in naval engagements against France and Spain. Yet, the excesses of liquor and promiscuous living practices led to an early end to their once promising careers. Both men were overweight. Their once resplendent uniforms, now worn and soiled from spilled liquor and leavings from the table, gave stark evidence of a decadent, or debauched life style.

Approaching the two men John McCaffrey introduced himself. "Gentlemen, my name is John McCaffrey; I am here to finalize the arrangements for my family to travel to America on the *Isle of Jersey*." He offered forthrightly, and then turning to Captain Sinclair, added, "I believe that is your ship, Captain. I talked to your first mate. He told me I would find ye here."

"McCaffrey, hey, good, I'm always glad to discuss the crossing with the uninformed." He replied seriously. "By the looks of you, I take it you're a farmer?"

"Yes, I am, sir."

"Well McCaffrey, landed gentlemen have no idea of the hazards one might encounter crossing the North Atlantic, particularly at this time of year. Sit here and we will talk." He offered and John McCaffrey sat directly across the table from the two men.

"How is it that you know me?" Sinclair asked with a scowl, then after a glance at his fellow captain, added, "You don't look familiar McCaffrey. Have we met before?"

"Yes, it was many years ago in Galway."

"I don't remember you; McCaffrey, you say. In what business were we involved? I was an officer in Her Majesty's Navy stationed in Galway in the forties. But I do not remember you."

"Nor I," Captain Smyth interjected. "Just what business would we have had with you at Galway, McCaffrey?

"Ye both were involved in the business of sedition and treason." He said quietly, looking at Sinclair first and then to Smyth.

The two former naval officers appeared stunned at the charges leveled against them by this stranger; nevertheless, Sinclair reacted quickly.

"Ye Irish son of a bitch," he bellowed, drawing a small revolver out of his coat pocket, pointing it directly at John McCaffrey.

"You will tell me McCaffrey what your real name is and what you hope to accomplish with such a foul accusation. If you don't I'll blow the top of your head off, right now."

"You stupid Irishman, McCaffrey!" Captain Gordon Smyth roared, enraged by their visitor's unsettling charges. "What the hell are you up to?" He demanded taking out his own weapon from his coat pocket; it too was a small revolver.

John McCaffrey merely nodding his head responded quietly. "Yes, Gentlemen, we in fact met several times in 1842 on the Naval Pier at Galway. That's when ye gave me these documents." Slowly he reached into his coat pocket and passed two Royal Navy monthly ship manifests dated September 1842, each signed by one of the two former naval supply officers.

In examining the documents, the two appeared surprised, even somewhat astonished, but apparently untroubled by these for neither man yet fully grasped the role they were about to play in this encounter.

"Just who the hell are you, you Irish bastard?" Captain Sinclair demanded.

"Ye knew me in those days as, 'The Irishman from Limerick.' Does that not help ye to recall what ye did to further the cause of The Movement? Ye knew what we were doing. Eventually the Galway Constabulary took us down, but by that time, we had smuggled a thousand weapons and millions of rounds of ammunition, and tons of explosives into Ireland from France. Ye two provided a clear path for us to do that."

"Why you Fenian bastard!" William Smyth roared. "I ought to kill you here and now." He said cocking his revolver and pointing it directly at their visitor.

"No! Not yet!" Gordon Sinclair growled. "He's got more to say, I can tell by the look on his face. He is mocking us. Spit it out McCaffrey or you will not walk out of here alive."

"I have sixteen documents just like these with ye signatures on each and everyone. If ye will take the time to review the Galway papers, ye will note that each of our forays into Galway occurred after the Royal Navy took on supplies and returned to their base on the Aran Islands. We knew, thanks to ye two traitors that after the Navy set off for the Kilronan anchorage we would have at least two days to move our guns safely through Galway." Then pausing for a moment, he added. "Gentlemen, if I do not walk out of here, or if ye do not do as I request those documents shall be dropped off at the Crown Prosecutor's office in London."

"Keep talking, McCaffrey," Captain Sinclair responded grudgingly, his face contorted with a contemptuous smile.

Ignoring the threat from the two men holding handguns pointed directly at him from across the table he continued. "Ye two heroes have involved my children and my sister's children in a capital crime scheme; if discovered it might very well land all of them in Kilmainham Jail. It is already underway, so it is too late for me to stop it. Captain Smyth, ye will have the stolen cattle ye talked these children into stealing to pay for their passage to America. They will be within your cattle byre by this time tomorrow. And as for ye Sinclair, the stud ye have talked my son into taking will be delivered dockside as ye requested."

"You sound like you have more to say, McCaffrey." Captain Sinclair growled. "Let's have it all. What do you want from us?"

Turning directly to face the enraged man, he responded grimly. "Safe passage to America, Captain, for my family, first class, that's it. Because of the war in America, ye have several uncommitted First Class cabins available on this upcoming crossing. I want four of them reserved for my family and my sister's family; twenty people all together. Without exception, ye shall provide these accommodations at steerage fare."

"Those are outrageous demands, completely preposterous." Captain Smyth bellowed, slamming his fist down on the table. "Why should either one of us adhere to such demands?"

"Because I will do what I promised and the Queen's men will hang ye both for treason if not for theft of livestock."

"I think you are bluffing." Captain Sinclair growled.

"Think what ye will, Gentlemen," he responded quietly. "Today ye let a total stranger come and sit at your breakfast table not knowing the man's purpose; ye would not be hard to kill." At this time, John McCaffrey stood up; to both men's surprise, they discovered that during this meeting their visitor held a loaded and cocked revolver pointed at them under the table.

"I will repeat myself, so there is no misunderstanding, if my children are harmed in any way I will turn the rest of these papers over to the Crown and if they don't hang ye, I will kill ye both myself."

With this last threat on the table, both men grudgingly acquiesced to the safe delivery of the Malone and McCaffrey families, as demanded. When his meeting with Captains Sinclair and Smyth ended, John McCaffrey walked out into the cool morning air of the quay, pleased with what he had accomplished, and then he headed off to his sister's home near Queen's College.

Pushing back from the dinner table that evening, John McCaffrey felt good about today's encounter with the two former naval officers. He had no doubt but that they would carry out their agreement; should they not do so he was quite sure both would hang. The men who manage The Queen's Navy do not take treason lightly. Besides his sister, Margaret's dinner of fried chicken and dumplings was delicious. Taking out his corncob pipe, he filled it with tobacco and taking a bit of burning turf from the fire to light it, settled back into the comfort of a straw-cushioned rocking chair. His sister brought him a cup of tea and then sat across the table from her brother while her daughter Shannon and nephew Jimmy cleaned off the dinner table. Three years had slipped by since he saw his sister last, that was when she came to his daughter Joan's funeral. He thought at forty-eight years she looked so much older than at that time.

"Go with the children, Maggie." He said. "Take Shannon and go with the twins; start a new live for all of ye in America. There is nothing here for either of us anymore. Your husband and two of your boys are already dead and my Mary Kate will be gone before the end of the month."

"What would I do?" Maggie Malone asked her brother. "And Shannon is only a baby."

"I am not a baby, Momma!" Shannon Malone exclaimed loudly. She pretended to be cleaning the floor near the fireplace, but she and Jimmy McCaffrey had quietly listened in on every word spoken by her uncle this evening. "I'm eighteen and working nearly fulltime now. I could go and I would find work in New York or Boston. With Kevin and Donald, we would get along just fine. The boys could get good jobs in America and not be out rustling cattle; that's all they've talked about since they got out of jail."

"Our brother Paul would take care of all four of ye until ye have a chance to find your own way in America."

"You should have gone when Daddy was alive, Momma." Shannon said, scolding her mother. "I told you that before, but you always said you didn't have the money. Well I have it now." She offered, proudly, "I have saved enough for passage and I want to go with Jimmy and Katelyn and the boys."

"I'll not tell ye what to do Maggie," John McCaffrey responded kindly. "But I made arrangements today for your travel, should ye decide to go. The boys will come by a week from Tuesday next. Take only what you need, including food for the crossing. It will not be an easy trip, but ye and the women folks will have a first class cabin together and ye can fend for each other while aboard ship."

"We'll see," she answered quietly, but this non-committal response did not set well with Shannon.

"No, Uncle John," she said forcefully, then turning to her mother added, "We will be on that ship." Her mother smiled, but did not respond.

En route back to Mallow and home, John McCaffrey was comfortable with the way things worked out for him and his family today. If the young men who entered into an admittedly unholy alliance with Captains Sinclair and Smyth, escaped detection, they may well accomplish their mission and soon be safely on their way to America. Nevertheless, he was still concerned for he knew that the risk of detection, capture, and imprisonment was extremely high. Too many people knew of their plans and too many youngsters in the group looked upon the cattle raid and the theft of one of the Queen's prize studs as an exciting adventure, an adventure where the chance for failure never entered their mind.

It was past midnight when the two of them arrived back home where they found Oliver Jackson's cart and Connemara pony tied-up at the front door and the house alight with candles. Jackson, a trained veterinarian was the nearest thing to a physician available to tenant farmers. In the past twenty years, his wife Angelina assisted him whenever his patient was female. Upon entering the house, Louise Haggerty greeted them with a "Shush," and a single finger held to her lips. She was holding Katelyn asleep in her arms while the two youngest boys, Thomas and Daniel were sound asleep on mats near the fireplace. Speaking softly she said, "John, Jimmy be quiet. The children have just gotten to sleep." Then with a whimper, as tears formed in her eyes added, "Mary Kate's gone. The Good Lord took her in her sleep this afternoon. I am so sorry, John. Ye were so in love and she was such a grand person and she was my friend."

"But Daddy she can't be," Jimmy responded woefully. "She was fine yesterday when we left. She can't be gone now." He sobbed quietly.

"Who was here, when she went away?" John McCaffrey asked quietly.

"Angelina and I, Colleen was with us. The children came and got me. I sent them after Father Sullivan and Mister Jackson. Angelina came with him. However, she was gone before they got here. I am so sorry for ye and the children John. Father Sullivan gave her the Last Rites of the Church and he will be back to ask God's Favor for Mary Kate at the wake. Angelina is preparing Mary Kate now."

"There will be no wake, Louise." John McCaffrey stated quite forcefully. "Mary Kate did not want some total stranger in our home keening over her dead body. Moreover, there will be no church service. Father Sullivan can lead the prayers at the cemetery if he chooses, but Mary Kate made her peace with her God a longtime ago. Her only interest was in her children. Two of them have gone on ahead to make way for her and she knows the rest of them will soon be safe in America."

"But John, what about the Church; what will the priest say?"

"I don't care about the Church anymore or what Father Sullivan might say, Louise. What I care about is our children and I have made arrangements this very day to take them away from this hell on earth. We are living in a time and place of horror, conceived by the Queen and Parliament. They hope to resolve the 'Irish Problem' as they call it by killing our people. The Church has remained silent while our children have died right here for lack of common decency. The Queen's henchmen are very efficient in carrying out her dirty work. They deliberately starved to death over a million of our fellow citizens, while another two or three million fled the country where they were born. That bitch has taken our land, our livestock and stolen the heritage that our children should lawfully enjoy. Consequently, Louise, I am not interested in what Father Sullivan thinks or what anyone else thinks about this. I will bury my Mary Kate here and she will become a part of Ireland, a part that was denied her while she was alive."

At the cemetery near Saint Joseph's Church, Father Michael Sullivan held gravesite services for Mary Katherine McCaffrey. Nearly one-hundred young men and women that she and Louise Haggerty brought into this world were there to honor her. Not surprisingly, more than a score of Protestant English men and women also attended the service. Methodists, Anglican and Presbyterians of all ages from Cork, Clare, Limerick, and Galway Counties, all recipients of her nursing skills, came to pay tribute to her. Many in the crowd however, were confounded when Lord Willingham and his family stepped out of a splendid coach, drawn by four beautiful black geldings. No one could remember Lord Willingham ever before attending the funeral of a tenant farmer's family member. Indeed, this was quite unusual. Yet some remembered that Mary Katherine provided lifesaving care to the Willingham family's firstborn grandchild when the boy fell from the back of an unruly Connemara pony.

At the end of the service, death provided Mary Kate her due; she became forever the sole owner of her little piece of Ireland, something denied to her in her own lifetime.

CHAPTER 3

RETRIBUTION

Early Tuesday morning, a crowd began to gather around the five ships tied-up along the Quay. Before the day was over, at high tide, Ireland would add the names of nearly another eight-hundred or more of its citizens to the long list of over two million who in the past twenty years fled their homeland. Both relatives and friends alike, along with the curious came to Cork to see them off. They would travel on four of Great Britain's merchant ships and one ship sailing under the French flag.

The presence of the French vessel with its huge masts and steam driven paddle wheels drew nearly as much attention from the visitors as that given to family members waiting to board. In comparison to the English merchant fleet, the *Villeneuve* was a huge vessel that overshadowed both the *Isle of Jersey* and the *Hampton Court* tied-up nearby. After Napoleon Bonaparte's disastrous defeat at the hands of the British at Waterloo, the French removed from office the man who would be ruler of all of Western Europe. Now their challenges became less draconian. After the war both nations moved swiftly to repair their economies and gain the lead over the other by taking full advantage of the rapid growth in the maritime industry. That industry provided the industrial world with the means to move people and new products to even the most remote corners of the world. In the race to capture the trade routes to and from the Americas, France soon became a threat to the Island nation's rule of the seas by developing one the largest maritime fleets of any country on the European continent. During the American Civil War, the French took an active role in supporting the Union Forces of the United States. As opposed to the British, they also provided both guns and ships to the American Navy; the *Villeneuve* would be the largest battle ready warship sold to the Americans during the war.

The French ship and its crew were a mere curiosity to most in this huge crowd, but not to the French Ambassador to England and the ambassador's staff who were on hand to see their newest ship take on passengers and cargo for the North American market. The *Villeneuve,* (named after Admiral Pierre de Villeneuve defeated by Lord Nelson in the Battle of Trafalgar in 1805) with France's colors flying from its tallest mast, towered over the four British merchant ships tied-up nearby. Although nearly fully loaded with French citizens heading for their settlements in Quebec, it was about to take on additional cargo and a few English and Anglican Scott-Irish first class passengers destined for Canada.

The French ship however, was more than a curiosity to the dozen or so British Naval officers present at the Quay. There was no mistaking the ship for what it was, a poorly disguised "Man of War" destined for delivery to the United States. While the English continued to trade with the Confederacy, a French representative struck a deal to deliver the Villanova to the U. S. Navy. It was obvious to the French that the rebellious secessionists would lose the war and France was vying to become a major player on the world stage. They were about to challenge the British at sea and compete for the largess offered by the American dollar.

By mid afternoon, all five ships began taking on first class passengers. Before doing so however, from atop the gangway of the *Villeneuve*, Cork's Lord Mayor Robert Allison, standing beside the French Ambassador, Louis des Champs and the ship's Captain Claude de-Beaupre, delivered with much flare a rousing speech. The overweight red-haired politician with the huge mustache and loud voice, speaking to the crowd, began by calling out to them "My beloved Irish brethren." He then added, with his voice reverberating off the walls of the Customs House, "The thought that so many of my fellow citizens find it necessary to leave your homes and cross this great ocean is a sad day for all of Ireland. Nevertheless, I applaud your courage. I know that in the Americas ye shall make a new home for yourselves in the great American wilderness. That will be a challenge, but a challenge that I am sure ye, our beloved citizens are capable of accomplishing. We shall miss each and every one of you."

When the Lord Mayor paused someone in the crowd yelled, "Ye turn-coat bastard; the Brit's drove our people out and you did nothing to stop them!" The crowd yelled their support for the anonymous heckler, many with contemptuous comments of their own aimed at the Mayor and the Crown. Unperturbed the Lord Mayor continued, "I congratulate the French Government, Ambassador des Champs and Captain de-Beaupre for providing such a fine ship *to carry our family members* to the new world." He made no comment on the worthiness of the British merchant ships.

Although the Lord Mayor praised the fine qualities of those about to emigrate, two things he did not mention, first there would be no Irish steerage passengers taken onboard the French ship. The second was the primary purpose of bringing the ship to Ireland, for France was in fierce competition with Belfast ship building firms to capture the fast growing American market for merchant and warships alike. In the last year, England sold three naval warships to the Confederate

States, while the French were doing their best to support the American Navy. Taking on passengers in Ireland was their way of telling the industrialized world that France would be a staunch competitor for the North American ocean-going trade route. However, the *Villeneuve* was much more than a poorly disguised merchant ship.

Once Captain de-Beaupre off-loaded his cargo and passengers in Quebec and steamed beyond the territorial waters of the Crown's most cherished colony, his crew would change into their military uniforms and hoist the insignia of the French Navy. Moreover, before sailing into New York Harbor, more than fifty cannon, removed from the cargo hold, and mounted on deck, would transform the innocent merchant vessel into a formidable warship. To counter Great Britain's support for the Confederacy, Captain de-Beaupre on behalf of the French government was to deliver one of France's largest and finest warships to a nation at war with itself.

Late in the afternoon, John McCaffrey and an entourage of twenty family members arrived at the Quay. They came out onto the docks in groups of two or three at a time so as not to attract attention and quickly mingled with the growing crowd of emigrants, well-wishers, and the curious. Mathew and Louise Haggerty and their girls were there; daughter Colleen and Donald Malone escorted eight-year-old Katelyn McCaffrey. The four younger McCaffrey boys arrived separately, with one of them coming onto the pier with his Aunt Margaret Malone and her daughter Shannon. One of the Burke boys and Michael Ryan drifted toward the *Isle of Jersey* accompanied by two Ryan girls and Patrick Kennedy's sister. There was no sign of Bobby Burke or Leo Gordon.

After raiding the Queen's horse barns at Mallow Castle, Jimmy along with Kevin Malone and Patrick Kennedy planned to approach the city from along the water's edge, their route would take them through the back streets of Cork. They hoped to arrive after sunset, but in time for boarding.

John McCaffrey went directly to the roof of the Custom House where he was in a position to observe anyone approaching either Captain Sinclair or Captain Smyth's ship. More than a dozen members of the Constabulary and two Fusiliers officers from the Cork Garrison appeared early in the afternoon, yet they, like their fellow Irish visitors appeared more interested in the French ship and the passengers boarding that vessel. They took particular note of the young women dressed in their Sunday finery and paid little attention to the common and poorly clothed Irish peasantry waiting to board the British merchant ships.

As dusk settled over the Quay, the merchant ships began to take on their cargo of steerage passengers. Before these souls got a good look at the dismal lower deck facilities they would occupy for the next few weeks, they would be far out to sea. The newly boarded, guided by members of the crew carrying lanterns made their way down into the bowls of the ship. For the children and most of the adults it was a frightening experience and after depositing their food and luggage rushed back onto the deck to get that last glimpse of friend or relative who came to see them off.

As John McCaffrey's family gathered at the foot of the gangplank, he came down from the roof of the building to say goodbye. The younger boys, Michael, Joseph, Thomas, and Daniel all tried their best to be brave but were unable to hold back their tears. "Why Daddy?" Daniel asked. "Why won't you go with us?" He said while weeping and holding onto his father. "Please Daddy," cried Michael with tears rolling down his face. "At least tell us why you won't go with us."

This strong-willed father, a man who could never show his humanness suddenly discovered something about himself that he had successfully repressed and concealed from his family for so many years. He was terrorized by the fact that he was about to lose them, for he knew he would never see his family again. Now for the first time his children would see their father cry.

"I cannot go with ye because I love ye," he whispered quietly to the five youngsters gathered around closely, holding onto him. "I would be a burden to all of ye which ye cannot understand now, but ye will. Some day Aunt Margaret or Jimmy will tell ye why; but I cannot do that now. So ye be off." He said, turning to his sister, he kissed her goodbye. "Take them aboard Margaret and take care of them. I must go and make sure that Jimmy and the other boys get on-board."

"John, do not fret, I shall care for all of them as if they were my own." She said quietly. "Ye take care of yourself," she added, as tears began to run down her cheeks. She knew that with her brother's deteriorating physical condition this was a final goodbye. The ravages of late-term consumption, was literally eating her beloved brother alive. He was never a tall man, not much taller than she was, but always solidly built, straight backed, muscular and strong as a bull. However, the death mask, the drawn face, and obvious deteriorating physical appearance of her once beautiful brother was no stranger to Margaret Malone, she had already lost three members of her own family to this not so silent death, so common among the Irish. No one needed to tell her he would not live more than a few weeks at most.

Doctors in Dublin said he would not make it through the year; and now it appeared that this tough middle-aged Irishman had only days or weeks left on this earth. He had the look of a man near death's door, losing so much weight that he was the spitting image of a local farmer's scarecrow. His skeletal frame was clearly visible through his ragged clothing and his gaunt features; the bulging eyeballs, sunken cheeks, and bad teeth gave him the appearance of a cadaver. Notwithstanding his frail health, Maggie Malone knew her brother well enough that in the short time he had left on this earth, he would lash out at those he held responsible for driving his family out of Ireland. Then like Mary Kate, he too would get his little piece of Ireland, but only from the soil at Saint Joseph's cemetery.

"Ye best get home now, John." She added, shaking her head in grief. "Ye look worn out. We will pray for ye." When they parted, Margaret Malone and daughter Shannon gathered up the brood of youngsters and led them up the gangplank; she never looked back. As the family went aboard a small band of musicians, friends and relatives of some of those leaving, with tears in their eyes began playing a medley of old Irish tunes. It was their way of saying goodbye knowing that they would probably never see their loved ones again.

Hearing a commotion at the end of the pier John McCaffrey saw his son and his two nephews leading four horses toward the *Isle of Jersey*. The boys smiled as they approached with Jimmy calling out excitedly, "We did it Daddy. We didn't have any trouble at all. We cut their fences before we went into the horse byre to get the stud and these brood mares. We untied every horse there, then we opened all the gates and the byre doors and I used your gun to scatter them. They took off like crazy in all directions." He laughed, "And we rode like hell."

"Uncle John," Kevin Malone chimed in laughing, "those army guys will have a hell of a time explaining to their commander just what happened. They came out shooting but

I do not think they even saw us. The more they fired the more they scattered the herd." He clearly was satisfied with his part in this dangerous game of rustling the Queen's livestock.

"It really was funny Uncle John." Pat Kennedy added, with a chuckle.

Holding up both his hands to quiet them, Jimmy's father admonished the boys, "Quiet down all of ye. We need to get these horses to the aft loading gangway and get ye aboard. The ship is due to sail in less than an hour."

"Okay, Daddy," his son replied, still smiling.

"Did either of you see Burke and Gordon?" He asked.

"Yes, Daddy, we saw them about a half hour ago they were waiting until just before midnight to board Captain Smyth's ship. They told us a cadre of military people was questioning everyone going aboard and they were waiting until the Army left. They should be aboard by now. Bobby asked us to stay alert until the *Hampton Court* pulled away from the dock."

"If the Army is searching just their ship someone onboard must have betrayed them." His father angrily responded, shaking his head, "otherwise they would have posted all four ships. Ye be careful now. Stay alert, make your way aboard and go to your compartments, and stay out of sight until the ship pulls away from the dock. Aunt Margaret and Mathew Haggerty have taken care of the children." Then placing his hands on the shoulders of his two young nephews, he hugged both of them. "Goodbye boys, God Bless ye both—take care." He then turned to his son Jimmy, but again was unable to control his emotions. "Goodbye James." He said quietly. "Take care of your brothers and look after Katelyn. Your Uncle Paul will put ye up until ye find your way."

"Goodbye Uncle John," Kevin Malone called out as he headed for the cargo-boarding ramp, his voice tinged with sorrow.

Jimmy McCaffrey grasped his father throwing both arms around him and held on to him until his father pried his son's hands loose, "Ye must go now, Son," he said trying hard to hold back the tears.

"You better take this, Daddy." Jimmy said as he handed the revolver back to his father. John McCaffrey gave the gun to his son cautioning all three before they left on their escapade that they must not use the weapon unless their lives were in danger. "If ye are caught with this, they will hang ye for certain; throw it away if ye find yourselves trapped."

John remained on the dock until all three youngsters disappeared inside the cargo hold and then returned to his vantage point on the roof of the Customs House. From there he had an excellent view of both the *Isle of Jersey* and the *Hampton Court*. Shortly before the *Isle of Jersey* sailed, a large horse-drawn carriage pulled by four beautiful iron grey horses arrived on the dock. Two armed men on horseback accompanying the carriage dismounted when it stopped at the foot of the gangplank.

Most everyone in Cork County cringed whenever this rig, with its barred windows and armed escort came into view for this magnificent outfit with its stunningly beautiful horses also belonged to Sheriff Solomon Reed. He and the Crown prosecutor used it to provide transport for dispossessed farmers and businesspersons on their way to jail in Dublin for resisting the Crown's repressive property confiscation policies. In recent years, six young members of the Malone/McCaffrey Clan, unable to appease the Queen's Court became acquainted with this magnificent team and unusual coach. They ended-up in the Deportation Yard in Kilmainham Jail.

John McCaffrey watched closely for he had seen this scenario played out many years ago on this very dock. When the Crown deported the O'Sullivan Clan to Australia, the army shackled the men and marched them to the prison ship while their womenfolk and wee ones came by carriage. A group of women got out of the coach tonight and it looked like a repeat performance. However, this evening a middle-aged woman accompanied by a group of eight young *women of the evening* stepped out onto the dock; some of them appeared to be as young as fourteen or fifteen years of age. He thought to himself that Captain Sinclair would not be happy to have this problem dumped in his lap. Yet the women would probably be better off, they would no longer be subject to a system of justice that treated animals better than their own citizens. Two crewmembers escorted the woman and her charges to steerage.

At midnight, an order came down to haul-in the gangplanks to the four British merchant ships, however, the French ship had long since completed its loading process and was well on its way out to sea, but still visible in the moonlight. There was a loud clattering of metal and wood grating across the dock as sailors and dockworkers yelled or cursed while removing the gangplanks. With people shouting goodbye to their friends and loved ones, the sounds drifting up to the roof of the Customs Building along with music from the small band of musicians, loyal to the last.

As John McCaffrey was waiting for the ships to depart, he heard a loud commotion coming from the *Hampton Court* with men yelling and cursing, then shots rang-out from the nearby dock. Several members of the Constabulary along with an Army officer began shooting at two men in the water. It was his two nephews Bobby Burke and Leo Gordon. A fellow passenger had betrayed the two; the culprit identified them as the two escaped convicts the police were looking for. Once identified the two men knew if they stayed on the *Hampton Court*, prison awaited them upon their arrival in Canada with an eventual return to England to hang.

John watched as the two men swam desperately, soon disappearing from sight beneath the dock. Shortly thereafter, he saw what he thought were his son and Patrick Kennedy on the Port side of the *Isle of Jersey* pulling something out of the water, but he was too far away to tell what was going on.

He stood watch in the moonlight until he saw the last of the four merchant ships disappear beyond the quay en route to the Irish Sea. It was nearly daylight when he came down off the roof of the Customs House; still there was no sign of his two nephews. Perhaps, he thought, they could have gotten away unscathed. It was cold and he shivered in the night air yet at the same time he experienced an incredible sense of satisfaction and contentment. With his children en route to America, he believed they would soon be in safe hands.

Before returning home, John McCaffrey traveled to the village of Mallow or Mala, as it was called in Gaelic where he arranged for a stonemason to produce a headstone for himself and Mary Kate; he then stopped by Saint Joseph's to visit his wife's grave. His grandparents and his father and mother's resting place was nearby in the McCaffrey family plot, their headstones now long weathered by age. Members of the constabulary killed his Grandfather John Timothy McCaffrey when they came to take possession of the McCaffrey ancestral lands. Later that year they hanged John's father, William at Kilmainham Prison for killing one of the Crown's men involved in seizing his grandfather's land. John Joseph

McCaffrey the second, named after his grandfather was just a boy when that occurred.

He and his brothers would not forget what took place in the Kilmainham prison that year, for the authorities hanged four members of the Malone, McCaffrey, and Burke clan on the same day. The Crown brought members of their families to Dublin to bear witness to the executions. John McCaffrey was one of them and he would remember to the day he died the efficiency and cold-bloodedness of the Queen's men. The event was to be a reminder to all of Ireland's citizens that 'these ancestral lands' belonged to the Crown not to the Clan. John and his brothers would remember the brutality of that day as long as they lived. When it was over, they brought their father's body back to Saint Joseph's and buried him beside his mother; the year before she had become yet another victim succumbing to The Great Hunger.

Realizing that he had not eaten for two days, upon arriving at his house he found some leftover food in the scullery and gobbled it down. He was famished. Then taking out his corncob pipe, he filled it with tobacco, but before lighting, took the precaution of once again, securing his revolver in the hideout in the fireplace. Weary from his recent hectic activities which led to the successful embarkation of his family and most of his living relatives in County Cork he set his pipe aside and laid down to rest. Exhausted, he experienced another croup attack, a hacking cough one severe enough to double him over, his sputum laced with blood. The episode left him thoroughly fatigued; when it ended, he quickly drifted off to sleep.

He awoke suddenly to find four men hovering over his bed. It was early morning and the sun was shining through the open front door to his house; he had slept for more than twenty-hours. One of the men was, His Lordship Oliver Willingham and the other, the man's overseer Martin Quigley.

"Good morning, John." Willingham said to him, his tone of voice and manner grim. "Where is your family, John?" He asked.

Getting out of bed his tenant responded quietly, "They're gone, Willingham," he said, purposely omitting His Lordship's title.

"What the hell'd'ya mean, they are gone?" Martin Quigley demanded angrily, interjecting himself into Lord Willingham's inquiry. "We can see they're gone. The damn livestock are out and scattered all over hell. Where are your sons?" Quigley demanded his tone of voice ugly. "They didn't show up for work on the Cunningham_place this morning either."

"No, Quigley they won't be showing up to work for ye or Willingham, ever again. They are well on their way to America by now." He smiled grimly. "From now on ye and your Lordship here," he added contemptuously, "shall have to do that dirty work all by yourselves."

"Why you Fenian bastard!" Martin Quigley yelled. "I told His Lordship that he should have kicked you and your clan off his land years ago."

"Just a minute, Mr. Quigley," Lord Willingham interjected, "I want to talk to John alone. You and your men see to the animals."

Martin Quigley chagrined by this sudden and obviously unanticipated dismissal by His Lordship, glared at McCaffrey but without further comment turned, and taking his two men with him left the house.

"John, I am sorry to hear that you sent your family off to America all alone; that you didn't go with them surprises me.

However, why you did not go is none of my business; but we have worked together for several years without a harsh word between us. Moreover, Mary Kate was special to my wife and family. No other servant has been so kind and generous to my family. My wife truly misses her; but surely we could have discussed any grievance that you had with me and maybe we could have worked something out."

"No, Willingham ye and the rest of your Queen's henchmen don't get it. Ye have stolen our land and our children's inheritance; our very existence has depended upon your benevolence ever since the blight. Ye even made a servant of my wife. Do ye think that her service to your family for more than twenty-years for paltry wages justifies the injustices that her absence has wrought upon my family? She lost two lovely daughters while ye and your family had the best medical help available in London; yet ye never offered to help her. Now these last two years she has lain in this very bed, too weak to stand; we had no money to bring a doctor here from Dublin, let alone London and neither ye, nor did your wife so much as lift a little finger to help."

"But, John, we came to her funeral." Lord Willingham stammered after this litany of venomous charges leveled against him by one of his long-time tenants.

"Ye did that alright, but ye didn't fool anyone. That was all show; ye wanted to show your fellow Prods and your tenants and outsiders that ye were always the caring property owner. No, Willingham, do not be a lying hypocrite and tell me what ye have done for me family. Ye killed my wife and I will soon be gone; and while I lay asleep in my bed this morning, I see your henchmen ransacked my home in your presence. Look what they have done." He charged bitterly. "Ye have scattered our belongings, what there is left of them, looking for what, money, or would it be my gun? Ye are a fool Willingham. Thanks to you and the Queen, we have no money and as for my gun, your people will only get it if they kill me, but I will take some of them with me before that happens."

"By God, that's enough John. I'll take no more of your scurrilous lies." Willingham cursed.

"No, ye bastard, I am not finished with ye yet Willingham," John McCaffrey responded angrily, "ye will hear me out. My family will soon be free in America away from the wrath and cruelty of your tyrant Queen and her lackeys in their red and blue uniforms. When ye return to London, ye can tell your fellow high and mighty lords in Parliament that ye lost another twenty constituents today. Only this time ye did not get a chance to hang them, or even starve them to death; they escaped you and your tyrant's wrath."

Shocked that a lowly tenant farmer should accuse him with complicity in such monstrous injustices, injustices that civilized men would find completely reprehensible left His Lordship near speechless. This was too much even for him. No one ever dared to speak to him with such contempt and loathing, had they done so they would not have lived to repeat these charges. John McCaffrey also committed the unpardonable offense, accusing the Queen and he, a Member of Parliament of such crimes was a one-way ticket to the whipping post at Kilmainham Jail, if not to the gallows.

Willingham shook his head and walked away. At the front door of the cottage, he turned back to his tenant, and then quietly responded, his voice cold and ugly. "Damn you, John McCaffrey!" He cursed. "You have stepped over the line! You be gone from my property by this time tomorrow. If you are still here when I return I will see that you hang." John McCaffrey would ignore Lord Willingham's threat; after all what could they do to a dying man. However, he knew His Lordship well enough that he was sure the man would try to carry out his threat. More than one member of the McCaffrey Clan who crossed swords with this man in past years, ended up tied to the whipping post in Kilmainham Jail. One mistake that John McCaffrey never made was to underestimate the barbaric nature and viciousness of his landlord.

Removing the two small stones from the front of the fireplace, he recovered his revolver and a box of cartridges; what money he and Mary Kate normally kept in this *safe place* was in the hands of his children so there was little of value left in the house.

On his way to the cattle barns, he could see Lord Willingham's men on Mathew Haggerty's nearby fields rounding up the livestock that Haggerty turned loose before leaving for Cork. Taking the boys' Connemara pony from the stall he saddled it, put warm clothing, food from the scullery and a handful of matches in two saddlebags, and tied them onto the cantle. Returning to the barn, he checked the huge facility and all of the out buildings to make sure that none of the animals turned loose the day before had come back inside. Finding the building clear he lit a match and dropped it into a pile of dry hay near the door. The barn, the largest in the county, built by his grandfather and father would soon no longer be available for use by His Lordship.

Returning to what at one time was his grandfather's house and for a short time his fathers, he walked through it slowly, vividly picturing the events of a lifetime of joy and pleasure this home brought to his family. Even though it was not without its share of unhappy events that so many other Irish families had experienced in recent years, it had been a home of love and kindness that no one who lived under its' thatched roof would ever forget that. Striking another match near the front door, he touched off the thatched roof. Then he walked away, and without looking back mounted the pony and rode off toward Mathew Haggerty's farm. As he approached the Haggerty farm buildings, smoke from his burning home and barn, began billowing in the wind, rising high in the air where Lord Willingham's men saw it. This put an end to the livestock roundup as the men hurried off toward the fire.

Riding through the Haggerty barn and finding no livestock inside, he once again dropped a lighted match into a pile of dry straw. Moving on to the house, he examined the building to make sure no one was inside then set the thatched roof afire. John McCaffrey continued on his arson spree over the next two days. Riding across Lord Willingham's huge estate he visited more than a dozen farms formerly owned by Clan members who chose to follow the McCaffrey and Malone families and were now aboard one of the four merchant marine ships bound for North America. At the end of the second day, he moved into the Boggeragh Mountains to avoid both the Constabulary and the Army now on their way to the fires. Climbing to the top of Mount Seefin, he could see for miles as a huge pall of smoke drifted over the countryside. Many of the fires would burn for days for there was no way to stop them.

The next morning he came down off the mountain for he had three more targets in mind before he would end this carnage. In the village of Mala, Lord Willingham's' Overseer Martin Quigley would pay a price for his vicious attacks upon John's loved ones and upon the ordinary people of the village who quite often suffered more from His Lordship's men than the tenant farmer did. More than one villager went to the whipping post at Kilmainham Jail for slighting his lordship or his henchmen; often the charges brought against a citizen were completely bogus, yet he or she ended up in Kilmainham Jail based upon false testimony often provided by Martin Quigley or one of his men.

Quigley lived in a splendid two-story building located at the edge of the village on property seized from the Malone Clan by the Crown. He was a retired Fusilier sergeant and when he left military service Lord Willingham employed him to manage His Lordship's acreage now totaling more than forty farms, farms formerly owned by clan members. Quigley employed a half dozen young men and women as domestics or farm hands from the village at starvation wages; they would serve the needs of he and his family under threat of the loss of their parent's jobs at Lord Willingham's woolen mills in Mala.

Upon knocking on the front door a young woman responded; "What is it you wish, Sir?" She asked politely then recognizing the visitor said, "Oh, Mr. McCaffrey it's you; It's nice to see you." She offered, "Master Quigley is not home, but the Mrs. is here. Do you wish to see her?"

"Yes, please Young Lady," he replied politely recognizing the girl from one of the village families. He remained standing on the stoop until Blanche Quigley came to the door. When she stepped outside, she appeared upset with her visitor, for hired men particularly hired tenant farmers never dared to come to the front door of the overseer's home. Such indiscretions were punishable by reprimand or a thrashing from the overseer.

"What is it you want?" She demanded of her visitor. "My husband is not at home. If you have business with him I suggest you come back tomorrow."

"No Mrs. Quigley, I'll not be back tomorrow. I will find your husband and deal with him later. Are your children in the house?" He asked, his voice threatening.

"What business is that of yours, McCaffrey?" She demanded. "Oh yes, I know who you are. My husband has told me all about you and your kinfolk. But if you must know, my children are away and only I and my servants are here."

"That is all I needed to know Mrs. Quigley." He said, taking his revolver out of his coat pocket. "I am here to burn down your house."

"No." She screamed and tried to run back inside the building but he stood in the doorway blocking her entry. Upon hearing the woman scream, the servant girl reappeared at the door.

"Ye must get your personal things together and get out of this building young lady," he said to her. "Ye have three minutes, so hurry along now for I am going to burn this building."

With Blanch Quigley and her servants running toward the village, he entered the building and set fire to the curtains in every room on the main floor. Within minutes, the house originally built by his grandfather's brother was ablaze.

In the summer Lord Willingham and his family lived in what was at one time the Desmond Tower built in the thirteenth century; and rebuilt as Mallow Castle in the seventeenth century. Desmond Clan members torched the structure in 1690 during the War of the Three Kings along with most of the farm buildings. In 1845, the Queen gave it and the surrounding land holdings to Lord Willingham as a gift for his twenty years of faithful service to Her Majesty in India and Africa. Lord Willingham rebuilt the castle and updated the living quarters with all the amenities of a modern London townhouse. His family came to Mallow Castle at this time of year to enjoy the wonders of Ireland. In the winter, the entire family vacationed on the Mediterranean Sea coast in Spain, with Willingham returning to London when Parliament convened. From the tower of Mallow Castle a visitor could see Willingham's entire estate; it encompassed the farms of more than a dozen members of the McCaffrey, Malone, Haggerty, and Burke Clans.

After watching the huge cloud of dark smoke beginning to drift across his land Lord Willingham and a servant climbed the stone stairwell to the tower outlook; from there, they had an excellent view of all the land between the castle and the Boggeragh Mountains.

"What the hell is going on down there?" Lord Willingham shouted at the servant. "One of those damn Irish croppies probably got drunk and set one of our cattle byre's ablaze. You get down there and find Quigley and find out what happened," he ordered, his voice grim.

"I think there is more than one fire, Your Lordship." The servant responded excitedly. "I see smoke coming from McCaffrey's home place and from the Haggerty farm. In addition, if you look over there toward Mount Seefin that would be in the area of Burke or Malone's place, there are three and possibly as many as five more columns of smoke. It looks like the whole valley below us is on fire."

"Get my horse saddled." Lord Willingham yelled as he ran down from the tower. On his way to the barn, he stopped at his gun cabinet to pick up his revolver and an extra handful of cartridges.

Leaving the village, John McCaffrey traveled through the nearby woods and pastureland avoiding the roadway from Mallow Castle. He stayed out of sight as much as he could to avoid Army patrols now moving back and forth on the roadways in increasing numbers. When he did come out of the woods, an Army patrol spotted him. Spurring his mount into a gallop, he raced into a bog and down into a ravine of thick brush that concealed his escape route. He continued toward Willingham's home without being challenged again, arriving there shortly after noontime. Tying the pony to a post behind the castle, he entered the ancient structure, quickly walking through the building he came out at the back of Lord Willingham's magnificent living quarters where he quickly entered through the back door.

His sudden entry into the house startled a young maid attending to her chores; she screamed and made a hurried exit from the room. A moment later Dame Alice Willingham came into the room; although surprised at finding John McCaffrey standing in her kitchen, she smiled and greeted him kindly.

"What can I do for you, John?" she asked; "I understand there is a problem between you and my husband." However, her smile quickly faded when she took a closer look at her neighbor. With his gaunt and unshaven skeletal appearance and soiled clothing, she immediately became concerned for his wellbeing. "Are you all right, John? You look terrible; tis no wonder ye frightened my poor girl." She said. "Come sit down, are you hungry?" She asked. Her kind-hearted response was not what he expected from Lord Willingham's wife, particularly after his rude and unlawful entry into her home to do harm to her husband and to his property.

However, Alice Willingham was not one easily frightened, even by a neighbor whose ill-tempered behavior and sudden appearance in her kitchen was unexpected. She knew all of her husband's tenants, including John McCaffrey. She respected the man, and his wife Kate particularly, for their kindness and support shown when her young grandson fell from his

Connemara pony. Kate nursed the boy for several days. Lady Willingham was also well aware of the food and assistance the two of them provided to their less fortunate neighbors; that support continued even after the dreaded consumption took their two oldest daughters, and their eldest boy went to prison.

Alice Willingham was different; she was kind to everyone she met and at the time of The Great Hunger, much to the consternation of her husband, she vilified Parliament and the Prime minister accusing them of, "Abandoning the Irish Peasant in their terrible time of need." She pleaded with the London Press to pressure the government to stop exporting livestock and grain and to set up a relief program to feed and care for those suffering from the ravages of the famine. Lord Willingham's colleagues in Parliament became "Most distressed" by her actions and persuaded Lord Willingham to silence her. He thought he accomplished that when he sent her off to the family's winter retreat in Spain. However, unbeknown to Lord Willingham his wife arranged for passage on to Rome where she found a sympathetic ear in the Catholic Pope, Pius IX. The entreaties from Rome however, requesting Queen Victoria to intercede came too late, for by 1850 more than one million Irish men, women, and children had already become victims of The Great Famine.

"Hello Alice," John McCaffrey said quietly. "No I am not well, but I thank ye for asking. However, I am not here to do ye harm personally; I came to destroy Lord Willingham's property, the property he stole from my family. Then I shall leave ye and go about my business."

Alice Willingham could scarcely believe what she was hearing; yet made no effort to challenge her uninvited guest. "I don't know what your grievance is John but whatever it is, it will wait and you can discuss it with my husband when he gets home. However, right now you are going to sit down and rest. I will fix you a bite to eat, you drink a cup of tea, and then if you feel like it you may tell me what troubles you. I take it that it has something to do with these fires; Oliver said he thought you may behind them, is that true, John?" She asked.

"That's true, Alice. I am responsible for all of them and I came here to burn ye out of your own home."

"Well John, we'll talk about that later," she responded, not appearing in the slightest to be concerned for what this tenant farmer was threatening to do. "Right now you sit down here," she said sympathetically, taking him by the arm and leading him to a table and chair. "Whatever it is that's troubling you, it will wait until we get some nourishment into you, you look like you are about to collapse."

For the first time since his family left for America, John McCaffrey found himself in a quandary, he came here to burn Lord Willingham's house down and kill His Lordship if he posed a threat. Notwithstanding that, he now found himself unable to attack or harm Alice Willingham, a woman who had never lifted a finger against him, yet who did nothing to help prevent the death of one of her most faithful servants, his wife.

"I will not harm ye, Alice." He said quietly, as she placed a cup of tea and plate of sweet tarts on the table before him. "Yet I'll have no truck with the Crown and His Lordship; they have taken our land and nearly destroyed my family. They killed my grandfather, hanged my father and now the sickness that haunts all of Ireland can be laid at the doorstep of Parliament and the Queen. They have also taken your servant Mary Kate, my wife, but it ends here. The Crown shall never again be in the position where it will be able to assert a claim against my family based upon stories concocted for depriving my children of their true inheritance. We may only have our good name left, but my family will take that to America, and they will thrive. Furthermore the world will know of the viciousness of this tyrant queen of yours and I promise that before I die her henchmen will pay a price for their brutality and inhumanity to my family and to the Irish people."

In the thirty years, that Alice Willingham had been married to one of Her Majesties' most decorated soldiers she witnessed the catastrophic aftermath of the Queen's conquests in India and Africa. Yet she would be the first to accuse the Crown of committing the cruelest of all tragedies right here in Ireland. More than one million citizens starved to death when food was plentiful throughout the lands governed by her Queen. Much of this travesty occurred even after her Prime Minister Robert Peal publically chided Parliament warning that this would happen unless the government acted quickly. He warned that a monumental disaster was in the making in Ireland and the reputation of the Queen and all those who did nothing to avert the starvation of millions of their citizens would suffer; yet, his warning went unheeded.

"I best be going, Alice." John McCaffrey added quietly, as he got up from the table to leave. "I am sorry to have troubled ye, but I thank ye for your kindness. I will do ye no harm."

"You will not wait for Oliver?" She asked, appearing relieved that the inevitable confrontation that was bound to occur when John McCaffrey and Lord Willingham met would not occur here in her home.

"No Alice. Ye do not need to become involved; if he and I meet again it will be by his choice; I am going home now."

"But your home is gone, John. What will you do?" She asked as he mounted the Connemara pony.

"I will be with my Mary Kate, Alice." He replied quietly, nodding his head as he rode away from Lord Oliver Willingham's home.

"What do you mean he was here?" Lord Willingham virtually shouted at his wife upon returning home when she informed him of John McCaffrey's visit. "That man has burned every building on our land. Nothing is left and you tell me he came here! I will kill him myself."

"Do not be hasty, Oliver." She replied. "He's dying. He came here to set fire to our home. We shared a pot of tea and talked. Before he left he told me that he would not burn down our home; why I don't know, certainly he had cause."

"Cause! What cause, Alice?" He demanded angrily. "That man is a murderous scoundrel; the Army will hunt him down and kill him. Quigley and the men are looking for him now. If we find him before the Army gets to him, we will hang him. Do you know where he went?" Willingham demanded.

"He said he was going to be with Mary Kate; so I assume he will be at Saint Joseph's Cemetery."

It was nearly dark when Lord Willingham, accompanied by Martin Quigley and a group of hired men arrived at Saint Joseph's church where they confronted Father Michael Sullivan. The priest was standing on the small balcony leading to the front entrance to his small church where he quietly greeted Willingham and his men.

"I take it Lord Willingham you're looking for John McCaffrey," Father Sullivan stated forthrightly.

"That we are Priest." Willingham responded gruffly. "Is he in your church?" He demanded.

"If he were here Lord Willingham that would be none of your business, however, you do not have to worry about that. John McCaffrey has not been inside of this church for more than twenty years and I believe that is some of your doing."

"Do not lecture me Priest," Lord Willingham yelled at the man; then turning to Quigley he said, "Get some of your men in there and find him."

"You and your armed mob are not welcome here, Willingham," Father Sullivan said, moving to block Willingham's men from entering the church.

"Out of the way, Priest," Lord Willingham, screamed as Quigley and four or five hired men climbed the steps at the front entrance.

"No, your men shall not enter this holy place." Father Sullivan responded harshly, trying to stop Lord Willingham's men.

"Kill him!" Lord Willingham yelled at Quigley; then again, "kill the Priest."

Yet even Martin Quigley, for all his brutishness and violence that he participated in at the direction of Lord Willingham was reluctant to carry out this order. He stopped short of the entrance to the church and turning to Lord Willingham who was still sitting astride his horse, said, "No your Lordship, I cannot do that," his voice wavering and a look of anguish crossing his face. "There has got to be a better way, Sir." He said. "We'll find McCaffrey and deal with him."

"If you can no longer carry out my orders Mr. Quigley, I will find someone who can." Willingham shouted angrily, and then drawing his revolver, he fired a single shot that struck the priest in the forehead; the man fell backwards through the front doorway of the church. "Now you men get in there and find that man." Willingham shouted. A few minutes later, the men emerged from the church, with one of them exclaiming, "There is no one in here Sir."

"Then burn it!" Willingham yelled at the group standing around him. "Burn the church and destroy the cemetery; we'll turn this whole acreage into pasture land." Within minutes, the building erupted in flames.

"Now aren't ye the brave ones, Willingham," a man said loudly as he approached the group from the cemetery across the road from the church. As he came into the light from the fire, the men with Willingham recognized the speaker as John McCaffrey.

"Look at ye," he said. "Ye call yourselves Irishmen and now ye conspire with the Queen's henchmen to kill a fellow Irishmen, and a priest at that; one who has made no threat of violence against ye. Ye should be proud of yourselves." He said, contemptuously. Then speaking directly to Lord Willingham and Martin Quigley he stated quite adamantly, "This is your opportunity Willingham for ye and Quigley are here to obtain retribution. Ye both are armed and so am I."

"Kill him," Lord Willingham screamed and immediately began firing his weapon. Martin Quigley found this to be an opportunity to regain favor from his master and he too began shooting. With this burst of gunfire, their adversary went down on one knee, and then taking careful aim at Lord Willingham, clearly outlined by the flames from the church, John McCaffrey shot his former landlord. The man fell from his horse. Then turning his attention to Martin Quigley, he emptied his gun at the overseer and killed him, but not before being hit in his lower chest by a bullet from his opponent's weapon. Other members of Lord Willingham's men began firing at him until they noticed that both Lord Willingham and

Martin Quigley were down. Moving back across the road into the cemetery John McCaffrey reloaded his revolver; yet there was no further need; with the death of Lord Willingham and Overseer Quigley, the men quickly fled into the darkness.

When members of the Constabulary arrived the next morning, they found four dead men. Lord Willingham and Overseer Martin Quigley lay in front of the now burnt-out church where they fell the night before. They also found Father Sullivan's scorched body in the ashes of Saint Joseph's church and located John McCaffrey's bullet riddled corpse next to his wife Mary Katherine's unmarked grave; the grave still covered with flowers.

A week later in Dublin, the Royal Army buried Lord Willingham and Martin Quigley, both with full military honors. Several representatives from Parliament and one or two of Queen Victoria's staff attended the elaborate military ritual. Meanwhile, in Mala an outdoor service, near the burnt-out church at Saint Joseph's cemetery, the Bishops of Limerick and Cork concelebrated a funeral Mass for Father Michael Sullivan and John Joseph McCaffrey. More than two thousand people attended the service.

CHAPTER 4

THE CROSSING

John McCaffreys' carefully planned exit for his children from Ireland appeared to be in jeopardy when the police opened fire on two men in the water near the *Hampton Court*. As it was pulling away from the dock crewmembers on the deck of Captain Sinclair's ship rushed to the starboard side to watch the flurry of activities near their sister ship. Two passengers had climbed the railing of the *Hampton Court* and jumped into the water. They swam under the dock and came up on the port side of the *Isle of Jersey* where Jimmy McCaffrey and Pat Kennedy were waiting. The two younger boys quickly pulled their cousins Leo Gordon and Bobby Burke on board and rushed them into Jimmy's cabin.

"Get out of those wet clothes," Jimmy said. "Be quick about it; someone may have seen us and they'll be looking for both of you. Take these, put them on and we'll throw the wet ones out the porthole." He handed the two men clothing their father gave to them for the trip. Then with the admonition, "There's no heat in steerage and you may need these."

"What the hell happened over there, Bobby?" Kevin asked his cousin Bobby Burke as the two men changed into dry clothing.

"Somebody on board the Hampton recognized me; I've seen that man before tonight, but I don't know his name. When I saw him talking to the constables, I knew we would not be going to Canada. Unfortunately I won't ever have the opportunity to get even with that traitorous bastard."

"Nor I," said Leo Gordon. "I would make sure that he never made it to Canada."

"Let's not worry about that now," Jimmy said. "Get rid of those clothes and we'll break out a deck of cards and get a game going here in case an officer or crew member looks in on us. After awhile we will get you into steerage and it is unlikely that they will ever know that you did not book passage. However, you have to be careful; Daddy told us that the captain takes a head-count at least two or three times a week at breakfast. That's how they keep a count of how many passenger meals are served and the number that die en route or commit suicide by jumping overboard."

"Yes, and some will die, Jimmy boy," Leo Gordon interjected. "Some of those folks had no business getting on board these ships, let alone taking a long ocean voyage. We found out that neither one of these boats has a doctor onboard; some of the older folks are not well."

"Well we can give them a nice religious send off if they die aboard." Bobby Burke added bitterly. "The Archbishop has sent four of his young priests to America; soon there won't be anyone left here in Ireland to pray for."

"They're here; they have a cabin just down the passageway a bit. I saw them when we came aboard. Hopefully we won't have a need for the Last Rites before we get to New York." James said with wry humor.

After Kevin Malone and Pat Kennedy returned to their cabin, James's younger brothers climbed into their bunks and were asleep within minutes. Burke, Gordon, and he played cards by lantern light until well past midnight, then the two men made their way quietly into steerage.

"Good morning Jimmy McCaffrey." Colleen Haggerty said to him cheerily as she approached along the railing. "Good morning Colleen," he replied. "What are you doing up and about this early in the morning?" He asked her, smiling.

"Silly boy, we always get up early, when there's work to be done. I have some bad news however, Mother and Katelyn have been seasick ever since we left the harbor; they have made a terrible mess of things. Even Daddy is not feeling well, but he is better this morning after coming out on deck. The fresh salt air must be good for him."

"Is Katelyn better this morning?" He asked, concerned for the well-being of his baby sister.

"No, Mother's better, but Katelyn has not eaten and will not drink a thing. Each time she tries, it keeps coming back up on her. I'm worried about her," she added with a look of concern. "She's sleeping now but you best look in on her this morning."

"I will Colleen. Maybe I can get her to eat some oatmeal; that's on the menu this morning and Mother always fixed it for us at home. Mister Winters the First Mate told me Captain Sinclair insists that we eat with steerage passengers. He's afraid that his first class passengers may take offense; most of them are Prods, he says and he does not want any trouble between us on his ship." Jimmy smiled. "Did you look in on Aunt Margaret and Shannon?"

"Yes, they are doing just fine; neither of one of them has gotten seasick."

"How are the boys taken to the ship? Did they get sick?" She asked.

"Oh, I think a little bit, but they are too busy to worry about it. Mr. Winters put all four of them to work caring for the animals; they love it and they will earn a bit and get some extra food. They will not have time to worry about the crossing. Michael and Joseph love the horses, but the stud can be a handful. Daniel and Thomas have the responsibility to feed the chickens and turkeys and they even have about ten piglets to take care of. And this morning they took more than a dozen eggs to the chef."

Colleen Haggerty laughed, "I knew we had horses on board but I didn't know—chickens and pigs, oh that's funny."

"You won't think it's funny when they butcher them out here on the deck." He laughed.

"Oh Jimmy, do not speak of that. It's too nice a morning to talk of such things," she responded quietly. Although dressed in a warm, but threadbare winter coat passed down to her from her mother's youngest sister, she felt the chill of the cold wind off the water and snuggled close to him. However, her frayed and worn coat and cobbled shoes could not hide the stunning attractiveness of this young Irish beauty. James noticed that more than one crewmember found a need to work on some nearby maritime fixture on the *Isle of Jersey* each time she appeared on deck. This was particularly noticeable after the evening meal when there were fewer passengers around. One tough looking seaman however, with many tattoos on his body began to show more than a passing interest in Colleen Haggerty. Jimmy marked the man as someone that would bear watching.

"I wonder if it will be this cold all the way across." She said not really expecting an answer from her novice seagoing friend.

"It may get a little colder as we get closer to Newfoundland; that's where the *Hampton Court* leaves us and goes on up to the Saint Lawrence. However, this time of year it should be nice and warm in New York. Look there," he said pointing in the distance. "That's the *Hampton Court*. You can just make out the mast and sails on the horizon. One of the crewmembers told me they would move in closer if we do not run into fog, but at night, they keep their distance. He said too many ships have collided when the lookout misjudges distance in the dark."

"What happened to the French ship?" She asked, "I don't see it anyplace."

"No, it's too fast for us. The French will arrive in Quebec at least four or five days ahead of the *Hampton Court*. It is much faster than either one of these. This really is an old run-down bucket," he laughed. "The Jersey first went into service with Her Majesty's fleet transporting slaves from Africa. The crew said it was revamped a little to transport the Army to and from the Crimean War in the 1850s, since then it has hauled wheat, corn, barley, coal and even livestock; steerage smells like one of our cattle byres at home. It is not very nice."

"Oh, Jimmy," she said, "you know all about the ships and the ocean, I'm proud of you."

"No Colleen, I just ask a lot of questions." He grinned at her.

"Did you and your two cousins really steal those horses, Jimmy? Is that how we got our cabins?" She asked, innocently. "That's what one of the passengers said."

Startled by this question, he responded quietly. "Colleen, whatever you do don't mention that to anyone. Too many people onboard already think that we did something underhanded. They know we did not have any money so when it comes up, if I cannot avoid it, I just tell 'em our fathers' traded livestock and vegetables for our passage. I do not try to dissuade them otherwise.

"Nevertheless, as you know the amenities offered in steerage are not nearly as nice as First Class so you can understand why they ask the question. To travel that way is quite an ordeal, especially for some of these older folks. The damn rats and lice do not make it any easier on them. A rat has already bitten one youngster. And the bed bugs are nearly as big as the damn rats."

Colleen bit her lip and merely nodded her head, saying no more about how she and her family obtained first class passage. She had seen the cold, dark quarters for steerage passengers with their rough wooden platform bunks stacked in tiers and men, women and children all crowded in together like animals in a cage. She was sure she would not be tough enough to survive the crossing were she confined to such wretched accommodations.

"Catch!" The man yelled at James as he threw a rugby ball across the deck of the ship. "You're Jimmy McCaffrey aren't you?" The man said, smiling. "I saw you play in the Galway games against the Army. You fellows won, too bad the Crown's people did not see it that way. We did everything to keep you and your friends from going to Kilmainham, but it was not enough. I am sorry." The man offered apologetically. "The Queen doesn't take too kindly to priests meddling in the affairs of state." He laughed extending his hand as he approached the younger man. "I'm Father Kirk O'Herlihy."

"Hello Father; it is nice to meet you. How is it you happen to be aboard this ship?

"Well," he replied, "the Archbishop thought that as he was losing another thousand or more of his flock that he had better send four of his priests along to look after them. However, by the looks of things you don't need us to look after you." He offered with a grin.

"Maybe we do, Father. Some of these folks might not make it all the way to America; but if they do, all of us will end up right in the middle of a Civil War. From what I hear, not everyone will come away from that unscathed. Looking at the Dublin papers before we came aboard we are going to be right in the middle of it when we land in New York."

"That could happen, Jimmy, but it's been going on now for two years and it looks like Lincoln's people have the upper hand. Maybe it'll be all over by the time we arrive."

"Well I hope you're right, Father, but there are a whole bunch of Irishmen on their way to Canada instead of to Boston or New York because they don't want their families involved in someone else's fight."

"I understand that, Jimmy," the priest offered, "but you can bet if there is a fight going on someplace in the world and our people are there, most of them will want to get involved." He laughed. "We Irish are a strange breed aren't we now? Notwithstanding that, maybe those who have chosen to go to Australia or Canada have made the wiser choice. However, there's a problem with going to either one of those places; the last I heard both country's are still flying the Union Jack." He was deadly serious.

"That's what my father said," James responded quietly. "The Queen's people killed my grandfather and his father. My father will never forgive her for that."

"Are your father and mother with you, now, Jimmy." The priest asked.

"No, my mother died last month and Daddy will be gone soon. The doctors' told him he has the consumption and will die before the end of the year." Jimmy shook his head, his facial expression grim.

"I am sorry to hear that, Lad. I did not know either of them but I knew of the battles your father and others waged against the Crown to hang onto your lands. I really believe the prime minister did all he could to support the Land League folks, but it cost him his job and he fell out of favor with the Queen. When that happened the Conservatives took over Parliament." The priest appeared to be well aware of Parliament's cruel and insensitive response to the plight of the Irish and of the fact that the Queen completely ignored the consequences of these decisions.

"That fight is not over yet, Father O'Herlihy." James added forcefully. "If I know my father, before he's gone he will take another run at the landlords and it won't be pretty. However, he wanted to make sure that my brothers and sister would be safe in America where the Crown could not touch us and he put me in charge of getting them there. I will go back when the kids can take care of themselves."

"Don't do that, Jimmy. They shipped my younger brother off to Australia from the Deportation Yard at Kilmainham Jail. I was already in the priesthood by then and on my own, so my folks cut all ties to Ireland and started a new life in Australia where they could be near him. You should think long and hard about that. I'm afraid the Ireland that our grandparents knew is gone; there is no going back."

"You mentioned the Archbishop sent four young priests along as he thought that members of his flock might need a little spiritual guidance. Is that right?" James asked candidly, yet his tone of voice clearly revealing more than a casual interest in the Archbishop's motivation for sending these young priests to America.

"Well we are not all neophytes, as you might suspect, Jimmy. Most of us have a year or two of parish experience behind us. I was at Saint Anne's in Dublin for two years; that was a rough and tumble part of the city, so we do have a fair grasp of the needs of parishioners."

"You may have, Father, I'll grant you that." James responded straightforwardly, "but the Archbishop, Cardinal Paul Cullen, if that is who you're talking about, is completely ignorant of the needs of the Irish people."

"Why would you say that, James?" The priest asked, somewhat taken back by this young man's response.

"Because my father and some of his associates, I think would have killed him had they the opportunity to do so twenty years ago. He opposed everything they stood for. He worked against the Young Ireland Movement and opposed the Fenian attempt to reestablish the Irish parliament. This all happened before I was born, but in the McCaffrey clan it was as if it happened yesterday. The Crown hanged my grandfather for protecting his own home and family; and now has driven us out of Ireland. These things will not be easily forgotten."

"I realize that, Jimmy, for my parents, believe as you do. They however, expected more of the Archbishop than I believe he was capable of providing. He is and was a fine churchman, but a terrible politician. Although, he has accomplished more toward the education of our people than any other church official in the history of our country has. He built three universities and hundreds of primary and secondary schools, but in doing so outraged parliament and tested the mettle of the Prime Minister and the Queen."

"That may be so, Father, but he will not be forgiven by members of our family and certainly not remembered as a friend of the Irish."

"Under the circumstances, that's readily understandable; but his eminence was opposed to any and all secret societies.

He condemned both the Young Ireland group and the Fenian movement. He believed they should have chosen to redress the crown's usurpation of our parliament through lawful means."

"That was pretty hard to accomplish, Father," James responded grim faced, "particularly when the crown hanged or deported the opposition. However, that's behind us for now; but God help those we leave behind, they will not escape the queen's henchmen."

The first to die in steerage was a six-year-old boy; frail in appearance when he came onboard, he became seasick almost immediately and quit eating. No matter what his mother tried, or those who offered to help, the boy soon became lethargic; five days out from Cork, he died in his sleep. Captain Sinclair, to his credit, lowered the ship's flag to half-staff and provided from storage a body bag for the family. It appeared that the crew was better prepared to assist the dead than the living and well they might have been. Over their many voyages, death among wounded soldiers and the weak and innocent traveler was a frequent visitor on the *Isle of Jersey*. Father Kirk O'Herlihy administered the Last Rites of the Church before they took the child from steerage. Unexpectedly the captain ordered the crew to suspend routine work and maintain quiet throughout the ship for ten minutes to allow the priest and the family that private time to bury their child. O'Herlihy complied, completing the service in the time allowed. There was no wake and no keening by the womenfolk; the child's family returned to steerage to grieve in silence.

Members of the McCaffrey clan took serious notice of the death of the boy in steerage for a member of their own, Katelyn had eaten little since coming on board; she too was near death's door. No matter what Margaret Malone tried, short of force-feeding the child, she was at a loss as to what she could do. Colleen and Shannon tried their best to entice the girl to eat something, but each time she did it soon came back up. One week out of Cork, she suffered a seizure and no amount of praying helped. Her brothers James and Michael, Louise Haggerty, and Margaret Malone accompanied by one of the priests kept vigil at her bedside around the clock.

First Mate Jason Winters paid a visit to the compartment on behalf of Captain Sinclair. "The captain wishes to express his prayers for a speedy recovery of your child," he said. Maggie Malone suspected that the captain might have been more concerned about his own wellbeing than about John McCaffrey's daughter. Father O'Herlihy had told her the captain's license could be in jeopardy if passengers or a family member filed a complaint in New York of ill-treatment of his passengers. Since the days of the *coffin ships,* the American courts had taken more than a passing interest in the wellbeing of its future citizens. Yet she accepted his charitableness at face value. "Please thank the Captain for us," she answered kindly. A few hours later Katelyn Mary McCaffrey died.

By the tenth day at sea, the breakfast count of healthy souls willing to come out on deck to take nourishment of oatmeal mush and bread, dwindled rapidly. Boiled potatoes and stewed yams with turnips brought aboard by the farm families offered a little variety for steerage passengers in the evening, nevertheless, the number of persons coming on deck for meals continued to get smaller. Several of the elderly passengers were too weak to climb the stairs and lay in their bunk all day with members of their families selflessly caring for their needs. The McCaffrey, Malone, and Haggerty families had long since given up the food they brought on board; they divided it and gave it to those considered most vulnerable. Notwithstanding that, the lack of nutritious food was not the primary culprit for the continued deteriorating physical condition of steerage passengers. Few, if any of these people had ever been to sea; round-the-clock confinement in the bowels of this strange vessel and the continual pounding of the sea on the wooden bulkheads became a never-ending, persistent, and unremitting oppressor. Carl Wiggins, the father of five, whose wife lay ill in her bunk went up on deck one evening after dark and disappeared. Hazel Grant, the mother of two young daughters hanged herself from an overhead bulkhead in the middle of the night. Her grieving children's father, at the age of twenty-six had died six months ago in Cork. Megan O'Toole, the youngest of Molly Carson's charges got up in the middle of the night and was seen climbing over the rail by a First Watch officer but before he could get to her she jumped. She was sixteen years old; Molly confided to Colleen Haggerty that the girl, a runaway from an orphanage, began working as a prostitute at the age of fourteen.

On the morning of the fifteenth day at sea, only one-hundred and sixty-two of the two-hundred and nine officially listed passengers in steerage that embarked on this voyage from Cork picked-up their breakfast tray. In addition, another dozen or so, disheartened or too weak to brave the elements remained in their bunks.That afternoon Jason Winters knocked on James McCaffrey's compartment door. "Good afternoon to you, Jimmy," the first mate said. "The captain would like you, Mrs. Malone and Miss Haggerty to dine with him this evening. Would you please extend that invitation to the ladies? Father O'Herlihy will join us."

Surprised by this invitation, Jimmy responded, "I'll be glad to Mr. Winters. I will ask them. I am sure they would like to do that. We'll be there."

At eighteen hundred hours, or four bells as Mr. Winters called it, the three guests arrived at the captain's mess. He greeted each by offering his hand. "Mrs. Malone, Miss. Haggerty, thank you for coming and Jimmy it's nice to see you again." He said kindly. Father O'Herlihy was already there. He and Captain Sinclair were enjoying a glass of red wine. "Ladies, you know Father O'Herlihy? Good. Please take a seat," he said offering each woman a chair on one side of the long rectangular dinner table, now covered with white, spotlessly clean linen, with napkins and set with silverware of the highest quality.

"Jimmy, please sit here near me." The captain suggested, pulling a chair back next to the priest, opposite the two women. He offered his three newly arrived guests a glass of wine that the women declined, Jimmy accepted, whereupon the captain called upon his steward to pour tea for the two women.

Over the next few minutes, the captain engaged in small talk without a hint as to his true purpose for extending this invitation. These folks were what the crew called "highfalutin" passengers, for they had seen this many times before. This group though did not have the wherewithal to pay first class passage. The crew knew that it was customary for the disgraced politician, actor, or even the most notorious criminal on his or her way to prison to hang or heading into exile from his homeland to receive the honor of dining with the captain. On these special occasions, those passengers involved in the most bizarre or inexplicable of incidents, were more apt to receive that invitation than the common, unsophisticated Irish emigrant was.

This evening the captain served his guests roast pork, with carrots, potatoes, and cranberries. Many of his passengers had gathered above the afterdeck that very morning to watch the ship's cook kill and dress the carcasses of three pigs. Although raised on an Irish farm Colleen Haggerty had no stomach for what the captain called a delicious cut of meat—she had heard the squeal of the animal as the master chef cut its throat. Jimmy McCaffrey made sure that the beautiful cut of meat on her plate did not go to waste.

After raising his wine glass in a toast for a "safe passage," Captain Sinclair said, "I assume all of you are wondering why I invited you to dine with me this evening. The answer is quite simple. The captain of any seagoing vessel is a lonely man, in a lonely job and I enjoy being with people. Over the years I have sat right here and dined with some of the finest people in the world and some of the most vile. I have transported murderers, traitors, spies and some of Briton's most corrupt men to England to hang. I have even transported politicians, who have fallen out of favor with the Queen, to Australia, New Zealand, or South Africa, exiled forever. "However, it is always much more enjoyable to dine with good folks like the four of you. I must admit I admire the Irish who gave up their land, in many cases they left their loved ones behind, and built new countries out of what in most instances was nothing but a wilderness. Take Canada and the United States for example. I have been to these two countries many times, both in my capacity as a member of Her Majesty's Naval Service and as captain of this ship. I have seen how Her Majesty's former citizens transformed what in reality was one of the most inhospitable regions on this earth into centers of learning, food productivity and even created industrial wonders. America's growth has been phenomenal; great cities are developing all along the East coast. Moreover, I envy you. Had I the opportunity to live my life over I would have emigrated without a moment's hesitation."

While the captain was talking, James could not help but study the faces of his fellow dinner guests. Colleen Haggerty appeared mesmerized by the seafarer's stories of the ruffians that came aboard his ship and the exploits that led to their demise on the gallows in one of England's many infamous prisons. Although cloistered in a religious school for girls, the Church insisted that all their charges study English history, in that process the Haggerty girls learned of the many prominent members of the realm who fell out of favor with the Crown and ended up in the Tower of London awaiting execution.

Try as he might however, Jimmy could not understand his Aunt Margaret. She never took her eyes off of the captain, studying him as if trying to decide whether or not he was a good man or a cruel and uncaring villain—a traitor to his own country, a fact known only to her and two others on this ship. Yet when Katelyn McCaffrey died, the captain sent his condolences to members of the family so James was at a loss to understand what if anything she would say or do about this man when they arrived in New York. He made up his mind that whatever she thought, he was sure that her judgment of him tonight would have a bearing on how she would dispose of the Royal Navy records of the Galway incident, files that Margaret Malone carried on her person at all times.

By all outward appearances, Father Kirk O'Herlihy was the typical young priest who saw only virtue in all men. Jimmy thought he knew what the man would tell him in private; he was sure O'Herlihy would claim that the captain was a good man, a man placed in a very difficult position by the ship owners and insurers. Thus, the institution of seafaring was responsible for Captain Sinclair's imperfections.

However, when the captain spoke next it became clear why he invited these four passengers to dine with him. He spoke quite softly while looking directly at Jimmy, "We, as you well know, Jimmy, from your family's tragedy on board this ship, that too many of our dear passengers have died on this crossing. The toll has reached eleven, with another young woman jumping overboard last night. This cannot continue and I am seeking your help in curtailing any further loss of life. We are six or eight days out from Newfoundland and maybe ten days yet before we reach New York; however, as you can see, the ship has not moved for these past two days.

"It is not unusual for the polar easterlies to becalm a sailing vessel at this time of year, yet if you look to the North there are thunderstorms gathering and by morning we should be moving again. If we receive favorable winds, we could arrive in New York Harbor in seven or eight days.

"However, my crew, including my steward and the staff assigned to the galley are prepared to feed all two hundred steerage passengers one additional meal each day until we reach port. I have ordered that we will butcher all the livestock, save the horses, over the next few days and empty the scullery; but you have to realize there is a risk to operating a ship under such circumstances. Should the winds fail us as they have this week, it could be another ten, or twelve days before we make landfall. We do not have enough provisions for such an eventuality. What our ship needs is a gift from the Almighty to hurry us along on our journey; in the meantime, we need something to lift the spirits of those passengers depressed because of this most difficult voyage. This has been a very trying voyage for all of them, and more so because of the weather.

"Therefore, I have given Father O'Herlihy permission to hold religious services on the Quarter Deck every morning before breakfast for the remainder of the voyage and it will be up to you folks to encourage attendance. Yet from what I know of the Roman Church that should not be a problem. I also encourage you women to organize an evening entertainment program. As we move south, from Newfoundland, the weather should warm and you may find it quite enjoyable on deck. I know that there are several musicians on board, I have heard them and I encourage their participation, but it must end at eight bells. I'm sure you know by now that's eight o'clock." He smiled. "My crew work around the clock and we must maintain a quiet time after eight bells. Do any of you have a problem with this?" He asked, turning his attention to all of his guests.

Jimmy and the two women were stunned; never before, certainly not since the end of King Charles' Reign had the Monarch allowed formal Catholic services on the deck of a British ship. This undoubtedly was a history-making event. However, Kirk O'Herlihy was not surprised by this turn of events. Before departing Ireland, Archbishop Cullen of Dublin ordered him to report to Archbishop John Hughes of New York any instance of mistreatment or wanton neglect of ship passengers or crewmembers while en route from Ireland to America. One way to head off any complaints would be to allow this nearly all Catholic group of passengers the freedom to attend church services of their choosing.

Archbishop O'Conner directed, "If there is substantial evidence of ill-treatment, abuse, molestation or serious injury of passengers or crewmembers you shall take whatever evidence you find to Archbishop Hughes in New York. His Excellency has assured me that his office will file a complaint with the American courts in New York. I hope that the days of mistreating a passenger or crewmember by ships' officers are behind us. Neither the Americans nor the Irish people will tolerate the return to the era of the *coffin ships*."

Captain Gordon Sinclair was well aware of the Archbishop Cullen's position on this matter as were the owners Andrew Shaw and Oscar Seville & Co. and their insurer Lloyd's of London. Should a ship's captain or a crewmember assault or kill a passenger on the high seas, they knew American authorities may seize the ship in New York and it might be months before the Maritime Courts would rule on the case. In the meantime, the State of New York, or the federal authorities would hold the *Isle of Jersey* in impound until the court handed down its decision. With the country at war with itself, there was no telling when that would occur; any extended litigation would delay their return to England.

Colleen Haggerty and Shannon Malone took it upon themselves to organize the entertainment program that would follow the evening meal and to begin this very day. Colleen approached Molly Carson and two of her girls as she had heard them singing one night and thought it was beautiful.

"Molly you have a wonderful voice," she said smiling. "You must have had lessons; I've never heard anything so beautiful." Carson appeared surprised by the compliment and Colleen added. "No I mean it, it's lovely. Did you have formal training; you sound operatic."

"Oh, Colleen what a wonderful compliment; yes, I trained and sang professionally for nearly ten years in London, Berlin and Paris. However, as you get older there is not too much demand for middle-aged women in that business. My husband died in the Crimean War and we had no children. I took to drink and ended my career singing in cafes and bars in Dublin and East Belfast. I do not drink any longer but I could not go back. If you were up the night we sailed you would have seen the Sheriff put the girls and me on board; we have been exiled to America. But at least I have family there; maybe I'll find them and start over," she said pursing her lips and nodding her head as if to say, yes I can do that.

At first the turnout for the entertainment was small, not more than two dozen or so passengers came out on deck that first evening, but nearly all of the Malone, Burke, McCaffrey, Haggerty, Kennedy, Gordon and Ryan families and Father O'Herlihy and his fellow priests participated. Two men with violins joined them. With Colleen Haggerty directing the program, she and Molly Carson led the group through a medley of old Irish songs common to every household in Ireland. The following morning Father O'Herlihy and his fellow priests conducted church services on deck and afterwards administered Communion to more than a dozen persons too weak to participate, now confined to their bunks in steerage.

"What have you planned for tonight, Colleen?" Jimmy McCaffrey asked as the two of them sat on deck enjoying the morning sunshine. "We'll sing more songs and Mr. Mohan and our uncle Joe Ryan will entertain us with their violins and Shannon and I and my sisters, we'll do an Irish step dance or maybe two and a light Jig. Toe-stomping that's what Daddy calls it." She laughed. "With your mother's death and all the sickness we haven't danced for weeks, so we're out of practice. I hope we do not fall. Daddy says we have our sea legs now and none of us gets seasick any longer. Molly and a couple of her girls will help us out and she has agreed to sing two or three solo bits. She's really good Jimmy." Colleen responded excitedly. "She used to sing professionally."

"Yes I heard that. You gals will do just fine," he replied, smiling. "Did you bring your costumes along?"

"Yes, but Mother says we can't wear them until we are settled in America. I think she's afraid we'll show too much ankle; besides she doesn't trust all these seamen," she smiled.

"Neither do I Colleen," he replied grim-faced. "There are some pretty hard cases on this ship and Daddy warned me about them. The Royal Navy kicked a lot of them out of the service, including the captain. So pay attention to your mother."

"Oh, silly boy; let's talk about something else." She replied with a grin. "What are you going to do when we get to New York?"

"Well the first thing is to look-up Daddy's Brother Paul. We have his address, so we will see what he suggests. Maybe the war will be over by the time we get there. I will get a job, somewhere, and maybe you and I can see the sights. Moreover, we most certainly have something to celebrate, a new home in a new country. I think it'll be just grand."

"Are you including me in that celebration, Jimmy McCaffrey? She asked coyly.

"Of course," he responded, smiling. "I can't think of anyone I would rather be with; after all we've been friends for years."

"Is that all we are Jimmy McCaffrey, friends?" She responded coolly. "I thought we were more than that."

"We are Colleen," he said apologetically, nodding his head. "We are much more than that."

The appearance of members of the crew working under the direction of the Chief Steward interrupted their conversation. They began to set up tables to carry out the promise made by the captain to provide the first full meal to steerage passengers since leaving Ireland. Although the portions were small, the meal was both nutritious and well received by all who put in an appearance. Almost immediately, one could notice a sense of wellbeing arising within the group. More passengers came out on deck to the point that the first mate found it necessary to limit the number allowed to stay to eat as the crowd was hindering the free movement of the crew. That evening over one hundred passengers from steerage and nearly the entire first class passenger compliment came to listen and watch the entertainment. Colleen Haggerty and her sisters accompanied by more than a dozen others joined in, singing, and dancing to the Irish music. A small group of crewmembers, displeased by the captain's permissiveness in allowing steerage passengers such freedoms remained skeptical. Yet, others, remaining on the outer edges of the crowd clearly enjoyed the show.

When it ended the crowd quickly returned to their quarters as the wind picked up and skies darkened—a storm was moving in from the North. Colleen Haggerty made a last trip about the deck to assure that they left neither clothing nor instruments behind then made her way through the darkened passageway to her cabin.

The McCaffrey boys heard the scream, followed by a man cursing and a loud thumping sound like a body hurled against the cabin bulkhead, then someone running down the passageway. James and his brother Michael were the first to respond, followed closely by Kevin and Donald Malone. They found Colleen Haggerty, unconscious at the end of the passageway bleeding from a head wound.

"Quickly Michael," James McCaffrey yelled, "get her into the cabin, and get Aunt Margaret to take care of her. Kevin and Donald let's go get this son of a bitch."

Running the full distance of the passageway, they quickly came out onto the Quarter Deck, but did not see anyone; with only the light cast from two small running lanterns it was near impossible to make out the ships mast or even the railing.

"We better report this to the captain or Mr. Winters," Kevin Malone said, "we won't be able to find him in the dark."

"You go and report this to whomever you can find in the wheelhouse; but I'm going to keep looking. We know he has to be up toward the bow because he cannot get to the crews' quarters unless he comes back through this passageway and he will not go into steerage. Donald, you stay here at the passageway entrance and I'll go forward and see if I can find him."

"You be careful, Jimmy." Donald offered quietly. "He knows his way around the ship and you don't."

"I know most of it; we've been on this damn thing for three and a half weeks and I have a pretty good idea where he could hide. You just keep a sharp watch until Kevin gets back."

As the storm hit with its full furry James moved quickly along the starboard railing toward the fore-end of the ship. The bow of the ship soon raised high out of the water and slammed down with such force that the entire vessel shuddered causing a huge spray of seawater to come cascading onto the deck. Holding tight to the railing, he inched his way along trying each hatch as he moved on finding all of them locked down tight. Working his way around a lifeboat, he saw the glint of metal before he heard the man curse; but it was too late. Colleen's assailant was in the lifeboat above him and the downward thrust of the man's knife cut into Jimmy's shoulder. Having missed a fatal thrust the man raised his arm to stab his victim once again but James was too fast for him. Sidestepping the knife, he grabbed the man's arm pulling him out of the lifeboat and slammed him down hard on the deck.

His assailant lay motionless, stunned by the violent reaction of his victim, James taking the knife put it to the man's throat.

"Don't do it Son," the voice said. "He's ours now." It was First Mate Jason Winters accompanied by two seamen both carrying lanterns.

It was near midnight when Captain Sinclair and two of his officers visited James in the McCaffrey cabin. Margaret Malone had just finished bandaging her nephew and was cleaning his blood from the floor and off the small table in the center of the room. The younger McCaffrey boys were sound asleep in their hammocks by this time.

"How are you, Lad?" Captain Sinclair asked showing concern for this young man's well being.

"I'm fine Captain." Jimmy replied respectfully.

"He's weak Captain." Mrs. Malone interjected. "He's lost a lot of blood."

"I can see that Madam." Captain Sinclair responded nodding his head. "Do you feel well enough to tell us what you heard or saw of this incident?"

"Certainly Sir," James replied and then described what he and his brothers heard occurring outside their cabin and his pursuit of the culprit.

"Good Jimmy, I think we have a good idea what took place here tonight. Mr. Winters will look in on you tomorrow. You get some rest now." He offered quietly.

When the three men left the cabin Jimmy could hear the Captain and the two officers discussing amongst themselves the incident as they moved off to the Haggerty cabin.

Colleen was sitting up in the bunk when Mr. Haggerty admitted the three men to his cabin.

"I am sorry," the captain said to Mr. and Mrs. Haggerty, "to bother you this late, but we must know tonight what your daughter heard and saw, if anything, about the one who attacked her. Under Maritime Law whenever we have an incident such as this aboard ship it is always, best to question the parties involved as soon as practical. Would you mind, Miss Haggerty telling me just what took place."

Colleen Haggerty had little to offer owing to the fact of the darkened passageway and surprising swiftness of the attack. "I came in off the deck, Sir" she responded quietly, "and as I walked down the passageway to our cabin I heard someone behind me. I started to turn around when he hit me and grabbed me from behind. He put his hand over my mouth; I never saw his face, but he had tattoos on his arm. That's about all I can tell you." She said. "I'm sorry Captain; that's not very much is it? I am sure I would not know the man if I saw him again. But he was very, very strong."

Captain Sinclair responded, "Don't you worry about it. We have enough information to take care of this fellow. You get some rest now." He said quietly, then turning to his two officers asked, "Do either of you have any questions for this young lady?"

"Yes, I do Sir." One of the officers replied. "Did you cry out Miss Haggerty or fight back, could you have hit him or scratched the person that attacked you?"

"I know I screamed Sir and I was scared; I did not hit him--he was too strong for me but I bit his hand. He cursed at me and tore my dress and then hit me again."

The officer smiled; Captain Sinclair with pursed lips nodded his head and replied. "I think we have all that we need now young lady; you get some sleep and we'll look in on you tomorrow."

The following morning as the passengers began to assemble on deck for the morning meal Jason Winters approached James and Mathew Haggerty. "Good morning gentlemen," he said.

"Good morning Sir." The two men responded politely.

"The Captain would like you folks to witness the punishment of Seaman Henry Lanscove for his violation of law last evening. He was convicted this morning at Captain's Mast on charges leveled against him under the law." Mr. Winters said. "Lanscove was charged with Gross Personal Violence toward your daughter Mr. Haggerty and yourself James. His sentence of thirty-five lashes will be carried out at eight bells."

By eight bells, the storm had passed, but the seas were still running high and most steerage passengers chose to remain in quarters, some not even venturing out earlier for breakfast. Still Molly Carson and a few men came on deck to watch the ship's officers administer what to naval personal was an accepted form of physical punishment for a serious breach of maritime law. James was surprised that nearly all the first class passengers, including Father Kirk O'Herlihy and his three fellow priests gathered on deck to watch this most unusual event.

With the man tied to the mast, Mr. Winters read aloud the charges brought against Seaman Lanscove and of the findings of the Officers' Board whose members now stood on either side of Captain Gordon Sinclair. The chief boatswains mate, under the direction of Mr. Winters carried out the captain's order.

"I saw this at Kilmainham Jail, Mr. Haggerty," James said to Colleen's father. "And I am disgusted by such cruelty. I did not think it was proper then nor do I now. I'm angry for what he did to Colleen, but I don't think its right to treat anyone with such brutality."

"I understand that Jimmy and maybe you're right, but there are no courts or police out here to protect the innocent. He could have easily killed Colleen last night. I think this is the seafarer's way of preventing such conduct from happening again—at least it certainly sends a message throughout the ship that those who are at sea and violate the law will be dealt with not only quickly but also rather severely."

The whip with its nine knotted leather thongs and stout handle wielded by the powerfully built boatswain's mate quickly shredded Landscove's shirt and drew blood. Yet the man never cried out until Mr. Winter's verbal count of the number of lashes reached thirty. By this time James noticed that Molly Carson and most of the first class passengers had returned to their quarters; a few of the younger men from steerage lingered nearby until the seaman was untied and taken below.

The next day, James came on deck to calm seas and warm weather and was surprised to find the *Hampton Court* within hailing distance. Mr. Winters and the watch officer shouted a hello and wished fair sailing to Captain Smyth and his crew aboard the *Hampton Court.* Shortly thereafter, with the wind picking up, the *Isle of Jersey* turned south and within the hour, the watch shouted "Land Ho off the Starboard bow."

"That would be Newfoundland, Jimmy." Mr. Winters said as he came down from the wheelhouse. "That's all you'll see of Canada on this trip, Boy." He smiled. James thought Mr. Winters seemed relieved that they were within four or five days of reaching the end of their journey. Yet, he was also sure the First Mate was not pleased with what happened on his ship on this voyage. Eleven steerage passengers died en route from

Cork and Seaman Landscove's vicious attack upon Colleen Haggerty, followed by his punishment appeared to have left both crew and passengers alike dispirited.

This morning Jimmy thought crewmembers were less friendly toward him and many of the other passengers, with some even going out of their way to avoid any conversation at all. He could understand that, for if Colleen had gone directly to her cabin last night after the entertainment ended, the attack probably would not have happened and their fellow seaman would not have suffered as he did.

Passengers on the other hand appeared reluctant to leave the imaginary security of steerage. Less than one hundred ventured out to pick up a tray for the breakfast service. All of them knew that the crew avoided entry into steerage for fear of exposure to some unknown malady or affliction carried by these untouchable creatures below deck. Today however, those unwarranted fears of crewmembers would provide the weary and seemingly defenseless passenger with a perceived measure of physical security. They were quite sure whatever strange malady reigned supreme in steerage, it would protect them from harm by an unfriendly or angry crewmember.

"Did some of your family decide to go on to Canada on the *Hampton Court* rather than coming to New York with you folks?" Mr. Winters asked.

"Yes, some members of our clan did Mr. Winters. My father and mother however, wanted us to come to America. You may be aware of my family's ongoing fight with the Crown over our land; they thought it best if they got us away from all that. However, the Church had something to do with their decision also. My parents and almost all of the Clan opposed the involvement of parliament and the queen's people in our church's affairs; it appeared that it would be a never-ending conflict. My Daddy told me not to go to Australia or Canada. And he didn't want any of us kids to get further involved with the crown's men where we might end up in prison or be deported to one of the colonies."

"That's too bad, Jimmy. I met your father. I actually took him on a tour of this very ship; he came to me to arrange for your travel and I sent him on to Captain Sinclair. That must have been quite a meeting because the captain hasn't been the same since."

"Yes, I know about that. But my father and Captain Sinclair go way back to when he was an officer with Her Majesty's fleet."

"Oh, I didn't know that." Jason Winters responded, obviously surprised by this disclosure.

"Yes, Daddy was a member or the Movement twenty years ago and involved in some pretty violent clashes with the constabulary; the Navy was also caught up in it. That is where they first met. Captain Sinclair was a supply officer at Galway and if I am not mistaken the Movement brought guns in from France and got into a battle with both the Marines and the local constabulary. It was long before my time. I know that members of the constabulary hanged my grandfather and several members of the Movement at Kilmainham because of these and the Land Rights incidents before that. It was the type of violence our parents wanted to shield us from."

"That's too bad, Jimmy. I think under different circumstances he and I could have been friends; he seemed to be such a nice person, but those things happen. Unfortunately, for the folks you left behind in Ireland they will have to contend with those problems for years to come. Yet I cannot help but think that you jumped out of the frying pan, as they say, into the fire. Right now America is tearing itself to pieces. I was here two years ago when the war started and it was a sad thing. It was as vicious as anything that we have experienced in Britain. I don't think it will be over when we arrive but I hope it is."

Later that day as James and Colleen sat on the deck of the *Isle of Jersey* he told her of his conversation with Mr. Winters. "He is a good man, Colleen. It is too bad he never ran for a seat in Parliament. He could have made a difference."

"Maybe it was meant to be, Jimmy because he did make a big difference in our lives. I certainly will not forget him or Captain Sinclair's kindness to all of us. Even your Aunt Margaret has changed her opinion about the captain." She smiled. "She said, 'for an Englishman he is a pretty good fellow.'"

James laughed, "That's quite a change for Aunt Maggie."

As the weather continued to improve, more and more steerage passengers came out on deck to take advantage of the warm sun. Many women chose this as a chance to wash their long hair and then to lean back over the railing to let it dry in the wind. Some of the women used fine-toothed combs to remove the lice from their hair, while others sat in the sun and picked these vicious little creatures off one another. Unfortunately, their comfort was short-lived, for the infestation spread throughout the ship. An invasion of bedbugs further exacerbated their problems. The insects took up residence in their bedding turning this most arduous voyage into a near nightmare for many. A few men drew salt water for their families to bath and clean vomit and excrement from their bunks and bedding. James bathed and shaved using the soap his father insisted that he take on this voyage, yet he could not wait to get ashore where he could bath in hot water.

On the afternoon of the thirty-second day out from Cork word passed quickly throughout steerage that they were near the Maine coast. With favorable winds, the crew said they could arrive in New York Harbor within forty-eight to seventy-two hours. After lunch, James and Colleen moved to a somewhat secluded and comfortable position on the starboard side of the vessel that provided some limited privacy.

"What are you going to do, Jimmy, when we land?" She asked her tone of voice signaling a concern that the two of them could lose track of each other in the confusion of several hundred souls arriving in New York at the same time. "How will I find you if my folks don't connect-up with the family?"

"Don't worry about it Colleen," he said, "All the men have Uncle Paul's address and if we get separated we agreed that we would meet there on the fifteenth of the month. Moreover, if no one is there, that person is to leave a note telling everyone where he or she is staying. It will work out fine. So stop worrying." He smiled, and then added. "I am not going to lose you. We have come through too much to walk away from each other. Besides, young lady I love you."

"Oh, Jimmy! She exclaimed loudly. "You never said that to me before."

"No I didn't, because I didn't love you. I thought you were a spoiled little brat." He laughed and kissed her squarely on the mouth.

In the middle of the afternoon the watch called out, "Ship off the port bow." Shortly thereafter Captain Sinclair entered the wheelhouse. Colleen and her family and Jimmy and his brothers all went forward to watch the approach—it was a steam driven ship, well armed with uniformed crewmembers clearly visible on every deck. It was flying an American flag. An officer on deck hailed the *Isle of Jersey*, "Heave-too," is what James thought the man yelled, then added, "stand-by for boarding, you are entering a war zone."

Captain Sinclair's men quickly lowered the sails on the *Isle of Jersey*; and the ship slowed almost imperceptibly. The American Navy officer's announcement had a disquieting effect upon many of the passengers. Parents who longed for a better life for their children and who struggled for years to protect them in a country torn apart by conflict, suddenly found that the place they chose to take their children was still at war with itself.

"God help us, Louise," Mathew Haggerty complained bitterly to his wife when he heard the American officer's challenge. "What have we done? Our children would have been better off had we stayed in Ireland."

Although Louise Haggerty was somewhat shocked that the war was still going on, she had no regrets about leaving Ireland. "Be still Mathew," she commanded quietly. "Ye can't say that. We do not know what has happened in America and it may not be as bad as you think. What would ye do? We cannot go back, so we will make the best of it and make a home for ourselves. We will be free Mathew; free to live where we want to live, work where we want and to send our daughters to whatever school we think will be best for them. The land that we build our home on will be our land; it will not belong to the Crown. So Mathew Haggerty, ye just remember all of those things that we wanted to do in America, with God's help we will accomplish them. So say no more about it. Ye go over there and meet the Americans when they come aboard this god-awful ship and tell them we will be good neighbors."

Shocked by his wife's sudden outburst Mathew Haggerty merely looked at his wife and replied, "Yes Dear." In twenty-five years of marriage, Louise Haggerty had never challenged her husband's decisions; but today was different. They would build a new life for their family in America and there would be no going back.

Captain Sinclair and his officers greeted the American officer and five members of his crew amicably as they came aboard.

"This is a routine inspection, Captain. I am Lieutenant Byron Adams." The American officer said, acting friendly but business-like. "Our purpose is to interdict weapons and supplies that gun-runners from Canada and two or three unfriendly European powers try to smuggle to the Confederate States. We will not delay you longer than necessary."

Captain Sinclair and the boarding officer retired to the Captain's quarters while Mr. Winters escorted the four enlisted men to the main deck where more than a score of passengers came forward to greet them. James McCaffrey, Colleen Haggerty, Kevin, and Shannon Malone almost immediately stepped up and introduced themselves. As it turned out the Americans seemed pleased to meet the passengers yet at the same time appeared appalled by the unhygienic image they presented. The men were gaunt, unshaven, and their clothing dirty and disheveled. The women offered a less than feminine image, many standing back afraid that these strange uniformed men would spurn them because of their dreadful appearance and filthy clothing, clothing that reeked of the stench emanating from steerage.

The Americans soon found themselves mobbed, as more passengers from steerage, eager to meet these foreigners, rushed forward to introduce themselves. Still, the sailors seemed to enjoy this unexpectedly pleasant reception, even though deluged with dozens of questions about the United States. The most often asked was, "Is the war over?" During this period, the Americans continued with their duties making sure they inspected the smallest of compartments on the *Isle of Jersey*, all the while casually strolling along with small groups of passengers. Many of the passengers were eager to show their quarters, insisting that the American sailors come in and look at their cabin or bunk in steerage. The Americans found the friendliness and excitement of the passengers almost overwhelming. The Navy men had apparently never experienced such extraordinary affection from foreign arrivals, all of whom appeared eager to meet and talk to them.

Yet there was considerable hesitation on the part of the Americans to come forward and embrace this large group of Irish men and women. Although no one mentioned this to these soon to be new citizens, the American sailors to a man, were shocked at the physical condition of the passengers. A score or more were too weak to get out of their bunk; and the personal hygiene of many of those who greeted the Americans with hugs and kisses was deplorable. Both men and women were un-groomed, with many covered with sores encrusted with lice; and the stench from steerage revolted the senses of the sailors, a stench that lingered in the passengers' clothing and exuded from their body.

After about one hour, the Americans returned to their ship, yet neither vessel prepared to get underway. As Colleen Haggerty and James McCaffrey watched and waited on deck, along with more than one hundred other passengers, there was a flurry of activity on the American ship. Within an hour of their departure two small boats returned to the *Isle of Jersey*, fully loaded with fresh produce. Much to the surprise of both the crew and passengers alike, the boat crews hoisted on board crates of fresh fruit, bread, eggs, candy, and several gallons of milk. Captain Sinclair ordered it distributed immediately to those in most need.

CHAPTER 5

NEW YORK

On the morning of the fourteenth day of July, thirty-four days out from Cork, the *Isle of Jersey* sailed up the Hudson River into New York harbor.

"Ladies and gentlemen, please," Mr. Winters called out to the passengers assembled on deck near the bow of the ship, "There are too many of you here. You are hindering the safe operation of the ship. Please move away from the railings and the bow so the crew can do their job."

He might as well have been talking to the wind however, as the passengers paid little heed to the man's demand; they wanted a better view of the cities lining either side of the river. The deck crew needed to pull men, women, and children away from the railing so they could secure lines to the side-wheeler tugboat approaching from upriver.

Yet, what the passengers were looking at was not that *golden city on the hill* they envisioned, for a cloud of dirty grey and black smoke hung over the entire urban area and drifted across the Hudson to cover much of the New Jersey Coast line.

"What is it Jimmy?" Colleen Haggerty asked her friend. "I don't know, Colleen," he responded, quietly. "At first I thought the entire city was on fire; but I don't think so. Those are isolated fires; it looks like they must have been set at specific locations in the business blocks. The only thing I can think of that would appear as these do is the war; it must have come to New York."

"Oh, God no, Jimmy." She cried, "We didn't come all this way to end up in the middle of a battlefield. What have we done?" The anxiety in her voice was evident.

After being taken in tow the *Isle of Jersey* continued to move slowly up the Hudson when a navy gunboat pulled alongside and a uniformed officer with a trumpet hailed the captain.

"Captain," he called out to Sinclair who was standing on deck near the wheelhouse, "two leagues ahead you will find six or seven foreign-flagged ships off the Jersey coast, drop anchor there. Do not disembark. The Governor has declared martial law and no one can go ashore today. A representative of the port will contact you as soon as practical; he will see to your needs."

"I have passengers in need of medical attention," Captain Sinclair declared aloud. "It's imperative that we come ashore immediately."

"We will notify the authorities of your emergency, Captain, but no one must come ashore. If you do so you will place your people in harm's way and you shall be arrested."

There was no need for the captain to explain his predicament to the ship's crew or to the passengers. Those on deck clearly heard and understood the navy man; word quickly spread to steerage casting a gloom over the entire group that had remained below out of the rain.

"What do you suppose is happening, Jimmy?" Colleen asked her friend, "Surely if the war was being fought nearby would we not hear gunfire or cannons or explosives or something like that?"

"I think you're right Colleen, it's very quiet, and maybe it's all over. You can see several ships at anchor over there,"

James responded, pointing up river. "I count at least five and maybe more. We'll see when we get closer."

With the tugboat taking the *Isle of Jersey* in tow, the crew lowered the main sales on the ship and the ship moved slowly against the current of the river, coming to stop near the New Jersey coastline where the captain dropped anchor. The nearest ship, a Dutch flagged merchant vessel the Het Paleis out of Amsterdam lay at anchor nearby. Several members of the Dutch crew were intently watching the fires and the active movement of many horses and carriages on the New York waterfront.

"What's happening on shore?" One of Captain Sinclair's officers called out to the men on the deck of the tugboat.

"It's an insurrection," a seaman yelled back. "It's been going on for three days; riots and heavy street fighting at night and lots of military activity. The storm that came in yesterday quieted things down a bit, but the violence picked up after dark; there was a lot of shooting."

"Has there been any indication from the authorities when it will safe to go ashore?" The officer asked.

"They told us maybe late today or tomorrow, but it will probably depend on whether or not the Army is able to secure the docks. As you can see rioters set three or four piers on fire last night."

During this conversation, a heavy rain blanketed much of the river and the cities on either shoreline, yet several passengers braved the elements to come on deck and listen intently to the two seamen discussing the unfortunate situation occurring ashore. Standing outside the Wheelhouse Captain Sinclair took this all in and then tried to calm his passengers who had listened intently to this exchange between the two seamen.

"Ladies and gentlemen," he began in a calming voice and soothing manner, "do not fear, we are safe in harbor and we have enough food and water for all of you. By the time this storm is over we should be in a position to begin offloading."

Yet it was obvious that Sinclair was worried for he expressed his concern by repeating to the assembled passengers the warning he passed on to the naval officer earlier. "I know that several members of your families are very ill and in immediate need of medical care; I am sure the naval officer understands our predicament as I told him of our medical needs. He will take my warning seriously. So please bear with me for a period and give the authorities a chance to respond." When he finished speaking most of the passengers returned to their quarters.

Coming in out of the rain, Colleen returned to her cabin and James to his. When he entered, he found his cousins Bobby Burke, Leo Gordon, Pat Kennedy, Mike Ryan, and the Malone twins all crowded in the confining area along with his younger brothers.

"What do you think, Jimmy?" Leo asked. "I don't like this; we need to get the hell off of this bloody bucket. By the time these Americans quit killing each other we'll all be dead if we stay here."

"What are you suggesting, Leo?" James asked.

"We could get off the same way Bobby and I got on. We are only about two-hundred yards from the Jersey shore. We could slip over the side at night and swim."

"You can't be serious about what you've just proposed." James responded harshly. "I'm not going to start out in a new country by breaking the law; we did that to get out of Ireland remember. You go if you want but my brother's and I will enter this land legally."

"I don't know Jimmy," Bobby Burke added. "You're not sleeping in steerage like the rest of us. There are more than a dozen people there who will not live the week out; if they do not get medical care they will die right where they lie."

"Well you do what you have too Bobby, but our family is staying put, at least for now. I will go talk to Mr. Winters and tell him about those folks. I know him well enough that I'm sure he will do his best to get us ashore as soon as possible."

"Ok, Jimmy," Leo replied, "I'll wait until tomorrow night but if we are not on dry land by then I'm leaving."

"You're a selfish bastard, Leo." Kevin Malone said accusingly, interjecting himself into this conversation. "Why don't you think about someone else besides yourself? Our parents went through hell and gave up everything to get their kids to America. Pat and Jimmy pulled you two out of the bay at Cork and saved your asses from the hangman. If the Brits caught you, they would have hanged both the boys right along with you and Bobby. It is time to do something right, we protected you when you made your escape from Derry; that could easily have spun out of control and jeopardized our families' future. If you go, I will see to it that the clan cuts you lose, and from here on you will be on your own. You will be a stranger in a strange land and I do not think you will find it too easy. This country is at war with itself and you will not have a choice on which side you want to support. One side or the other may look at you as a traitor or interloper, or at least, someone not to be trusted. So you just suit yourself and do what you want but Donald and I will stay with Jimmy."

Chagrined by this stern tongue lashing from Cousin Kevin, Leo Gordon muttered, "Okay, I'll stay for awhile." Yet he could not leave without firing off a warning to his younger cousin. "I'll stay the day, Jimmy but all bets are off if we don't get off this god-forsaken ship by tomorrow night." Bobby Burke nodded his head as if in agreement with his cousin and followed Leo out of the compartment.

"Thanks, Kevin," James responded with a grim smile. "He had that coming, and I think he got the message."

It was near midnight when gunfire erupted in the city wakening most of the crew and passengers on the *Isle of Jersey*. Going out on deck, James found the entire Haggerty family and most of his cousins listening to the gunfire and watching as fires flared up along the waterfront. At one-point cannon fire erupted followed by explosions that sent glowing embers high into the night sky. The fighting continued for nearly an hour with pronounced movement of troops throughout the darkened streets, intermingled by the sound of bells from horse drawn fire suppressant apparatus. However, by three o'clock in the morning, quiet had returned to that part of the city visible to those on board the *Isle of Jersey* and most of the passengers returned to quarters.

When James awoke, the next morning the sun was shining brightly and there was only a faint smell of smoke lingering in the air from last night's fires. When he came out on deck, he found Colleen and Shannon Malone unashamedly removing lice and fleas from their hair; both girls looked wan and drawn. When they saw him, they pulled their coats closed and tried unsuccessfully to hide the scabs and open sores on their bodies that were clearly visible in the bright sunlight. As he approached, James sensed uneasiness about the two; he could tell they had been crying.

"What is it Colleen?" he asked quietly reaching out to touch her.

"Don't. Don't do that Jimmy," she responded pulling away, "don't touch me."

"What is wrong?" He asked sympathetically.

"You know what's wrong Jimmy McCaffrey; I am sick, I am dirty and I am hungry but mostly I am sick to death of this ship and everyone on it. Our salvation was to have been there in New York City, but it is not. It is just another hellhole, worse than home. We would have been better off had we stayed in Ireland." With this explosive response, tears began to flow down her cheek. Shannon Malone remained mute but soon she too was crying. She got up and returned to her cabin.

James could no longer bear to watch this pitiful creature suffer; he knew no amount of cajoling or playful banter would help alleviate the devastating and humiliating distress this young woman was experiencing. She had suffered in silence for a month then when the opportunity came to escape the hardship and distress of the crossing she found herself virtually imprisoned in a miserable lice and rat infected ship, a circumstance worse than anything she could ever have imagined. James was at a loss for words that might console her; but he knew what he had to do.

During the crossing, he had deliberately stayed out of steerage for there were some hurt feelings as the McCaffrey Clan, unlike their neighbors were fortunate to have traveled first class. Now however, it was time to take stalk of the conditions his fellow citizens contended with on this pigsty of a ship, as Bobby Burke called it.

Taking a pencil and paper he walked the full length of each of the two steerage compartment decks quietly asking questions of family members confined there and making a note of their responses. The task took most of the morning but when he was finished he had an exact count of the number of passengers in steerage who were either too weak to go on deck for their meal or too sick to get out of their bunk. He found that twenty-four adults and seventeen children fit his criteria. Although the number shocked his senses, he found that family members continued faithfully to care for their loved ones, both feeding them and handling their bathing and toilet necessities.

"What are you doing in here, Jimmy?" Leo Gordon asked as James prepared to leave steerage. "Did you come down to see how the other half lives? I didn't think you would stoop to visit your black-sheep relatives."

"Come with me Leo and I will show you what I am doing."

"Where are you going?"

"I am going to see Captain Sinclair. Come on, get off your ass, and let's try to help the Captain do something about this before we see more death in this god-awful place."

Reluctantly and still complaining Leo Gordon went with his younger cousin to see Mr. Winters.

"I would like to talk to Mr. Winters." He said to a seaman blocking his entry into the wheelhouse.

Jason Winters saw him coming and called out to him, "Good afternoon, Jimmy. What have you got for me?" He inquired kindly.

"I would like to show this to the Captain, Sir." He said politely. "This morning I took a body count, Sir, or inventory, if you would of all steerage passengers and I think the Captain should know what is going on down there."

"You don't think the Captain knows what's happening down there Jimmy?"

"I do not know, Sir." James responded candidly. "But as the crew has been reluctant to enter steerage I thought a first-hand account of the health of the passengers there, might be of value to him."

"Oh I am quite sure he knows what is going on down there, but let's look at what you have."

"Yes, Sir," James replied, handing his written notes to Mr. Winters. "We had over two-hundred people in steerage when we left Ireland, eleven of them, as you know died en route, and I know the Captain is aware of that. However, what he may not know is that twenty-four adults and seventeen children are in various states of physical distress. Most of them have not been out of their bunks in the last seven days. Two of the adults and three of the children have not taken food in nearly a week; Father O'Herlihy and Aunt Margaret believe that at least one child will die today or tomorrow. He is unconscious now and not responsive; he is six years old."

When James was talking, Jason Winters nodded his head his face grim and he looked first to Leo Gordon then to one of his officers standing nearby.

"That's it, Sir. I just thought the Captain should know about it."

"I'm glad you came to me, Jimmy." He responded quietly. "Yes the Captain should know about this and I will bring it to his attention immediately. It could be that after last night's fight, the rebellion leaders have had enough and will quit fighting and all of our passengers could go ashore. We'll see." He said, again nodding his head. "But whatever happens let me tell you that the captain is well aware of the serious need for medical attention for our steerage class passengers."

"Well that was a waste of time, Jimmy boy." Leo Gordon said as the two left the wheelhouse. "You don't expect Mr. Winters or Sinclair to do anything about this, do you?"

"Give them time, Leo. Mr. Winters is a good man and if he can get medical help to these folks, he will do so. Let's just wait and see what happens."

"Well you won't have long to wait Jimmy. A couple of those kids are darn near dead."

Within the hour Captain Sinclair, accompanied by Mr. Winters and four oarsmen were en route to shore in the Captain's gig. Two hours later, they returned on board one of the tugboats that brought the *Isle of Jersey* up river. Within the hour, the tug moved the ship to a pier near the Battery, a former artillery defensive gun position used by the British and Dutch in Colonial times on the south end of Manhattan Island. Just blocks away a dozen burnt out buildings continued to emit heavy smoke that rose above the tallest buildings in the afternoon sunlight. Unexpectedly a huge crowd of police officers, firemen and military personnel and hundreds of curious citizens gathered to greet the ship and its passengers. James taking Colleen by the hand moved close to the dockside railing to watch. The size of the military contingent surprised them. With the ship secured, eight or ten horse-drawn ambulances began to move out onto the dock.

"Look at this Colleen;" James said excitedly, "this is a sight none of us will ever forget. There must be four or five hundred people out there. We are going to go ashore today."

"Oh, my God Jimmy I can't wait, but what about our fellow passengers who are too sick or too weak to walk? What will they do?" She asked.

"From what I see Colleen I don't think any of us need worry about that. It looks like our new country has planned for just such a contingency. Look at 'em there must be twenty or thirty nurses and as many doctors down there. When you are sick there is nothing more gratifying than to see a woman in white waiting to come in and care for you."

While he and Colleen watched the activity on the dock, a uniformed officer appeared at the top of the gangway and began to issue orders to those onboard the *Isle of Jersey*.

"Ladies and gentlemen please step back so our doctors and nurses may come aboard to attend to the medical needs of those unable to care for themselves. No one shall come ashore until our doctors have examined every one of you. This will take some time so please be patient. Our immigration authorities will then process each of you."

"Well Jimmy, what do you think of Captain Sinclair now?" Mr. Winters asked. "I sensed that Mr. Gordon was quite skeptical that the captain would respond appropriately to this medical emergency. Am I right?" He smiled.

"Yes Sir, you are right." Jimmy acknowledged politely. "He and a couple in our party were not convinced that the Captain would be sympathetic to our families' needs. Yet I think there is a reason; none of us really realized until the last week or two just how difficult this crossing would be. I certainly did not. Notwithstanding that, Sir, you, and the crew have been kind to us on this voyage; we appreciated that. If not for that this crossing could have been much more difficult."

"Thank you, Jimmy. There are always a few passengers who believe they could manage our sailing better than we did; you might pass that on to your family, particularly to your two stowaway friends, Gordon and Burke." He grinned.

"You knew, Sir?"

"Of course, Jimmy; there are not many things that occur onboard a ship that a competent captain is unaware of. Had your friends been hardened criminals he would have locked them up. Whatever you say about him, he is a fair-minded man. You saw that when the Crown's people tried to kill those boys in the water while they were only trying to escape.

The captain will not countenance such conduct. That's why Gordon and Burke got a free ride; however I would not push his patience to the limit." He grinned.

"Thank you for telling me this, Sir. I will be sure to pass that on to them. However, tell me please, how did Captain Sinclair get such a swift response from the New York authorities? The ships that came in before us are still at anchor off the New Jersey shoreline."

"The captain has been here before, Jimmy; he's an old hand at this business. He told the man in charge, that he approved Father O'Herlihy's request to begin funeral services at first light tomorrow and that we would bury our dead in the traditional manner." Then he added, his face grim, "They did not want to see dead children floating out to sea on the Hudson River. The last thing they need is to have the public watch such a dreadful spectacle."

"Look over there, Jimmy!" Colleen exclaimed excitedly to her friend pointing to a sign held up in the crowd. "It's our name; somebody is holding up a sign with our name on it."

"I saw that Colleen and look, there's a woman holding up one with the McCaffrey name; she's way in back. I also see Burke, Malone, Kennedy, and Ryan signs. There is a whole bunch of them. How could they have known we were coming? We didn't even know it ourselves until last month."

Margaret Malone accompanied by her daughter Shannon following closely behind the McCaffrey boys, stopped at the top of the gangway and went over to say goodbye to Captain Sinclair. James waited and watched but because of the commotion was unable to hear their conversation; he did however see her reach inside her coat and hand the captain a large envelope. He suspected it contained the documents that his father talked about, the naval manifests from the Galway incident. If disclosed these papers could very well have determined the future of this sea captain. The man looked at the contents then smiled and shook Maggie Malone's hand. James could hear his parting farewell, "Thank you, and good luck to you Mrs. Malone," he said.

"Watch your step, ladies and gentlemen," a uniformed officer called out. "Those of you who have family may join them; for the rest of you I suggest the ladies and small children follow our people to Saint Mary's hospital where they will delouse you and you may attend to your bathing and toilet needs. You men folk are welcome to do the same at the Annex next door to the hospital."

Although Colleen Haggerty and James McCaffrey and their families were sorely in need of the services offered, both he and Colleen wanted to find out whom their mysterious greeters were. James approached the middle-aged woman holding the McCaffrey sign and introduced himself, "Good morning Madam, I'm James Robert McCaffrey from the village of Mala, were you expecting me?" He asked politely.

"Hello James," she responded smiling, extending her hand. "Yes, we certainly were. I am Ruth McCaffrey, your aunt, your Uncle Paul's wife. We are so glad that you have come."

"It's a pleasure to meet you Aunt Ruth."

"Are these your brothers?"

"Yes, Mum, this is Michael, that's Joseph, and that's Thomas, and Daniel, he's the youngest."

The boys set their bags down on the dock and politely extended their hand, each mimicking their older brother.

"Where's Katelyn? I must see her."

"Katelyn died on the crossing Auntie Ruth," Michael replied quietly.

"We buried her in the ocean." Daniel responded innocently.

"Oh no!" Ruth McCaffrey exclaimed sorrowfully, throwing both hands up as if trying to fend off this dreadful news. "And your mother and father, James, where are they?" She asked.

"Mother is dead too, Aunt Ruth. She died last month."

"Oh my God!"

"We buried her at Saint Joseph's cemetery, Auntie." Daniel chimed in once more.

"And your father?" She asked hesitatingly. "Is he not with you?"

"No, he saw us off, but the doctors told him he only had a few weeks left and he didn't want to leave Ireland. He wanted to be buried with mother."

This was too much for Ruth McCaffrey; she held both hands to her face in a vain attempt to hold back the tears.

Changing the subject, James was curious, "How did you know we would be on this ship Aunt Ruth?" He asked.

"We didn't of course. One or two members of our extended families have been here to meet every ship that has arrived from Cork over the past year. We only knew that you were coming soon, but your father never mentioned in his letters when you would be here. Therefore, it has been a long vigil; but come with me, I have a coach waiting, we will go home; your Uncle Paul should be in later tonight. This awful rioting has nearly consumed him these last four or five days. I hope it is behind us now. The Army hit them real hard last night."

"First, I'd like to say goodbye to the Malone and Haggerty families Aunt Ruth, but don't you think we should go with the other men to the hospital Annex to bath and get out of these dirty clothes?"

"No." She responded firmly. "You go say your goodbyes, but the Haggerty and Malone families all live within a block or two of our place so you will have plenty of opportunity to see them later this week. You can bath when we get home, but all five of you have to bath outside in sulfur and lye water and we may have to burn your clothing, we will see. Do not worry you will be fine. Every poor soul that gets off one of these dreadful ships has the same problem."

After finding that the Haggerty family was safe, James kissed Colleen goodbye. She was all smiles, "You promise, Jimmy. I want to see you tomorrow."

"Don't worry Colleen," he grinned, "I promise I'll check on you every day."

Mathew Haggerty watched his daughter as she said goodbye to James, then responding to his wife's persistent nagging, intervened. Alice Haggerty insisted that her daughters were spending entirely too much unsupervised time in the company of the McCaffrey boys. She had warned her husband several times while they were still on the farm in Ireland of the potential consequences, should this conduct continue. During the crossing however, she quickly found that aboard ship the problem worsened as her daughters sought to escape the monotony of the voyage and the confining conditions of their small cabin. However, with all of the ship's mysterious holds, compartments and lifeboats, Alice Haggerty had very little control aboard ship over when her daughters chose to meet clandestinely with a member of the opposite sex. She was quick to reassert that control the minute the family set foot on dry land. Mathew Haggerty however, the good and easy-going husband, without comment took it all in stride, for he liked James and looked forward to the day his daughter quit delaying the inevitable and married the young man.

"We need to go Colleen, your mother is waiting, and we cannot keep the family waiting. They are anxious for us to be on our way."

"Yes, Daddy I will be right there," she responded with a smile and a wink for her father; she knew he was only trying to placate her mother.

It was nearly ten o'clock in the morning when James awoke to find all four of his brothers still asleep, the two youngest on cots in the same room and Michael and Joseph in an adjoining room. Red and blue wallpaper and, Princeton, and Yale university banners hung from the walls along with photographic pictures the like of which James had never seen before. There were also pictures of young boys and girls and of two young men in Army uniforms. Although his father never talked about Paul McCaffrey's family in America, James surmised these were probably his cousins, Paul, and Ruth McCaffrey's children.

Lying across a footlocker were several pairs of underwear, shirts, stockings and trousers; he quickly shaved and dressed anxious to explore this huge house and to meet his uncle Paul McCaffrey. Coming downstairs, he could hear dishes rattling and laughter coming from the kitchen; when he entered, he found a middle-aged cook and young Irish woman apparently a maid, giggling and laughing.

"Good morning Lad." The woman said in broken English, which James thought, had to be a German accent. "Good morning, ladies," he said politely. "I'm James McCaffrey; I'm Uncle Paul's nephew."

"Oh we know who you are young man." The cook responded. "I'm Gertrude Metz and that little scamp is your cousin Sarah. You sit down here and eat. Mrs. Mac told us all about you kids. She said my job was to fatten you up because she said you all look like a bunch of scarecrows." Gertrude Metz laughed.

"Hello James, yes I'm Sarah Flynn" she offered extending her hand. "I work for Mrs. Mac as we call her. She's really my Auntie Ruth too; she hires me to help out when school is not in session."

"Hello Sarah. It's nice to meet you." James replied.

"Gertrude says that if she weren't my aunt Mrs. Mac would fire me." She grinned. "But you sit down and eat and I'll get your brothers up and dressed. Auntie says they are really cute." She was smiling. "Mrs. Mac has gone shopping and will have lunch with Uncle Paul; she will be home by the middle of the afternoon. You kids are on your own until then, but I was to warn you, you are not to stray too far because the riots may not be over. Uncle says most of these people are cowards; they just come out after dark to do their devilment then hide behind their wives and children in the daytime. Auntie said Uncle would be home for supper if things quiet down. He is the boss of all the uniformed officers in this part of the city, so he is busy. The police commissioner was hurt the other night when a mob attacked police headquarters. That's why, if you have not seen 'em there are two uniformed officers out front this morning. Uncle said they will be here until the riots are over."

After eating a huge breakfast, Sarah showed James and his brothers the immediate neighborhood, never wandering farther away from the McCaffrey residence than four or five blocks. She pointed out her school at Saint Thomas church where the youngest boys played on the swings while James and Michael visited with their newest kinfolk. While there an Army patrol, accompanied by two police officers came by.

"Good afternoon folks," one of the officers greeted the three youngsters as he got down off his mount. "Are you boys enrolled?" He asked James and Michael. The boys looked at one another without a thought of what the officer was asking.

"No they are not enrolled, Officer Sweeney." Sarah replied coldly. "They just arrived here yesterday from Ireland."

"Do I know you young lady?" The office acted surprised by Sarah's response to his question.

"Oh you certainly do John Sweeney," she responded indignantly. "I'm Sarah Flynn, Commissioner McCaffrey's niece and I go to school right here with your kids."

"Oh! Hello Sarah." He seemed a bit surprised then smiled, his tobacco stained teeth just visible behind a huge mustache. "I am sorry I did not recognize you. How are you?"

"I'm fine; these are my cousins Jimmy and Michael McCaffrey, and they did just get off the boat from Cork, that's the truth."

"I believe you Dear." He smiled. "Hello boys, welcome to New York." He said extending his hand.

"Thank you Mr. Sweeney," James replied politely.

"How was the crossing?" He asked. "Pretty rough, I imagine?"

"Yes Sir," Michael replied. "We lost our little sister and ten others. It was bad."

"I am sorry about that, Son, but you are in good hands now. Although it looks like you need to put some meat on those bones of yours. If you are staying with Commissioner McCaffrey, Gertrude will take care of that. She's the best cook in the neighborhood," his grin indicating he spoke from personal knowledge of her fine cuisine. "But we must be off. You take care now. Do not wonder too far from the neighborhood; if the Commissioner has not mentioned it, under the provisions of the Enrollment Law you young fellows have to register for the draft. That is what this ruckus is all about; it is the law of the land and the police have to enforce it. Have a great day, take care, Sarah." He smiled, then mounting, waved goodbye and rode off with his partner and the Army men.

On their way back to the McCaffrey residence James asked Shannon about their Aunt and Uncle's family. "There are pictures of two boys in uniform in the bedroom and also some others; are they Uncle Paul's children?"

"That's your cousins, the twins Emmett and Ray in uniform and the girl in the picture is their sister Emily. She died when she was fourteen and the boys were killed in September at Antietam."

"Where is that, Sarah? What happened?"

"What happened? The war silly; our army battled the Rebs there near Sharpsburg, that's in Maryland." She responded surprised that he and Michael did not know about this terrible battle that cost so many lives.

"Oh," James responded quietly, "we know a little bit about the war, but I guess we just had other things to worry about. Nearly everyone knows where Maryland is, but unless the Irish had family in the army, most did not follow the war news. The *Cork Examiner* had some stories on the front page once, but that was months ago."

"Well Emmett and Ray were in college when the rebellion started; they left school and joined the Army. It was their first battle and it was terrible. Mrs. Mac won't ever get over it, and Uncle doesn't say much about it anymore."

Sarah and her new friends were sitting on the front steps of the McCaffrey home when their uncle arrived in a calash driven by a uniformed officer. James and the boys studied the man as Sarah ran out to greet him. He was a big man; well over six feet tall and very heavily built with bushy red hair and a large mustache.

"Hello Sarah," he boomed, giving his wife's niece a kiss, then looking at the five boys now standing near the front stoop, asked, "I take it these are our boys from Ireland? Hello boys," he said shaking hands with James and the others in turn. "You're James; I know that, you look just like your father. And you must be Michael?"

"Hello Uncle Paul, yes I'm Michael and this is Joseph and that's Thomas and this little guy is Daniel."

"Boys I am very glad to meet you and so pleased that you came to our home. I am sorry about your mother, and that your father could not come; and I am so sorry about dear Katelyn. For them she was a dream come true after your sisters died."

Listening to his Uncle, James noticed that he spoke the way of the old Irish; it was like being at home again for he sounded just like his father.

"Your mother wrote a wonderful note about her when she was born." He continued. "However, let's get a bite to eat; you too Sarah. We need a snack before supper," he smiled. "I need to catch up on family and ye have to tell me about Mala and County Cork. I left there before ye were born Jimmy."

As they entered the McCaffrey back yard, the boys noted that their Uncle Paul turned and waved to the two uniformed officers standing across the street. They had been there ever since Sarah and the boys left for the playground at Saint Thomas's school that morning.

Ruth McCaffrey and Gertrude had been busy while they were away; the two of them prepared a late lunch for the family, with sandwiches from a large cut of roast beef, along with coffee and lemonade.

"Boys, do you know what ice cream is?" Their aunt asked, with James and Michael responding.

"Yes, Mrs. McCaffrey, I know." Michael said. "Mother took us to Cork when we were small and we had some there."

"Good, but first things first; I am your Aunt, please call me Aunt Ruth or Auntie. I am after all your Uncle Paul's wife. Okay?" She replied kindly.

"I will do that, Auntie Ruth," Michael responded with a smile.

"That's good, Michael. Now, I want you to tell me what you see sitting there on the end of the picnic table. Do you know what that is?" she asked, pointing to a large wooden barrel on the end of the table.

"No, I'm afraid I have never seen such a contraption, maybe Jimmy knows."

"I know what it is Auntie," Daniel responded enthusiastically. "It is an ice cream maker. I've seen pictures of it."

"Good boy Daniel, now you are going to get your first chance to make ice cream. Sarah put Daniel to work here, and when he gets tired let the other boys take a hand." The boys' obvious innocence amused her.

Before the family sat down to eat Paul McCaffrey left the group for a few minutes and returned in a few minutes accompanied by the two uniformed officers on guard at the McCaffrey residence.

"Fix your plates, gentlemen, please." He said to the two men.

"Right here, boys." Gertrude called out, handing each a plate and silverware. "Start with the roast beef and potato salad and whatever else you find tempting." She smiled. "Cups, and the coffee are over there, help yourself." The two men took ample amounts from every dish, and then poured themselves a cup of coffee before returning to the front yard.

"A blessing Paul, please," Ruth McCaffrey interjected, "and a prayer for John, Mary Kathleen and Katelyn."

"Yes, Mother." He responded.

When the backyard picnic ended, the boys helped Gertrude and Sarah clear away the dishes and take things indoors. Paul McCaffrey and his wife Ruth marveled at the energy and excitement on the faces of their young niece and nephews.

"Memories, Mother?" He asked.

"Yes, Dear; maybe if we are lucky we could start again with Thomas and Daniel. They are too young to be out on their own. The other boys will have to enroll this week. The Governor has declared Martial Law and the federal government activated the Guard as part of the regular force. If we do not enroll them, the Army may arrest them. They have had enough trouble in their young lives, they do not need that."

"Paul, at our ages, do you really think we can handle two young livewires like Thomas and Daniel?"

"Yes, if you are asking me, I think both of us can do what needs to be done. I could not put them in an orphanage, nor would I adopt them out. Sarah can help and they will be in school most of the time."

"Nor would I let you, Paul." Ruth McCaffrey responded warmly. "Yes we'll take them, but let's do it slowly and let them think it's their idea, okay?"

"That's a great idea, we can do that. When you go in, Dear, send James and Michael out, I want to talk to them about their dad, okay?"

When the boys came outside he greeted them with a smile and said, "There is more ice cream there fellows, help yourself. Then come and sit by me. I want to know about the family. How old was Katelyn and your two older sisters when they died? Did the Crown take everything or were you still on the home place? Just bring me up to date; your Dad was not that great at keeping me informed. We received his last letter about three months ago."

Over the next three hours, the two boys brought their uncle up to date on just what happened to the farm eked out of timber and scrubland in County Cork by Paul and John's father and grandfather. James filled him in on his father's activities with the Land League and the Movement and the Crown's response to the organizations in which his father was so active. He told his uncle of the continuing violence directed toward those in the Movement by the government.

"Father often talked to us about the Prime Minister's efforts to help our families when you were still in Ireland. But as you know, the Queen fired Mr. Peel and Daddy said things got worse for him and Mother after you left."

"I am only too aware of that Jimmy," Paul McCaffrey responded with a note of sadness in his voice. "Yet if we continued our resistance they would have come after all our families; the older folks feared that the Crown would either kill us or deport the entire clan. Therefore, we had no choice.

When ye children came along your mother persuaded your father to quit the Movement for fear that all of ye would be deported; that happened with two of the Movement's most active families. It was a sad day for all of us."

The boys continued with their story, only pausing long enough to answer their uncle's frequent and probing questions for Paul McCaffrey hungered for information about his brother and his beloved Ireland. The boys talked openly of their sisters' deaths and how their mother suffered before she died, having been bedridden for nearly two years, then about their father's illness.

"I don't think Daddy will last much longer." James responded. "It took nearly all his strength to get us onboard the *Isle of Jersey*, and it was hard on both he and Mother. I spent two years in Kilmainham, Uncle Paul and we did some bad things to get enough money to pay the fare. Daddy told us that if they caught us, we would have gone to the whipping post or the Deportation Yard, the thought of that nearly killed him.

"Leo Gordon and Bobby Burke robbed the Army paymaster in Belfast and after being sentenced to hang, they broke out of the gaol at Derry. The constabulary almost caught them going aboard the *Hampton Court*; they jumped overboard and the police fired on them in the water. Pat Kennedy and I pulled them aboard the *Isle of Jersey* just as we left dockside. If it were not for Captain Sinclair, they would be dead by now. His first mate told me the Captain was a fair man and even though he got kicked out of the Royal Navy he didn't think it was right for the Queen's men to kill people like that."

"Well good for him. I read that Burke and Gordon had escaped. We still get the Cork Examiner and occasionally see The Irish Times out of Dublin. Both of them are always a month or two late but over the years we have been able to keep track of some of the old clan members."

"But that name Sinclair is familiar, James. How is it that I would know him?"

"Daddy said Sinclair and Captain William Smyth were Royal Navy supply officers at Galway when you and he were running guns into Ireland."

"Ah, yes I remember those two gentlemen quite well," he smiled. "They were a couple of real scallywags. We bribed them to help us bring the guns into Galway Bay. But by what stretch of the imagination would they help you or your father unless there was some monetary gain for them personally?"

"Maybe you remember Uncle Paul, Daddy kept the British ships' manifests from that time; they identified when the Navy would arrive and depart Galway. From these he said you could tell whether-or-not Marine detachments were on board the ships. If the marines were not on board, members of the Movement felt it would be safe to bring the guns ashore; that was until an informer entered the picture."

"Ah, yes, and I suppose he held these over Sinclair's head as a threat, right?"

"Yes, Sir he did that."

"Your Dad would do that, James. Good for him," he smiled.

It was near bedtime when the three men reentered the house but before saying goodnight Paul McCaffrey turning to James said, "I understand you, Michael and Joseph are aware of the Enrollment Law; is that right?"

"Yes sir, we are." James replied. "Sarah and Officer Sweeney told us all about the new draft law and of our responsibilities under that law."

"Good, then I want you to go with me tomorrow to the precinct to register to avoid any problems for yourselves. Then if this ruckus is over by this weekend, we will have a barbecue in the back yard after Mass on Sunday. What do ye think of that?"

"That will be just fine, Uncle Paul; I don't think we have ever been to a barbeque." James responded, hesitantly not being too sure just what a barbeque entailed.

"I want you and Michael to round-up everyone that made the crossing with you; we'll roast a pig and celebrate your arrival in America. We will have a great party, and that Father O'Herlihy, I would like to meet him. In the meantime, start thinking about what you would like to do and how we can take care of Thomas and Daniel. This fall we will need to get them into school."

On Friday night, rioting spread to several nearby cities including Philadelphia, Trenton, Buffalo, and Baltimore. At police headquarters in New York, Paul McCaffrey after meeting all afternoon with his intelligence staff and US Army command staff, briefed his commanders on what lie ahead for his men. The group of borough and precinct commanders included the top staff of the detective division along with several military command personnel. His tone was ominous and he spoke plainly when telling his staff what he expected of them.

"As you gentlemen know, the National Guard troops are now federalized and will be directly under the command of the War Department in Washington so I want all of ye to get acquainted with their commanders in the field. Ye have met Brigadier General Richard Johnson, he and his headquarters staff will work out of my office. As you are aware, the rioters have both muskets and short firearms, along with nitroglycerine, and all manner of weapons including paving stones. I do not need to tell ye what those things can do to our men when dropped from the roof of a building. They are particularly deadly so it will be up to your men to look out for the safety of our infantry boys and troopers on horseback not accustomed to policing large cities. Most of our military are boys from farms or small villages throughout the country so do not expect them to know what the risk is from these stones. Take them aside and clearly show them that these are very deadly weapons.

"Our federal friends came well prepared. President Lincoln, at the request of the War Department sent several thousand additional troops into the city this week. After what has occurred here during the past several nights and the carnage spawned by arson fires and looted buildings, our hospitals are overflowing and with the dead and injured numbering in the hundreds neither the governor nor the mayor are in a mood to concede even one more block or building to these thugs. The intention of the mob has been clear from the beginning; they want to stop the draft and do what they must to disrupt legitimate government functions.

"That shall not happen in our city gentlemen. General Johnson has advised Washington that if the mobs are successful here in New York the government will not be able to enforce the Enrollment process anywhere else in the country. I might add that he has assured Washington that it will not happen on his watch. Nor gentlemen shall it happen on our watch; we shall meet violence with force if that becomes necessary."

That evening the police, working in conjunction with the Army, posted armed personnel at every major government building in the city, with a reserve force of police and Army units stationed at several strategic locations throughout the metropolitan area. From these locations, troops could respond in a moment's notice to any part of the city.

Shortly after dusk, the gangs began to form at multiple locations with two groups coming together in what was obviously a preplanned attack upon government buildings. Officials estimated that more than 50,000 people were on the move in groups of five to ten thousand each, with the largest group moving on police headquarters. They coordinated their attack, opening fire at nearly the same time from both ground and rooftop locations.

Some members of the mob had gained access to the roof of a building across the street from the main entrance to the police building and opened fire on officers on the street below. With bullets ricocheting off the front of the building McCaffrey ordered his officers to return fire immediately. The police response ended the attack as quickly as it began with the mob dispersing quickly, running in all directions. In the aftermath the officers counted seven dead rioters and at least thirty-five others lay where they fell, too badly injured to flee.

In other locations the results were similar, the mobs ended up in complete disarray, quickly putting an end to their unlawful activities. By three o'clock in the morning, it was all over, the gangs scattered like so many leaves in the wind. When the sun came up Saturday morning, detectives and uniformed officers had in tow more than fifty of their leaders and chief instigators. While the Army and Fire Department ambulance crews picked up over two-hundred injured for transport to the nearest hospital. Saturday afternoon the County Coroner's Office issued a statement to the press that the body count had reached sixty-two; sixteen of these were uniformed police officers. However, he told the newspaper people the count would continue to rise as reports came in from local hospitals. Still it was over; the streets of New York City were once again quiet.

Before returning home, Paul McCaffrey met with his colleagues from the Army, including Major General Charles Sanford, and members of his command.

"It's over Paul." General Sanford said. "It appears that they have had enough, thank God."

"I believe you're right, General. We have most of their leaders in jail and we decimated some of the real hardcore criminal gangs. Your people did such a magnificent job. Had it not been for the Army those people could have taken control of our city. Hopefully several of them will pay a high price for what they have done."

"They should hang, Paul but they won't; the American people are too forgiving; the bleeding hearts will soon surface seeking clemency for these thugs. Such is life in these United States of ours." He smiled grimly. "They really have no idea of what they almost accomplished. Had they won it could have been the end of the Union. The irony of it is that before this war is over our good citizens will be petitioning the President for amnesty for all of them."

"I suppose you're right, General. However, I will not forgive them. A whole lot of these buggers are Irish Nationals, they came here to escape a corrupt system of government, and the people of these United States welcomed all of them. Granted, some have faced tough sledding in the job market, but that is no reason to turn against one of the few countries in the world where they accept the Irish without preconditions. All this country ever expected of us was that we would work and pay our own way and that we would defend the country in time of war. Well these people could care less about our country and I for one hope that Congress and the President have the backbone to send them back where they came from. I am thoroughly disgusted with all of them."

"Don't be too hard on your own people, Paul." The General responded reflectively, "Congress and the President are responsible for this mess. The Enrollment Act should not have allowed the rich and the politically connected to buy their way out of the draft.

"That's why I say don't be too hard on your Irish brethren, for I'll remind you that several of our lads who were killed tonight were Irish through and through; they certainly gave a good account of themselves."

Paul McCaffrey knew this professional soldier was right, of the sixteen police officers and several soldiers that died in these riots, many of them were of Irish stock. Notwithstanding that, he could not help but feel that this week the crimes committed by the rioters dishonored the Irish nation and brought much pain to a great American city.

Sunday turned out to be a beautiful warm day in New York City and nearly two dozen members of the Malone, McCaffrey, and Kennedy Clan would be together at Paul and Ruth McCaffreys home for a good old-fashioned American pig roast. Most of them lived within Saint Thomas's Parish and attended ten o'clock church services where the newly arrived Father Kirk O'Herlihy assisted the parish priest at the Mass. Afterward they walked the short distance to the McCaffrey home where Officer John Sweeney working with Gertrude Metz was making final preparations for lunch.

"The pig is ready to eat, Mrs." John Sweeney called out to Ruth McCaffrey.

"Oh it smells delightful, John." She responded, smiling. "If Gertrude ever leaves us I want you to retire from the force and become our personal chef."

"I would do that, Mrs. Mac," he laughed, "but my wife may have something to say about that."

"I think that's a great idea, Ruth." Paul McCaffrey added, interjecting himself into this light-hearted conversation. "I could retire and John and I would enjoy a Guinness or two in the evening and entertain you with heroic stories on how we saved this great city from itself and still managed to survive for twenty-five years doing the peoples' work."

"No, on the other hand I think maybe I'll do the cooking myself." She said. "I've heard too many police stories already. John you'll just have to go to work someplace else." John Sweeney smiled.

As the family settled into a chair or on the lawn with their food their conversations took on a more personal tone with the adults and children pairing off with someone near their own age. Colleen Haggerty, her sisters Catherine and Mary, and Shannon Malone staked out a quiet corner of the yard with Sarah Flynn. They wanted to learn from her everything they could about American girls, from what they wore, to hairstyles, availability of schools and job opportunities for young women in New York City.

The five former inmates of Kilmainham Jail and recent Crossing survivors Pat Kennedy, Mike Ryan, Donald and Kevin Malone and James McCaffrey, each with a glass of Guinness and their food in hand gathered around one another where their thoughts and conversations never strayed far from Ireland. However, Bobby Burke and Leo Gordon wanted to put Ireland behind them; they could not forget that if they went back home there was a Hangman waiting for them. They would not drift too far away from Paul McCaffrey for these two young men were interested in a new career; they hoped to learn from this man where the greatest opportunities existed for the newly arrived immigrant.

Margaret Malone, Ruth McCaffrey, Louise Haggerty, and the Kennedy and Ryan women sat at one of the tables enjoying each other's conversation; they were particularly interested in Maggie Malone's news of Ireland. For some of them more than thirty years had passed since their parents left there. While the women visited, they made sure their maternal instincts would not fail them should the young McCaffrey boys need looking after. The youngsters appeared to enjoy this unaccustomed motherly attentiveness.

Late that afternoon John Sweeney and Gertrude Metz called the young men over to take the last cut of meat from the carcass on the spit. By the time they had their fill, only the pig's head and soup bones remained; John Sweeney would take this home. There was little doubt but that this week the men in his precinct would be eating headcheese, ham, and pea soup for lunch. But it was time now for their host to have a few words with his guests before these family members departed; Ruth McCaffrey, Mathew and Louise Haggerty and Father O'Herlihy were in agreement that these men and women needed an experienced counselor to get them off on the right track to succeed in this new land of theirs. They chose Paul to do this, which as it turned out was exactly what he wanted.

"Before ye all head off for home I want ye to gather around and listen for a moment to what lies ahead for ye. This is a tough time for a new immigrant to arrive in New York and I am going to suggest some things that you may not understand right now, but if you follow this advice, it will keep you out of trouble. First, you young men must enroll for the draft; that is the law of the land. As you have seen since you arrived, these riots caused the death of nearly one-hundred men and women; there are over two thousand wounded, some of whom will die in a hospital. Many are our own people from Ireland, along with many others who resisted this draft; they have paid a terrible price for that resistance. Therefore, I suggest very strongly that you young men enroll first thing tomorrow. Ye can do that at the precinct. Mr. Sweeney will get you in and out in just a few minutes, but it is imperative that ye do that right away.

"Also, the police and the fire services are in desperate need of young men; we are hiring now. It is a good job. However, let me warn ye, it does not pay very much and there are some unpleasant tasks that go along with the territory. As a police officer, ye will spend most of your career on the night shift and ye will have to do some things that you may not like to do, such as taking action against your fellow citizens. In spite of that, these are wonderful, exciting service organizations to belong to and I think you would enjoy the job very much.

"Third, every hospital in the city is in need of nurses and nurses aides. They are full with our wounded soldiers, including many from the rebel army. Your Aunt Ruth has talked to the Administrator of Saint Mary's Hospital and they could put all of you young women to work this week. Still, like the police service, it does not pay a great deal of money, but everything I said about police work applies equally to the nursing service. I think ye would enjoy the work; these are professional people and serve this city well. I also understand from Father O'Herlihy that there are positions available in both the Army and the Navy and they are actively recruiting right now. Ye should also know that Father O'Herlihy joined the Army yesterday."

"Good for you, Father," Maggie Malone called out, interrupting her brother's closing remarks. "Hopefully you will not be required to carry a gun, will you, Father?" She asked.

He smiled and shook his head. "No Mrs. Malone, I think I will only be carrying my prayer book."

"I am sure Father O'Herlihy will have something interesting to tell ye about that later." Paul McCaffrey added. "However, that is all I have to say and I am sure ye are glad of that?" He said with a smile. "Just remember ye are always welcome in our house. Good night everyone and thank ye for coming."

Upon hearing that the priest joined his adopted country's military service, the five former inmates of Kilmainham Prison quickly gathered around the man. The boys were eager to learn what to expect should they follow his example. He remained behind for more than an hour fielding their questions.

On Monday morning when Paul McCaffrey left for work, he found Bobby Burke and Leo Gordon waiting on the front step. "Good morning boys," he said cheerily, "what brings you out so early?"

"Do you have a few minutes Uncle Paul?" Bobby asked. "We would like to talk to you about the possibility of Leo and me joining the force."

"Good, you bet I do. What would you like to know?"

"Both of us are wanted by the police in Ireland; we escaped from jail in Derry and the Crown's people may come after us. Do you think that precludes us from being police officers?"

"What did ye do to be in jail in the first place?" Paul McCaffrey asked his tone of voice now grim.

"We robbed the Army paymaster in Belfast, Uncle Paul." Leo Gordon responded sheepishly.

"Did you hurt or kill anyone?"

"No Sir."

"What did ye do with the money?

"We bought passage for our brothers and sisters and our folks, they are to sail from London for America next month. In addition, we spent some of it on ourselves for our passage from Cork to Canada, but the Army caught up to us when we went aboard the *Hampton Court* at Cork. We jumped overboard and Jimmy and Pat Kennedy pulled us aboard the *Isle of Jersey*."

"And what money do ye have left?"

"None, Sir, we had some but it is in Canada by now; we left the *Hampton Court* in kind of a hurry."

"I see," Paul McCaffrey responded reflectively, nodding his head recalling his own clandestine departure from Galway nearly a quarter of a century ago.

"What do you think, Sir?" Bobby Burke asked timidly. "Will that preclude us from joining the force?"

"No." Their uncle responded firmly, his lips pursed as if contemplating future possibilities for his two young nephews. "Ye go home; it's only six o'clock and too early to do what we need to do. Shave and get yourselves a haircut and be in my office at two o'clock sharp; I think we can find ye a job. One other thing, ye are never to mention the Belfast incident again and this conversation never took place. Is that understood?"

"Yes, Sir," the boys responded candidly.

"What do you think, Pat?" Kevin Malone asked his cousin. "We're too young to join the police force and none of us have a trade. The police department has already accepted Bobby and Leo. I talked to them last night and they are to report for duty Wednesday. The rest of us are too young and there is not much demand for farm laborers in this city, maybe joining the Army is not such a bad deal."

"How about it, Jimmy," Pat Kennedy asked his cousin, "are you going to join the Army?"

"I think so, Pat. Michael, Joseph, and I talked about it and we spoke to Mr. Sweeney; he figures the Army will draft us because we do not have a job and really no family responsibilities. Thomas and Daniel would like to live with Auntie Ruth and I think she would take them, so we would have no ties. I would rather volunteer than wait to be drafted."

"I'm going to join," Mike Ryan said. "We'll get a chance to learn a little bit about this country; I didn't realize it was so darn big. If we got into the cavalry maybe, they would send us out West. I think I would like that."

"What about your girl friend, Jimmy? Donald Malone asked, grinning at his cousin. "You'll have to leave her behind; maybe if you got married she wouldn't let you go."

"Go the hell, Donny! We have not even discussed that. She and her sisters and Shannon have all gone to work at Saint Mary's Hospital. They want to be nurses. I think that's great. Sarah wanted to go along with them but she is too young. When the war is over and Colleen finishes her training there will be time enough to start thinking about marriage; but neither one of us has time for that now."

"Well I know what I think we ought to do," Michael responded firmly. "Uncle Paul and Auntie Ruth have taken us all in, no questions asked so whatever we do I think we should talk to them first, we owe them that. Then each of us should decide what he wants to do. I think we ought to join the Army, but I also think we should stick together. So let's talk to Uncle Paul tonight when he gets home, okay?"

"Fair enough Michael; you're right." James replied. "What do you say Joseph?"

"I'm all for joining the Army," Joseph responded innocently, "but I am not mad at anybody and I certainly haven't killed anyone but I don't want to go to jail for refusing to fight. I don't think you fellows do either."

"If you're going, Michael, I'm going too." Thomas responded quite forcefully in his high-pitched young voice.

"You are not going anyplace, Thomas," James replied authoritatively. "You're only fifteen years old. You and Daniel are going to get an education. Auntie Ruth has already signed you up a Saint Thomas' school. You will be going with Sarah. That's settled."

"No it's not," Thomas replied heatedly. "I'm old enough to decide that for myself."

"No way, Thomas, Uncle Paul, and Auntie have already made that decision, so live with it."

Thomas glared at his older brother, but said no more.

"Can we talk to you tonight after supper about the enrollment, Uncle Paul?" James said as the five boys sat down for supper with their aunt and uncle.

"We shall do just that, Jimmy; right now and right here while your Aunt Ruth is present. She and I have already talked about your future and we want Thomas and Daniel to stay on with us until they are out of school. What do you think of that Thomas, Daniel? Does that sound alright?" He asked smiling at his two young nephews.

"That sounds great, Uncle Paul," Daniel responded with a huge grin. "Can I sleep in Jimmy's bed when he goes away?"

Paul & Ruth McCaffrey both smiled at this, with Ruth responding. "Daniel you can sleep in any bed you want to, but this fall you will have to get up and go to school very, very early with Sarah."

"That's okay Auntie; I like Sarah." He smiled.

"I want to go with Jimmy and Michael and Joseph, Uncle Paul." Thomas blurted out. "But Michael says I can't go 'because I'm too young. I'm almost sixteen now and I've seen young guys like me in uniform at the armory; so I could go too."

"No Thomas," Paul McCaffrey replied gently. "Those youngsters at the armory are sent there by the courts; most of them have committed a crime and they are on probation and working off their sentence in lieu of going to jail. They did something bad and they must pay a price for that. If they do not get into any further trouble, the Army will take them when they turn eighteen. So you don't want to be associated with those young men." Then turning his attention back to the three older boys, Paul McCaffrey continued. "The chairman of the Borough Draft Board told me today that ye boys would be called up next week. It has been nearly a month now since ye registered so they are anxious to move on ye. I've been able to stall them for awhile to let ye recover from the crossing, but I'm afraid that next week ye will get your notices to report for training at the 69th Infantry Regiment's Armory in Manhattan."

"We're ready to go, Uncle Paul," Michael replied. "We are certainly willing to fight for this country, but I guess I don't understand it. We are not angry with anybody on the Confederate side; Momma and Daddy taught us long ago that slavery was not right but many of the people fighting for the South are Irish kids just like us. It doesn't make any sense to us."

"Unfortunately, Michael war does not make much sense. However, think about your daddy and your grandfather. They fought the Brits for more years than ye have lived, their reasons were the same as what ye see here. The black man wants to be free to choose his own way in life just like your daddy and grandfather did. Moreover, here, we think the Good Lord is on the side of President Lincoln and the Army."

A few days later as Paul McCaffrey was preparing to leave for work he suggested to his wife that with the boys leaving next week they should get everyone together again for another backyard barbeque. "You know, Dear," he said quietly, "what the risks are; we may not see some of them again." He was dead serious.

"Oh God no, Paul, don't say that!" She cried out. "They've only been here a little while; you and I have just gotten to know them. If they have to leave let them go off quietly, I do not want to pretend. I cannot celebrate when we know what they may face in the upcoming months. This war looks like it will go on for years and I can't take it anymore." She turned away from her husband so he would not see the tears.

"The celebration would not be for you and I Dear, ye know that. These kids have lost everything, first their older sisters, then their mother and Katelyn, and now their father, not to mention their home and country where they were born. Celebrating their departure should send a message to all of them though that they would always be welcome in our home."

"You didn't mention to the boys what *The Times* said about their father, did you?"

"No. How could I, the Queen's people accused their father of being a cold-blooded murderer; they say he killed Lord Willingham, a priest, and several others. Neither you, nor I believe that for a second. I have no doubt that he may have torched all those farms; that is what I would do. Nevertheless, the boys do not need to read that. Before they leave for training, I will tell them their father has died. When they are older, they can learn of the circumstances of his death on their own. I am sure that by that time it will be public knowledge as to just what really happened and the Brits will not be able to cover it up."

"What about Thomas and Daniel?" Ruth McCaffrey asked with a worried look. "We'll have to tell them something."

"I'll tell the older boys when I see them off at the armory next week; but I won't show them the stories in the press. We can tell the little ones later. Eventually the truth will come out."

"Don't you think they may see a copy of the Examiner or the Times in Camp?"

"No, no one except a few of us older folks are interested in what is going on in Ireland and rightly so. These youngsters will have enough to worry about right here. Our boys will join The Army of the Potomac and from what I hear they will move into Southern Virginia. The Rebs were on the run after Gettysburg but it looks like they are going to stand and fight in Virginia. General Sanford told me yesterday that Lee is forming up for another assault on Washington."

"It sounds very ominous, Paul."

"Yes, it does, Dear. I am afraid it will be a long time before this war is over."

CHAPTER 6

FIRST BATTLE

"Lieutenant Kelly, just what in the hell are you doing? Where were you last night? You're three miles behind the lines and your people have been moving in circles all night; your platoon was supposed to be on the company's right flank."

"I don't know sir. It was raining so hard I guess I got a little confused on our directions."

"A little confused, that's a laugh. Your men have been shooting at anything and everything, except the enemy. For what purpose do you think the Army issued you that compass? We are moving South Lieutenant; that is the opposite direction from where that little needle points, so let us move this bunch of dumb Irishmen toward our enemy. Do you think you can do that today?"

"Yes, Captain, right away, Sir."

"And put those fires out. The Rebs can spot them for miles. "But my men were wet, Sir. We were just trying to dry their clothing."

"Well, we're all wet Lieutenant; that's what happens when it rains in Virginia, so put them out and move this bunch of knuckleheads out of here."

"Yes, Sir Captain."

"Geez Jimmy, did you hear the general? He really chewed out Lieutenant Kelly. We were lost last night, right? It was so dark I couldn't see a thing."

"He is not a general, Michael;" James responded smiling. "That was Captain Swartz, the Company Commander. However, I couldn't see a darn thing either, but our lieutenant is an officer and has a compass so he should have known where we were going. It sounds like we were just moving in circles."

"Well I thought somebody was shooting at us; every once in awhile our guys would unload a round or two into the woods. But I never saw anybody."

"Nor I, Michael, I think they were shooting at shadows."

"I don't care Jimmy; after we got the fires going I got most of my clothes dry this morning, so I think our lieutenant is okay. He may have gotten us lost but at least he did not get us killed in our first battle."

"Are you okay?"

"I'm okay; and you Jimmy, what do you think of the Army now?"

"It's okay, but we'll see what happens when we run across the Rebs."

"I heard Captain Swartz tell the lieutenant that was just a scouting party we ran into the other night—strange isn't it, we are looking for them and they are looking for us and when we find each other we are going to try to kill each other."

"But we didn't find anybody last night, Jimmy. Maybe we were lucky."

"Well they wounded a couple of our people; but I'm not convinced that they weren't shot by our own men. It was dark and raining so hard that we could not see anything other than the flash from our own rifles. How are your feet holding out, Michael?"

"Fine, the boots are great, certainly better than anything we ever saw in Ireland. And our uniforms are fantastic; maybe a little too heavy for this weather, but at night it gets pretty darn cold."

"Do you feel comfortable with the rifle?"

"Sure it's great, certainly better than what Daddy had before the Brits confiscated everything. We were lucky to have Daddy teach us how to shoot. Most of these kids from New York never fired a weapon before they joined up; they can't hit the broad side of a barn."

"How is Joseph doing, Jimmy?"

"He's fine; actually I think he enjoys all of this. You know him, he has always been an outdoors kid and loved the farm; he also likes Lieutenant Kelly. Kelly was born in Ireland but he grew up in New York and he is a good person. The two of them get along well together. Captain Swartz assigned Joseph to B Company. He will train with the sniper teams under Kelly; the lieutenant manages the teams for all three companies, he has an eye on using Joseph as the lead trainer."

"Yeah, I heard that."

"Michael with this new Springfield, he can outshoot just about anybody in his company. He has picked off targets well beyond 500 yards. He's good."

"Oh, I know he is good Jimmy, but don't you think there is something unholy about killing someone from a great distance. The poor bastard doesn't have a chance and most of the time his fellow soldiers have no idea where the shot came from."

"It would be nice Michael if the three of us come through this god-awful war without killing anybody, but I'm afraid that's not going to happen. However, if we kill them up front, face to face or from a great distance, it does not really matter; they will be dead and if our luck holds out, we will still be alive. You have to keep in mind what they told us in training at the Armory, 'The rebels will kill us unless we kill 'em first.' Hopefully Lieutenant Kelly and Captain Swartz remember that and do everything in their power to keep us alive."

"Have you heard or seen anything of Pat Kennedy or Mike Ryan?" James asked his brother. "No, not since we got off the train. They did such a good job handling the horses I think the artillery people were going to get them transferred into their unit. Mike wanted to get into the cavalry, but artillery may be as close to a cavalry unit as he will ever get."

"What about the Malone twins, are they still with Joseph's company?"

"Yes, but Joseph does not see much of them except at night as he is tied up at the range most every day. I talked to them at the mess tent a couple of days ago; they are doing well. Kevin looks much healthier now. Remember how very sick he was when we arrived in New York. He must have gained twenty or thirty pounds since then. He and Dennis both like the Army and it looks like it has been good for them. They get letters from Shannon and the Haggerty gals and that helps."

Michael chuckled. "I had my eye on one of Colleen's sisters, but it looks like the twins are way ahead of me; I should have written a letter to either Mary or Catherine when we were still in training."

James smiled, but made no comment; however, Michael's mention of the women in their lives quickly reminded him that he needed to respond to Colleen's latest letter.

"Where do you think we are going, Jimmy?"

"I don't know, the sergeant mentioned a place called Chancellorsville. He said they were in a big battle there in May of last year and the Army run the Rebs off, but he thought we might bivouac in that area through the winter to keep those people from infiltrating our lines and moving North again. However, I really don't know anymore about this country than you."

"Well we should know pretty soon, it looks like we may be taking another train ride; there are at least four trains over there on the siding. That would be nice, boots or no boots, my feet are in need of a rest."

"Did you get a good look at the horses that came through here yesterday there must have been nearly a thousand or more troops and a remuda of another two hundred or so?"

"Oh you bet I did, Michael; they looked like Morgan horses. I can picture Daddy, how proud he would have been to have owned one or two of those."

"If he still had Granddad's old place, we would have had a whole herd of them and you and I would be riding in the Derby."

At the mention of their father, both boys turned away from the other for fear they would be unable to control their emotions. "What do you think happened after we left home, Jimmy, any thoughts on that?"

"At one time Michael that's all I thought about, both during the crossing and while we were staying with Uncle Paul and Auntie Ruth. However, after joining the Army I just made up my mind that I would not think about it anymore until we get a copy of the Cork Examiner or the Times. They'll do a story on him; the press people knew all about his battles with the Crown and it would be too big of a story not to print it."

"I thought when Uncle Paul came to see us off on the train at Madison Square that he knew more than he was telling us. He did not seem to want to say more and neither one of us asked how he died. I think we just assumed the consumption took him. Be that as it may, we'll find out what happened before this war is over."

"Good morning Sergeant O'Malley." Lieutenant Jack Kelly said authoritatively, "breakfast at six o'clock; we'll start loading troops at seven thirty. Make sure they are squared away and ready to go. We're heading south."

"Yes, Sir Lieutenant."

"The cavalry has gone on ahead to secure the track so we should be there in four or five days. This will be the troops' last hot meal until we set up camp along the Rapidan River. We may be spending the winter there."

"They'll be ready Lieutenant." Sergeant O'Malley responded.

"What's your problem, McCaffrey?" Mike O'Malley asked James as the young soldier approach his boss who was sitting with another sergeant near the end of the coach.

"No problem, Sergeant; but it is mid afternoon and the supply and artillery units with their caissons, wagons and draft horses have yet to be loaded."

"I can see that, McCaffrey; so what do you want me to do about it."

"I just thought, Sir that we could get off the train and maybe play ball or something."

"Go sit down, McCaffrey. If the Captain wanted us off the train, he would have told us to get off. But I don't think he wants us out there playing games; we are on stand-by and I'm sure we will be on our way before too long."

"Yes, Sir Sergeant." James replied politely and turned around only to bump into Lieutenant Kelly. "Sorry, Sir."

"No problem McCaffrey," the lieutenant replied, then turning to O'Malley said, "Sergeant O'Malley let's get these folks off of this damn train and get them fed and then some close-order drill. They need the exercise and the training." Then turning to James, added, "That's good thinking McCaffrey, some day you might make corporal." He smiled.

"What time is it, Jimmy." Michael asked his older brother.

"I don't know, Michael; it must be near midnight, why don't you go back to sleep."

"How far have we traveled? It seems like we just go a few miles and then we stop and sit. This is a crock."

"Relax Michael; it's raining and we're undercover and warm so just go back to sleep and I'll wake you if anything happens."

It was daylight when the troop train again came to a sudden stop awaking most of the sleeping troops.

"Good morning Joseph, how'd you sleep?"

"Jesus Jimmy this is crazy; but I slept good. However, I'll bet we didn't go a hundred miles last night. My platoon detrained twice, to repair the track. Our captain said the Rebs spike the rails to slow us down."

"Well they don't want us to get through and every time they stop the train it gives them more time for their forces to get set-up. They've got to take a stand somewhere or we will go right on into Richmond."

"Is that where we want to go, Jimmy," Joseph asked, curious that his brother would know so much about their expected destination. "How do you know about all of this?"

"I just listen. Lieutenant Kelly and most of the sergeants are Americans; except for the lieutenant, they were all born here, so they know the country. That is something we are going to have to learn, but if you listen carefully, you can learn a lot from those fellows about the geography and history of Virginia. If we take Richmond the Lieutenant said the war will be over."

"Well it doesn't look like that is going to happen anytime soon at the rate we are traveling. By the way, did you get a look at the two Rebs the cavalry captured? They caught a couple of them just after daylight; all they had were their rifles and a couple of crowbars. Their shoes have holes in them and the uniforms are not much to look at. Actually they look like hell."

"Maybe so, but obviously they know how to fight. Our cavalry never caught them until after they spiked the rails; two young Rebs successfully delayed more than five thousand enemy soldiers. At that rate this war may last longer than Uncle Paul expects."

"Good morning, Michael."

"Hi Jimmy; have you been outside since we arrived?"

"Yes, I woke up before daylight and it's cold out there. It froze last night."

"You've got to be kidding me; it's only October, isn't it."

"It tis that, Michael, but we're not in Ireland now, remember? "Incidentally, I ran across Mike Ryan and Pat Kennedy. They were on the supply train. The Regiment has assigned them temporarily to the artillery. Mike said their officers were impressed with the way they handled the supply wagon teams, so they are going to transfer them to an artillery unit. The two of them are happy about that; Mike wanted to go with the cavalry, but at least he will be working with horses."

"Soldiers," it was Sergeant O'Malley yelling at his troops, "Get your gear together and fall-in, outside. We have a long march ahead of us today."

"Where are we going Sergeant?" One of the men asked.

"To the Rapidan River, it's about twenty miles as the crow flies; we will eat when we get there and set-up a camp. We may be there for several weeks."

"Twenty miles," someone yelled, "oh crap; that's crazy Sergeant."

Sergeant O'Malley's retort was swift and threatening. "Knock it off soldier; you volunteered to join this man's Army and you will take the bad with the good. So all of you pick up your gear and prepare to move out with the regiment."

The recent heavy rainstorm, in Virginia left its mark on the roadway from rail's end to the Rapidan River. Deep wagon ruts, many still overflowing with water forced the troops to wade in ankle deep mud and slush with the trek to the river turning into a nightmarish march. It was near dark when the Army arrived at the Rapidan campsite.

"Pickets out, Lieutenant Kelly, I want ten men across the river at fifty yard intervals. Tell them to keep it quiet; anyone else seen in that area will be a rebel, but I want prisoners, not just dead bodies until we know just what we face here."

"Yes, Sir, Captain.

"Sergeant O'Malley, take ten men for picket duty and move across the river; find a site where we can ford, but be careful, the water's running high."

"Yes, Sir, Lieutenant, we will find a good location; we have lots of rope and a couple of good swimmers."

Returning to the platoon, Sergeant O'Malley selected the nearest ten privates, calling them by name including James and Michael McCaffrey. "The rest of you pile rifles and let's get our tents set up before dark; straight line, one-hundred yards from the bank of the river." Then turning his attention to the ten men selected to cross the river he addressed James and Michael. "Did you McCaffrey lads learn how to swim in Ireland?" He asked.

"Yes, Sir, Sergeant," James responded. "We swam every summer in the lough on our Granddaddy's farm."

"We call them lakes here, McCaffrey; but no matter. I want you to strip-down and find us a shallow crossing; take rope with you and secure it on both sides then lead the squad across. Be careful, it will be cold and we don't want to lose anybody."

The two boys found a suitable crossing where the water was only waist high where they quickly secured two ropes from shore to shore to aid the none swimmers. The men crossed without incident carrying their weapons and clothing above their heads, with Sergeant O'Malley cautioning everyone to keep their clothing dry. After two years of duty in the field, he knew he could lose men from pneumonia just as easily as from enemy fire.

"Pair up by twos, fifty yards apart along the bank with two hour watches and keep it quiet." He warned.

James and Michael stayed together and before digging into their rations laid-out their rubber blankets on the wet grass and shrubbery along the edge of the riverbank. Even with their overcoats on and their blankets wrapped around their legs, the boys were cold and nearly famished. They quickly downed a piece of smoked beef and a hardtack biscuit then washed it down with water from their canteens; within the hour Sergeant O'Malley came by to check on them.

"Did you two keep your clothing dry when you came across?" he asked solicitously, showing concern for the welfare of these two young men from Ireland.

"Yes, Sir, Sergeant," Michael responded. "Maybe it won't rain anymore tonight, the moon and the stars are out so the river should be down by morning."

"Good observation, McCaffrey; by the way which one are you"

"I'm Michael, Sir, that's James, and Joseph is assigned to B Company."

"Michael, James, and Joseph, hey," he smiled in the moonlight. "I suppose if there were more of you your parents would have named them Peter and Paul?" He laughed quietly.

"Not exactly, Sergeant," James offered quietly, "our younger brothers are Daniel and Thomas."

"Ah, yes, I might have guessed that." He replied still smiling. "Anyway, stay awake and keep it quiet; I'll be back to check on you before morning. Remember Captain Swartz wants these Rebs alive, so we can find out what we are facing. We know that Lee has at least two brigades somewhere south of us and plenty of cavalry; so just stay alert."

"Yes, Sir," the boys replied in unison.

It was past midnight when James whispered to his brother as he held his hand over Michael's mouth for fear he may make a noise when he awoke. "We have company coming. There are two of them about seventy-five yards straight out; look about twenty degrees to the left at the top of that ridge. They're on their belly and heading for the river."

"What will we do, James?" Michael replied in a whisper.

"Take your rifle and just stay put; they should crawl right past us and when they get between us and the water we'll take them. I'll go for the first one in line and you get the number two fellow."

"Will we stick 'em, James?" Michael whispered.

"Only if we have to; but if they turn on you, or don't do what you tell them, stick 'em."

The two dark shapes continued advancing slowly, their route if continued, would take them within twenty or thirty feet of the boys position on the riverbank. Just before reaching the water's edge, the first soldier stopped and waited for his partner.

"Now," James whispered, "let's go. Hold it right there, Soldier!" He yelled thrusting the point of his bayonet at the dark shape lying on the ground now not more than ten feet away. The man did not move.

The second soldier stood up and moved swiftly to attack James from behind, aiming his Enfield musketoon rifle, with bayonet attached at James' back. Michael moved quickly to block the attack, thrusting his bayonet into the soldier's upper torso. The man merely gasped but before collapsing, fired his weapon the bullet missing his intended victim.

"What have you got, McCaffreys?" Sergeant O'Malley arrived within seconds of the shot fired by the rebel soldier.

"We have two rebels, Sergeant," James replied, "one here, he's alive and Michael got the other; but he is in a bad way."

"I think I killed him, Sergeant. I am sorry."

"Don't be sorry, soldier; just be glad you're still alive. Tie that one up James and we will take him across the river in the morning. Let's look at this fellow."

"I stuck him in the side, Sir just above his belt. He has lost a great deal of blood."

"He is still alive McCaffrey, but apparently not for long. What's your name, soldier." Sergeant O'Malley asked.

"Private Peter O'Brien."

"Oh, God, not another Irishman!" Sergeant O'Malley exclaimed. "What outfit are you with son?" The young soldier his eyes wild and flashing back and forth between O'Malley and Michael did not answer the sergeant's question.

"Am I going to die?" He asked, his voice beginning to fade.

"Yes, young man, I'm afraid you are." Sergeant O'Malley replied.

"Will you tell my parents' please?" He pleaded, then, quite suddenly quit breathing.

Since the time of the "River Incident" as the troops called it, the entire brigade was involved in a concentrated training program. They worked out on a makeshift parade ground that served the duel-purpose of rifle range and a close-order drill arena. Nearly fifty-five thousand infantry, cavalry, and artillery troops were encamped along the Northern shore of the river for as far as the eye could see. There was no doubt in anyone's mind that the Army of the Potomac was preparing for a spring offensive, but this was Saturday night and the camp was quiet. Captain Swartz's company no longer had the responsibility for supplying pickets for security of the camp, but no one in the cavalry or infantry units escaped the hazards of the patrols across the river. Their job was to seek out enemy positions and capture or destroy their probing units.

"I don't want to go out on anymore patrols or picket duty assignment, Jimmy." Michael said to James and Joseph as the three brothers got together on Christmas day. He could not forget the river incident that led to the capture of one rebel scout and the death of a young Irish boy, no older than he was. "I just want to go home and forget that this ever happened to me, but they won't let me forget it. The captain brings it up whenever he gets together with his fellow officers and he always calls me over and says, 'That's my man, gentlemen; he took care of Johnny Reb' and then he laughs."

"I took care of him alright; he was just a dumb kid at the wrong place at the wrong time and they gave me a medal for killing him. It would be funny except it's so awful." He shook his head, sadly.

"Stop it Michael," James said quietly. "Quit beating yourself up over that, if you had not killed him he would have killed me and that's what he was trying to do. That is war Michael and there is going to be a lot more killing as soon as this weather breaks; Lieutenant Kelly said the entire Army would move against Lee's people in just a few weeks. He said we should all write our folks or loved ones a letter 'cause it may be our last. The last time the Army hit Lee's people the Lieutenant said they lost over ten thousand men; he wasn't here then, but he knows all about what happened here last year."

"What's going on with you, Joseph, are you still training to be a sniper?" James asked.

"No, I'm all finished training, mainly because the ammunition is hard to come by; but I can hit a coffee cup at 800 yards, so they figure I don't need any more practice."

"Does it bother you, Joseph?" Michael asked, curious as to how his brother viewed his new duties.

"No, why should it? At a thousand yards or even five hundred, all I will see is a target and I will not be able to hear anything other than the sound of my rifle; so why should it. Although I know what you are driving at, I may feel differently before too long. We're going across the river three or four days ahead of the Army and they will drop us off at strategic locations where we are to hide out until the opportunity arises where we can put our skills to work."

"You'll find out then Joseph that you are not killing a target, it will be a man or as in my case a young boy." Michael responded with a note of sadness in his voice.

"Change the subject guys," James intervened. "Write that letter the Lieutenant was talking about. All of us owe letters to Thomas and Daniel and Uncle Paul and Auntie Ruth too and I'll tell Colleen that you guys are going to write to her sisters." He grinned. "But for heaven's sake do not mention anything about fighting; Auntie and Uncle Paul don't need to hear anymore about that."

"Who are those old men out there marching, Jimmy?" Michael asked as the two brothers walked across the parade ground toward the mess tent.

"Look at them close, Michael. Those are real soldiers. Look at their uniforms, specially their boots; they certainly don't look like ours."

"No I haven't shined mine for a week; but everything about them is neat and clean, but they are old men."

"They are retired soldiers from the American Army and some of them are from France and Germany and Poland.

There are even some Brits in that group. Lieutenant Kelly said most of them were immigrants and were so happy with this country, they volunteered to enlist, but were too old. Despite that, the Army thought their skills were too valuable to waste so they brought them in to help train guys like you and me. They really are good, Michael. They shoot better on the range than most of us. They also know a lot about tactics so the young officers are happy to talk to someone who has a wide range of experience behind them. However, because of their age they will work mainly with the ambulance crews taking care of the wounded."

"Well I hope they live through this, war is no game for the old." Michael added thoughtfully.

"It is no game for the young either, Michael; just pray that you and I live through this thing."

"Fall-in soldiers," Captain Swartz yelled, with the command relayed across the parade ground by his three platoon commanders then to the sergeants, who in turn ordered their men to fall-in and stand at attention. The command, repeated up and down the North bank of the Rapidan set in motion the movement of nearly fifty-thousand infantry troops, accompanied by cavalry, artillery units, and supply wagons on their trek south. Their first objective was to move across the river with infantry troops leading the way over the five pontoon bridges built by the engineers to accommodate the Army of the Potomac. Artillery, supply, and ambulance wagons formed into two huge columns to follow. The swift moving water slowed the crossing of the cavalry now in the process of fording the river downstream from the bridges.

Infantry troops from Company C led by Captain Brian Swartz were the first to move across two of the bridges, followed by Company B commanded by Captain Amos Butler, and they in turn by D, E, and F Companies. It was mid-morning before the entire regiment reached the far shore of the river, where they began to set-up defensive positions alone the South bank. The artillery units with their large draft horses and heavy cargo moved out next onto two of the bridges at approximately the same time. Slowed by the weight of the huge draft horses, and their ponderous caissons and fully loaded limbers, the artillerymen still made good progress crossing on these somewhat unstable pontoons. Supply and ambulance wagons formed up in columns to follow the last of the artillery units.

However, when the artillery units approached the South end of the bridges, Confederate snipers opened fire on them bringing the long convoy to a halt. Within minutes, three of the bridges became impassable. Dead or injured horses, their handlers, along with the disabled caissons effectively shut them down, cutting off infantry troops from their support units. The eerie and blood-curdling screech of the wounded or dying horses and curses or cries from injured soldiers echoed across the river.

With the closest bridges effectively blocked, Confederate troops suddenly appeared at the top of the ridge above 'C' and 'B' Company and opened fire on the Union soldiers crowded together along the South bank of the river. With the bridges blocked, the Union forces could not use them to withdraw. Nor could they retreat across the water, as the river was still too high and dangerous, and running swiftly due to the recent rains. However, neither Captain Swartz nor Captain Butler considered retreat as an option; they intended to engage the enemy wherever they found them and ordered an attack. For the moment the Rebs' appeared to be distracted by the cavalry units, now stretched out in column formation fording the river below the bridge.

Captain Swartz was the first to react, "Pickets out," he yelled. "Take positions along the top of the bank and find our enemy." Then to his lieutenants, "Conceal your troops along the river bank as best you can; have them drop their packs and fix bayonets. We will carry ammunition and canteens only. Upon my order we shall move against those on the ridge above."

"You heard the captain," Jack Kelly called out to his sergeants, adding, "Let's get it done, gentlemen."

"Jesus Christ, Jimmy!" Michael exclaimed to his older brother as the two dropped their heavy packs on the ground. "I didn't want to get that close to the Rebs again where I would have to stick anyone. The captain is going to lead us right to them; don't we get to shoot first?" He said, shaking his head, with a worried look on his face.

"Michael don't worry about it, we will get plenty of opportunity to shoot; we may never get closer to them than one or two hundred yards. They will be shoot'n at us as soon as we stick our head above the riverbank and we will shoot back. Hopefully we will hit more of them than they will of us."

"I don't know, Jimmy, they are darn good, look what they did to our people on the bridge."

"I know Michael, but I heard Lieutenant Kelly tell the sergeant that some officer is going to get his ass chewed for not sending out scouts and probing units before we began our move across the bridge."

"I heard that, too, Jimmy. Although Joseph told us last week that his team was scheduled to be deployed early; they're probably located somewhere beyond this group of Rebs."

"I would guess so, but it's terrible what this group of Rebs did to our artillery units Michael," James commented, shaking his head. "However, I don't think that they killed too many of our people, because it looks like they concentrated their fire on the horses."

"That's awful, Jimmy, killing innocent animals like that."

"I know it's a terrible thing we just witnessed, Michael, and the Rebs couldn't miss our people from up there on the ridge. However, they wanted to stop the column and they did that. A downed horse will block a bridge quicker than a dead soldier will. Whoever that Reb Commander is he knows his tactics and he might teach all of us another lesson or two about warfare before this day is over."

"Did you make sure you got your required sixty rounds, Jimmy." Michael asked as he removed his pack and checked his weapon and ammunition. "I have over two-hundred in case you need some."

"Two-hundred rounds, what the hell are you doing, Michael? You should only be carrying sixty; that's regulations."

"I know. Sergeant O'Malley chewed me out the other day for carrying so much. I told him I did not want to stick anyone again and that I would rather just shoot the Rebs, if I have too. He just laughed and said I would eventually get tired of carrying that much weight around. Well he might be right, but I don't think so."

"C Company, prepare to move out." Captain Swartz called out.

"B Company, stand ready in reserve to support C Company;" Captain Butler shouted his order. "Relay the orders gentlemen,"

"Skirmish lines out," Lieutenant Kelly ordered as his sixty-man platoon moved in unison, three men deep, covering an area nearly fifty yards wide and parallel to the river. The First, Second and Third platoons moved as one, extending the attack mode even further along the riverbank, with the line continuing as the regiment took up similar positions up and downstream from the bridge. Their plan, as explained by Captain Swartz and Butler was for Company B and C to lead the assault on the Confederate position. As the attack developed, the regiment was to envelop the Rebs by flanking their position on the ridge above.

Captain Swartz explained he and Captain Butler's plan to their lieutenants, later, Kelly made an unwise comment about it to his sergeants, a comment overheard by Captain Butler, a West Point graduate. "It looks good on paper, gentlemen, let's hope it works." When Butler made mention of this to his fellow company commander, Captain Swartz called the lieutenant aside.

"We do not need that from you Lieutenant Kelly. If you do your damn job, it will work and we shall carry the day. Therefore, if you would like to offer any suggestions on how we should command these companies either tell me directly or keep it to yourself. Is that understood, Lieutenant?" Lieutenant Kelly's only response was a muted "Yes, Sir."

"Stay close, Michael and we can do as we have always done since we were kids; as they say here in the American Army, we will protect each other's backside." James offered his tone of voice grim.

"I will, Jimmy and we better say a prayer; maybe it will help." He replied quietly.

"Company C, forward." The command came from Captain Swartz and Lieutenant Kelly, who passed it on, in turn to their sergeants.

All along the river a wave of blue clad men, armed with Springfield rifles, bayonets attached moved up the riverbank, a short climb of less than fifty feet onto a low-lying plateau of shrub brush and knotty pine and fir trees. Much to their surprise there was no enemy in sight, for once enmeshed into this clutter of brush and trees it blocked their view of the Rebs positions on the hilltop. Yet it soon became obvious, Confederate troops were now hidden in this same wasteland with sight distances often limited to a few yards in this hostile wilderness.

"Keep moving forward," Captain Swartz called out. "Keep your lines straight and make sure you keep sight of the man on your right and one on your left and move forward together."

The lieutenants and sergeants repeated the captain's orders and the company moved slowly in mass through this maze of small trees and shrubs with its limited sight distances. The company progressed less than a half mile when a volley of canon fire erupted in front of Captain Swartz and shouting rang-out from rebel positions across the entire frontline. A barrage of rifle and pistol fire quickly followed. The rebels, well concealed in the heavy undergrowth had waited for the Union forces to move forward, and then fired their weapons as they came into sight.

Captain Swartz went down almost immediately; Lieutenant Kelly responded quickly, yelling, "Fire your weapons!" For those in his platoon involved in earlier engagements with the enemy the order was altogether unnecessary. Several recent recruits however, remained standing out in the open totally surprised in this their first encounter with an armed enemy soldier. "Fire your weapons, goddamn it." He yelled again.

"Shoot, Michael." James yelled at his brother as two rebels both armed with musket and bayonet suddenly appeared from behind a nearby bush. The two moved against James, yet Michael did not fire his weapon. James shot the nearest man who toppled over just yards from his intended target. Then once again, James yelled at Michael as he tried to reload his weapon. "Shoot him, Michael, for Christ's sake. He will kill us both." Still Michael hesitated long enough that a fellow trooper had time to rush in bayoneting the confederate soldier from behind.

"What the hell is wrong with you, soldier?" The young man asked, "You want to get us all killed; you better wake up, or you won't go home when this war is over." He added, scornfully.

Yet reloading would have to wait as a score or more rebel troops emerged from the brush yelling; with bayonets fixed, they attacked Lieutenant Kelly's platoon. Moving to protect his brother, Michael got off a shot felling one soldier then with bayonet engaged three more, killing two before a rebel soldier struck him in the face with a rifle butt. He went down hard. By this time, James and others from their platoon intervened and a wild and vicious, hand-to-hand bayonet wielding melee followed. James bayoneted two more men yet while engaged with these two, a confederate officer emerged from the brush armed with pistol and sword and moved to attack him. Michael although still down on the ground and dazed from the blow to his face grabbed his rifle and fired one round at the officer. The bullet struck him mid-waist, yet he was still standing and now tried to bring his pistol in line to fire at Michael when

James bayoneted him, his blade going clean through his chest. The man went down hard. (Later, James would recall this incident as the most horrendous and personally revolting act he participated in during the war, for he needed to brace his foot against the man's chest and wrench-out the embedded bayonet. The officer was still alive at the time but died shortly after that).

With the death of the Confederate officer, the rebel soldiers pulled back, quickly retreating into the heavy undergrowth of stunted trees and bushes. The atmosphere, now laden with a near impenetrable mantle of gun smoke further restricted visibility. Even though an occasional gunshot continued to ring out in the distance, it appeared that both sides were content to retire from this violent encounter of two great armies.

Although wounded, Captain Swartz was still alive after taking a rifle ball to the side of his head. His men carried him out for transport to the field hospital yet to be setup on the near shore of the Rapidan River. C Company Lieutenants Art Ronan and Shawn Murphy died in the attack, along with four sergeants and sixty-two privates. A rebel bayonet left Lieutenant Kelly with a gaping wound in his left arm, yet the man refused to leave the battlefield and quickly took command of C Company. Forty-seven other members of the company-sustained wounds, some of these men would not survive their trip to the first aid station. B and C Companies lost more than one-third of their trooper strength.

Union commanders estimated their troops killed more than three-hundred rebel soldiers in this short encounter. They captured another hundred or more, including sixty-three wounded rebels, left behind on the battlefield. The Confederate officer, had he lived, could have claimed success in this engagement with enemy forces, for this day his smaller force decimated the ranks of three Union infantry companies. Sitting down with the surviving non-commissioned officers Lieutenant Kelly's first order of business was to post pickets far enough out in the brush to give adequate warning should the rebels mount another attack. Then it was a matter of taking care of the wounded.

The surviving troops had sufficient supplies of ammunition, water, food, and warm clothing to last them through the night or until they could withdraw from the field or be relieved. However, Lieutenant Kelly was not about to withdraw from this fight. He called out to Michael, "McCaffrey, take ten men and go back to the river bank and bring up our packs. Strip those dead cavalry and artillery men of whatever ammunition and guns you can find and be quick about it." Then calling to James, he said, "Gather up a squad and retrieve whatever ammunition you can from our dead and wounded; then distribute it to those people we have left. We don't know what Johnnie Reb may be up to, but I want our people ready for an attack."

"Jesus, Lieutenant," one of the remaining sergeants from Company B exclaimed, "they won't come after us after dark, will they?"

"What the hell do you think, Sergeant? After the losses we suffered here today, if I were the Reb Commander as soon as I could muster all my people I would come back and wipe us out; so you better get back to your company and prepare your people for another attack."

"I will do that, Lieutenant." The man responded wearily. "But I am not even sure where most of them are."

"What's your name, Sergeant?" Lieutenant Kelly asked, "And where is Captain Butler and your lieutenants?"

"I'm Sergeant Dennis O'Hare, Sir and Captain Butler is dead and our lieutenants are shot-up so badly they may not make it through the night."

"Well I suggest Sergeant O'Hare that you start the ball rolling and get your sergeants together or appoint a few temporary sergeants and start preparing to defend yourselves as soon as you can. We cannot retreat and leave our wounded unattended and even if we did; we would have no place to go. The Rebs would catch us at the river and kill us all. Therefore, I think you better get started. If you can hold our left flank we'll hold the bastards off until we get our wounded out and maybe by tomorrow Division will be in a position to relieve us." Although Jack Kelly was an experienced veteran of more than two years fighting the confederates, he was aware that the likelihood of being relieved was indeed remote.

With dusk approaching, Michael and his ten-man squad returned to the battlefield with a wagon-load of backpacks, ammunition and several canteens of water along with a score or more of Spencer rifles stripped from cavalry dead or wounded along the river bank.

"Where did you get the wagon, McCaffrey?" Lieutenant Kelly asked as the men began to distribute water and rations to company personnel.

"We borrowed it from Supply, Lieutenant." Michael responded with a grin. "Some of them made it across the bridge after it was cleared and nobody seemed to be using this one so I figured we could put it to good use."

"Good man, McCaffrey. You will make a good soldier someday. By the way which one are you?"

"I'm Michael, Sir."

"Well you're Acting Sergeant Michael McCaffrey, now. Get that gear distributed, but hang onto those Spencer rifles. Nobody here knows how to shoot them so let's not get ourselves killed by our own people." James, who was standing nearby and listening to his brother and his lieutenant's conversation responded, "I know someone in Company B, Lieutenant who could teach us real quick."

"And just who might that be, McCaffrey."

"Our brother Joseph in B Company, Sir, you taught him. With your permission, I'll go find him."

"If we survive the night, you do that at first light. It looks like our boys brought enough ammunition with those Spencer rifles so we could equip two or three squads. Those weapons will triple our firepower. That's the only way we're going to stop these rebel bastards."

"You're James, aren't you?" Lieutenant Kelly stated matter-of-factly.

"Yes Sir, I am, Lieutenant."

"Okay James, now see to it that our men are ready in case the Rebs hit us again tonight?"

"Yes, Sir. We distributed water and ammunition as you ordered and I have four men handing out the food we took from the backpacks Michael brought in. Everybody should be fed by dark; but our pickets tell us that there must be twenty or thirty wounded men beyond our lines and I need your permission to go after them."

"It's tough, isn't it, to hear men cry out for help James and not be able to go out and rescue them?"

"Yes, Sir it is, but I believe two or three of us could get out there after dark and get to them, Lieutenant." James replied, his face grim.

"You probably could, McCaffrey," Lieutenant Kelly answered, nodding his head. "We'll go after them; but remember this; you do not know whether they are our men out there crying for their mothers or Confederates. What do you think the Rebs will be doing after dark? They will want to rescue their own. The Reb Commander knows we will come for our people after dark and he will be waiting to kill you. Nevertheless, you can go McCaffrey; pick six men you know, no rifles, bayonets only. First Aid kits and water for the wounded, but canteens wrapped or inside your coats, no noise, or you will be a dead man. Good luck, McCaffrey. If you can bring any of them out, do it; but you will have to make some tough choices out there."

"How's that, Lieutenant?" James asked, not sure what this officer had in mind. "What choices are you talking about, Sir?" He asked, innocently.

"You will know that when the time comes, McCaffrey" was Lieutenant Kelly's only response.

"Jesus, Jimmy what are you going to do?" Michael asked as the two men sat propped up against one of the wheels of the supply wagon with their rubber blankets wrapped around themselves to ward off the cold night air. "The guys tell me the Lieutenant has ordered you to go out tonight to rescue our wounded. Our pickets say the Rebs are thick as flees on an old dog out there; you'll get yourself killed."

"No, Michael, he didn't order me to do it; if he wasn't the only officer left in the company he would have gone out himself, but he knew he could not do that. I volunteered to go along with six others. Someone has to at least try to bring some of those people in while they are still alive."

"But how do you know they are our people, Jimmy? Could some of them be Rebs? Michael asked, obviously worried for the safety of his brother.

"Undoubtedly, some of them will be Rebs and if we can help them we will, but our objective will be to find our own and if they can walk or crawl we'll bring 'em out."

"Oh, I don't know, Jimmy that sounds like a death trap to me. I would not want to go along with you."

"Don't worry about it, Michael, we'll be okay. By the way, congratulations, you saved the day for this company. Although, I'll bet the supply boys are not too happy with you requisitioning one of their wagons." He laughed.

"No they weren't. They hollered like hell, but we were too fast for them."

"Incidentally, join me tomorrow morning, I got the lieutenant's permission to go get Joseph and have him teach our people how to handle those new Spencer rifles you brought back."

"That's great, but do you think the company commander will let him go? I understand they lost almost a third of the company. Do we even know that Joseph is alive?"

"He's alive, Michael. I talked to a couple of people that saw him after the battle and they told me he is just fine. For some reason, command did not deploy his unit and Joseph fought with B Company; so he was out there on the river bank with the rest of us."

"That's a relief."

"The lieutenant told me to take several of those Spencer rifles and some of that food you requisitioned, Michael, and give it to Sergeant O'Hare. He said to tell him it was a gift from him and I shouldn't have any problems."

"I saw O'Hare talking to the lieutenant, what was he doing over here so far away from his own people?"

"He got lost; it's as simple as that. Yes, even sergeants get lost occasionally," James smiled. "By the way, congratulations, Sergeant," he said reaching out to shake his brother's hand. "That's fantastic; I am glad that Lieutenant Kelly selected you. You will do a great job."

"It's only an acting position until we get relieved." Michael replied quietly.

"I do not think so, Michael. The Rebs killed several of our Company sergeants and two lieutenants and five or six others were injured. I do not think any of our wounded NCOs will be back. We will need several sergeants to bring the Company up to full strength. Anyway, let's get some sleep, we move out in about three hours."

Shortly after midnight, James and his six volunteers quietly reentered the wooded area where so many of their comrades died yesterday morning. Their first sense of the tragedy that took place here just twenty-four hours earlier was the weak and muffled moans of the wounded and their cries for help or for water. Then, the all-pervasive smell of death came over them with a terrible sensation that only a seasoned veteran of the war had experienced before. To James it was almost like a blow to the stomach. However, it was not until they closely examined the terrain around them that any of them realized the enormity of the disaster that took place here. With the moon, casting its eerie light through the scrub brush they saw these low-lying shadows of the grotesque figures of hundreds of dead soldiers scattered throughout the battlefield as far as one could see.

"Oh my God!" One man blurted out.

"Knock it off," James said quietly; if you want to live through this night keep your mouth shut." There was no misunderstanding the deadly seriousness of his order. Then he whispered, "Down, there's movement ahead. Look to the left of that thicket straight in front of us. There's two Rebs carrying off one of their own."

"How can you tell it's one of theirs, Jimmy?" One of his men asked, his voice hushed.

"Don't be stupid," another responded quietly. They sure as hell won't be rescuing one of ours."

"What do you want us to do, Jimmy?" Another asked his voice muffled.

"Nothing, sit still and keep quiet and stay alert. Let's give them a chance to get back to their own lines then we'll move out."

As the six men sat huddled together, James examined the battle scene around him that stood in stark contrast to the grandeur and splendor of the night sky. He thought it ironic that the moon and the spectacular view of the Milky Way, both shining in all their splendor shed light upon one of the most gruesome scenes ever brought about by man. A question from David Young, one of his fellow soldiers, a young man from Yonkers, New York interrupted his musings. "What are you looking at Jimmy?" The soldier whispered.

"Nothing, David; I was thinking how beautiful this spot must have been before our two armies tore it to pieces yesterday. Did you notice the trees, their cannons completely stripped the bark off some and there are hardly any leaves left on any of the bushes. The Rebs' canister shot did that. It's no wonder our soldiers were ripped apart; we will be lucky if we find any of our people alive out here in this godforsaken wilderness."

"Look there is movement in that clearing just to the right of where we saw Johnnie Reb," one of the men whispered.

"Let's take a look and see who it is," James replied quietly.

"He's one of ours," one man said as the six men approached the clearing, yet what they found sickened all of them. More than two dozen bodies, some mangled, and others mutilated beyond recognition, lie entwined together in the most grotesque of positions. Most were Union soldiers, unrecognizable due to injury, bloating, or putrefaction. About a half dozen Confederate dead lay among them, recognizable only by the color of their uniform. Yet one Union soldier was still alive; he had apparently used whatever strength he still retained after the rebel attack to crawl a short distance from the heap of dead men tangled together in the clearing.

"Help me, please." He pleaded his voice a mere whisper. His rescuers quickly attended to the man's wounds; he suffered severe injuries to both legs, possibly from canister shot.

"Two of you pick him up and move him out." James ordered, quietly.

"I'll go, Jimmy." One of the soldiers offered, "But I am all turned around. I don't know the way back to our lines."

"David, go with him, please. We came in from the West and we were facing the moon, all you have to do is keep your shadow in front of you. Keep your back to the moon and you will come out of where we entered this terrible wasteland. Move quietly, but don't surprise our pickets, let them know who you are."

"Let's go guys," he said quietly, "we have a lot of area to cover and not too much time." The four of them set off again in their quest for more of their wounded comrades.

"It looks like two more of our guys over here, Jimmy," one of the soldiers whispered and moved off a short distance from the clearing. "They are ours, Jimmy and there's a Reb here with 'em." The rescue party gave each man a drink of water, then began to dress what wounds they could see in the moonlight.

"What outfit were you guys with?" The soldier asked, with one of the wounded responding, "I'm Sergeant Coleman, Company B, Sixty-Ninth Regiment and you, soldier?" The man asked.

"Keep your voice down, Sergeant, please. The Rebs are all around us."

"Yeah, I know they paid us a visit; they took my boots and left me bare foot. They took one of their own who was not too badly hurt. Private Mitchell and I pretended we were hurt more than we really are." The sergeant grimly responded, motioning toward the injured Confederate soldier and the nearby Union man. "The Reb's name is Johnson, he's dying." Yet the injured enemy soldier was alert enough to respond with a guttural laugh and comment directed at Sergeant Coleman.

"Go to hell, Sergeant, you blue belly Mick bastard."

"As you can see, gentlemen, he and I have become friends since we met here on this manure pile." The sergeant grinned. "Can you get us out of here boys and maybe take him with us? He is a pretty good guy for a Reb."

"No, we will bandage him up and leave him a bite to eat and a canteen; his people may be back when the sun comes up. I think we are fairly close to the Reb camp."

"We'll get you out of here, Sergeant. That big guy over there will pick you up and put you in a fireman's carry and you will be back with our people by sunup."

"What about Mitchell? Who is going to carry him?" Sergeant Coleman asked, now no longer smiling.

"Sorry, Sergeant, Mitchell stays here; he is dying."

"What's your name and rank, Soldier?" Sergeant Coleman demanded of James.

"I'm Private James McCaffrey, Sergeant, with the Sixty-Ninth, C Company."

"Then I am ordering you Private James McCaffrey to take Private Mitchell out of here."

"Sorry, Sergeant, you have no authority here, my job is to rescue the living. Unfortunately, dead men are of no further use to this man's army."

"He is not dead, soldier."

"No he isn't Sergeant, but he will be before morning."

"You're a cold blooded bastard, aren't you, Murphy?" Sergeant Coleman responded gruffly.

"It's Private McCaffrey, Sergeant and yes I guess I am what I am. Now let's get moving."

One of James' team picked-up Sergeant Coleman, hoisted him over his shoulder like a sack of corn, and began the slow trek back to the Union encampment, now setup above the river.

With the three men on their way back to their lines, James sent two men north, paralleling the edge of the Confederate camp, their campfires now clearly visible. "Keep the Reb camp on your right and you'll be fine." He said. "Count your steps, about two-hundred yards; we will move south and meet you back here in about an hour, okay?"

"Okay," one of the men replied quietly; "but we are awfully close to the Reb lines, Jimmy."

"I know, but just be quiet, they won't be watching for us this time of the morning. It will be daylight in a couple of hours; they should be asleep by now."

"What's your name, Soldier?" James asked as he and the last of his charges continued to look for more of their own men.

"Cameron Halleck, Jimmy. They call me Hal."

"Okay, Hal, let's see if we can find anymore of our people out here."

The two continued quietly, cautiously examining each corpse in the moonlight for any sign of life. However, it was not until Private Halleck stumbled over a Union soldier that they found anyone alive. The man, either asleep or unconscious was aroused enough to utter a harsh-sounding groan, then the word, "Water."

"He has a face wound, Jimmy," Private Halleck commented after giving the man a drink from his canteen. "But he is not bleeding now."

"Are you people, Rebs?" He asked after taking another drink from Halleck's canteen.

"No, we are from C Company; we came out here looking for you. We'll get you to hell out of here, but you have to keep quiet, the Rebs are all around us."

"I know, they came by earlier and gave me a drink of water. I cannot see but I could tell they were Rebs by the way they talked. My friend is over there somewhere," he said waving his hand in a circular motion where his two rescuers soon spotted the prone figure of another Union soldier. "He said they carried two or three of their own guys away, but my friend must be sleeping now because he hasn't said much in the last hour or two."

James walked over to the now still form and found the man dead; he apparently bled to death from his wounds.

"Can you walk soldier?" James asked the man.

"I'll walk if you show me the way," the man replied obviously pleased that someone would lead him out of this horrible place. "They took my boots, but I'll be fine."

"Let's head back, Hal. We'll meet-up with our people and get the heck out of here before these Rebs start waking up."

Returning to the clearing, they found that their comrades had rescued two more badly wounded soldiers. James was pleased with his nighttime adventure, that so far had resulted in the rescue of five Union soldiers, soldiers who might return to fight another day; yet he wanted to do more before returning to camp.

"You guys take off for our lines," he said quietly, "remember follow your shadow, and don't surprise our pickets."

"What are you going to do, Jimmy?" Private Halleck asked. "Aren't you going with us?"

"No, Hal, you, and I have more work to do before we leave. As long as we are here, I think we should scout out these Rebs and see what they are up too. Maybe Lieutenant Kelly and whatever officers are still alive would like to know what these people are doing."

"You're playing a dangerous game here, McCaffrey," one of the men stated quite matter-of-factly.

"Yeah, Jimmy, I didn't sign on for that. I don't like that idea."

"Come on, Hal all we have to do is to get a little closer to those campfires and maybe we can get a count on how many guns and people the Rebs have. All of you know that our regiment is coming after these people either today or tomorrow and it would be nice to know just what we are up against."

"Okay Jimmy, one quick look and then we get the hell out of here, but I don't like it one bit."

As the rescue team headed back to their campsite, Privates McCaffrey and Halleck quietly and with great caution moved closer to the Reb encampment. As they crawled to within one hundred yards of the nearest campfire, James whispered, "Look at these guys Hal, they're all sleeping. There is not even a picket out, anywhere. They must be confident that we won't attack today."

"Well even I am sure of that, Jimmy. We got our asses kicked yesterday. Our people are in no shape to attack anyone; but we better get the heck out of here Jimmy it's starting to get daylight."

"Wait, look down the line to your right, there must be sixty or eighty guns all set up down there to greet us. If we come back here tomorrow they'll kill us all."

"Let's go, Jimmy."

"No, wait. I have to make a sketch of this."

"You're out of your damn mind; we haven't got time for that."

"We must take the time, Hal." He responded, as he continued drawing a rough sketch of the area and the location of the encampment.

"Look over there beyond where those horses are tethered, Hal."

"Yeah, I see them, but what about it?"

"Look at the size of that bonfire compared to those farther on. What does that tell you?

"Somebody has added firewood, so they must be cold and I'm cold, Jimmy; but let's get out of here before one of those guys spots us."

Okay, Hal however with those fires burning down I think everybody is sleeping over there. Now look just to the left of the fire, there is a guard there and he appears to be asleep and look close at what he is guarding."

"Jesus, Jimmy those are our people, they're prisoners."

"You bet they are and you and I are going to go and get them."

"You're nuts, Jimmy. If we wake up that guard we're dead."

"Well, Hal we will just have to do it without waking him. That is why we have these bayonets. Let's get it done."

Private Halleck became the reluctant infiltrator in this most dangerous undertaking. After watching his partner crawl off toward the sleeping Reb guard, he muttered quietly to himself, "You're a crazy bastard, McCaffrey. You will get us both killed," then he too began to work his way through the thick tangle of brush. When they got to within a few yards of the Confederate soldier, the man suddenly slapped his bare neck as if bitten by a mosquito. He got up, stretched, examined his sleeping prisoners, and then turned around to find a Union soldier holding a bayonet to his throat.

"Keep quiet, soldier and you will live," James said quietly to the startled guard as he grabbed the man's musket; "If you move, or cry out, you're a dead man. Do you understand that, Soldier?" The man nodded his head in response to James' threat.

"Wake 'em up, Hal and move them out, quietly."

Taking the rebel soldiers' Enfield, James removed the attached bayonet, unloaded the musket, and gave the empty gun back to the Reb soldier. "Shoulder your musket, Soldier." James said quietly to the man, and then added, "You are going to take all of us for a walk right into those bushes. Just remember if you yell or make any quick moves, I will kill you with your own bayonet. Do you understand?" James asked his tone of voice deadly serious. Once again, the man nodded his head in agreement with his captor.

Upon again attaining the relative seclusion of the thick brush, the rescued soldiers turned on their guard. "Kill him," one man said.

"No." James replied forcefully. "You people keep quiet or you'll have the Rebs down on us. Use some common sense and we may get out of here alive. Two of you gag him and tie him up, and watch him closely. We will take him back with us. Now let's move out, my partner will lead the way. How many, Hal?" he asked quietly.

"Eleven, Jimmy. Two of them are in bad shape. They won't be able to make it on their own."

"We will carry them if necessary." One of the rescued soldiers responded.

It was nearly eight o'clock in the morning and the sun was already high above the eastern horizon when Privates James McCaffrey and Cameron Halleck arrived back at the Union encampment. They found Lieutenant Kelly reviewing a map of the area with Captain Brian Swartz. A huge bandage covered the side of the Captain's head and he appeared pale and gaunt. Notwithstanding that, his smile gave no hint of his discomfort from the Minie ball that struck him down just twenty-four hours earlier.

Lieutenant Kelly was the first to welcome them. "Good work, McCaffrey," he said shaking James' hand. "You too, Halleck; the boys told us what happened, it looks like you two must be the Pied Pipers of the regiment. How many people did you bring out?" He asked.

"We have eleven; Sir and one prisoner and I believe our team brought out five wounded, Sir."

"They did, McCaffrey. We sent them on to the aid station at the river; I think they will all make a full recovery, but one of the boys will probably lose his eyesight."

"Congratulations, Private McCaffrey, Private Halleck." Captain Swartz said with a smile, shaking hands with both soldiers. "However, you two need to get over to the mess tent and get a bite to eat and get some rest."

"If you don't mind, Sir," James responded politely, "I drew a sketch of the Rebs encampment and I probably should give that to our intelligence people first."

"Right you are, McCaffrey." Captain Swartz responded. "Give me your map and you two go over to the mess tent and grab a bite. I will assemble the staff in an hour for a briefing; we have several new men on board and they will want to hear from both of you."

CHAPTER 7

SECOND BATTLE

"Are all our officers assembled, Captain Swartz?" Colonel John Bream Sixty-Ninth Infantry Regiment Commander asked his newly assigned executive officer.

"Yes, Sir," Brian Swartz responded. "We have commanders from C, D, E, and F companies and two acting captains, Lieutenants Edward Jones and Glen Michelson. Jones and Michelson will command A and B Companies until Division replaces the men we lost yesterday."

When Swartz mentioned the lost men, Colonel Bream stood mute then shook his head slightly as if trying to control his emotions before inquiring further of his executive officer on the status of the regiment. Captain Swartz waited patiently for the man's response. He was aware that Captains James Anderson of A Company and B Company Commander Amos Butler were both friends of the Bream family. In 1860, John Bream and his wife attended their graduation from West Point. Then, putting the death of his two friends aside, the colonel asked, "What about platoon commanders, Captain, are we set to go there?"

"Yes, Sir. With your appointment of the six acting lieutenants from the non-commissioned ranks, we are up to full strength with our platoon commanders; but as you know, the regiment has yet to address those acting sergeant positions. However, from the five hundred replacements that came in this morning, we picked up an additional ten or fifteen experienced NCOs and a half dozen acting lieutenants. So we will be in good shape and ready to move against Johnnie Reb by the end of the week."

"Unfortunately, Captain Swartz we do not have until the end of the week. I plan to hit the Rebs tomorrow morning before daylight. Therefore, your people have about twenty hours to fill these vacant supervisory positions, assign and equip the replacement troops and let company and platoon commanders become acquainted with their people."

"With all due respect, Colonel," Captain Swartz responded, forcefully. "That is a near impossible task. The readiness state of these new troops is unknown. The time frame shall limit our unit commanders' ability to assess their capabilities and to see that they're properly supervised and equipped."

"Then I suggest, Captain that you get at it." He responded brusquely, beginning to show his impatience with this captain of infantry by slapping his boot with a riding crop. "Where are these two privates we want to talk to?" He demanded.

His cavalier response stunned Captain Swartz. Just hours ago, Confederate troops cut a swath of destruction through the Sixty-Ninth Infantry Regiment, decimating the NCO and officer corps ranks. Now Colonel Bream planned to take the surviving members into battle within a few hours along with nearly five-hundred newly arrived replacement troops.

Knowing the pompous temperament of his commanding officer, Swartz realized any further objection on his part would be futile. Colonel Bream would not tolerate a challenge or captious response from a subordinate.

"They are outside, Sir. I will have them come in."

It was midmorning when Privates James McCaffrey and Cameron Halleck entered the large mess tent escorted by their platoon commander former Lieutenant, now the new

C Company Commander Captain Jack Kelly. The enlisted mess crew had long since cleaned the facility after the early breakfast, and departed making room for nearly one hundred non-commissioned and commissioned officers brought together for a briefing by Colonel Bream. Colonel Robert Jenkins and several of his staff from the Second Regiment also attended the briefing. Colonel Bream wasted no time on introductions other than to acknowledge Colonel Jenkins then introduced Privates McCaffrey and Halleck.

"Gentlemen, Captain Kelly sent a squad out last night to reconnoiter the Rebs' position and take a Reb prisoner or two if possible. As you will see from these reports, they successfully accomplished that mission. However, they went beyond that, they entered the Rebs encampment, freed nearly one dozen of our captured soldiers, and rescued six or eight of our wounded. We can learn something from this raid; first, our enemy is vulnerable. They are pretty good soldiers and we should not forget that for a moment, but they make mistakes just like the rest of us and we will learn from their mistakes and take full advantage of those errors in judgment. Secondly, they do not have unlimited resources; they are short of food, warm clothing, including shoes and coats and have a limited supply of ammunition.

"Notwithstanding all of that, with the heavy loses of both Union and Confederate troops yesterday, they will be expecting us to take care of our wounded, regroup, and resupply our forces before we attack again. That is what they taught our military professionals at West Point; General Lee's people sat in those same classes with many of your commanders. That is why we will not pursue that course of action; we will not give them the opportunity to take care of their wounded, nor to resupply nor to regroup. We are going to hit them again tomorrow morning at daybreak." The directive, delivered by this tough talking, and apparently no nonsense regimental commander gave rise to an audible groan from the assembled group.

Completely ignoring this negative reaction of his commanders, he continued, "Yes, tomorrow at daylight we will attack and destroy or capture General Lee's Alabama Regulators. General Grant would like to offer President Lincoln this prize before the end of the week. However, the General knows this is not a game, but he also knows that if we do not defeat these boys from the South or capture them, they can still destroy the Union. He has faith in you men from this brigade, that you will not let that happen. Yet, do not think for a minute that we will be fortunate enough to catch these people unawares. They will be waiting for us, but hopefully they will not be expecting an attack this soon." Colonel Bream ended his short presentation by introducing Privates James McCaffrey and Cameron Halleck.

"Private McCaffrey," he said, "start at the beginning and tell us what you found and what transpired on your reconnaissance of the Reb camp last night. We have enlarged your sketch of the camp, here on the board. Please use that in your presentation so all of us may have a clearer understanding of both the terrain and the layout of the encampment."

At first, James was nearly tongue-tied; never before had he been required to make a critical presentation before such a large group of men. At home in Ireland, thousands of sports fans came to watch he and his fellow Galway Ravens play rugby and they could often be very intimidating, with some using the most foul language imaginable directed at he and his teammates depending upon the city where the game was played. Nor was it unusual for a disgruntled fan to hurl a rock or two out onto the playing field, luckily the perpetrator often had too much poteen in his belly, and such missals usually fell wide of their intended victim.

However, here before this large number of American military officers he immediately thought about the New York City draft riots where the mobs consisted primarily of young Irish immigrants of his age. That mob of thugs challenged lawful authorities including the Army of the United States of America. Now, several months later this newly arrived Irish transplanted immigrant was about to suggest a course of action that the American Army should pursue that may help end this terrible civil war.

When he began speaking, James quickly recognized that even though everyone in that tent outranked him and many were not of the Irish, they all wore the same uniform and were in effect, on "his" side. Besides he and Halleck successfully participated in a highly dangerous, some said foolhardy, military rescue, something that few soldiers ever experienced or lived long enough to tell about it. They entered an enemy encampment, freed several of their fellow soldiers, and returned safely to their own lines. The inner feeling of satisfaction from that experience now emboldened James's self-confidence. Any misgivings he may have had about his own inadequacies, quickly faded.

Colonel Bream's staff accurately reproduced the sketch made by James that included the number and location of enemy gun positions and pickets encountered. Captain Swartz handed James his riding crop to use as a pointer.

For the next hour, Privates James McCaffrey and Cameron Halleck were the focus of attention for the Brigade's officers and NCO staff. Several of them asked specific questions about estimates of enemy troop strength and horses, both cavalry mounts and the larger draft horse used for supply wagons or gun caissons. Halfway through his presentation an officer sitting in the front row asked, "Private McCaffrey, how many Quaker guns do you estimate the Rebs may have mounted to confuse us?"

James paused, as he did not know what the officer was talking about, and then responded, politely. "I am sorry, Sir, I do not know what a Quaker gun is."

A smattering of laughs erupted from a few in attendance until the officer who asked the question, responded bluntly. "That's alright, Son. Some of these fellows in this group have never seen them before either. Nevertheless, we all know and the Rebs know that they will lose this war because the South is incapable of meeting the needs of their men in the field. Therefore, their soldiers try to confuse us; and they do just that. They are tough and clever. They cut down trees, paint the logs black, and prop them up behind a breastwork, where they look like a real gun. This trick has worked in the past to our disadvantage. My question to you then, is how many guns that you counted were attached to a caisson or carriage?"

"All of them, Sir." James responded, quietly, surprised by what he just learned.

"Good. Thanks to you and Private Halleck, we know what the Rebs have planned for us tomorrow." Then standing, the officer turned to his fellow soldiers, his voice harsh and grave, "Don't any of you forget what this soldier said here today. Thanks to these two young men we know what the Rebs have in mind for us when we move on them."

When the two privates finished their presentation, Colonel Bream thanked them and went right into the plan he and his staff worked out for the attack that would begin that very evening with the early deployment of the sniper teams.

Privates James McCaffrey and Cameron Halleck were to play a part in that attack.

When the conference ended, Colonel Jenkins walked over to the two privates and congratulated them for, a job well done, as he put it. "You two be very careful out there tonight and tomorrow," he warned, while shaking hands with the two men. "They will be ready for you this time so don't take any unnecessary risks on your own. Just remember there will be over five-thousand other men there to support you; so rely upon your fellow soldiers. They will take care of you.

All you need to do is to lead them through the wilderness to the Reb guns." Then, before rejoining Colonel Bream and his staff, he added quietly, "Good luck to both of you."

When James left the mess tent, Michael and his brother Joseph were waiting for him.

"Jimmy," Michael yelled out, "look who found us. I went over to B Company this morning looking for him and he was here looking for us." He laughed. "Anyway we're all together now, at least for awhile."

"Hi, Jimmy," Joseph responded with a smile and huge hug. "You've been pretty busy haven't you? The whole camp is buzzing about the two soldiers that rescued some of our people, that's you Jimmy. You did that. What a way to spend a night; did you just go romping through the woods and accidentally come across our guys?" He asked with a grin. "Our company lost a lot of people, but you brought ten or fifteen back that we wrote off as either dead or lost in the woods. I tell everyone, 'that's my big brother, James.'" Joseph smiled grabbing his brother playfully around the neck.

"What's going on Jimmy?" Michael asked. "What have they got planned for us now? Do you know? Joseph said his team is heading out at dark. Do you know where we are going?"

"We're going back through the woods; the colonel plans to attack the Reb camp at daylight tomorrow."

"Geez, Jimmy," Joseph responded quietly, "I didn't know that. If that is the case, I guess I will have a ringside seat on this show; but what do you know about the attack? How many companies are going and who is going to lead the attack? Do you know that?"

"I think I know more about the attack than I should be telling you. Both of you should find that out from your platoon leaders. However, it is no secret. Private Halleck and I will take the point and guide a squad of experienced soldiers to the Confederate camp. It will be the squad's responsibility to take out any Reb pickets along the way. The General promoted Lieutenant Kelly to captain and he will lead the company. Captain Swartz will go along as an observer only; he is very weak, but insisted on taking part in this upcoming clash with the main Confederate force. Colonel Bream appointed him as the regiment's executive officer. As Halleck and I have already gone into the Reb camp we will lead Captain Kelly's men; his people plan on taking-out the Rebs' heavy guns before they can raise a defense."

"Jesus, Jimmy that's pretty risky; don't you think the Rebs will be waiting for us to come at them?" Michael commented.

"Maybe not, Michael, our cavalry units will move out just before dark. They are going to go south with the hope that the Rebs will see them leave and conclude that they are returning to Division. Eventually they will swing around to the West and attack at daylight when Captain Kelly's company moves on the Rebs' artillery positions."

"What are you up to, Michael?" James asked. "Have you been assigned yet?"

"I sure have. I am the newest sergeant in the Second Platoon of Company B. I have a squad of twenty soldiers. They all young guys from New Yorker and all of them are Americans. I think there was some resentment at first when they found out I was a foreigner, but they are all Irish and I think I can win them over. The oldest one is twenty and the youngest is only sixteen, but some of them have already seen action so I can learn a lot from them. My lieutenant is young also. He just graduated from West Point. I understand they lost so many platoon commanders in combat during the last two years that they are running them through an abbreviated course. I think he was there less than two years; he's only twenty-one."

"Well it looks like we have something to write home about." James said. "The colonel told us that we all should sit down and write a note to our families as he believes the next eight or ten days will be very tough on all of us. He said we would be very busy. He also said something else that struck me as odd. He said the Reb losses have been higher than ours have and they may not wish to stand and fight. They could still pull out, however they hold the advantage and all the high ground east of our positions here; if they do withdraw our cavalry will attack their columns and try to delay their retreat until we catch up to them."

"Lord, Jimmy, you really were in with the top brass today. They let you in on all that information and you're only a private?" Joseph commented innocently. "Our sergeant doesn't tell us much of anything other than order us to 'Clean your weapon, Private,' he says to me every time he holds an inspection. Heck, I think that's all I have done since our last encounter with the Rebs. Captain Kelly is different; he is a great firearms instructor and really a good guy."

Before nightfall, the cavalry units made an open display of preparation to depart the regimental campsite. While the cooking fires slowly ebbed, troopers packed their bedrolls, watered their mounts at the river, and saddled up. With the sun setting, a long column of nearly one thousand mounted troops moved out, and was soon lost to view as they made their way over the low-lying ridge south of the river. Union commanders hoped the Confederate spies hidden along the ridgeline east of the river saw this orderly withdrawal of Union cavalry and would report this to General Lee's people.

At the same time two squads of snipers, one from B Company and another from E Company, their long guns primed for action slipped away from the campsite and disappeared into the wilderness. Their objective was to quietly locate and kill any Reb snipers that may be ensconced on the ridges above the river then provide fire support in the morning when Union troops moved on the Confederate campsite. If everything went according to plan, Joseph McCaffrey would spend his eighteenth birthday shivering in the cold night air awaiting the attack. He was sure of only one thing; tomorrow, irrespective of what may happen to him, the American war guaranteed he would experience the most fascinating birthday of his lifetime. He prayed that at the end of the day he would still be alive.

"Are you ready, Private McCaffrey?" Captain Jack Kelly asked as C Company personnel formed up into two columns, in preparation for their return trek into the heavy brush.

"Yes, Sir, Captain," James, replied.

"Then let's move out," he responded. "It's time, gentlemen, keep it quiet," he said to a lieutenant and two Sergeants standing nearby, "pass it on." With those words, James and a squad of ten men, all of whom had participated in earlier engagements with the rebels quietly moved into the brush, bayonets at the ready. Captain Kelly followed accompanied by two platoon commanders and one-hundred and forty infantry troops. In the background, Colonels Bream and Jenkins' men stood fast. They would await a signal from Captain Kelly that the expected enemy pickets had been disposed of and then move into a position to attack the rebel campsite at daylight. When that signal came, Colonel Bream, accompanied by Colonel Jenkins would lead nearly ten-thousand troops into the fray.

As James and his squad moved into the wilderness, they once again experienced that terrible nauseating stench from the dead; it filled the night air with its sickening odor. Although all members of his squad experienced this loathsome, stomach-churning smell before, one man delayed their forward movement by his involuntary retching and vomiting. The noise he made was loud enough to warn an alert enemy picket should one be nearby. James held up his hand stopping the squad's advance; he waited until the soldier pulled himself together then quietly moved on. After traveling more than halfway through the heavy brush toward the Confederate campsite he was about to send a runner out to advise Captain Kelly of their progress when he detected something different from that ever-pervading smell of death. He signaled for everyone to stop and get down.

"What is it, Jimmy?" one of his men whispered. "I don't see anything, do you?"

"No," James answered quietly, "but what do you smell?"

"Just death, Jimmy; we are in the middle of a cemetery. What did you expect?"

"No, I smell horses and tobacco smoke. There has to be a Reb patrol or picket nearby."

"Jesus, Jimmy, are you sure? I don't smell a damn thing other than dead bodies."

"Be quiet and bring our people in, pass the word." Within moments, all ten men gathered around James, curious as to what was holding them up.

"What have you got, McCaffrey?" One of the older men asked. "Did you see something?"

"No, but I smell it. What do you smell?" He asked.

"I smell tobacco smoke; you're right, we got a Reb close by," he whispered.

"More than one I think," James responded, quietly. "We have horses too. It could be a patrol or possibly a Reb sentry; they may be changing watches, or possibly someone brought food out to a picket. I'll take three men, you two," he said to two young men squatting nearby and, "you," placing his hand on the shoulder of an older soldier. "We will work in pairs. Take them with your bayonets; if there are horses, we must get them. If they get back to the Reb lines without their riders, it will alert the camp." Then turning to the remaining members of his squad, he whispered, "If we do not come back in half an hour, send a runner to advise Captain Kelly what happened here. What's your name, Soldier?" he said to the older soldier.

"I'm Edmund O'Toole," the man replied softly.

"And you?" he asked of another.

"I am Peter Means," the private responded quietly.

"Peter, you come with me. Edmund take this man," he said placing his hand on the shoulder of the soldier standing next to him, adding, "Peter and I will move in from the right, you come at them from the left. You will have to kill them without firing your weapon. If you fire your weapon, we may be dead men before this night is over."

The three men all nodded their heads; they were experienced soldiers and knew what James said was probably true. They would not survive this night if their attack alerted the Reb campsite, which was now less than five or six-hundred yards distance at most.

Working their way forward on their bellies, the four soldiers got close enough to make out two Confederate soldiers in the moonlight sitting on the ground smoking, and talking. Tethered nearby was a grey and black cavalry mount. James signaled to Private Means to get the horse and he and the other two men would take the two Rebs. It was over in seconds, both rebel soldiers died quickly from the trio's deadly bayonets. Private Means seized hold of the startled mount.

"Bring the rest of the squad in," James said to the men. When they gathered, he whispered to O'Toole, "take two men, and move north two or three-hundred yards and search for another picket." Then turning to Private Halleck, he said, "Cameron take two men with you and search south; go out about the same distance and be on the lookout for another picket or patrol. There are probably a few more here on the west side of their camp. Find 'em and kill 'em, and do it quietly. The rest of us will move in where we can get a good look at the Rebs. We will meet back here in a half hour. You need to move quickly, it will be daylight within an hour or so."

As Privates O'Toole, and Halleck and their men disappeared into the brush, James and the remaining members of his squad moved quietly toward the Confederate campsite. They crawled the last several yards until they were in a position to observe much of the rebel base. What they saw startled James.

"Look to the south and tell me how many guns you see," he whispered.

"I see twenty-five, or possible twenty-eight," Private Means replied.

"That's what I count," another man replied quietly. "How many were there last night, Jimmy when you and Halleck came through?"

"There were twelve to fourteen batteries, probably about eighty to one-hundred guns, all pointing west and ammunition limbers lined up behind them as if they were expecting our assault to come from the west. However, most of the ammunition wagons are gone, and I do not see any sign of the cavalry and no horses at all. The Rebs must figure we will be coming from another direction. They may not have fallen for the colonel's ruse with our cavalry. We have to get a message to Captain Kelly and the Colonel right away. Let's move out of here, find cover, and wait for our troops. When they get here, we will have accomplished our immediate task."

Returning to the rendezvous, they found Halleck and O'Toole's men waiting for them; however, it quickly became obvious something was wrong, one man was missing, and O'Toole and another soldier were attending to a man propped up against a small tree.

"What happened, Edmund?" James asked, with O'Toole responding, "There were two Rebs, they heard us and actually came after us. They are dead, but they killed Private McKinsey, and Clark here took a bayonet to his leg. We got the bleeding stopped; he will be okay. They were good Jimmy and strong as hell," he said quietly, shaking his head, saddened by this loss of a "good man" as he called his fellow soldier.

"I know, Edmund, it's sad, but right now we have to move quickly. Get Clark on that horse with another man; we have to get word to Captain Kelly right away. We have to notify him that the Rebs have repositioned some of their guns; although it looks like they have moved some larger guns into position here that were not here yesterday."

"Could those be the Quaker guns they were talking about at our briefing, are they that large, Jimmy."

"They are, but at this distance they certainly look real; we will have to assume that they are real."

Turning to the two on the rebels' horse, he warned them, "don't you guys go busting in on the company, or you're apt to get yourselves killed." Then to Private Means he said, "Go on foot, Peter, just in case our horseman here runs into trouble; you are our ace-in-hole. Tell the captain what we found; but be quick about it. It will be daylight before long."

When the two messengers and the wounded man disappeared into the thick brush, James sat down next to Private O'Toole to rest. Until that moment, he had not realized he was so completely exhausted. When he lay back on the ground and looked at the clear night sky, it reminded him of his home in Ireland. On clear summer evenings he and Colleen Haggerty, and their friends, much to the chagrin of their parents, often slipped out of their homes at night to enjoy each other's company.

One warm summer night, after he got out of Kilmainham prison, he and Colleen slipped away from the group to a haystack on Haggerty's home place. They lay entwined together for hours watching the Milky Way, playfully counting shooting stars and completely oblivious to the rest of the world.

"Where does it end, Jimmy?" Colleen asked with a note of sadness in her voice.

"Where does what end, the Milky Way? On the other side of the earth I suppose." He laughed. "I don't know."

"No, silly boy, where does it end for you and me; both of your parents are dying and that's sad, but how will it end for you and me?" She asked.

He remembered that he had no answer for her at that time. As consumed as he was in planning his escape to another continent, the imminent death of his mother only entered into his consciousness when he thought it might not interfere with his planned journey. Now however, in this moonlight setting with all of its beauty arrayed above it seemed that he was still involved in his journey, a journey that had turned into a nightmare in this wilderness. He could not believe the number of dead and the extent of the destruction and devastation brought about by this war. The scope of it was beyond his ability to comprehend. Never before had he seen such terrible decimation visited upon human beings, and now his journey from a small farm in Ireland ended in the middle of all this chaos and mayhem.

"Jesus, Edmund," he said, "I'm tired. I am shaking like a leaf and sweating like crazy; yet chilled to the bone. What the hell is wrong with me?" He asked the older man, "I don't understand it. I have never felt this way before."

"What you are experiencing, Jimmy is quite normal. You should be tired, nervous, and upset. Any normal human being would feel the same after what you have gone through. You didn't get any sleep yesterday and none today; you have tangled with the Rebs and killed a human being yesterday and another one tonight. Besides that, the Army has placed you in an untenable command position. You have no rank, yet you are making decisions that would be a challenge to even one of our officers. If the colonel's plan works out, it will be because of the advice you gave to him. If his plan fails, the Army may hold you responsible.

"If we win, you might be a hero, but if we lose, you may find yourself in a most undesirable position; so pray that it works out, Jimmy. If it does, then as Colonel Bream has suggested we will eliminate these Regulars from any further threat to the Union. Maybe then, we can all go home. I have a wife and two small children that I have not seen for nearly three years and as far as I am concerned, I am finished with this damn war. I pray to God that that poor fellow over there," he said quietly, nodding his head toward one of the two dead Confederate soldiers, "is the last man we will ever kill. So soldier boy, if I were you I would try to relax and get some sleep. You have done all you can tonight for our cause; let Captain Kelly and Colonel Bream do the worrying from now on."

Before Edmund O'Toole finished talking Private James McCaffrey was curled-up on the ground, sound asleep. Taking a Reb blanket from near the two dead confederate soldiers, O'Toole threw it over his sleeping colleague.

"Wake up, McCaffrey," the quiet yet unmistakable voice of Captain Jack Kelly came with a not so gentle kick to the rear of Private McCaffrey jolting him out of a near dead sleep. When James looked up at the man who kicked him his first thoughts were that his assailant was a Confederate soldier and he grabbed his bayonet and bolted upright his bayonet at the ready.

"Easy, James," Jack Kelly responded, his voice quiet and pleasant. "It's time to go back to work. Private O'Toole filled us in on your mission. You fellows did a fine job, but we have to move now. My men are ready to go after those guns and I want you to join us. I have looked at the area and if we strike fast and hard we should be able to take most of them out before the Rebs can muster a strong defense. If they force us to retire before the regiment arrives, we will use grenades to destroy the guns. However, we shall do whatever we can to hold onto them. Is that clear?" He said. "We may need them before this day is over."

"Yes, Sir, Captain," James, responded. "Sorry about the bayonet, Sir, but we were all a little bit spooked after the Rebs took two of our people out last night."

"That's understandable, but don't worry about it, James. I want you and O'Toole to stay with me. The rest of your people can rejoin their regular units, as the regiment is close on our heels. We will attack all along the western perimeter of the Reb campsite and our cavalry will move in from the south. So let's move out."

Captain Kelly's company had already deployed along the western perimeter of the Confederate campsite with the assault teams from the First Platoon awaiting a signal from their captain to attack. Behind them two squads from the Second Platoon were to follow on their heels, each man armed with four Ketchum grenades, more than enough to spike the Rebs' guns if it became necessary. After crawling to the edge of the Confederate campsite, Kelly suddenly bolted upright and with a loud voice bellowed, "C Company attack!" Moving quickly, he covered the short distance to the Reb campsite in less than a minute, closely followed by McCaffrey and O'Toole. When James looked back, he was thrilled to find a wave of blue-clad men following closely on their heels. Loud shrieking yells erupted from several veteran troops, who gave vent to their emotions by mimicking their rebel adversaries. Confederate soldiers routinely hollered and screeched quite profanely whenever attacking a Union stronghold; yet such displays of bravado were not common within the ranks of Union forces.

However, James had little time for contemplation of such an ostentatious display of emotion, for Union soldiers suddenly found themselves face to face with a score of Confederate infantry. The first volley of enemy musketry took down a dozen men from the First Platoon, but before the Confederate soldiers could reload C Company troops unloaded a withering barrage of fire wounding or killing every Confederate soldier in sight. Those that lived through this onslaught of Union firepower tried in vain to reload their Enfield muskets, before falling prey to a bayonet. These Union soldiers, mostly veterans of earlier encounters with the Reb forces were experts at dispatching an enemy with the skilled use of a bayonet.

Soldiers from the Second Platoon quickly passed through this thin defensive line of Confederate soldiers and attacked a large group of artillery battery soldiers, killing many and forcing the others to retreat from their weapons.

The attack thus far went as planned and better than Captain Kelly expected; more than one-hundred Confederate corpses littered the battlefield. The attack signaled Colonel John Bream to move against the Alabama Regulars with C Company personnel cheering when nearly five-thousand Union troops emerged from the wilderness. Bream, riding a black mount led the way accompanied by Captain Swartz and four other officers of his immediate staff. His first words to Captain Kelly, were, "Where are our cavalry units, Captain? Any sign of Colonel Evans and his troops?" He asked, obviously concerned, for Colonel Lawrence Evans was to have moved in on the Confederates from the south with the first indication that the attack had gotten underway.

"No, Sir, nothing at all. During a lull in our situation here, my people tell me they heard gunfire that they thought came from some distance to the south of us; so it is possible that they ran into some trouble from the rebs."

"Well, we cannot wait for them Captain; by the looks of this camp the Rebs pulled out pretty quick; so we've got them on the run. We shall continue to attack until they are no longer a threat. Pass the word we move out in thirty minutes."

Colonel Bream was prepared to lead the remainder of the regiment on a final assault upon the retreating Confederate force without waiting for Colonel Evans' cavalry units or supporting artillery. It would take at least another twenty-four hours to finish cutting a road through the wilderness large enough to accommodate the artillery and supply wagons. "We dare not wait." Colonel Bream said. We cannot afford to lose the spirit, and dash and outright imaginativeness shown by our infantrymen today. So let us proceed to destroy these people."

Captain Kelly could not quite believe what he was hearing. The location of more than half of the Confederate artillery was yet to be determined, yet Colonel Bream planned on a full-scale frontal assault upon the Reb line. Kelly glanced at Captain Brian Swartz, still sitting astride his mount; he also appeared surprised by the regimental commander's order. Swartz however, made no comment; nor did any of the dozen or more other officers present.

Nevertheless, Captain Kelly believed that he had already seen too much death and destruction of his fellow soldiers and could not remain silent.

"Colonel Bream, with due respect, Sir, without our cavalry we may never corner the Rebs. I suggest that we wait for the artillery to make their way here and that we send out scouts.

We need to find out what the Rebs are up to, and learn what happened to our cavalry units."

"I appreciate your concern for our troops and our situation, Captain," Colonel Bream responded unwavering in his decision that this was his day "to finish off these secessionist traitors" as he called them. Notwithstanding that, the fact that this newly appointed infantry captain would question his decision to go ahead with the attack clearly annoyed him.

"You did an excellent job today, Captain Kelly," he snapped, "but I do not think you appreciate what is at stake here. If we do not finish this business today with this Alabama group, we shall have to fight them another day. I do not wish to do that, Sir; but I do appreciate your suggestions. Now if no one else wishes to discuss my decision I suggest we go about destroying these Confederate traitors and be done with it. We shall use their guns against them. Your people did such a superb job here, Kelly, that I want you to take the point on this attack. Your attack was a near perfect textbook example for these younger officers to emulate. They can learn from your noble and prodigious experience. Please move your people out."

"Yes, Sir," was Captain Kelly's only reply, clearly aware that the colonel was not about to follow his advice. Yet, he was sure that the recent West Point graduates had learned another, and longer lasting lesson today; that was you question your commanding officers' orders at your own peril.

Within the hour, company commanders lined-up their units in parallel lines in a double assault formation stretching north and south through the abandoned rebel camp for nearly a mile. Captain Kelly and C Company taking the lead quickly disappeared into the heavy growth of brush on the eastern side of the camp and were lost to view by those who were to follow.

Privates McCaffrey and O'Toole, following both Captain Kelly and two company sergeants at a discrete distance, quietly discussed what they overheard at the officer's meeting with Colonel Bream.

"From what you heard there this morning, Jimmy, what did you learn?"

"That's an easy question to answer, Edmund. We are lucky to be with Jack Kelly's company. Did you notice that no one else challenged the colonel's orders? I have known him only a short time, but he always looks out after his men. Even in training earlier this year, he tried to do the right thing. I believe he was responsible for improving our food; he took the mess galley sergeants to task over the poor quality of food served and that improved markedly. He also got us ammunition for practice on the range. My brother Joseph was training to be a sniper and the Quartermaster limited the men to twenty rounds per day. That's no way to train a soldier; I just respect him one heck of a lot."

"Well that's good to hear, but he hasn't done us any favor here in the field. He stepped on the colonel's ego, in front of his fellow officers. From my experience, West Point graduates do not like that. For his reward, he shall lead C Company in every crappy detail that no one else wishes to take on. That is you and I, Jimmy boy. If we live through this next encounter with Johnny Reb we will be awarded the grand prize; we shall be given the honor of leading the next attack and the one after that."

It came without warning, a grinding, screaming roar, like a million hornets, followed by an explosion in the trees overhead that took off the top of a scrub oak nearby along with nearly all its leaves. Men all around the explosion screamed and fell to the ground. Jimmy's only hint at what actually was taking place came from a warning shouted by Captain Kelly. "Reb artillery, down, get down," he yelled. Privates O'Toole and McCaffrey and a hundred others nearby hugged the earth as the ear splitting buzzing began anew, followed by one explosion after another. The entire company of men stopped in their tracks, frozen in place, completely terrorized by the screeching, buzz saw like explosions that took nearly all the leaves off the small trees and uprooted or tore apart the stoutest of oak. In the process men died, torn apart by the cruelest of all weapons in the field, shrapnel from explosives and canister shot, projectiles with hundreds of small pieces of steel that cut down everything and everyone in their path. It stripped the bark from the trees and tore away the thick cover of leaves from bushes. Colonel Bream had found the Rebs' missing artillery.

The shelling continued for nearly twenty minutes, when it stopped the screams and moans of the wounded and dying extended throughout the entire battlefield. Smoke lay across the brush filled gullies and the small rises in the terrain with those lucky enough to have been in one of the many low lying areas on the battlefield largely unscathed. However, soldiers caught out on the higher ground had no way to escape these deadly missals.

Captain Kelly, along with one of his lieutenants crawled back to a group of soldiers, including Privates McCaffrey and Edmund O'Toole who lay huddled together in a sheltered hollow.

"McCaffrey, O'Toole," Kelly called out, "I want you two to contact Captain Ed Jones in A Company and find Captains Michelson in B Company and O'Leary in D, and tell them we are in trouble here. We cannot do it alone. Tell those gentlemen we are completely exposed and the Rebs will eventually kill us all unless we take those guns out."

Before he could finish issuing his orders to the two soldiers, the shelling began again and no one dared to move. All of them lay crunched together in the same hallowed out space in the terrain while a terrible withering barrage of rebel artillery fire tore away both trees and bushes, and turned ground cover into shreds where men died. As with the first barrage, the firing lasted for approximately twenty-minutes. When it stopped and the smoke and flames from a hundred small fires started by the exploding shells, ebbed, the cries of the wounded and dying rose to a near crescendo. At this moment, no one could do anything to relieve the suffering.

"Go now, quickly," Captain Kelly, said to the two soldiers. "Tell them that based on what the Rebs are doing we may have at most, one-half hour before the next barrage. We will attack with every able-bodied man we can raise. We must destroy their infantry and get to those guns or we are all dead men. Tell them to be ready to move on my signal. Move quickly," he added, his voice harsh and grim.

A, B and D Company Commanders, Captains Edward Jones, Glen Michelson and Andrew O'Leary, as planned, held their men in reserve in the event C Company ran into trouble. When Privates McCaffrey and Edmund O'Toole contacted them, they were ready and more than willing, even anxious on such short notice, to join in the attack. Within minutes the three companies of nearly five-hundred and fifty men, dropped their backpacks and quickly moved forward joining ranks with Captain Jack Kelly's scarred and battered force.

Upon arrival the three company commanders, along with their platoon lieutenants conferred with Captain Kelly for but a moment, promptly recognizing the gravity of the rebel threat they agreed to Kelly's plan of attack. It called for an immediate, classical infantry/bayonet assault upon the rebels, with the view of destroying the Confederate infantry and capturing or destroying their artillery. Unfortunately, within minutes of the commanders returning to their units, the rebel barrage began again. This time however, B Company took the brunt of the artillery barrage; resulting in the loss of more than thirty men.

When it ended, not waiting for another barrage, Captain Kelly yelled to those within earshot, "We attack now," and signaled his intent to company commanders. Within minutes, nearly a thousand Union troops, members of A, B, C and D Companies, formed-up into three huge skirmish lines nearly a quarter mile across. They began moving forward through the heavy brush where they ran into a withering barrage of rebel musketry. Notwithstanding that, members of Kelly's force were determined to push on and quickly overran the rebel infantry positions.

Yet, almost immediately, Captain Kelly sensed that something was amiss. Several Reb enemy infantrymen gave up secure positions without firing a shot; their sudden retreat gave all the appearances of a near rout.

"Hold your positions, take cover, pass the word," he yelled, having to repeat his command a second time before he was able to halt the attack. "Pickets out--one hundred yards," he yelled, whereupon platoon commanders halted their men, sending one or two soldiers from each platoon forward as ordered.

Captains Jones, Michelson, and O'Leary came in to confer with Captain Kelly and shortly afterwards Colonel Bream and his immediate staff arrived.

"Why did you call off the attack, Captain?" Colonel Bream angrily demanded from astride his horse; his tone of voice clearly indicating he disagreed with his company commander's decision. To those standing nearby, the man's tone of voice and truculent behavior unmistakably signaled his annoyance with Kelly's failure to pursue the Confederate troops.

"You had these people on the run. I expected you would put a finish to this business of Confederate forces escaping once again, only to fight another day at a place of their choosing." Without giving his captain a chance to explain his action, he relieved Kelly of his command. "I want you to report straight away to Captain Swartz for reassignment. I shall take charge, and gentlemen," he said turning his back on Kelly to face his personal staff, "We shall continue the attack at once. Captain Jones, bring up the rest of the regiment and follow on. I want to finish off these Rebs." Turning to the company commanders, he virtually shouted; "Return to your commands and form up behind me. We will put a finish to this business today; we shall attack immediately."

Bream's tempestuous demeanor and his decision to lead an entire regiment in a frontal assault upon Confederate forces, when no one was sure of the enemies' strength nor the number or exact location of their field guns, was too much even for Captain Swartz who was nearby. Moving his mount in close to the regimental commander, he warned the man. "Colonel, Bream," he began quietly, "two days ago, Private McCaffrey's squad counted over seventy-five heavy weapons in the rebel inventory; yet today in our initial assault upon the Confederate campsite Captain Kelly's troops came across only about a third of those guns. We do not know the exact location of those other guns. Nor, Sir, do we have an accurate picture of their strength. The quantities of artillery support equipment we captured would indicate we are up against a Confederate force of seven to ten-thousand men. It could even be more than that as the Reb travels with much less equipment than we do. Therefore, I respectfully recommend, Sir that we hold up our attack. If we send out our scouts now they could be back before nightfall; by that time we should know what the Reb is up to."

This was too much for the colonel. First, one of his company commanders, refused to pursue an enemy force that Bream believed was retreating in complete disarray, now his executive officer appeared to have lost his appetite to do battle with this fleeing adversary. Colonel Bream knew such opportunities to trounce an enemy seldom occurred in battle; yet when they did, he was convinced the aggressor needed to take full advantage of that situation.

"Captain Swartz," he responded angrily, startling those around him. "What is wrong with you people? Your enemy has once again presented you with the opportunity of a lifetime and you have failed to take advantage of his mistakes. These circumstances always work to the advantage of the aggressor, but only if the attacking force is willing to immediately pursue the retreating force until the enemy surrenders or is annihilated. We attack now," he said, repeating his order once again to the three company commanders.

"Jesus, Brian," Jack Kelly said, grabbing onto the bridle of Captain Swartz's mount. "He's going to get a bunch of our people killed; we cannot just sit here and watch."

Stepping down off his mount, Brian Swartz and two or three other members of Colonel Bream's personal staff gathered around Jack Kelly.

"I know, Jack. He is playing a dangerous game here. If what he plans on doing, works out okay, the War Department will love it, but if it goes awry, a lot of good men will not go home to their families when this battle is over."

"What do you suggest, Brian?" Jack Kelly asked his concern for his men evident in his voice. "We've got to do something."

Swartz, the most experienced and senior officer in the group, moved quickly. "Stay with your company, Jack. Even if he sees you the colonel will be too busy now to do anything about it; if he says anything, tell him I ordered you to give him whatever support the colonel needed." Then turning to the remaining staff officers he rapidly issued a series of orders, "Quickly, bring in all of our people, hold two companies in reserve and send one infantry company in close-order support to Colonel Bream's attacking force. In addition, send out a scouting party to find out what happened to our cavalry; if anyone is alive in that outfit, we need them here now. Also, send a runner to our artillery command; tell them we have fifteen or twenty Reb guns with a limited amount of ammunition and we need men who can fire them. The cannon are 12-pounder Napoleon field guns. Let's get it done, gentlemen, before this damn think blows-up in our face and gets us all killed."

Captain Kelly first heard and then saw what he feared may happen, a trap. The Confederate commander's ruse worked; his forces appeared to have fled the field of battle only to move into preplanned defensive positions. The Reb troops dropped over the bank of a small dry creek bed that provided near perfect cover for their infantry where they had previously constructed a long series of protective breastworks to protect their troops. Beyond the creek, the missing artillery pieces Captains Swartz and Kelly worried about began firing again in mass over the heads of their own soldiers taking out a wide swath of Union troops. Among the first to die was Colonel

John Bream; a canister round killed him and his mount while he was still astride the animal. A score or more men to the left and right of the colonel died with him in the barrage.

"Oh, God Almighty!" Jack Kelly exclaimed loudly as he raced to reach this nearly decimated group of Union soldiers. "Stay down all of you," he screamed. However, as he made his way through the carnage created by the bombardment, toward the front of the column, he quickly became the Rebs' immediate target. When he came within range of those concealed behind the breastworks, several riflemen climbing to the top of the protective barricade opened fire on him. He immediately slipped into a small crater, where aided by thick gun smoke that permeated the battlefield was lost to view by his would-be assailants. Calling out to a couple of sergeants he found crouched behind a small tree, he asked, "How many men do you have that are uninjured?" He asked.

"About a dozen, Captain. Maybe thirty or more wounded and over one-hundred dead." The man responded grimly. "They did a good job on us, the bastards."

"Bring two of your best men forward and put them in a position to cover our withdrawal. Tell them if they cannot find a target, to shoot low into the smoke from the Rebs' weapons. We need to pull back at least five-hundred yards, if we get that far away, the Rebs' infantry will have to show themselves to fire on us. Tell your people to keep down; when the smoke clears, put snipers to work on anyone that tries to come over the barricade. Pass the word, quickly," he yelled over the hail of Confederate musketry tearing through the thick scrub pine and brush foliage.

A half dozen soldiers, ignoring the shouted orders from the two sergeants, dropped their weapons and fled the battlefield, only to run into members of the Second Regiment heading into the fray. Taken in tow by both officers and NCOs and brought before Captain Swartz, he questioned two or three of them briefly. "What happened?" he asked without a trace of enmity or acrimony in his voice toward the would-be deserters. "Tell me what happened out there, quickly."

Satisfied with what he learned, he said to his company and platoon commanders, "Strip the dead of their weapons and give them to these men; we will need every weapon we can get our hands on to extricate our people from the trap our southern boys have set for us."

CHAPTER 8

THE AFTERMATH

"Are you all right, Private McCaffrey?" Captain Kelly asked, as he came across James and a small group of C Company soldiers trying to administer aid to two wounded men.

"Yes, Sir, Captain, I am fine."

"Well, James you do not look fine; you have blood all over you. Where did you get hit?"

"It is just a scratch, Captain. Most of this blood came from this fellow here. He's a bleeder; we had a tough time stopping the blood flow, but I think he will make it okay."

"Good. Did you get a good look at the number and location of the Rebs' gun?"

"Yes, Sir, I did," James replied. "They are laid out in a line about four hundred yards beyond and parallel with the creek bed. There are at least eight and possibly ten batteries of six cannon each and it looks like the guns are the same caliber as the ones we seized in their camp, both 12- and 20-pounders."

"Did you see where their mortars are set up?"

"No, sir, but my guess is they are probably in the creek bed."

"That's the way I read it McCaffrey. With the mortars and that many guns, they can blow us right off the damn planet. I want you to report all of this to Captain Swartz and identify the coordinates. If he can get those Reb guns working that we captured this morning tell him we need concentrated fire on their gun positions first, then on the troops hold-up in that creek bed. Tell him we cannot go forward and I will not pull out of here until we can evacuate our wounded. Do you understand all of that?"

"Yes, Sir, Captain." James replied.

"Move out then, Private; let's get it done."

Within one hour of Private James McCaffrey's arrival at Captain Swartz's location, the regiment had two rebel guns firing a limited supply of shells into the Confederate positions on the eastside of the creek bed. While this continued throughout the rest of the day Union soldiers scrounged the former Confederate campsite for ammunition and made ready ten additional rebel guns, bringing them to bear on the Confederate forces. Captain Jack Kelly's men continued to attend to the injuries and evacuation of nearly three-hundred of their fellow soldiers. Their toughest challenge was leaving behind the dead and their soon-to-die comrades.

The arrival of Union supply and artillery units before dark, at the former Confederate campsite could not have come at a more opportune time. Second Regiment rescue teams evacuated nearly all the injured soldiers from front line positions and loaded-out nearly every wagon with the wounded. With the sun setting in the west, a line of thirty-five or more wagons began the long trek back to the Regimental Aid Station on the river. The horse-drawn column of wagons stretched out for nearly a mile along the newly created roadway cut through the thick underbrush.

"Move your people out tonight; the Reb artillery will no doubt have zeroed in on this location by morning." James recognized the voice, although the man stood facing the small campfire with his back to the young soldier. It was Brigadier General Owen McMahan issuing orders to Captains Brian Swartz, Jack Kelly, Edward Jones, Glen Michelson, and Andrew O'Leary.

"We will setup camp in the Rebs' former campsite. There is water there and we can use it as a staging area. I have ordered Colonel Jenkins to move his entire regiment here. Colonel Will Terry and the Thirty-Second Regiment are also en route. If we have as many Confederate soldiers here as is indicated, we shall need them. They should start arriving here within forty-eight hours. Right now, we need to integrate replacements into our ranks. Captain Swartz, your report indicates the Sixty-Ninth lost more than thirty non-commissioned staff, four lieutenants, and two captains and if I read this correctly, we experienced about three hundred casualties. Is that right?" He asked, quietly.

"No, Sir, as a result of the Rebs' ambush here today, Sir," Captain Swartz replied, his voice muted and nearly inaudible, "over five-hundred men have been killed. We also have another two-hundred, or more wounded and several of these men will undoubtedly die before they reach the Aid Station. Approximately two-hundred others are missing. The best our people can come up with right now is a total casualty count of approximately nine-hundred, Sir."

"Jesus Christ!" General McMahan exclaimed, "That son of a bitch has a lot to answer for. He was a goddamned political appointee of the governor and nobody in the War Department objected. The Department assumed the publicity of his return to the Army would encourage others to sign on for this war. He served in the cavalry for two or three years after graduating from West Point, then resigned his commission to enter the political circus. Well it is over. However, when the press catches up to us, I want all of you to be kind and put in a good word for him. It will not do his family any good by telling the press he was an incompetent ass whose reckless leadership led to the slaughter of five-hundred young Americans boys in a battle that we will have to fight again tomorrow. God help us all," he added, solemnly.

"What about Colonel Evan's lads, how many cavalry troops did we lose? Are they included in this body count?"

"Yes, Sir, as you know, Colonel Bream sent them out early to fake a withdrawal and to circle south where they planned to hit the Rebs' left flank. Unfortunately, the Confederates did not fall for this and bushwhacked Colonel Evan's men. Their casualties are included in our total count. Seventy-two horse soldiers died and another seventy-five or eighty suffered wounds serious enough to require medical aid."

General McMahan made no further inquiries; he just shook his head slowly from side to side. "Five-hundred young boys!" he repeated the number quietly as if he was having a difficult time comprehending the enormity of this debacle. "We can lie to the press gentlemen, but this was a disaster that need not have happened. This war will be over soon and most of us will go home physically unscathed, yet the truth of this catastrophe will come out; and that is what it is, a dreadful catastrophe. Moreover, how do we explain to the mothers and fathers of these young boys that they need not have died, except for the incompetence of their leader?" He shook his head again and quietly walked away from the assembled group of officers.

General McMahan wasted little time in attending to the needs of the Second and Sixty-Ninth Regiments. Captain Brian Swartz, after conferring earlier with the other officers present, submitted a list of enlisted men and officers that the commanders wished to have promoted through the Army's field commissioning process. There was an urgent need to replace the dead, missing, or wounded officers and NCO staff. Swartz presented the names of Lieutenants Dan Hanrahan, and Robert McAfee for promotion to the rank of captain. Also on the list to be elevated to a higher rank, were eight sergeants and forty-five enlisted personnel, to fill existing vacancies, all casualties of the botched Sixty-Ninth Regiment's assault upon the entrenched rebel force. This would bring the regiments supervisory and officer corps up to near full strength. He handed the list to McMahan.

General McMahan studied the list of names and proposed promotional rank of each, quickly noting the recommendation to promote one private to the rank of lieutenant. "What's that all about, Captain?" He asked, not recognizing the private's name.

"That's Private James McCaffrey, Sir. You may recall meeting him and Private Halleck after they led a raid into the Reb campsite. They brought out several of our wounded and freed fifteen or eighteen of our soldiers taken prisoner by the Rebs. Captain Kelly tells me he is one of a kind. He is a tough Irish immigrant kid; a rugby star in Ireland, locked-up by the Brits for assaulting a British officer during a game in Galway and one hell of a soldier. Besides, we are still short four lieutenants."

"I see that, Captain, but you might be creating a problem here; your sergeants may not agree with you. Whenever we do something like this, we generally have a personnel problem somewhere within the ranks."

"I realize that, Sir, however in this case the recommendation for this came from our sergeants who have seen this young fellow in action. I do not think we shall have a problem."

"And what about Private Halleck, Captain?" General McMahan inquired.

"You'll note we recommend he and Private O'Toole be promoted to the rank of sergeant, Sir."

Nodding his head McMahan responded with a slight grin. "It looks like you folks have done your homework on this; so let's run with your list and promote all these people today. After the horrendous beating they took yesterday, a promotional ceremony may be a morale builder and just the ticket that will help turn our past leadership mistakes around." Then turning to his personal staff, he said, "Get it done gentlemen; we shall have a formal promotional ceremony and personal equipment inspection at noon tomorrow. We need to get these young soldiers thinking about something besides the death and destruction they suffered here this week." Although there was general agreement among the officers on the candidates selected for promotion, they did not agree that a formal inspection was in order. Notwithstanding that, wisely, no one cared to object to the general's proposed formal promotional ceremony.

"We need one more name on that list, Captain Swartz," General McMahan added. "Have you any idea who that should be?" He asked, smiling.

"No, Sir, I do not, Sir." Captain Swartz responded; he was in a quandary, he had no idea what General McMahan was talking about.

"Put your name on that list, Captain. I am promoting you to the rank of colonel. You Sir, as of now, are the new Sixty-Ninth Regiment's commanding officer. Congratulations Colonel," he added, coming over to shake Brian Swartz's hand. Upon hearing this, the officers stood and began to applaud, with several shouting their approval. The men quickly lined up behind General McMahan to congratulate their newly appointed regimental commander.

"Jesus, Jimmy we finally got a day off; ever since the general brought in all three regiments, we've been in a training mode. Our sergeant has run my ass off; we are either drilling or out on the range firing or policing-up the area."

"I know, Joseph," James responded with a smile. However wasn't it nice the Rebs built this great campsite for us before they pulled out?"

"I suppose you're right. At least we didn't have to cut the trees down to make room for all our tents." He laughed.

"Joseph, after the promotional ceremony and inspection I didn't even get a chance to come over and talk to you and Michael. However, the shellacking we took at Dry Creek was enough for the War Department to get involved and things got rather hectic all of a sudden."

"I'll agree with that, Big Brother," Joseph responded, with a grin. "They have been running our butts off from daylight to dark since the general's arrival. He even came out on the range to check us out. Did you get to talk to him, Jimmy?"

"No, I'm just repeating what I heard, or what Captain Kelly passed on to us. He said he warned the command staff that General Grant was anxious for us to defeat this Alabama bunch for they were holding up the Army's move beyond the Rappahannock. General Grant told him he would not accept an excuse for failure. General McMahan tells it like it is. He is planning to hit them again next week. The Sixty-Ninth Regiment will take the lead under Colonel Swartz; and Colonel Jenkins will lead the Second into battle. Colonel Will Terry and the Thirty-Second Regiment will move out tomorrow and circle south and hit them on their left flank when we commence the attack."

Michael, who came by to congratulate his older brother on his promotion and to spend as much of his day off as he could with James and Joseph, responded. "You are talking about a full-fledged donnybrook, Jimmy."

"Yes, we'll all be involved, all three regiments. However, we are ready. The training you and Joseph are getting now is what should have happened before the Dry Creek battle. Had that happened, a lot more of our guys would still be alive."

"I agree with Jimmy," Michael replied, "but Jimmy and me are going to have it easy compared with what you and the sniper teams are going up against, Joseph. We will have support, but you will be all alone out there, so be careful. We all want to go home when this is over."

"Speaking of home," Joseph interjected. "I received a couple of letters; one from Thomas and one from Auntie Ruth. The boys appear to doing fine in school; Auntie Ruth says they will not have a problem going on up to the next grade. Their grades are good and they like their teachers. How about you, have you heard anything from Colleen or her sisters?" He smiled, knowing that Colleen wrote James every week. Sometimes it took a couple of months for her letters to come through, and some longer than that, but she was a faithful correspondent.

James responded with a smile. "Yeah, you know I did. She sent me a birthday card; she said everyone was fine. She and Shannon have moved in together into a flat in Brooklyn. The girls are working full time at the hospital and enrolled in a night school nursing program. By the time this war is over, Colleen said they expect to graduate. They are getting lots of practice; the New York hospitals are overflowing with wounded soldiers."

"Geez, Jimmy, I forgot all about your birthday." Michael responded. "Nevertheless, the Army gave you a present, didn't they? You received your promotion to lieutenant on your twenty-first birthday. I'll bet you're one of the youngest officers in the regiment, aren't you?"

"No, most of these young fellows coming out of West Point are twenty to twenty-two years old."

"Captain Kelly told us that most of the Confederate officers are West Point people, too, is that right, Jimmy," Joseph asked his older brother. "How's that possible?"

"That's what they say. Nearly three-hundred former West Point graduates resigned their commissions in the Union Army and signed on with the secessionists. I do not know that anyone can answer that question, Joseph. It seems to me that this country was darn good to these people; they gave them a free education for a commitment to serve their country and they turned against their own. It doesn't make any sense to me."

"Are you going to stay with Captain Kelly, Jimmy?" Michael asked.

"Yes, he's a great guy; most of his men are from New York. Sergeants O'Toole and Halleck will be there also, and Peter Means; those three guys saved my butt when we went into the Reb camp."

"I don't envy you," Joseph commented. "When I told my sergeant that you made lieutenant, he just shook his head. He said the survival rate of infantry lieutenants is lower than for any other rank in the Army. I do not like that; you have to be very careful. He said he thought you were lucky at Dry Creek;

the Rebs were using canister and explosive shells there. That canister ammo is designed specifically to take out infantry troops, specifically front line people and their officers."

"Don't worry about it, Joseph. So far, things have turned out pretty good for all five of us, particularly when you think of what our mother and father put up with in Ireland at our age. Uncle Paul said when Daddy was only sixteen he was in a gun battle in Dublin with the Brits. They caught him and two or three others trying to free some of their people from Kilmainham; the Crown was going to hang all of them when Irish Regulators came to their rescue. Moreover, he and Mother just barely survived the Great Famine, so our problems here do not seem quite so bad. We are living in a tent, we have the best clothing and weapons money can buy and we get three meals a day and thirteen dollars a month; what more can you ask for. Besides, most of our officers are graduates of West Point and they are good people. They try very hard to look after their men. Some of them served with Colonel Swartz when he was a platoon commander at Gettysburg."

"I've been meaning to ask you about the colonel, Jimmy. I am curious," Michael said. "How did a fellow with a German name become an officer in an Irish American regiment?"

"Well I never asked, but I too was curious. I know that his mother came from Ireland in the forties, probably at the time of the Great Famine, but he is quite a man in his own right. This was his fourth major clash with the Rebs; his fellow soldiers thought so highly of him early in the war that they voted to have him appointed as a platoon leader."

"I didn't know they did that, Jimmy."

"Yes. In the early days, here in America it was a common practice to elect your own commanders. After Gettysburg, the Army promoted him to captain and assigned him to command a company. At home it was always more formal and the Crown, of course controlled all appointments in both the Army and Navy. The service academies here provide most of the officers now for both services, graduating several hundred each year. Although since this war started the Army officer casualty rate has been so high, they have to reach down in the ranks for replacements. So," James responded with a smile before continuing, "that's why I was promoted. They needed more platoon commanders."

"Probably for cannon fodder," Michael added solemnly, shaking his head.

"I bet they would have selected you anyway, Jimmy," Joseph responded with a smile. "You earned it." "I agree with you Joseph," Michael replied, grimly, "I was wrong to suggest such a terrible thing."

"We move on the Rebs tomorrow, gentlemen," Brigadier General Owen McMahan announced to his commanders and staff officers. "We've had three weeks now and our people are equipped, rested and all replacements are on board. We believe Colonel Evan's cavalry units, working with Captain Ryan's infantry company have interdicted most of the Rebs resupply efforts. However, some shipments, particularly food and ammunition have gotten through our blockade along the river. Colonel Evans men have captured more than two-hundred Confederate soldiers and seized or destroyed, as many as thirty field artillery pieces; these were mostly twelve and twenty-four pounder field guns. However, as these guns are easy to disassemble and move, a few mules can transport a whole battery; the colonel believes some may have gotten through. He suggested that with what they already have we might be facing upwards of two-hundred heavy weapons.

"The Second and the Sixty-ninth Regiments' field artillery units shall begin our assault with a sustained artillery barrage beginning at six o'clock tomorrow morning. Colonel Terry's Thirty-Second is in place and ready to attack the Rebs' left flank. Our infantry units will move out at nine o'clock. Colonel Evans' cavalry shall be in position to harass the Rebs should they retreat to the South or try to escape by crossing back over the Rappahannock.

"Gentlemen, before you all leave to undertake your duties I believe I should mention again that this endeavor shall be very challenging. Lee's people will not give up one yard of this state without a fight. We have a long hard road ahead of us and I fear our men will suffer greatly. Yet if we coordinate our attack, move rapidly with maximum firepower, and overrun their defensive positions, I am confident that you and your men shall prevail. God speed to all of you."

"Jesus, Jimmy, how long are they going to continue the bombardment?" Sergeant O'Toole asked his platoon commander Lieutenant James Robert McCaffrey. "I know what it must be like for those poor bastards over there I was on the receiving end of that in Sixty-three."

"Yes, Edmund, you, and I both know what must be happening to those people; I remember what they did to us a few weeks ago, they killed a lot of our soldiers. However, look around and tell me how many of our people survived that bloody confrontation with the Rebs; then think about how many Rebs will still be alive to greet us when we attack."

"I know what you're talking about, Jimmy. When I look back on that, I should be praying that our artillery boys keep shelling those guys all day long."

When the artillery fire ended, no one was surprised to see the officer who would lead the Sixty-Ninth Regiment into battle. Colonel Brian Swartz, riding swiftly to the front of the column called out, "Forward, we attack now! Follow me."

Yet Swartz was no swashbuckling bravado leader out to make a name for himself; his fellow officers and the enlisted men respected him as a true professional soldier. A soldier they trusted, one who they believed would not risk their lives needlessly in battle; an officer who would seek ways to minimize suffering for a soldier if there was a way to do that. Platoon Commander James McCaffrey felt the same way about Captain Jack Kelly.

"You heard the Colonel, gentlemen," Lieutenant McCaffrey called out to C Companies' Second Platoon, "let's move."

Reentering the heavy growth of brush, scrub oak and pine from which he retreated just three weeks earlier made James' skin crawl. Evidence of that earlier confrontation with Confederate troops was everywhere. Except for the smoke drifting across the terrain from dozens of small fires once again ignited in the underbrush by exploding shells, he was surprised by the distance he could now see through this once nearly impregnable landscape of brush and trees. Last month, visibility was limited to mere yards; today however, with most of the leaves missing from the brush, and trees toppled or decimated by the massive barrage laid down by artillery fire, that problem no longer existed. Notwithstanding that, even though both Union and Confederate forces had long since recovered, and buried their dead, the smell of death had not left the battlefield. James took this all in, even noting that much of the torn and burned ground cover had begun to return. Nature had gone about repairing the damage done by these two great armies, armies that fought each other here such a short time ago.

He was aroused from his musings when all around him men stopped in obedience to the raised arm of Captain Jack Kelly; C Company troops were nearing Dry Creek, the area where just three weeks earlier the Rebs repulsed Union forces with such terrible losses. Yet there was something quite different about the area. Captain Kelly signaled for his platoon leaders to come forward. By the time they arrived Colonel Swartz, aware of the lack of forward movement of C Company signaled a halt to the forward movement of the regiment and approached Captain Kelly.

"What is it, Jack?" Colonel Swartz asked quietly. "What's the hold up?"

"Look there, Colonel, through your glass." Captain Kelly said, "The Rebs have built a second breastwork of timber and rock and possibly bunkers along the creek bed. Lieutenant McCaffrey and Sergeant O'Toole are looking at it now. They should be back in a few minutes. We cannot afford another ambush."

"I agree with you, but we cannot wait too long either, we must take advantage of our artillery barrage of this morning or we lose the benefit our heavy weapons have given us. We will wait only a moment, and then we must resume the attack."

"It's another trap, Sir." James reported to Colonel Swartz and Captain Kelly. "There are twenty or more mortar batteries hidden along the bottom of the creek bed and log bunkers line the full length of the creek for at least five-hundred yards. They have both field guns and howitzers inside the bunkers and behind the breastworks, although it looks like our artillery destroyed many of those that were out in the open. They have suffered a lot of casualties, and are busy moving the wounded out of the forward bunkers and gun positions."

"Thank you, Lieutenant," Kelly replied, "good work. We will continue to move forward, quietly. They know we are here and expect us to attack, but let's first take your men and go after those mortar batteries. Come at them from both sides; and let me know when you are in place. I will hold E and F Company in reserve and the rest of us shall move with the Sixty-Ninth on their main force when your people take out those mortars."

"You got that, Jimmy?"

"Yes, Sir Captain; we are on our way. Second Platoon will enter the creek bed from the south. Okay?"

"Okay, James. Lieutenant Waitt, take your men in from the north. Good luck to both of you."

Twenty-five minutes later, after moving cautiously for the last one-hundred yards, C Company's Second Platoon was in place. When the Sixty-Ninth and Second Regiment artillery began firing on the rebel bunkers C Company's Second Platoon soldiers, emitting loud rebel like yells followed their lieutenant and quickly slipped over the side of the creek bank and raced toward the nearest battery of mortar men, rifles, and bayonets at the ready. Providence was shining on James's platoon as the Reb infantry assigned to protect the artillery units were still engaged in moving their wounded back from the front to an aid station; with most of their muskets piled near the line of mortars. A score of Confederates tried to escape. They ran north along the creek but were intercepted and captured by First Platoon troops moving south into the creek bed.

Shortly thereafter, a withering barrage of rifle fire coming from Reb bunkers pinned down both the First and Second Platoons in the creek bed. The Rebs' principal target however, was the Second Regiment led by Colonel Jenkins. Yet Lieutenants McCaffrey and Robert Waitt's people, now holding a score of prisoners, found themselves trapped in the creek bed between the two armies.

"Bobby," James called out to Lieutenant Waitt, "my people will concentrate our fire on these bunkers immediately in front of us, if you move these prisoner out the same way your platoon entered this creek depression, you should make it. Once you get beyond these bunkers, I'll put a squad to work destroying the mortars; when that's done we will follow, okay?"

"Let's do it, Jimmy, but you need to get out of here as soon as you can. They can trap you down here if the Rebs send in their infantry. It will be like shooting fish in a pond; so do not delay your withdrawal. Get the hell out of here as soon as you can."

"I will, good luck, Bobby."

"Good luck to you, Jimmy, you will need it. Just remember what I said, there is no cover here for you; you've got to get out of here before the Rebs send in their troops."

Yet, even Lieutenant Waitt's escape from this Confederate controlled battle area dragged on longer than planned, hampered by the delay tactics of the two Confederate officers taken prisoner. The Reb officers realized that if they could delay the platoon's progress out of their territory it could result in a rescue attempt by their own forces. However, Lieutenant Waitt soon solved the problem, for after a second warning to the two Reb officers, one of whom attempted to flee, Waitt shot the man. Turning to the second officer he growled, "Pick up your buddy, and move out. You are next if your men do not do as I have directed, tell them that if anyone else tries to escape or further delays our progress back to our lines they shall be shot." The rebel officer complied and Lieutenant

Waitt's platoon experienced no further delay caused by a Reb prisoner's unwillingness to accept the inevitable.

Meanwhile James positioned his men below an aperture of one of the many Reb bunkers built along the creek bed. The occupants of these mini-fortresses could not fire down on his Second Platoon troops without putting themselves at risk to fire from both Second Platoon soldiers and Colonel Jenkins's troops approaching from the west. Unfortunately, by this time Confederate artillerymen began to bring into play the many field guns General McMahan's three-hour barrage left undamaged. Their withering barrage of canister shot and explosive cannonade brought Colonel Jenkins's and members of the Sixty-Ninth to a halt, forcing them to seek whatever shelter the terrain had to offer. The Rebs' field guns continued their barrage for nearly twenty minutes without a response from Union forces.

Colonel Swartz, mindful of the precarious position of both his force and that of Lieutenant McCaffrey's platoon, called for artillery support. Unable to move forward, nor able to extricate Lieutenant McCaffrey's platoon from an untenable position, he had no other choice. Union artillery zeroed in on the Reb positions keeping Confederate infantry from entering the creek bed while they silenced several above ground artillery batteries. In spite of that, Confederate artillery, sheltered in the near impenetrable and well-protected bunkers and revetments along the south end of the breastworks, continued to fire on Union forces forcing troops all along the front to halt their advance and take cover.

While the horrific artillery duel between two of the worlds' largest armies raged across the wilderness, from their relatively safe haven in the creek bed C Company's Second Platoon went about the business of destroying the Reb mortars. When finished with their handy-work, James and his men hunkered-down along the creek below the Reb bunkers. Yet, when the artillery duel ended, the platoon found itself in the untenable position Lieutenant Bobby Waitt warned him of, they came under fire from Reb infantrymen.

Keeping low and out of sight of the Rebs in the nearby bunkers, James crawled over to where two squads with their sergeants lay concealed directly below one of the Reb bunkers and behind a series of large boulders.

"We cannot stay here, gentlemen," he said to Sergeants Wayne Hennessey and John Nestor. "Nor can we pull out without taking out two or three of these bunkers. The minute we climb that bank our men shall be exposed and vulnerable to both the Rebs' infantry and artillery fire."

"That's true, Lieutenant, what do you have in mind?" Sergeant Hennessy asked. "We are in a damn precarious position here; you're not suggesting a direct infantry assault upon those bunkers, are you?"

"Nothing that foolish Sergeant; that would be suicidal, however, we still have a couple of their mortars and a good supply of ammunition. Let's put it to work. All of our sergeants and most of our experienced men have at least a rudimentary knowledge on these weapons. As long as our people keep shelling the Reb positions, their infantry cannot move on us, so let's take out two or three of these bunkers using their own mortars. Then before the smoke settles, we rejoin the regiment. However, get set up first so we can coordinate our attack, for Reb infantry will be all over us when they find out what we are doing. Our people will have a chance at the artillerymen inside those bunkers from across the creek bed and we should be able to get a charge in through a gun port. Then, we get the hell out of here before the Reb infantry decide to attack us in force."

"Let's do it Lieutenant." Sergeant Nestor responded. "My men will take this one right above us and the next one, to the south of us. Let's go," he said to his squad and they quickly followed him to a mortar battery position already set up by the Rebs awaiting the attack of Union infantry.

With the two sergeants leading the way, troops quickly moved into position below each of the five closest bunkers and awaited their lieutenant's signal. When it came, the attack teams fired mortar rounds at the gun ports of the artillery bunkers, where ensuing clouds of smoke and dust allowed the attack teams the opportunity to toss grenades through the gun ports silencing all five bunkers. Secondary blasts occurred almost immediately with a horrific roar destroying two of the Reb bunkers. Unfortunately, two of Sergeant Hennessey's soldiers who led the assault were unable to escape in time and died in the explosions.

The attack, carried out in minutes, left behind five demolished bunkers with uncounted dead, and injured Confederate soldiers buried in rubble. However, the attack was not without further cost to Lieutenant McCaffrey's platoon. Besides the two men who died in the secondary detonation that ripped apart one of the bunkers, Sergeant Nestor received multiple injuries to his torso when one of his men mishandled a grenade.

"Move out now," Lieutenant McCaffrey yelled to the remaining members of Sergeant Nestor's platoon. "We can't wait. Carry the wounded; we will have to attend to their wounds when we get back to our own lines." The lack of a breeze became a godsend to members of the Second Platoon for a grey/black pall of smoke from the rifle fire and explosives lay across the battlefield helping to conceal their hurried withdrawal. James moved south along the creek bed from where they entered the depression earlier, yet before they escaped the narrow channel Confederate infantry opened up on them from above forcing Second Platoon soldiers once more to take cover. This time it was as Lieutenant Bobby Waitt warned; like shooting fish in a barrel.

However, Colonel Swartz reacted immediately upon observing the destruction of the first Confederate bunker and before the second bunker erupted in a secondary explosion, he ordered his men to move forward.

"Our men are down below those bunkers; we must attack now while the Reb artillery is quiet," Colonel Swartz yelled, as he and Captain Kelly led their men in a frontal assault upon the Confederate fortifications. Captain Kelly's C Company troops were the first to arrive, now accompanied by Lieutenant Waitt and First Platoon members. Kelly and Waitt along with the First Platoon quickly slid down the north bank of the creek to linkup with Lieutenant McCaffrey's Second Platoon; they promptly came under fire from enemy troops deployed along the south bank. Shortly thereafter Colonel Jenkins entered the fray with over one-thousand troops from Second Regiment. With neither side yielding ground, by nightfall the battlefield took on the appearance of a massive slaughterhouse.

Darkness gave Union supply personnel the opportunity to bring in and distribute wagonloads of food, water, and ammunition; and then the gruesome task of loading out the wounded for transport to the Aid Station began. With this well underway, Colonels Swartz and Jenkins sat down with their staff to assess the results of the battle and obtain casualty data.

"Captain Kelly, please, what is the status of your company?" Colonel Swartz asked quietly.

"We suffered about one-hundred fifty casualties, Sir, or approximately one-third of my company. I do not have an accurate count, but it looks like fifty-five dead and slightly over one-hundred wounded. However, we shall be ready by daylight; my people are fed and resupplied with water and ammunition." Even though the Sixty-Ninth led the attack today, the Second Regiment took the brunt of the Reb cannon fire resulting in higher losses of personnel than that of the Sixty-Ninth and Thirty-Second regiments combined. Notwithstanding that, with each commander's report it quickly became obvious to General McMahan that Union forces under his command suffered a horrific number of casualties today. Unfortunately, they had little to show for it, except thanks to the early efforts of Second Platoon troops, they overran and destroyed nearly all the Reb bunkers.

"You men try to get some rest tonight," Colonel Swartz said quietly, "for we attack again at first light tomorrow. Our artillery will lay down a barrage for two hours, and then we shall move forward with our infantry; Colonel Jenkins has committed the entire resources of the Second Regiment to breaking through and to finishing these people off tomorrow. Unfortunately, Will Terry's regiment encountered a severe setback today, with heavy losses. It is now questionable whether the Thirty-Second will be in a position to protect our right flank should we push through the Confederate front lines tomorrow. I want you all to keep that in mind; the river will protect our left flank and Colonel Evans' men will keep us advised should the Rebs try to bring in more troops from the south. Tomorrow may be most trying for all our men, so say a prayer for all of us."

Unfortunately, neither luck, nor fate played into the hands of the Union forces that next morning, for it took ten more, bloody, gut-wrenching days for Union forces to destroy the Confederate Army they encountered in the Wilderness that summer of eighteen sixty-four. By the time the battle ended, thousands of Confederate and Union soldiers paid the ultimate price; and the stench of death extended over a one-hundred square mile area of the State of Virginia.

"How are you doing, Michael?" James asked his younger brother as the two of them got together for breakfast two days after Union forces accepted the Confederate general's surrender of the Alabama Regulars. The Reb general surrendered to General McMahan along with an assortment of rebel units decimated by Union forces. "You are not eating your breakfast, how come?"

"I am tired, Jimmy and I want nothing other than to go home, take a hot bath, and sleep for week."

"You and me, both," James replied. "I do not even want to own a gun or ever fire one again. God help me, Michael, but I have killed at least twenty-young men in the last ten days, and I am responsible for the deaths of hundreds more. I wonder what Mama and Daddy would say if they knew I did that." His face was grim and he shook his head, "what a waste," he added.

"You cannot look at it that way, Jimmy." Michael replied, soberly. "Remember, when we captured those two young Rebs on the Rapidan that first night? You told me to forget about it and not to beat myself up over what I did to that young soldier. Well I cannot forget it, but now when I think about it, I just tell myself, I was justified, for that boy would certainly have killed you. Therefore, I don't dwell on it any longer. I try to think of him as a target, you know, as Joseph does. He has certainly shot a lot more people than either you or I have, but he still looks at them as targets. However, I could never do that."

"If the truth were known, Michael I'm sure that by now Joseph has dropped that notion altogether. Although he seldom misses a target, have you noticed when you talk to him, how he has changed? He doesn't like to talk about his sniper duties any longer and he tries to avoid the recognition and fame he has generated within the army because of his marksmanship."

"I have seen that. He is only eighteen and we have not given him a chance to be a kid and enjoy himself. You and I played ball, Jimmy; we went to dances and even had a drink or two, but he was always home, either working or taking care of Mother, and then all of a sudden he's a soldier. When we get home, we owe our kid brother more than we'll ever be able to pay him."

"I suppose you're right, Michael; let's go find him. I know he was to go out on a patrol yesterday. Several Reb cavalry units have been shooting-up our supply wagon people coming across the Rappahannock and Colonel Evans wanted to put an end to it."

"Good morning, boys," Captain Kelly called out to James and Michael as they were leaving the mess area. I was looking for both of you. I just learned that your brother did not come back from a patrol with the cavalry yesterday. I am sorry boys; I would have contacted you earlier if I had known. He went out with a cavalry troop two days ago and they dropped him off where the supply wagons cross the Rappahannock. When they went back to pick him up, there was no sign of he or his partner. Colonel Evans is putting a troop together now to find them."

Although shocked by this news, James reacted quickly. "We're going along with them, Captain." He replied grimly.

"That's fine, you both need to get out of here, and under the circumstances I would do the same. I will clear it with Colonel Evans; take food and water with you. You never know how long you will be out there. Good luck, boys."

CHAPTER 9

THE RESCUE

"Okay, Lieutenant," the tall cavalry lieutenant with the red bushy hair and mustache growled, skeptical of this young infantryman's purpose and showing no respect for his visitor's rank. "You say you and your sergeant volunteered for this patrol. I am Lieutenant Mark Roberts and I will be leading the troop and we are very selective in who we accept from the infantry."

"No, Lieutenant, I guess I did not make myself clear; we are going along with your troop. My name is James McCaffrey and this is Sergeant Michael McCaffrey and as you might have guessed, yes, we are brothers." James responded politely.

"By whose authority, Lieutenant? The last I heard, in this man's army grunts could never learn how to ride a horse," the man responded, with a note of sarcasm in his voice. "It takes us nearly two years to train a cavalryman; what makes you think that you meet our standards?"

Ignoring the man's inhospitable attitude, James replied, "I think if you check with your commanding officer Sergeant, you will find that Colonel Evans authorized our participation in this mission."

"I will take your word for it, Lieutenant, the colonel must have a reason and I won't argue with him; he has already stuck me with two other infantry grunts. I take it you both know how to ride, however, this will be no pleasure trip; we ride hard and fast and Johnnie Reb will blow you right out of the damn saddle if he gets a chance."

"We are aware of that, Lieutenant, we undoubtedly do not have your vast experience, but we have come up against an occasional instance where we found it necessary to use our weapons. And yes, we do know how to ride." James responded deliberately playing down he and Michael's horsemanship capability and military experience.

"Okay, you and your brother pick out your mounts and saddle up; this may be an extended patrol so I assume you have the proper supplies, but you need to stop at the armory tent to pick-up a Spencer rifle and ammunition. I take it you both know how to handle the Spencer?" He commented, obviously skeptical that a couple of young infantry soldiers would be able to handle one of their oftentimes-unruly mounts, much less, the new Spencer rifle carried by the cavalry.

"Yes, Lieutenant, we have qualified with the Spencer," Michael responded straightforwardly and who by this time became annoyed by Lieutenant Roberts' condescending attitude toward him and his brother; prompting his next response with a touch of disrespect in his voice, he added, "We also know a little bit about horses. Furthermore, one of the men that you are going out to look for is our kid brother; he too was one of those infantrymen from my company that you folks relied upon to protect you and our supply convoys from Reb raiders."

"I apologize to both of you, gentlemen." Lieutenant Roberts replied, finding himself in the uncomfortable position of questioning the knowledge and expertise of his fellow soldiers and then finding them to be the brothers of one of the missing snipers from the Sixty-Ninth. "However, as I told you we are already stuck with taking two other guests who have been pestering their company commander for a transfer to a cavalry unit. So I shall be going hunting for Reb horse soldiers with two green-pea troopers and you two; God help us all," he shook his head. "Just remember the Rebs are expert horsemen and crack shots and they like nothing better than killing a Yankee horse soldier to get his mount and that rifle we carry."

"We will do our best, Lieutenant to hang onto both our rifle and our mount and find our soldiers in the process." James responded, quietly.

"If we can accomplish that, gentlemen it will be a good day; pickup your equipment, we pull out in an hour."

"Hi, Jimmy, Michael," the young soldier called out from on his mount. It was Kevin Malone. "Dennis and I thought that was you talking to old hard-ass Lieutenant Roberts." He laughed. "He gave us a bad time too; I bet these cavalry guys would never ask for help except they lost more than half of their people in last week's battle with the Rebs."

"Hi yourself, Kevin," James responded with a smile, grabbing the mount's bridle. "It is good to see you."

"Hi Kevin," Michael smiled, reaching up to shake his cousin's hand. "I have heard good things about both of you from Sergeant Meade."

"Yeah, Meade is a good guy; every time we get a break he wants to hear more about Ireland. He says he will go there for a visit when this war is over. His grandparents came from Dublin at the turn of the century and he wants to know all about the city. We told him the only part of the city we ever saw was the view from inside of Kilmainham prison; he always laughs when we tell him that."

"Where is Dennis?" Michael asked his cousin. "I don't see him here."

"No," Kevin replied laughing. "His mount's a two-year old filly and she gave Dennis such a bad time he is out for a run with Sergeant Moore. He has to prove he can handle the horse or they will not take us along. Knowing Dennis, he might even teach the sergeant something about horseflesh. Dennis and I volunteered when we heard that Joseph was missing. We figured you guys would be here."

"What did they tell you about the sniper teams, anything?" James asked quietly, as Dennis dismounted.

"Not much Jimmy. They took out five or six teams and they were to setup along the supply route at different locations where the Reb cavalry has hit the supply convoys in the past. The raiders move in fast, kill the mule skinners, run off the mules and burn the wagons then take off before the cavalry gets anywhere near them. The sniper teams have been successful; they have taken out a dozen or more Reb raiders, but yesterday the Rebs bypassed the convoy and went after the snipers. The cavalry people found two of them; the Rebs hate the snipers so badly they took time out to burn the bodies of a couple of them. They even hung two of them from a tree; that really shook up the escort teams."

"I can understand that, our people might do the same thing. You know what the Confederate snipers have done to our ranks; however, what about Joseph and the other two or three teams that were out there, any word about them?"

"Yes, Jimmy, we were told that two teams shot it out with the raiders. Two of our people died, but the cavalry rescued two others, however, there was no sign of Joseph and his backup man. They found a couple of dead Rebs near their location, but Joseph and his partner went missing. The escort unit believes that they might still be alive or they would have found their bodies and there was no sign of their backpacks, or weapons. The Rebs like the long guns our snipers use and they forage both for food and ammunition."

"Jimmy, Kevin, look over there," Michael, yelled, "If I am not mistaken we have a horse race in progress and no money to bet on the winner." He laughed, "That's Denny, I can tell the way he rides. I would bet on him any day!"

"Good ride, Soldier," the sergeant said as he and Private Dennis Malone's horses came to an abrupt stop at the corral gate, where both men slipped easily out of the saddle onto the ground. "You can ride with me any day of the week. Get your gear and be prepared to move out."

"Yes, Sir, Sergeant," Dennis replied with a smile then turning to his cousins, he rushed to meet them. "What is this?" he said, "a family reunion?" He laughed as the four cousins, all talking at the same time greeted each other.

"Gather around, troopers," Lieutenant Roberts called out to the fifteen-man troop that was about to embark on a search and rescue mission in territory along the Rappahannock River trail, all of which was hostile to Union forces. James and Michael and the Malone twins were about to learn how a Union cavalry troop operated in enemy territory. Lieutenant Roberts was no novice in this business having been with Colonel Evans' cavalry for more than three years, and as with this venture into hostile territory, their losses to Confederate forces frequently required them to recruit replacement personnel from wherever they could find them.

"This is what we know, gentlemen," he said straightforwardly. "The territory we will be searching is in effect no-man's land. We do not control it, nor do the Confederate forces, but it is necessary for our supply wagons to use about a thirty-mile stretch of the Rappahannock River trail. Our engineers have built two bridges across the river for our wagons, but the Rebs have destroyed both of these. Without the bridges, we can only ford the river in two places so we shall continue to be susceptible to attack along that stretch of the trail. Last week we setup six sniper teams on the high ground above the river crossings; our snipers shutdown a half dozen raider attacks until yesterday when the Rebs went after our boys. Unfortunately, my men, who were with the supply wagons, did not arrive in time; the Rebs killed or wounded a half-dozen of our sniper people. From the looks of things, they may have captured at least four and maybe more of our men. Our objective today is to find our people if they are still alive and to protect the next supply train which will come across the river sometime late tonight or early tomorrow morning. So that's where we are heading; let's move out."

With Lieutenant Roberts leading the way, James, riding a well-trained three-year-old Morgan gelding settled in on the trail alongside the cavalry lieutenant with the troop in column formation, following close behind. Michael and the Malone twins fell in at the end of the column. As the day progressed, they caught-up on family matters, discussing what they learned about home from those infrequent letters from friends and relatives in New York.

"Where did you learn to ride, McCaffrey?" Lieutenant Roberts casually asked of his fellow officer.

"On my father and grandfathers' farm, in County Cork; all of us kids had our own ponies from the time we learned to walk; that is until the Brits came."

"What was that all about?" Lieutenant Roberts asked. "I remember reading something about it, but I am not Irish, so I never paid much attention to what was going on in Ireland, or in Europe either. As you can see we have our own problems here with the secessionists."

"Principally, politics and religion all mixed together, but mostly over home-rule. The Irish have tried for decades to break away from the British Empire and our parents and grandparents pleaded with the Crown, argued with Parliament and eventually took up arms to gain their freedom. From what I have seen, it is not too unlike what you have here in America with the South trying to hang onto the old ways with the Negro."

"I suppose you're right," Lieutenant Roberts responded, nodding his head. "However, here in the U.S. the damn thing got completely out of control; instead of trying to settle the differences between the Union and the Confederate folks, we started shooting at each other. In some cases, it is brother against brother, with whole families split over the issue of slavery. Thousands of men on both sides have been killed or injured and whole families destroyed over what should have been resolved at the ballot box."

"My parents and grandparents tried that approach in Ireland, but were rebuffed by the British and now I am a fugitive in my own country." James responded. "However, my brothers and I are free now and except for this war, we love everything that we have experienced in this country. It truly is blessed, in every way, is it not?"

"Aye that it is," Lieutenant Mark Roberts replied.

For the next eight hours, the troop moved south along the Rappahannock River trail, eventually approaching the first river ford, where Lieutenant Roberts raised his arm to slow their approach. "Keep it quiet from here on. Pass the word." He said his voice muted.

Shortly before reaching the crossing, he led the troop into a thick grove of brush and small trees alongside the river where they began the steep climb up the southern bank, eventually coming to a small clearing. "Dismount and rest your horses," he ordered, giving his men the opportunity to get on the ground and stretch after the long march.

"Come with me, Lieutenant," Roberts said to James, "I want to show you something up here on the ridge. This is where we dropped off the first sniper team a week ago. From here, they had a near perfect view of the crossing. When the first wagons come out of the water, the Rebs hit the train, so we set up our teams along this ridge. When they came a second time, the teams took them out then moved further down river waiting for them to take another crack at our convoy. Our strategy worked twice here and at the other crossing, but one thing you can say for the Reb leadership, they are not dumb. They came back after dark and took out three of our teams. Therefore, this is where we make our stand at least for tonight. We will tether our mounts along the river and set-up here and hope they show when the wagon train comes though either late tonight or at first light in the morning."

Returning to the troop, and then directing his attention to James and Sergeants Moore and McCaffrey, the man said, quietly, "Two hour watches, no fires, no smoking, keep it quiet, and stay alert."

"Lieutenants," Sergeant Moore, on watch whispered, nudging Lieutenants Roberts and McCaffrey with his boot, as both men slept on the ground a short distance apart from their men. "It will be daylight soon and we have company. I heard the Rebs move in a short time ago; they are just beyond the rapids, down river from the ford. You cannot see them, it is still too dark, but they are there and now we can hear the wagon train people. If you listen close, you can hear the muleskinners cussing; it would be my guess they should be starting across the river within an hour or so. There is no sign of the escort, but these trains frequently stretch out over two or three miles and they could be anywhere back down the road a piece."

"Okay, Sergeant" Lieutenant Roberts responded, immediately wide-awake to his surroundings. "Wake the men, keep them quiet, and let's deploy as we discussed last night; we shall prepare that fine reception we laid-out for these bastards. The Rebs are hard pressed for troops these days, so they generally travel in groups of ten men or less; but you never know, stay alert for two or three squads or even up to a full troop."

"I will set-up my people across the top of the ridge as you suggested, Lieutenant," James responded quietly to Lieutenant Roberts' request, "We'll be ready if they come our way."

"Good." Lieutenant Roberts replied, then turning to Sergeant Moore, said, "Let's get to our horses and be ready. Just remember, let the Rebs make the first move. We want to know how many we will be dealing with and where they plan to attack. They usually let the first two or three wagons cross the river before they attack, particularly if the escort troops are not in sight. Good luck James," he said. "Remind your boys that we want one or two of them alive; we will never find their operating base and our men unless one of them talks."

"Good luck to you, Mark; we will do our best not to disappoint the cavalry." As the two men departed, James was sure that in this faint light of early morning he detected a smile on his colleague's bearded face.

"Jesus, Jimmy look at them. There must be a whole platoon of Reb cavalry there. I count thirty-two and it looks like there are a few more in the bush. We are going to have our hands full; I hope Lieutenant Roberts knows what he is doing."

"I do too, Michael; you, I, Dennis and Kevin are in for it if the lieutenant's plan does not work and the escort people don't respond in time. Even though we have these Spencer rifles, they have enough people that they could easily overwhelm us if it goes awry."

"Dennis, Kevin," James called out quietly to his two cousins positioned along the ridge behind a scattering of large rocks; "are you ready?"

"We're ready, Jimmy," Kevin replied, "bring 'em on." He smiled, yet his heart was pounding so hard he found it hard to steady his rifle.

"Just remember what Lieutenant Roberts said, give the Rebs a start, so our cavalry boys can get in behind them. This time, we set the trap for them and just maybe when it is all over we will find Joseph. Look sharp now, the wagons are already fording the river and Reb cavalry is moving in fast; but hold your fire until Lieutenant Roberts makes his move."

The Reb cavalrymen moved quickly; before the first supply wagon made it across the river, their entire troop stormed into the shallow riverbed, opening fire on the muleskinners and their teams. They killed or disabled several mules bringing the wagon train to an abrupt halt in the middle of the river. Yet the Rebs were in for a surprise for there were two or three Union soldiers concealed under canvas in each of the lead wagons. When the attack began, they threw off their cover and opened fire on the Reb troopers. Taken by surprise in this sudden response from soldiers in the lead wagons, the Reb attack faltered for a moment with the Confederates milling around trying to take stock of this unanticipated and violent opposition. Yet there were too few Union soldiers, thus the

Reb troop commander after but a moment of hesitation, rallied his men for a second assault on the lead wagons. He cried out, "There are only a half dozen soldiers in the wagons, take 'em' out!" However, that hesitation was all the time that Lieutenant Roberts needed to get his troop in behind the rebel unit and he and his troopers bore down on them at a full gallop while firing their weapons.

Before beginning their second attack upon the lead wagons, the Confederate officer in charge of the raiding party realized they were about to be caught between two groups of Union soldiers; those concealed in the wagons and Lieutenant Roberts' wildly charging cavalry coming up behind his force. With clouds of dirty grey/black smoke from musket and rifle fire beginning to obscure the battle scene there was no way for the Reb commander to determine the number of cavalrymen bearing down on his troops. Whirling his mount around there was only one choice left, "Retreat," he yelled, "follow me," spurring his mount with his troop following close behind he led the way toward the south bank of the river coming out of the water right below James, his brother Michael and the Malone boys.

In their wild flight from the battle at the river ford, the rebel commander had no opportunity to see the four Union soldiers waiting for them as they made the mad dash up the riverbank where they ran into a withering barrage of rifle fire. Confederate soldiers cursed as they went down, either shot out of the saddle or with the death of their mount from the powerful 56-56 rim fire cartridge loaded with 45 grains of black powder fired from a cavalryman's Spencer rifle. The rebel officer made it to the ridge above the river before his mount went down from a round fired at close range by Michael, throwing the officer to the ground into a heavy thicket of brush.

"Take him alive, Michael; we will hold here until our boys arrive." James yelled to his brother as Michael rushed into the brush to capture the fleeing man, now on foot. Yet, even with their officer down, the rebel cavalrymen kept firing their weapons; some in a desperate attempt to escape, concentrated their attack on the three Union soldiers at the top of the riverbank while others turned to fire on Lieutenant Roberts' troops now moving fast toward them from the water's edge. However, before Roberts' troop came within firing range of the wild melee on the south bank of the river, with only a handful of Reb soldiers remaining in the saddle, a Reb yelled, "Enough, enough, we surrender," the man cried out, waving his hat in the air.

"Cease fire," James yelled at Dennis and Kevin Malone, "cease fire," he yelled again as the boys had continued to shoot. "Denise, Kevin, hold it up. They have quit firing," he said. "Let's wait until Lieutenant Roberts' people get here to see what we have. Kevin stand ready here; Dennis take out after Michael, see if he has rundown that Reb officer yet. Be careful, the man may still be armed."

"Holy Christ, James!" Lieutenant Roberts exclaimed as he slid out of his saddle. "In my three years with the Army of the Potomac I have never seen anything like this."

"It is not a pretty sight, is it Mark?"

"I suppose that's one way to describe it; but you and your three men took out an entire Reb troop. Those men were the best the South had to offer; God help these poor bastards. Only a handful survived and several of those are wounded."

"I have no regrets, Mark," James replied resolutely to his fellow officer. "These are the soldiers that like to burn or hang Union snipers from trees. I did not want even one of them to escape. Michael and Dennis made sure you have the officer in charge of this piece of southern hospitality. However, you can thank 'Mr. Spencer' and his quick loading magazine tube for what we did here today. The Rebs did not have a chance; although I see some of them were also armed with the latest model Spencer."

"No, I don't have any regrets either, James. The Rebs that had those rifles took them off our dead soldiers, but you will have to admit that between us today we operated as only one could dream of; a mass killing by such a small number of cavalrymen is unheard of in the history of warfare."

"I find no joy in killing these fellows, Mark, but I recognize if an ambush will help shorten this bloody war and fewer Americans will die because of it then so be it."

"Good. You have no reason to apologize for what we did here." Lieutenant Roberts responded, bluntly. "These bloody bastards have killed a lot of our people."

"I realize you are in command, Mark and I will abide by your wishes, but I would like you to release that Reb sergeant and maybe one or two of his men."

"Why would you ask such a thing?" Lieutenant Roberts asked, somewhat taken back by James' unusual request.

"Let them go back and tell their leaders what happened here today; it may encourage them to stop or at least to cut-back on these raids."

"I understand that, but why the sergeant?"

Well, his captain led their troops into a trap, costing the lives of more than half their men."

"That's true, but they may not tell their superiors the truth about today's battle."

"The sergeant would have no reason to exaggerate or lie about their commander's failed leadership. Besides, Michael and I questioned the captain and his sergeant, and a couple of privates. They will not tell us the location of their camp, nor did we push that line of questioning and we did not mention the hanging of some of our men or the burning of their bodies. That could, in my opinion best be left to our intelligence people when they take custody of the captain. He spoke freely of capturing over one-hundred Union soldiers this past month. We pressed him hard about that. He admitted their men captured two or three of our sniper teams and was quite proud of that. He even gave us the names of some of them and my kid brother was one. He told us the Army immediately transferred all of his prisoners onto a Reb train bound for Richmond."

"Well at least now you know, James, that's a godsend, the war will be over for your brother."

"What are you thinking about, Michael?" James asked his younger brother as the two of them kept an eye on the Confederate prisoners digging graves for the casualties from today's battle.

"Don't you think it is kind of ironic, James that we are standing here watching a group of Confederate soldiers digging graves for a group of young rebels that died here today."

"Yes, Michael, but it is not only ironic, it is so sad, for the men wielding the shovels and most of the dead are of Irish or German stock. From the way those people talk out there, many of them must be recent immigrants themselves. Along with the Irish I recognize that heavy German accent."

"Maybe the secessionists gave these Confederate boys the same choices we had in New York; you either volunteered or went to jail." Michael added with a grim smile.

"James, I understand from Lieutenant Roberts that you and Michael did well on your recent experience with the cavalry" Captain Jack Kelly commented. "Congratulations," he added with a smile and handshake.

"Yes we did, Captain, thank you. In fact, Lieutenant Roberts asked Colonel Evans to keep all four of us on as troopers, but Michael and I declined. A ten or twelve hour trek in the saddle is not our idea of soldiering. The Malone twins jumped at the chance; they thought they might eventually get an opportunity to visit the West. I understand that the majority of our forces out West are composed of cavalry troops."

"Yes, that's correct, but I, like you did not relish those long marches on the back of a horse; I was glad to come back to the infantry."

"I didn't realize you started out in the cavalry, Sir." James responded.

"Yes, I did, but those extended trips on horseback and cold camps are onerous and sometimes very taxing on the body of middle-aged soldiers. However, James, I wanted to talk to you about something else; how would you feel about taking over the Company."

"C. Company, Sir?" James asked, taken completely by surprise by his captain's inquiry.

"Yes. Colonel Swartz's injuries from this last go around with the Rebs turned out to be worse than first believed. The medical people ordered him out yesterday. I will be taking his place as Regimental C.O. I need a good man to take over here.

You are respected and popular with the troops, and frankly I think you would do a superior job as company commander."

"But Sir, I'm not even a citizen," James protested. "I'm an ex-convict and if the Brits had their way they would have put a rope around my neck before I left Ireland. What about all these other young lieutenants and sergeants, surely they are more qualified than I and there are some really good men there."

"Yes, I agree there are some very good men there, but most of them are younger and less experienced than you. Besides, our older men are too wary to take on the challenges required of an infantry captain. I do not blame them for that; our infantry officers have experienced a hundred percent casualty rate, most of those were platoon and company commanders. The Reb sniper has also taken a huge toll, you have seen that within the regiment, but if we are going to win this war, we need intelligent and tough leaders who will be one-step ahead of the Confederates. Before he left, I told Colonel Swartz you were that man and that you could do the job for us."

"Wow, is all I can think of to say, Captain. However, this country has been good to me and our family and I will do my very best for you and the Army."

"Good boy. General McMahan will conduct a formal promotional ceremony for all our people when he gets back from Washington, but as of now Captain, you are in charge of C Company, Sixty-Ninth Regiment. Tomorrow the entire regiment will be relieved and we will return to camp to train our replacements; they should arrive sometime later this week. As you may have guessed, the Army is gearing up for a drive on Richmond and Petersburg; plans are well under way for a major confrontation with Lee's people somewhere beyond the James River. It shall be necessary for you to get your new people assigned and trained as quickly as possible. We may have less than thirty days to accomplish what needs to be done."

"Jimmy, did you hear that Colonel Terry died yesterday and Colonel Jenkins is taking his place."

"Yes, I knew that. When he led the attack on the Rebs two weeks ago, the Colonel was badly injured. I am so sorry; he was a nice man. I liked him. He was a lieutenant in the infantry when the war started, but promoted in the field to captain at Gettysburg. He was a West Point graduate, however he had not been home for nearly three years, and they tell me it was beginning to take a toll on his performance. Still, at the Officer's Council, he was always very professional and was certainly admired by his fellow officers."

"Good God, Jimmy; just think of the number of officers that have been killed since you and I came into the Army. It must be in the hundreds by now."

"It gets worse, Michael. The Rebs killed Colonel Evans the day before yesterday when his troops raided a Confederate campsite on the Red River; also two of his troop commanders suffered severe wounds. They brought the Colonel's body in last night, along with thirty or forty wounded troopers."

"Jesus, Jimmy that's terrible! What about the twins, did you hear anything?"

"I talked to Lieutenant Roberts this morning; he said they are fine; he also said they gave a good accounting of themselves during the battle."

"They would, but that's what scares the hell out of me. They are not afraid of anything or anybody. Even after what they have seen and done this past year, they still think they are indestructible."

"I know that, we saw it in their performance when we ambushed the Reb cavalry; it borders on recklessness, but neither you nor I, Michael can do a darn thing about it."

"What about Evans' attack, how did it end?"

"Roberts said it was just a damn mess. Their scouts reported there were approximately two to three-hundred Reb infantry encamped along the river, but another complete mounted battalion of troops arrived unexpectedly just as our troops attacked. He does not know how the scouts missed 'em. The battle lasted nearly all day. Colonel Evans died leading a charge into the middle of the Reb troop and snipers shot his two company commanders, Captains Brady and Rooney. They lost nearly their entire command staff."

"What about Mark, did he come out of it okay?"

"Yes, but he doesn't look good. The battle raged for hours, Mark said it was the fiercest encounter he ever experienced, and he lost a good friend. He and Evans had been together since Gettysburg. Of those who fought at Gettysburg, he is the only senior officer remaining in the regiment, the rest were either wounded too seriously to return to duty, or they're dead."

"I didn't know Colonel Evans, Jimmy, but Captain Kelly told me that he was a West Pointer and highly respected by his people."

"Yes, he was well respected and apparently a great leader."

"However, Michael I know something that you haven't heard yet."

"What's that, Jimmy?"

"The Army is going to promote you to Lieutenant today and you will take over a platoon in the Thirty-Second. Terry's people lost several field officers last week, and over seventy-five percent of their officers in the last year alone. So you be watchful out there, do not take any unnecessary chances. This war will be over soon and we need to go home together."

"I wonder why Captain Kelly didn't mention that this morning, if it's already out."

"I don't think Kelly knows anything about it; this just happened and besides as of yesterday you're no longer with the Sixty-Ninth Regiment, and Kelly's got his own problems to contend with."

"What do you mean by that Jimmy?" Michael responded confused by his brother's remarks.

"He is having one heck of a time finding replacement officers and noncoms to fill the existing vacancies in the regiment. There are sixteen officer vacancies that he has to fill, and more than two dozen NCO types, your former position is one of those, Michael. The high rate of casualties this last month has depleted the available pool of officers and most of the recent graduates from West Point are dead or wounded. He is having a hard time finding volunteers to take their place. Notwithstanding that, if they do not volunteer, he has the authority to select whomever he wants from the ranks. The people will not be given a choice like you and I were; he will appoint them and they will be expected to perform and you know Captain Kelly, he will go ahead and do that, but it will just tear him up inside. He does not support the concept of a military draft and believes Americans should volunteer to serve their country. He will be very reluctant to appoint a draftee to fill any one of his existing vacancies. Every NCO that he moves up puts him in the position of selecting a private to fill the empty slot and most of those folks are draftees."

"I guess Jimmy, what you are telling me, I shall soon find out that being an officer in this man's army is no bed of roses, as Mother used to warn us when we were kids." He laughed. "Remember when Daddy put us to work in the byres; before we could ride one of grandfather's Connemara ponies or even learn how to milk a cow he made us haul the manure out and work it into the garden. When we complained to Mother, she would sing her little ditty about life, 'Life is not a bowl of cherries or a bed of roses.' Remember that, Jimmy?"

"I won't ever forget that," James replied smiling, "but our day is coming. We will be going home before too long."

"By the way, Jimmy, after what you and I have experienced in the Army this past year, I am always very careful. I cannot forget that both of us are filling positions because the Rebs wounded or killed the former occupant. I do not want my name included on one of those casualty lists. Incidentally, the Thirty-Second is made up of nearly all German immigrants; that should be interesting." Michael laughed. "I don't speak any German; I hope they all speak English."

"They're good, Michael. I think they make better soldiers than the Irish. They outperform us on the range and they make us look sophomoric on the parade ground. I think it must be their background. We Irish are an independent lot, we think we can lick the world and maybe we could if we would quit fighting among ourselves. We could have whipped the Brits if we had combined our forces, but no, we had to squabble between our different groups as to who should govern our country; the Brits took advantage of that. The Germans seem to stick together though; they appear much better organized in the field. I think they will like you, Michael and you will learn a lot from those people."

"You remember what Daddy used to say about the Germans, Jimmy." Michael was smiling, 'When the Irishmen finish drinking their poteen they would go stand in the bread line, while the German would drink his hot apple wine, eat his strudel and Sauerbraten beef roast, then go to work.'"

"Aye, he did that, but he was talking about those lazy buggers who wouldn't work and expected someone else to carry their load. I don't see that happening here; some of the draftees, both Irish and American born, do a lot of bitching about the Army, but most of them do a pretty good job."

"I think you're right, Jimmy, we haven't done too badly; we've taken the lead in several battles and taken more territory and captured more Rebs than any other regiment in the Army. That is quite an accomplishment for a bunch of Irishmen, many of whom cannot even read or write. Did you notice how many of our people make their mark at the end of the month on the Paymaster's record; they cannot even write their own names. That doesn't bode well for the Irish."

"No, you're right and that's sad; but that's something that will change in time. Look at Thomas and Daniel's letters that tells you a whole lot about America. They are getting the education that Mother and Daddy dreamed was possible for all of us. So I think the Irish will do alright in this country."

"I hope Captain Kelly thinks my promotion and transfer is a good idea, but it's probably best for you, Jimmy; you can concentrate on running your Company and not worry about your kid brother any longer." Michael smiled.

"The Captain will be very pleased about your promotion, Michael. It is a great move, you have become such an accomplished soldier; I never worried about you. Ever since the Rapidan incident, the captain and I both knew, that you were the personification of the professional. You see, I learned from you and for that, I will always be thankful. I would not be a captain today except for you and Joseph as I was always trying to show my younger brothers how easy it was to be a soldier. I also pretended that I enjoyed every minute of it, just so you two would not become discouraged."

"I never realized that." Michael responded, surprised by his older brother's statement.

"I thought you saw through this thin veneer of mine, Michael. I really like the people that we are associated with since joining the Sixty-Ninth; they are a great bunch of soldiers. They taught me so much about the military and about this country. However, I could never be a professional soldier; I hate this war. Fortunately, I seem to have the skills needed to organize and carry out a military operation and maybe that's been good for us and our new country because nearly every battle we have been involved in, except our first, resulted in helping to defeat the Confederate Army."

"That's not bad, Jimmy. We came here to get away from what the Confederates profess to be right for the country, which is contrary to everything that you and I learned from our parents in Ireland. You cannot have a country where one group completely enslaves their fellow countrymen."

"I don't disagree with you, Michael; it's just that, I might become so skilled at killing that someday I may look at an enemy soldier as just another target to shoot. I do not want that to happen to me. When this is over, I want to go to some quiet corner of this great land and build a home for Colleen and me and our children and never kill another human being."

"I think you are more normal than you even imagine, Jimmy. Most all of us want that. This war should end within a few months and we will all go home. Captain Kelly tells me that when we get out of the Army we will qualify for citizenship and be able to apply for a homestead. We listed Uncle Paul and Auntie Ruth's home in New York as our home when we enlisted, but the Captain said in sixty-two President Lincoln signed The American Homestead Act. That law will allow us to stake out a homestead claim any place in the territories and if we improve the land, it is ours. And nobody can take it away from us." He smiled. "That will be great, Jimmy. I think we did the right thing in joining the Army. When this is over, we will find Joseph, and the five of us can go wherever we want."

"We can thank Daddy for that, Michael; he got us the hell out of Ireland."

"Let me have your attention, Gentlemen," newly promoted Sixty-Ninth Regimental Commander Colonel Jack Kelly asked of the assembled officers in the large mess tent. "You newly assigned and those of you who have been recently promoted have had nearly two months now to train your soldiers, get acquainted with your platoon and company commanders within the Sixty-Ninth and hopefully you feel confident that your men are combat ready. I also hope that you have a fair understanding of what I shall expect of you when we meet the Rebs on the battlefield. We must cooperate and coordinate every move on the battlefield with your fellow soldiers. Within forty-eight hours we, along with nearly every man in the Army of the Potomac shall move against Lee's Army of Northern Virginia now entrenched at Richmond and Petersburg. General Grant shall personally lead this mission; his objective is to completely surround Lee's Army and put an end to this horrible war. It will not be easy and many of you may die before it is over; but the General believes that if we can contain Lees' forces here in Virginia the Confederate Army will surrender, and the war will end. However, if they do not surrender, with God's help we shall see that they do not live to fight another day.

"General McMahan has been instructed to hold our entire division in reserve in support of Fifth Corps; the Fifth has moved into position south of Lee's troops and are advancing on Petersburg as we speak. We shall move out tomorrow and take a position where we can readily support the Fifth and eventually take the fight to the enemy in their own encampment. Good luck to all of you and may God help us to carry the day for the Union."

Luck appeared to be beyond the reach of the men of the Sixty-Ninth; on the third day of their march toward the Confederate fortress at Petersburg, the heavens let loose with a torrent of rain the like of which had not struck the State of Virginia in more than twenty-years. Fifth Corps, in the meantime positioned itself opposite the Confederate entrenchments striking out with skirmishers and snipers testing the strength of their enemy. However, if the rain continued at the present level, General McMahan's troops would never reach the front as scheduled to support Fifth Corps' planned advance on Petersburg. McMahan's troops soon bogged down on the roadways with caissons and supply wagons frequently buried up to their axles and troops wading through mud and water at times above their boots.

McMahan split his forces, leaving one regiment of cavalry behind to protect supply wagons and artillery battalions and moved the remaining cavalry and infantry regiments as fast as he could toward an engagement with the Rebs. The battle had been underway for more than three days and it was not going well for McMahan's forces. When they arrived at the front, his infantry began the offensive without artillery support and lacked adequate supplies and ammunition, yet he had no other choice. Earlier in the week, the Fifth Corps' attack ran into an overwhelming massed artillery barrage from more than four-hundred guns, decimating the center of Fifth Corps infantry. A Reb infantry attack followed with their troops punching a half-mile wide hole into the Union lines; General McMahan had to rush all three regiments in to stem the advance of the confederate forces.

Immediately upon arrival at Petersburg the Sixty-Ninth, lead by Colonel Kelly moved against the Rebs' left flank, while the Second and Thirty-Second, after circling around the battered remnants of Fifth Corps infantry struck hard at their right. Yet it was nearly dark before Colonel Jenkins, now handling the affairs of both the Second and the Thirty-Second Infantry, got his troops into position. The delay allowed the Reb commander to deliver the full furry of his assault troops upon Colonel Kelly's infantrymen.

Kelly threw all six companies into the fray, succeeding in halting any further expansion of the Reb encroachment into the breach and cutting off the attacking force from their support. Nevertheless, without artillery support, compounded by a shortage of ammunition, and no reserve force, the Sixty-Ninth troops suffered heavy losses of men and equipment in this valiant effort to retake and hold the territory reclaimed from the Confederates. Both Colonel Kelly and his company commanders welcomed the end of the day and the ensuing darkness provided the opportunity to rescue the injured and retrieve weapons and ammunition left behind by their wounded and dead comrades.

The responsibility for rounding-up hundreds of Confederate soldiers who ended up trapped in the no man's land area between Fifth Corps front lines and the Sixty-Ninth rested upon the shoulders of the men in Captain James McCaffrey's C Company troops.

"Offer them food and water, James, if they surrender peacefully; but take no chances." Colonel Kelly admonished his young captain. "We do not have much of either, and we are almost out of ammunition, but our supply wagons should be here in the morning. We need whatever guns and ammunition your men can gather. If our supplies do not arrive, we will be in trouble, so we need to finish these Rebs off tonight; we must either capture or kill them before morning. By daybreak it will become only too evident to the Reb commanders and we shall be hard pressed to hold off a counter attack."

"We'll get it done, Colonel. We shall tell them the obvious; that there is no way out except through our lines and that we will take care of their wounded if they bring them out with them. For a bunch of tired soldiers trapped between two armies that should be an enticement to surrender."

"I hope you are right, Captain, but these are tough men; some of them may choose to fight it out with knife and bayonet and others may fear reprisal from their own people should they try to surrender. So take care, be watchful; if I were to guess there has to be four or five hundred enemy troops trapped in this pocket between our forces and Fifth Corps."

"I would agree with that figure, Colonel; we shall be careful."

Returning to his troops, James called out, quietly, "NCOs and officers gather around, we have a long night ahead of us." When all were present he continued, "Our entire company has been tasked with rounding up the Rebs that are holed up between our troops and Fifth Corps front lines."

"Tell us you are not serious, Captain," one of the senior sergeants responded, expressing his displeasure with his commanding officer's charge.

"No, Sergeant, I wish I weren't, but that's what you signed on for when you put on those strips. We are going to talk these southern boys into surrendering, or kill them. I do not want a firefight here in the dark if we can avoid it.

"We know there are several hundred Confederate soldiers trapped between us and Fifth Corps front lines and you platoon leaders, as you move through this area it will be your responsibility to convince them to surrender. Let them know you are coming and call out to them; offer to take care of their wounded if they carry them out and tell them we have food and water for them. Our supply wagons should be here tomorrow along with the Medical Corps; that may be the only chance for survival for their wounded.

"However, be sure to get their weapons and ammunition; we are short of ammunition. If they resist you will have to go after them in the dark; if you cannot kill them at least scatter them. They have no place to go, and they know that, but they should not constitute a major threat alone in the dark. If we miss a few, the Fifth Corps will take them out in the morning. Any questions," James asked.

"Yes, Sir, Lieutenant Parks with the Third Platoon asked, "What about Fifth Corps people, Captain, will they know that's our people out there so they won't be firing on us?"

"Good question, Lieutenant; yes the Colonel has coordinated our incursion into no man's land with Fifth Corps. They will hold their fire until daylight. However, they took such a terrible beating the last few days there may be some skittishness on the part of their men, so do not take any chances. But don't return their fire, hunker down and let them know who you are."

"Jesus, isn't that a little risky?" First Platoon Lieutenant Tyler Yates asked. "If someone is shoot'n at you it's damn hard not to fire back."

"I grant you that, Lieutenant," James responded quietly, "but the Colonel selected us because he knows everyone of you and he has faith in your judgment. He is counting on your field experience to accomplish something that is very risky. If it works, it may save many lives. Just remember, we are damn near out of ammunition and our supplies are hours away if not days away, so if we can convince a large number of these southern boys to surrender, we will not have to go after them with a bayonet.

"I will join your platoon, Lieutenant Yates and we'll move south toward Fifth Corps' frontline positions. Lieutenant Parks move your men South-Southeast and Lieutenant Oliver set your sights on a South-Southwest course. We shall meet back here at daylight. Any other questions? If not, then let's move out."

C Company personnel called this Colonel Kelly's life or death gamble. The Colonel was gambling their lives, nearly three hundred Union soldiers, betting that they could move through a tangled mass of trees and brush, in which several hundred Confederate soldiers were now holdup, and try to convince them to surrender. Yet the odds were in favor of Kelly's men, as the Rebs, surrounded and trapped between two Union Armies had no hope of rescue. Kelly's ace in the hole was that he believed his men could convince the trapped men to surrender, for when Fifth Corps reentered the fray they would die.

On this warm quiet summer evening, just before midnight, Lieutenant Yates, smelling tobacco smoke brought his platoon to a halt, just yards away from a partially burned-out farmhouse. "You inside the building," he called out, "I am Lieutenant Tyler Yates United States Army, and you are completely surrounded and cut off from your troops. If you surrender, we shall provide you with food, water and our medical people shall care for your wounded. However, you must surrender now or we shall fire the building. You have three minutes to decide."

Listening to Lieutenant Yates' directive delivered loudly by this recent West Point graduate, James was impressed by the manner in which the young man conducted himself. There was neither grandstanding nor squeamishness evident, just an honest, straightforward command delivered by a professional soldier. He thought how lucky he was to have such men under his command.

"We'll fight you, you blue belly bastards," one man shouted only to receive a stern warning, "Shut the hell up, Webster. Stick a knife in him if he opens his mouth again," the unseen voice commanded. "Colonel, Stackhouse, here, I'm coming out. I am unarmed." The man said.

In the faint light from a million stars and a quarter moon that just begun to rise above the horizon, James got a close-up view of a tall, thin, emaciated Confederate officer who came out of the building to greet them.

"Good morning, Colonel Stackhouse. I am Lieutenant Tyler Yates, Company C, Sixty-Ninth New York Infantry Regiment. This is Captain James McCaffrey, Company Commander."

"Captain McCaffrey, Lieutenant Yates," the man repeated their names and then added, "May I sit, please, Lieutenant? I am not well and I am concerned that if I do not sit down I shall go to meet my maker, right here in your presence."

There was sufficient light to see that the man was in need of medical assistance, dirt and dried blood caked his uniform, and he walked with a noticeable limp.

"Certainly, Sir, please sit here." Lieutenant Yates replied and he and James squatted down beside the man.

Turning to James, he spoke quietly, "As an officer of the American Army, Sir, can you give me your word that if we surrender, my soldiers shall be afforded all necessary medical assistance and be cared for as prisoners of war as promised by your President?"

"I assure you of that, Colonel; every man that surrenders shall be humanely treated, and every man that has suffered injury shall be cared for by our medical teams. Our ambulances are as we speak en route to this very battlefield; they offer the finest and I might add the only medical assistance available to soldiers within a hundred miles of where we are presently located.

"Better than what we have here in Petersburg or Richmond?" The Colonel responded with a weak smile.

"Yes, Colonel, better than anything the Confederacy has to offer; for you may not know it but Petersburg is surrounded and Richmond and Atlanta are both now completely cut off. So yes, Colonel, to answer your question, the American Army is the only medical service available to your men."

"I realize that, Captain, although I was not aware that Richmond and Atlanta had succumbed to Union forces. Irrespective of that, on behalf of my men we shall surrender and trust our future to God. I have seventy-two men in the building Captain, all wounded. When your boys overran us before we could reach our entrenchments, I was injured and chose to stay behind and care for my men."

Upon entering the damaged home, now lit by one or two candles, it was immediately obvious to James and Lieutenant Yates that this was once an elegant mansion with multiple rooms on each of the two floors of the building. After securing the rebels' weapons, Lieutenant Yates' men took a quick count of the number of Confederate soldiers inside the various rooms in the building. There were in fact more confined here than the seventy-two soldiers that Stackhouse admitted to; unfortionately nearly a third of them were already dead with another dozen or more at death's door. The entire building reeked with the smell of death. After a quick walk through of the building it was obvious to James, that there was no way Lieutenant Yates's men could move or care for these critically injured men. Returning to the front of this old colonial mansion, he found Colonel Stackhouse sitting on an empty ammunition box, resting.

"Colonel, I am sorry but we cannot move your men. If we take them with us, many of them will die. Some will have a chance to survive if we leave them here and I send our medical teams in to attend to their needs. We shall leave our water and rations, a dozen or so of your men are ambulatory and they can take care of the injured until we get medical aid in here. However, I want you to put out a couple of those white sheets in the windows and caution your men; should anyone of them fire on our troops when they return, the results could be disastrous for your people."

"I understand that, Captain. I shall see to it that none of my soldiers shall initiate any action that may jeopardize their safety."

"Fair enough, Colonel; as soon as we secure this area I shall bring in our medical teams to care for your men."

"Jesus, Captain I did not expect to run into that, I thought we might run into a firefight or two but not a whole bunch of Johnnie Rebs left behind by their own forces to die. What the hell kind of an army are we fighting." Lieutenant Yates commented, shaking his head.

"It's a desperate one, Lieutenant," James responded, "I have only been at this business for a short time and you're just getting your feet wet, but I assure you it will get worse. I hate to think of what will happen as the South becomes more desperate to hold on, and the Union puts more pressure on General Grant to end this nightmare. It looks to me like this siege of the City Petersburg may continue for months and thousands will die before it's over."

"God, I hope you are wrong, Captain."

"I do too, Lieutenant, but I don't think I am. Listen!" James, exclaimed, "It sounds like one of our platoons has come across some of our southern boys that do not want to surrender."

It was near daybreak when C Company rejoined the regiment; with Captain McCaffrey reporting in to Colonel Kelly, "I believe we were successful in accomplishing our mission, Sir. We lost two men, with four wounded, yet we captured about three-hundred Confederate soldiers. Nearly all surrendered without a fight, they were scattered all over hell out there, many wounded among them from their encounter with Fifth Corps, with little or no medical assistance. I think most of them were glad it is over. They have been without food and in some cases water, for two or three days. Our people became involved in two firefights, and in the process captured about fifty soldiers that chose to fight including four wounded officers. We killed two others. One of the prisoners is a brigadier. Several of them need immediate medical attention or they probably won't survive long."

"That's too bad James, but they will have to wait, our artillery and medical and supply wagons are still bogged down by this mud; another day, possibly two before they get through to us. Fifth Corps has taken some of our critical injured, but the Rebs kicked the hell out of them last week and they are still reeling from that."

"Jesus, Colonel," James responded, his lips pursed and shaking his head, "We have nearly one-hundred wounded Rebs hold-up in an abandoned farm house about three miles into the breach; there was no way we could bring them out. I was hoping we could get our medical people to them right away; if we don't, I think most of them will die."

"Unfortionately James, that's the fortunes of war; they won't get much sympathy from Fifth Corps folks as the Rebs damn near decimated their infantry boys last week and that's Fifth Corps' territory. They will be going back into the breach today and taking out whatever stragglers your men missed last night. God help 'em. Get some rest, James. You look like you need it."

"Hi Jimmy," Michael called out to his older brother sitting on the ground in the warm sun with his back against a tree. Since their incursion into the breached lines of Fifth Corps a week ago, C Company, Sixty-Ninth Regiment had rested for two days then went into a resupply and retraining mode in preparation for a major move to breach the Rebs' defensive lines around Petersburg.

"Hi, Michael, come join me; what have you been up to?"

"Mostly what the Army does, Jimmy, waiting. By the time we got into position last week, the Sixty-Ninth had pretty well taken care of Johnnie Reb and right now, we are again into training and resupplying our people. With the amount of food and ammunition we are stock-piling it looks like the General is getting ready for another massive attack on the Rebs hold-up here in Petersburg."

"You're right, Michael, General Grant is here, and he will be leading our next attempt to breach their lines. You know what's going to happen when he is present, one hell'u've a lot of people are going to die."

"Yes, I know that, Jimmy, but I don't want to talk about it," Michael replied, with a note of sadness evident in his voice. "What have you heard from home, Jimmy? Since we have secured the rail lines again between here and Washington, our mail has caught up to us at a good rate. I received four letters the other day, they were from the girls, written nearly two months ago, but since then I got one mailed last month. Uncle Paul sent several clippings from the New York papers; they were all about the war and a small clipping from the Cork Examiner. It wasn't much, another sailing of the Island of Jersey for America with two or three-hundred Irishmen leaving the country, that's all."

"Yeah, I know, but I don't care anymore; as they say here in America that really is the "Old Country" and I don't care anymore what happens over there. What did the New York papers have to say about this war? Is there any hope that this damn thing will be over soon?" James asked his brother as if looking for something that would provide a glimmer of hope that this terrible conflagration would soon end.

"Not really, I brought them along; read them when you get a chance. They call this thing we are doing here, the Siege of Petersburg. I suppose that is as good a name as any for this mucked-up chaos we have ourselves into, it has been going on for weeks. It does not appear that this will end anytime soon. We all know what happens when General Grant takes command; the newsboys don't need to tell us that."

"Well, maybe he will end it soon and we can all go home." James replied wistfully.

"I heard what they are saying about what the Fifth Corps people did when they went back into no-man's land. I heard it was a real slaughter; did you hear that Jimmy?"

"Yes, I thought that could happen and I warned the Reb Colonel that if any of their people fired on our troops, it might happen."

"But, they say it was the Colonel himself, Jimmy that fired. Someone said he took the white flags down, then stood outside the front of the mansion, and fired on the approaching troops. That's when our artillery opened up and nearly leveled the entire building."

"I can only presume what happened, Michael. I told the Colonel that I would have our medical folks come in to care for his troops as soon as possible; it took five days Michael before Fifth Corps got here. By that time, most of his people must have died; can you imagine what he must have thought about us. Captain Kelly told me Stackhouse graduated from West Point; he was a professional soldier with the American Army before the war started. In effect he lived and died by a code of honor instilled in him at West Point; I violated that code and dishonored him and me in the process."

"Jesus Christ, Jimmy, it wasn't your fault that you never got back in there to get those people out. Moreover, what about him, he took an oath to defend this country from all enemies both foreign and domestic; he turned against his own people."

"I know, however I should have done more to insist upon rescuing those poor devils."

"We attack at sunrise tomorrow, gentlemen," Brigadier General Owen McMahan announced to all members of the Brigade command staff assembled in the Mess Tent for a briefing. General Grant shall lead the attack in person; the Sixty-Ninth, the Second and the Thirty-Second Regiment and the Fifth Corps, will take the lead. Our artillery shall commence firing on the rebel entrenchments on Boydton Plank Road here, where it intersects the *South Side Railroad* tracks," he said, using his riding crop as a pointer to indicate the area on a large map of the Petersburg area. "At the same time, as a diversion, the Second and Ninth Corps Artillery shall open fire on the Reb entrenchments at Fort Steadman, located here, two miles north of the railroad, at this location," he added, again using his riding crop as a pointer. "Our artillery shall continue firing until nine o'clock; when it ends we, along with the Eighty-Sixth shall attack; our objective is to breach the Reb lines on the Boydton Road rail crossing and enter Petersburg. Hopefully that will be the end of this deadly war."

CHAPTER 10

LETTERS

As promised the shelling of the entrenched Confederate troops at Petersburg, Virginia continued without let up for three hours. Captain McCaffrey and others of the Sixty-Ninth New York Regiment wondered if the American Army would run out of ammunition. Yet there was no fear of that, for in June General Grant decided Petersburg was the key to putting an end to this war. The capture and destruction of the Confederate rail links to the South at Petersburg would deny Richmond the ability to resupply their troops throughout Virginia. Grant needed that to put an end to the war and issued a priority message to his staff, "We must take Petersburg at all costs; it is the primary target that will open the floodgates into the Reb fortress."

For two months, the army moved tons of supplies into the two large ordinance depots established behind Union lines outside of Petersburg. From there, Conestoga supply wagons moved thousands of mortar rounds and 12 and 20 pounder shells including both explosive and canister shot directly to the front line troops whom, by this time encircled Petersburg on three sides.

When the shelling ceased, General Grant signaled his Corps and Division commanders to move against the Petersburg breastworks. "Let's move gentlemen," General Owen McMahan called out to Colonels Jack Kelly and Robert Jenkins regimental commanders who would spearhead the attack upon the Confederate soldiers entrenched at the rail crossing on Boydton Road. If successful in breaching the entrenched forces at this location, General McMahan's orders were to open a path and hold it, for Fifth Corps' thrust into the city.

Moving swiftly on a cavalry mount across an open field before his assembled regiment Colonel Jack Kelly called out in a loud voice, "You and I shall take the lead on this one, gentleman," he called out to James, and Glen Michelson. "However, let us send out two scouts first to test their strength. There is still no sign that they are prepared to stand firm and resist our attack. Let us see what they have to offer."

Neither Colonel Kelly, nor his two company commanders needed to wait long for the Confederate response, as the two scouts approached within rifle range of the defensive breastworks, both died in a hail of musket fire from within the Confederate lines. The sight of two of their own lying dead on the roadway ahead clearly indicated to the men of the Sixty-Ninth what lie ahead for them. Kelly, a veteran of several battles knew his only option was to attack; there was no other choice as his orders were firm.

"Let's go boys, let's put an end to this war here today. Give your best to Captain McCaffrey and Captain Michelson and to your country," he yelled, waving his hat in the air. His mount straining at the bit seemed to sense the excitement. "Rifles, ready, attack, attack now;" Kelly yelled, "let's get these bastards so we can go home."

A roar of support came from his troops as he, now on foot, accompanied by James moved at a fast pace toward the Reb breastworks, still no enemy soldier had shown himself. When they came within a few yards of the Reb fortification the breastworks across the roadway erupted into a roar of flame and smoke. Flashes of gunfire and black and grey smoke emitted from more than a hundred openings between the breastworks of logs and rocks set up across Boydton Road, stacked to the height of a man's head along the full length of the barricade.

Unfortunately, Colonel Kelly was hit almost immediately, the force of the missal spinning him around, where he went down on one knee, but he was back up quickly, yelling commands, ordering his men on and encouraging them. "Return fire;" he shouted, "shoot at the smoke from their muskets, or find a slot between the logs. Their gun ports are a foot or two above the ground and at eye level. Concentrate your fire there. Reload quickly and keep firing."

James rushed from one platoon to another repeating Colonel Kelly's orders. "Take careful aim and if you cannot see a Reb, fire into the smoke and keep firing at those open slots; remember, a foot or two above ground and also at eye level. Don't let up; we want to take these people down today." Fortunately, the weather worked to the advantage of Union forces. The dirty black and grey pall of smoke and dust, from more than five thousand guns across the battlefield proved to be of some benefit to the attacking force. Smoke obscured the area to such an extent that after the initial assault the Rebs could not see their attackers allowing Captain Michelson's men to move in close to the rock and log barriers and fire directly into the open gun ports.

While that was taking place, James climbed up on the wall of this fortress and signaled his men to follow; nearly one-hundred men followed their company commander, quickly scaling to the top of the revetment. From there they could fire directly down upon the Confederate defenders. With Michelson's men firing directly into the Reb gun ports and C Company seemingly well ensconced on top of the wall, Kelly ordered his remaining forces to move on over the wall and signaled General McMahan of his intentions. Yet before the Fifth Corps could mount this offensive move, the Confederates counter attacked. The Rebel Commander came to the aid of his badly mauled defenders first by firing a withering barrage of canister shot that stopped the Union advance in its tracks. Then, Reb infantry troops quickly finished off those Union soldiers who had penetrated the Reb fortress along with those yet to make it off the wall. James took a bullet that shattered his rifle stock and ricochet into his shoulder knocking him off the entrenchment.

Colonel Kelly, anguishing over the terrible mauling his men were taking, looked around for General McMahan and not finding him, ordered a retreat. "Retreat, retreat," he called out in a weakened voice from the base of the Reb fortress, which was quickly relayed throughout the Union ranks. "Jimmy, have them pick up our wounded and move back quickly," he said, yet by this time there were too few able-bodied men left unscathed to carry off the wounded.

"I will Colonel," James replied, but the man so many admired and respected never heard his captain's reply. Colonel Kelly died in a ditch along the Boydton Road, along with several hundred other young men in blue who perished in this early morning assault upon the Confederate stronghold at Petersburg.

With the dead and wounded members of the Sixty-Ninth mounting rapidly, Colonel Jenkins ordered the Thirty-Second in to support Colonel Kelly's troops, now pinned down in the ditches alongside Boydton Road and at the base of the Reb entrenchments.

However, it was not long before Jenkins people also faced the full force of the Confederate Army of Northern Virginia. When the Thirty-Second charged forward, the ferocity of musket fire from this desperate group of Southerners bent on destroying the Army of the Potomac nearly devastated the Thirty-Second Regiment. Nightfall provided a reprieve for both regiments from this failed assault upon the Reb lines. The daylong battle resulted in the near destruction of two Union regiments. Still General McMahan, complying with Grant's orders rushed the Fifth Corps into a night assault upon the Confederate fortress. By midnight, his men had once again breached the Reb lines in two locations, but were driven back by the 12 and 16 pound explosive shells and deadly canister shot fired at pointblank range from a hundred Reb guns. This withering barrage of concentrated cannon fire killed or wounded more than two hundred Union soldiers.

Among the dead were Brigadier General Owen McMahan, Colonel Jack Kelly, Sixty-Ninth New York Infantry Regimental Commander, and Captains Edward Jones, Commander of A Company, Glen Michelson, B Company commander, three platoon lieutenants, and more than two dozen non-commissioned officers, along with dozens of soldiers from the Sixty-Ninth. Over two hundred others suffered injuries of various degrees from bullet wounds to broken limbs. Captain James McCaffrey was lucky he suffered no disabling injuries; yet he still needed medical attention and reported to the Aid Station for the removal of lead and wood splinters from his arm and chest.

The following afternoon James walked out of the Aid Station and began looking for his younger brother. Earlier in the day while talking to officers from the Thirty-Second, he learned a Reb soldier shot Michael while he led his men in a desperate attempt to scale the barricade. Hoping that Michel was still alive; he walked the long lines of wounded men lying on the ground awaiting transport to the railhead to board the train for Washington. Not finding him, he began to call-out Michael's name, receiving no response he shouted, "Does anyone know where Lieutenant Michael McCaffrey is?" The answer came almost immediately from a man standing in front of one of the surgery tents wearing a bloodstained apron and smoking a cigarette.

"He is in here, Captain." The man replied, "I am Doctor John Hubbard; we are having some difficulties with him. What is your connection, Captain with Lieutenant McCaffrey?" The doctor asked.

"I am his brother, Doctor. He and I are with the Sixty-Ninth; what is the problem Doctor. How badly is he injured?"

"He was hit with a Minie ball in the arm and he has lost a lot of blood, the elbow joint is shattered and there is no way that I can save his arm and he won't let me remove it surgically. His chances for survival are good if we act now; if we delay he will probably die within a day or two."

"Jesus, Doc, isn't there any alternative? He's just a kid." James asked, quietly. "Isn't there something we can do?"

"Look around you, Captain and tell me what you see." Doctor Hubbard responded, "There are four-hundred injured kids here, as you call them; they are waiting transport out by wagon train to the railhead, that is four or five miles or so from here. Some of them will not be alive when they get there and others shall die on the train before they ever reach Washington. My options are limited, with surgery, he shall have a chance to live to a ripe old age and enjoy his children and grandchildren; without surgery, he will probably die within the month from infection or gangrene. He will not listen to me; if you want your brother to go home you best convince that boy, as you call him, that life without an arm is better than no life at all."

"Hello, James," Michael called out as his brother walked through the open tent flap to where he was lying on a wooden table set up on two saw-horses. "I knew that was you as soon as I heard you yell out there. Thank God, you're alive."

"Aye, Michael, yes we are both alive and we are going to stay that way; it's going to take more than a few bloody Rebs to kill us." James replied, quietly, reaching out and grabbing Michael's uninjured right arm, his other stroking his brother's blood smeared forehead. "The bastards nicked you pretty bad, didn't they?"

"I'm afraid it's more than a nick, Jimmy. Doctor Hubbard wants to take my arm off. I cannot let him do that Jimmy. How would I get by without an arm; hell I might as well be dead."

"Let's talk about it, Michael. There may be something more important in this world than an arm. You and I made a promise to Mother and Daddy in Ireland that we would take care of Katelyn and our younger brothers. You remember that, Katelyn is gone; we could not do anything about that. However, we have Daniel and Thomas to worry about when this war is over; and then there is Joseph. You and I promised each other we would go find him and bring him home and that is what I thought we were going to do; but I cannot do this alone. I need your help."

"I know, but Jesus Christ, Jimmy what can a one-armed man do. I won't even be able to tie my own shoes."

"You can learn how to tie your shoes; look at all the soldiers who we've seen this past year and a half that have gone home without an arm. If you think about it, a whole lot of them left this man's army without a leg and others with no arms at all. They all went home because that is where their loved ones are. Colleen's sisters and Shannon have been good about writing to you. All of them, Auntie Ruth, Thomas, and Daniel believe something good will come out of this war and that includes you and me and Joseph going home. So you think about that."

"I know what you are trying to do, Jimmy, but Jesus I don't want to be a cripple the rest of my life and wind up in the Poor House."

"You will not be a cripple the rest of your life, Michael. In this country of ours, Michael, and it is ours, we have earned the right to be here. You can be whatever you want to be, a farmer, a teacher a lawyer and even a priest if you want too and no one can stop you except yourself. However, Doctor Hubbard tells me that if he does not take your arm off, the downside of this is probably death within a month from infection or gangrene. Your elbow is shattered and they don't have the medical know how, nor the equipment here in the field to repair it."

"OK, James, I'll take Hubbard's advice," Michael responded weakly. "I won't like it, but looking at the alternative, I really do want to live out my life in this country of ours, as you call it."

"Good boy, Michael, I'll tell Doc Hubbard."

"You'll be here, James?" He asked, quietly.

"I'll be here, Michael I will go to the railhead and see you off on the train for home, so don't worry, OK?"

"I won't worry, James, after our go around with the Rebs yesterday, I won't be afraid of anything the future has to hold for us. Besides, I want to know how this thing here at Petersburg ends."

"We have your brother on board now, Captain and we are anxious to get this train moving; so you best say your goodbyes. He is in good hands; we will take good care of him." The young lieutenant serving in the Medical Transportation

Corps said to James as the two men watched the last of the ambulatory patients make their way on board the hospital train bound for Washington.

"How many injured men are you taking out?" James asked

"About three-hundred today; yesterday there were a few less, but of a higher priority than these men. Most of those soldiers were in immediate need of hospitalization; your brother and these fellows here are in good shape compared to those boys. It seems like every time General Grant visits the Petersburg battle group we need a greater carrying capacity to take out the wounded." He laughed.

James was aware of the charges of failed leadership against Grant espoused by some members of Congress and in the press, yet not amused by this soldier's disingenuous remarks so guilefully directed at their commanding officer. He could not countenance such criticism from a fellow officer without a response. He delivered a rebuke immediately, his voice cold and hard.

"General Grant fights, Lieutenant, he wants us to win this damn war and that's what these men have been fighting for; so let's not forget that."

The young lieutenant made no further reply.

"Are you okay, Michael, can I get you anything before the train pulls out?"

"No, I'm fine, Jimmy," he responded with a weak smile."I think Doc Hubbard has loaded me up with so much laudanum that I will probably sleep all the way to Washington."

"That's good, you need the rest, and don't worry. You are safe. I like what the Army is doing for our people. Doc Hubbard and his staff are doing their best under very difficult circumstances, for our injured soldiers."

"I know that, Jimmy, hell I feel fine now," his brother responded sounding more confident than just hours ago when he and James talked about Michael's future.

Still James believed it his duty to advise his younger brother of the tragedy that befell his fellow soldiers in this latest battle.

"Michael, are you aware that Captain Kelly was killed yesterday?" He asked, his voice muted and strained, for he knew Michael regarded the Captain as a friend and one of the best persons he had ever known.

"Yes, Jimmy, I know that. I just heard that from a couple of soldiers from B Company who were loaded onto the train with me. You and I will miss him and Joseph too. Joseph idealized the man. It's such a shame that fellows like him are taken," Michael responded, quietly as he began to drift off from the effects of laudanum. "It doesn't make much sense, but I guess it's God's will," he said as he drifted off to sleep.

Petersburg, Virginia
July 10, 1864

Dear Auntie Ruth and Uncle Paul,

I saw Michael off on the train to Washington today; he asked me to tell you that he is well, but shall be hospitalized for a week or two in Washington before he goes on to New York. It is with much sadness that I tell you he lost his left arm in our fight with the rebels here at Petersburg. Michael courageously led his platoon in an assault upon enemy forces in which we suffered severe casualties; he and his fellow soldiers performed heroically yet many of them died in their valiant attempt to dislodge General Lee's people from this city. The Confederate soldiers are well entrenched and it looks like we shall have a tough and prolonged struggle ahead of us. We have been on the line here for nearly three months now and there is no sign that the Rebs are willing to concede an inch of territory.

However, do not worry about Michael; right now, he is quite depressed over the loss of his arm, but he is a tough kid; he will do okay. The Army transfers most of our injured from the Sixty-Ninth to Saint Mary's Hospital in New York before they muster out. Should you have time I am sure he would like you to visit him there.

I stay well, and I hope this letter finds you two that way. Give Thomas and Daniel a hug for me and my best to Sarah and the girls.

Your nephew,
James McCaffrey

New York
August 15,

Dear James,

Your letter of July 10, reached us today so there has been some improvement in the mail service. Thank you for telling us about Michael. You may be surprised however, that we learned of Michael's injury yesterday from Colleen; she came across his name quite by accident on a hospital admittance roster. He arrived at Saint Mary's on Tuesday last. Even though he knew she worked there, he made no effort to contact her, nor me or Ruth. Colleen was quite distressed when she saw him; he was in the amputee ward with two or three dozen other soldiers from the Sixty-Ninth and Seventy-Second New York Regiments.

Ruth and I immediately went to the hospital to see him and at first; he was reluctant to meet with either one of us. The doctors told us he is doing quite well physically, yet is experiencing some emotional problems with his physical handicap. They assured us that what he is going through is quite normal and in time, he should overcome this challenge. We visited for nearly an hour and when we left, Colleen walked us out. She plans to drop in on him two or three times during her shift; as you may know she works nights in an adjacent ward. Michael does not want the boys to see him this way so we shall honor his wishes and wait awhile before we take Thomas and Daniel to the hospital.

In following the war news in the New York papers and after visiting with Michael, we of course are quite concerned for your safety. Michael told us that your regiment has lost nearly sixty-five percent of your men while serving under General Grant in Virginia. I am reluctant to say this but Grant appears to be quite callous or cold hearted in the use of his troops. The press is very critical of him, with his aggressive tactics and they allege he has needlessly cost the lives of thousands of our boys. I do not believe that, but the public knows very little about what you and your men are doing or have experienced at Petersburg. Michael is a firm supporter of the Army, particularly of those officers he knew personally. Even after all the stress and pain he has undergone he totally supports General Grant. With men like you and Michael, it bodes well for the future of our country.

Good luck to you, Son; I have enclosed some news clippings from the Irish Times and the Examiner in Cork that are very favorable toward your mother and father. You will learn from these, what really happened in Mala the day your father died. As you will see, Lord Willingham's people killed him after they forced him off your grandfather's land. The Crown's statements of your father's alleged criminal activities do not jibe with the facts; and surprisingly the press condemned the Crown's activities in this sad episode.

Your Auntie Ruth will fill you in on the boys in her letter; they are doing fine in school and are a credit to their Irish heritage.

Your Uncle Paul and Auntie Ruth.

New York
September 1, 1864

Dearest Jimmy,

I know your Aunt and Uncle have told you of me running across Michael accidentally here at Saint Mary's Hospital. I found him in the amputee ward; I really was surprised to see him and he was practically right across the hall from my station. I am still on nights and things are going well for Shannon and me. We have a flat in Brooklyn, not far from the hospital. She works the day shift in the orthopedic ward so it is convenient for both of us.

I did not tell you and Michael assures me no one else has told you this but you are the father of our baby, a boy who is almost a year old now. His name is John Robert McCaffrey; I named him after you and your father. I thought that you might have guessed something was amiss when I left home and Shannon and I found a place to live close to where we work.

My Father and Mother have been good to me and helped financially, so your son is well taken care of. I am sorry I cannot say I am pleased with the attitude of some of my other relatives toward me and our baby, particularly the older women; but you know the Irish, an unwed mother is a curse.

Notwithstanding that your Auntie Ruth, Uncle Paul, and the boys, including Father O'Herlihy have been supportive. However, with this terrible war now going into its fourth year, for most people here in New York it is a non-issue. Widows with young children are as common in this city as the proverbial summer breeze.

Father Kirk is still in the Army, but his ministry is here in New York where so many members of the Sixty-Ninth and Seventy-Second are receiving medical care in our hospitals.

I have enclosed a picture of your son, and have told you about him after discussing this with Father Kirk and Michael. Michael can be very persuasive when he wants to be. He told me all about the Siege at Petersburg, much more about it than what we see or read about in the newspapers. He warned me that you, as an infantry officer are much more likely, God forbid, to become a casualty in that horrible bloody, protracted siege in Virginia and that something could happen to you. He said I would regret it if you became a casualty and never learned that you are the father of the sweetest little boy you can imagine.

I love you James Robert McCaffrey

Colleen.

New York

August 27

Hi Jimmy, I thought I had better tell you that I am responsible for persuading Colleen to tell you about your son. I convinced her that she should not keep it a secret from you any longer. I have known about the birth of your son for more than six months, but I did not believe it was my responsibility to tell you about him. Both Shannon and Catherine wrote to me and told me that I should tell you about him, but I figured that was Colleen's decision, not mine. However, when I got home, I told her she was making a terrible mistake in not telling you. The boy is beautiful and Colleen has done a great job in caring for him; you will be pleased when you see what awaits you here.

By the way, I can tie my own shoes now, with one hand. Daniel showed me how and it is not that hard, he really is a smart kid. He must have grown at least six inches since we left and he acts like a typical young lad. He tells everyone that he is "almost" fifteen years old. I have to laugh at that. He and Thomas are both doing well in school and both have newspaper delivery routes in the city. I am back in civilian clothes now and feel a little strange about it and I have applied for a couple of jobs. A locale restaurateur has offered to teach me how to become a chef; I am not sure that is what I would like to do for the rest of my life. I still dream of us settling on our own homestead in the Northwest. We will see.

Uncle Paul gave me several clippings from the Irish press regarding the incident at Mala; I have not read all of them yet, but will soon. I am not surprised at what Daddy did; at least he took a couple of the Crown's henchmen with him; the dirty bastards!

The news from Virginia does not sound good; General Grant was in Washington a week or two ago but the press has indicated he has gone back to Petersburg. After our mishaps with him in July, I am not sure that bodes well for you or the people in the Sixty-Ninth. Take care, Jimmy.

Your brother,

Michael

Petersburg, Virginia
Oct. 24,

Hi Michael,

Thanks for your letter of August 27. I am happy for you that your rehabilitation is going so well and that you have improved to the point that you are out looking for employment. Keep it up and by the time Joseph and I get home you can teach both of us a new trade. However, I told Colleen that when the war is over, you and I were interested in filing for a homestead somewhere, possibly in the Northwest. She has looked into it and wrote that land is available for homesteading in Michigan, Minnesota, Wisconsin, and Missouri, and even out in the Territories. I would like you and Colleen to choose a place and we will discuss it when Joseph and I come home. I was hoping that the war would be over in a few more months; however, you may recall that is what I said at this time last year.

A lot of probing here at Petersburg for soft spots interspersed with heavy shelling and minor incursions into the Reb lines. Our Regiment lost about four-hundred men, and we are not yet up to full strength. Replacements are hard to come by. General Grant has returned from Washington so we expect to see some heavy fighting soon. Our artillery forces have pounded the devil out of the Rebs here but they still show no indication that they are want to give up. Their snipers have taken a toll on our troops, particularly among the officer ranks.

The Pennsylvania boys blew a huge hole in the Confederate entrenchment lines and the Negro regiments moved in as we did earlier this year; but they took a hell'u've a shellacking. The Rebs drove them back and then rebuilt their defensive structure; it looks like it soon may be our turn once again.

My best to Uncle Paul and Auntie Ruth and the boys; look in on Colleen and your new nephew for me when you can.

Your brother,

James.

October 25, 1864

Petersburg, Virginia

My Dearest Colleen (and our Son John Robert McCaffrey),

Thank you for telling me about our Son and sending his picture--he is beautiful and I am so excited and pleased that you told me about him. I have shown his picture to almost everyone here in camp, with lots of smiles and favorable comments about this newly born Irish/American kid. Some of them even say he looks like me. Wow, that is a real a compliment. Give him a hug for me. I am anxious to see both you and him. I hope that this bloody war will soon be over and we shall be together again.

We will be moving out tomorrow morning for another go at the Rebs hold up in Petersburg--it looks like we have enough people and supplies this time that we should prevail in driving them out from behind their fortifications and that should end this terrible war. There are lots of newspaper people here looking on so you should know the outcome before you receive this letter. Do not worry about me. I still have a minor medical problem with my left arm so they assigned me to limited duty for a few more days. By that time, the war should be over and we shall head for home.

I love you (and our Son),

James

Long Island, New York
November 1, 1864

Captain James McCaffrey
New York Sixty-Ninth Regiment
Army of the Potomac

Dear Captain McCaffrey,

My name is Ellen Kelly; I am the wife/widow of Colonel Jack C. Kelly formerly with the New York Sixty-Ninth Regiment, and from my husband's correspondence, I learned that you served in his command in the Army of the Potomac for the past two-years. He frequently mentioned you and your brothers in his letters telling us of your Irish background and your high principles and trustworthiness while the three of you served our country. He mentioned that when the war was over he would like to go the "Old Country" as he calls Ireland and see its marvelous wonders and picturesque lands and villages you described to him. He was nearly infatuated with that wonderfully enchanted land of yours and his ancestors. Although plagued by the injustices of a totalitarian ruler, the Irish never seemed to lose their love for Ireland.

This, Captain is my way of introducing myself so that you may not think I am a crazed Army widow when I ask you to tell our family about Jack's army experience in this terrible war and where and how he died. The receipt of the War Department's notification of Jack's death was a cold, mind numbing bitter experience. I shall never forget it. However, I want our children to know, and I want to know personally how he met his fate in this terrible war. I know he was brave, but I need to hang onto every moment that God gave us, even though it has been more than two years since we were together.

I would be forever grateful should you choose to honor my request; Jack and I only had six years together, yet for two of those years you were privy to his very presence, aware of his kindheartedness, compassion, love of live, and country and of his fellow soldiers. All I ask is that you share with us a small portion of those two years. I know that is asking much of you. However, even to acquire a bit of information on my husband's last days on this earth would be more than this cold cruel notification from the War Department that told us of his death in Virginia.

I pray for your wellbeing and hope that I may hear from you soon.

Sincerely,
Ellen Kelly

December 17, 1864
Army of the Potomac
Petersburg, Virginia

Dear Mrs. Kelly,

It is a privilege to respond to your request for information about your deceased husband and my friend Colonel Jack Kelly. It was an honor to hear that Colonel Kelly considered me a friend, and to have served with him in the Sixty-Ninth Regiment. Later I shall commit to paper and forward to you a complete history covering Colonel Kelly's exceptional career with the Sixty-Ninth. During these past nearly two years he and I formed a bond of comradeship that I shall always treasure.

However, may I suggest that you contact my brother Michael; he is presently in Saint Mary's Hospital in New York City. If upon receipt of this letter, he is no longer there, please contact Nurse Colleen Haggerty in the Orthopedic Section and she will know where he is. Both Michael and our brother Joseph and I were friends of Colonel Kelly. Michael and I were with the Colonel during his last hours. I shall write to Michael and tell him of your request. You will find him to be a wonderful young man and he will be happy to talk to you about your husband.

I hope that we may meet someday when I return to New York.

Sincerely,

James R. McCaffrey, Captain
New York Sixty-Ninth Regiment

Captain James McCaffrey was not the only company commander from the Sixty-Ninth Regiment to receive letters from complete strangers whose brothers, sons, or husbands died in the stalemated siege at Petersburg. Dozens of other Union Army commanders were also in receipt of such letters.

Returning to his tent after ten days on the front lines at Petersburg, James found the mail clerk holding 27 letters addressed to Captain James McCaffrey, C Company, Sixty-Ninth New York Regiment. On many of them his name was misspelled, either printed or in crude hand written form, or simply addressed Captain Mack, C Company, 69th Regiment, Virginia.

"I checked the return addressee's last name, against the old C Company's roster, Captain and it looks like the last name, at least in most cases, matches one of your boys that lost his life on the Boydton Road attack. I'm sorry about that, but our lieutenant says I must deliver all of them as addressed to their company commander."

"I understand that, Private. Just give me what you have and I'll handle them."

"Yes, Sir, but the lieutenant never told me what to do with those directed to Captain's Michelson and Jones. He said I was not to stamp them Undeliverable or Deceased."

"How many do you have, Private?" James asked the young man.

"About fifty, Sir, and I don't know what to do with them."

"Oh, God," James groaned, shaking his head, then responded. "Bring them all to me, Private; we'll work something out."

CHAPTER 11

AMBUSH

"Good Morning, General, I am Captain James McCaffrey, Sir." James saluted as he approached the one-star general, Charles Murray, a man he had heard much about, but never met before. The general was sitting at a makeshift desk inside the Quartermaster's tent.

"You sent for me, Sir?"

"Good morning," the general responded. "Yes I did, thank you for coming." He returned the younger man's salute then standing, extending his hand. "It is great to meet you. I have heard a good deal about you, Captain and it is my pleasure. Please sit here and we will have a cup of coffee and a bite to eat. Have you had breakfast yet?" General Murray asked.

"Yes, I have, thank you, Sir."

"I assumed so, you youngsters are up earlier than fellows of my age," the man added, smiling. "However, please join me; my orderly will bring us some coffee. I wanted to talk to you Captain about what has been happening here in the Sixty-Ninth Sector and what steps you have taken to prepare your people for our next assault upon the rebels ensconced behind these rather formidable entrenchments. I understand that you have taken over Captain Edwards and Michelson's duties also, is that Correct?"

"Yes, Sir General, there really wasn't anyone else available after the Boydton Road encounter with the Rebs, and Colonel Gibbs asked me to help out."

"Yes, Gibbs told me that however, I also want to know if you feel you have recovered sufficiently from your wounds to take on additional responsibilities."

"I am fine, Sir. My arm muscle is still a little sore, but it is healing quite well. I am ready and able to handle the Company. What few replacements we have received, are training with our veteran soldiers now; we shall be prepared to move against the Confederates when you call upon us."

"That's good to hear, Captain but because of the weather General Grant has rescinded his order for the next assault upon Petersburg. We shall continue our siege, but hunker down for the winter while we resupply and train our replacements. We will continue to harass the rebs at every opportunity. Moreover, as the Sixty-Ninth is most familiar with this area they shall again spearhead the attack in the spring. Once we have breached the Reb entrenchments the Brigade will mount a full-scale attack pushing through the breach in the Reb lines and move on into the City of Petersburg. Our tactics shall be somewhat similar to our earlier attack, except for two major differences. Three battalions of artillery shall lay siege to the Confederate forces with a continuous barrage with 12, 20, and 36 pounders, firing without let up for as long as necessary. We shall mount an assault upon Fort Stedman at the same time, using similar tactics.

"General Grant believes those two-pronged attacks shall overwhelm Rebs' defensive capabilities which will lead to a successful conclusion to this campaign. The Confederates have tied up nearly one-quarter of our resources here for over eight months and weather permitting we shall put an end to this in the spring and move on to Richmond. The General believes that the civil population here and the defenders are near starvation; our intelligence supports that. Their supplies are low and living conditions such that a massive assault upon the city's defenses should be enough to overwhelm them.

"However, it will take time to bring our troops into a full readiness mode and I believe that can best be accomplished with less experienced commanders. Having said that I want you to rejoin the Cavalry troops for a winter campaign to interdict and limit the Rebs' repeated efforts to resupply and bring in additional troops from Richmond and up from the Carolinas. During this period of inclement weather, Lee's people at Richmond are sure to mount an attack to save their forces entrenched here at Petersburg. We shall make sure that they fail in that effort. Even so, the Rebs will surely try to resupply their forces here.

"If during this winter we can cut-off supplies to both cities before our spring offensive, we will take Petersburg and Richmond; that shall put an end to this war. With that in mind, I want you to take command of Lieutenant Roberts and Lieutenant Moore's troops; I believe you were with them earlier this year at the River Crossing incident. I want you to move into Reb territory with the view of disrupting their supply routes, both road, rail and river barges. You will be on a hit and run mission. Move in quietly, avoiding their troop concentrations, attacking outposts along their major supply routes, demolishing whatever means of transportation they may be utilizing. It will not be a matter of simply attacking their supply centers, for I want you to find and destroy every bridge between Richmond and the Carolinas. We need to cut Reb supplies coming in from the surrounding states; we can do that if we lay waste to their railroad bridges between here and the Carolinas.

"Unfortunately, you will also have to put a torch to every ferry boat, barge, train, wagon, and building along their supply routes and kill whatever livestock you find; cattle, horses, pigs and whatever else that may provide sustenance for their troops. If we can starve them out, so be it, it shall save lives in the end, for we shall have fewer enemy soldiers to kill when we attack in the spring. If in this very dangerous incursion into enemy territory, your men are successful our troops might not have to face the horrors of another assault upon the breastworks at Petersburg."

"That would be quite a gift for our troops, Sir." James responded, quietly. "If we can pull it off, which I believe we can."

"Yes, Captain, I would not send a small contingent of our best troops into enemy territory unless I was convinced that they would be successful. You, and Lieutenants Moore and Roberts possess both the experience and wisdom, which I believe is necessary to operate successfully behind our enemy's lines. About one hundred heavily armed troops should be sufficient, moving fast and living off the countryside if necessary. We have two former railroad engineers, presently assigned to our engineering battalions who have prepared explosive supplies and other destructive devices that your men must master before you leave. It's not just a matter of burning their bridges, we must be assured of complete destruction of both their bridges and rails, and also the destruction of whatever is available to the Confederates to repair and restore that which allows them to continue supplying their troops on the battlefield."

It was dark, cold, and snowing lightly on Christmas Eve when a company of the 16th Cavalry, commanded by Captain James R. McCaffrey departed the Union Army's staging depot ten miles south of Petersburg. Army Commanders believed that at this time of year, with the temperature hovering around ten degrees most Confederate spies would be hold-up in a warm enclosure, either a tent, or damaged building in the City of Petersburg and not out in the Virginia hillsides monitoring Union troop movements. Captain McCaffrey, along with Lieutenants Mark Roberts and Stewart Moore headed-up a double column of mounted soldiers of ten sergeants and ninety-two troopers, accompanied by a dozen packhorses carrying supplies, including extra ammunition and more than two-thousand pounds of explosives. By morning, they expected to be miles from the Petersburg entrenchments, with any sign of their track obliterated by falling snow.

They moved silently throughout the night and as dawn approached stopped near an abandoned sawmill to set up a cold camp and rest. Lieutenant Moore sent out a scouting party of Sergeant Brad Adams and two troopers to explore the area west, and north of their present location. The stopover provided James an opportunity to visit with his all-volunteer force to see how they withstood the rigors of the nightlong forced march in the snow. It was a pleasant surprise to have these veterans of a dozen battles gather around as he walked through the bivouac area. Most troopers exhibited a positive attitude toward their new commander and Lieutenant Roberts was quick to note that even though James was half as old as some veteran troops, they appeared genuinely pleased to meet him. Yet it was Roberts himself, who just days ago worked hard to convince the troops that this young man from Ireland earned the right to command. Roberts' litany of successful raids into enemy territory and as a leader of troops that stormed the Confederate breastworks at the Rapidan river crossing and more recently at Petersburg laid the groundwork for this acceptance.

When James posed the question, why these men volunteered for this incursion behind enemy lines, it appeared some were just tired of the long tedious hours in training or the time spent on guard duty. They wanted to get back into the cavalry mode. Others however answered from a somewhat more pragmatic point of view, with one man responding to James' questions gruffly. "Let's get this damn thing over with, Captain. I want to go home to my family. Three years in this man's army is enough for one lifetime."

"We all feel that way," Captain, another man added, then continued. "These secessionist bastards have caused nothing but pain and death and it looks to us like we are going to have to kill 'em all before we get to see our families again."

In response to the man's harsh rhetoric James replied quietly, "I happen to agree with you, soldier. We are in the process of doing that now, and if we do our job right this war will be over soon."

"Wouldn't want to bet an Irish quid on that, would you, Jimmy?" a voice in the rear of the group asked, with Kevin Malone stepping forward, a huge smile on his weather-beaten red face. "Excuse me, Jimmy, I mean Captain," he added as he and his brother Dennis both stepped forward and reached out to shake their cousin's hand.

"What the hell are you two doing here?" James replied, pleasantly surprised to see two members of his family present. "I didn't see you yesterday at the staging area."

"No, we were late; we were off on one of the general's crappy details when we found out that you and our lieutenant were off to win the war all by yourselves."

"Does your sergeant know you're here?" James asked, glancing at Lieutenant Roberts, remembering very well that his two cousins were prone to ignore army regulations or protocols.

"Yes, Sir, Captain," Dennis, responded, "I think Sergeant Moore, excuse me, Lieutenant Moore was glad to get rid of us for awhile." He laughed. "But now that we are back he is happy again."

"I am sorry, Captain," Lieutenant Moore responded, "I neglected to mention this to you," He smiled, "I just assumed as these two jug heads were family and thought you already knew they had been assigned to the Sixteenth."

"No problem, Lieutenant." James replied. "By the way congratulations on your promotion," he added, with a grin. Then turning back to his two cousins, he cautioned them, "You two just remember who the hell your lieutenant is and no more two-man army heroics, okay?"

"We promise, Jimmy," Dennis replied, with a wide grin while glancing at Sergeant Peter Robinson, as if looking for a stamp of approval for their transgressions of the past.

"I'll see to it that they toe the line, Captain," Sergeant Robinson responded, aware of the twins' tendency to overstep army procedures. "Lieutenant Roberts filled me in on their daredevil proclivities."

Later James commented to Lieutenant Roberts, "Mark, you know what my concern is with those two, they are good soldiers, but they take too many chances. That may get them killed, heaven forbid, but in doing so I hope they don't do something foolish and jeopardize someone else's safety."

"I think they have learned a lot since the Rapidan attacks, but Lieutenant Moore already warned Sergeant Robinson they were a problem for him when he was

their sergeant. Robinson will keep a tight rein on them."
"Good."

"We saw no sign of life or rebel activity, Captain." Sergeant Adams reported as he and his scouts returned from their patrol and dismounted. "It was still snowing lightly in some places so our sight distances were somewhat limited; however we saw two columns of smoke, approximately twenty miles distance. It was hard to tell what it was coming from. If I were to guess, I would say it was more likely a farmhouse or small village, possibly a campsite, but not a train; at least there was no movement to indicate a train."

"What about track; any sign of the railroad yet." Lieutenant Roberts asked his sergeant.

"No, nothing, Sir. There was neither a depression, nor a trail cut through the trees or brush that we could see just lots and lots of snow. It was at least a foot deep in places with some drifts four to five feet high."

"Well let's take a look at the maps the engineers provided," James said as he unrolled a map provided by the former railroad men embedded with the Engineers. "We knew when we left base it would take us two to three days to reach the Danville, Richmond main rail line. However, there are a whole series of privately owned, short haul mine or farm to market lines that tie into the Richmond, Lynchburg, Piedmont line to Danville and Greensboro. We can follow any of these smaller rail routes to the main line." He said pointing out on the map what appeared to be the nearest railroad. "As there is no indication that the Confederate forces are patrolling this area, let's pack-up and move on while it is still snowing. It looks like we should run across one of these lines within the next eight or ten miles.

By the time troopers readied the packhorses and their own mounts, it was mid-afternoon when the column got underway. James estimated they had about three more hours of daylight. With Sergeant Adams leading the way, the column moved soundlessly, imperceptibly on. He retraced his earlier track, now nearly covered over by the persistent and sometimes heavy snow flurries. Their mount's hoofs stilled by natures quieting blanked of snow. Only the creek of leather and occasional outburst of a troop aggravated by his mount's failure to respond to rein or spur, broke the stillness of the day.

Near midnight, as the column approached what appeared to be an abandoned coal mine encampment Captain McCaffrey called a halt, sending Sergeant Adams and two troops ahead to investigate. Returning within minutes, Sergeant Adams reported, "It's abandoned, Captain. There are four or five ramshackle outbuildings and a few coal cars and a rail siding. It looks like they just dropped everything and moved off."

"Well, we have seen lots of that. The Rebs are hard up for soldiers; they take them from wherever they can find them. Let's move in and take advantage of the cover while we can. Cold camp, no fires, but be prepared to move quickly should we get company during the night."

Calling Lieutenants Moore and Roberts aside, he counseled them, his tone of voice grim. "This may be our last best opportunity for a rest before we encounter the Rebs so let's take full advantage of it. As we discussed, pickets out, at least one-thousand yards two-hour watches; have the men take care of their mounts, eat, and get some sleep. Tomorrow we shall follow the main rail-line and perhaps we shall find what we seek."

When James awoke, bright sunlight was streaming through the broken windows of what turned out to be an empty tool shed where he and Lieutenant Roberts had been sleeping. Looking out he could see Roberts readying his mount. James' mount, a three-year old Morgan, saddled and tethered nearby was ready to ride.

"Good morning, Mark," he called out to the man. "You should have woke me up."

"No, you haven't slept since we left Petersburg. An officer, like anyone else needs to rest if he is going to make the right call in the field." The soldier replied with a grin. "It's my job to see that happen so we can be sure to live through this little expedition we've taken on here. If I am not mistaken you are going to need it before this day is over."

Pulling on his gloves and hat, and then walking out into a deep snowdrift, James was quick to note that his two lieutenants had the entire troop saddled-up and were apparently waiting for orders.

"What did I miss, Mark?" He asked, solemnly.

"Our pickets have detected quite a bit of movement in a small village about three-miles to the North of us; more than would be expected from a small community here in the foothills. We even have a train there, or at least an engine. In this cold weather sound travels well and the men say they are sure they heard a train whistle and possibly a bell. It's not a mainline road, but all we have to do is follow these tracks, they lead right to the village."

"Good, that's what we came after. Let's you and I and Lieutenant Moore take a look."

Calling for Lieutenant Moore, the three men accompanied by Sergeant Adams rode out to get a better look at their target.

They moved closer spurring their mounts to the top of a brush-covered ridge that would conceal them from those in the small town.

"It looks like a freight train, Captain!" Lieutenant Moore exclaimed, looking through his spyglass, "Maybe, twenty or so cars, some freight, and a few empty coal cars possibly getting ready to load out."

"I don't see any sign of Confederate military, do you?" James asked while examining the layout of the village."

"No, Sir, nothing at all." Sergeant Adams replied.

"Good, let's take this on as our first objective and see how it goes. Lieutenant Moore, take your troop to the east end of town and block any attempt to escape by anyone, military or civilian with particular attention to the train crew should they try to move. Lieutenant Roberts and I shall come at them from here. Two hours should be sufficient to allow you to get into position. Then we shall move on the town from both sides at the same time. Just make sure you get everyone; move them toward the train depot. We will hold them there while we decide the best way to put their mine and this rail line out of business."

Several of the townspeople were pleasantly surprised to see in the early morning sunlight what they thought was a contingent of their own soldiers coming into their village. Their joy was short lived, for they quickly noticed the American flag and blue uniforms as the troops entered the town. Within the hour the train crew, mineworkers, and nearly fifty civilian resident families of the Village of Crystal Springs, some with small children gathered in the town square.

Before the last of them arrived, explosions set-off by members of the Sixteenth Battalion demolition teams reverberated throughout the village as troops destroyed both the above ground mining equipment and set charges deep within the two operating mines nearby. The sound of rifle fire accompanied the explosions as others killed both horses and beef cattle in a nearby stockyard awaiting shipment to Richmond; then set fire to outbuildings including a small warehouse of food supplies destined for the Confederate Army. Unfortunately, the fire quickly spread to other close-by buildings; soon the entire downtown section of the village was ablaze.

James in examining the destruction brought about by his troops was satisfied they had accomplished their objective as ordered by General Murray. Notwithstanding that, he had to fight to hold his emotions in check for never before had he experienced such loathing and hatred now directed at him personally from the residents of this small town. Nevertheless, no one died in the raid. One trooper shot a middle-aged coal miner after the man pulled a gun from his waistband and threatening the life of the soldier, but the man would survive his wound. Yet there was no time to commiserate with the town's citizenry; that could come after their last battle with this vengeful and powerful adversary. He knew the enemy could still do great damage to he and his troops should he forget for a moment the objective of their mission. There would be a time to express sympathy or offer condolences later.

Turning to his two lieutenants, he asked, "Have we taken care of the telegraph?"

"Yes, Sir," Lieutenant Moore responded. "The wires are down and we have their equipment."

"Then burn the depot. What about the train crew?"

"We have both the engineer and the fireman and two brakemen. A train this size should have at least four or five brakemen, but it looks as if two of them discarded their uniforms, such as they are and ran off. They are in that crowd somewhere. What do you want us to do, Captain?"

"Forget them and send these people home, we are finished here."

"What about the train, Captain?" Lieutenant Moore asked. "There is a bridge just east of town; we could fire the bridge with the train on it, and kill two birds with one stone, so to speak."

"That sounds good, Lieutenant, but let's look at the configuration of the freight and coal cars. Could we not haul horses on these? Why not ride the train on into enemy territory and burn the bridges as we cross them. It would be a heck of a lot quicker and could be quite rewarding. What say you, Gentlemen?" James asked with a wry grin on his face.

"Let's do it," Lieutenant Moore responded eagerly.

"I agree," Lieutenant Roberts replied.

"Captain, this is Mr. Williams, Sir. He is the train engineer," Lieutenant Moore stated, introducing a short, stocky gray-haired man dressed in the typical uniform of the American railroad man, blue cap, stripped coveralls, and a red kerchief tied loosely around the neck. "Those three men over there," pointing to three older men similarly dressed, "are what are left of his crew. Mr. Williams, Sir this is Captain James McCaffrey."

"How do you do, Mr. Williams?" James offered politely, yet before he could say more, the man launched into a bitter tirade against Union forces and at James personally.

"So you're the son of a bitch who is responsible for this." He cursed loudly, his arms flailing as if to encompass a sight these Southern citizens had never seen before, the burning and near complete destruction of their village, a village where the engineer knew nearly every person who lived here. "I have nothing but contempt for you and your Yankee cutthroats; but ye will not get away with this." He fumed, "Our boys will be here tomorrow, and you'll get what you deserve. I hope they kill all of ye, ye bastards."

"Good morning, Mr. Williams," James responded politely, his demeanor and tone of voice seeming to confound the railroad man. "If you will calm down just a bit, Sir I will give you a message that you can pass on to General Lee, when his boys arrive. It's a message directly from General Grant." James' reply quieted the man, now seeming unable to find the words he wished to use to continue to berate this enemy soldier in the blue coat.

"You tell your boys that the American army is here to stay and that General Grant believes that the only way we can bring an end to this terrible tragedy that has befallen us is to destroy the South's ability to wage war against our country. Moreover, we shall do that by destroying your precious railroad and food supplies that feed your young men who have taken up arms against their fellow citizens. The only alternative to such action is to kill your boys as you call them and all those who are engaged in the destruction of our country. We shall confiscate your train and use it to that purpose and you and your brakemen shall accompany my men until I see fit to release you. Should anyone of you attempt to sabotage or delay us in accomplishing our mission, it shall cost him his life. Do you understand what I am telling you, Mr. Williams?

"I understand, you bastard!" Williams exclaimed through clenched teeth, his face now nearly as red as the neckerchief that adorned his neck

"I pray that you do, now get up in your engine and fire-up the boiler so we can get under way." Then turning to Lieutenant

Moore, he ordered in a voice loud enough that the train crew could hear him. "Put a guard on each one of these men; should they be foolish enough to try to impede or obstruct our people, kill 'em."

"Yes, Sir, Captain; come along with me, Mr. Williams and bring your crew." Lieutenant Moore said to the railroad man. "You are going to teach me how to operate this iron monster of yours."

Turning to Mark Roberts, James said, "Let's get our people on board, Mark and get out of here. We cannot stay too long. Some of these good citizens will be heading cross country to find their boys and we do not want to be here when they arrive."

"Yes, Sir, Captain, we should be ready to move out in a few minutes."

"Good, did our people collect some of the Reb food supplies before we fired the warehouse?"

"Yes, Sir, grain, several slabs of smoked meat, salt pork and vegetables; we have a good supply."

"Great, as soon as we are loaded, get the men fed for we may be rather busy very shortly. The Rebs will see the smoke from these fires so I would expect their scouts to arrive here before dark. We should delay but a few minutes at the bridge east of town. Tell your explosive teams to hurry along; as soon as the charges are set, give Lieutenant Moore the high sign, and get your men back on the train. I don't want to leave anyone behind."

"They'll do the job for us, Captain."

"I'm sure they will, Mark."

"Let's move out, Lieutenant."

"Yes, Sir Captain, we're ready." The lieutenant responded. "Mr. Williams, please," motioning to the train engineer that it was time to move.

It was near the noon hour when the train slowly pulled away from the small, burned out train station and still burning warehouse and out buildings in what remained of the village of Crystal Springs, Virginia. With soldiers standing in the open doorways of the boxcars or open coal car a few responded verbally to the curses leveled against them from the townspeople; many of whom stood outside their homes watching the Union soldiers leave.

"What are your thoughts on this, Captain?" Lieutenant Moore asked as the two soldiers moved closer to the firebox to warm themselves and still stay out the way of the fireman now busy attending to his duties.

"You mean using the train to accomplish our objective here in enemy territory, Stewart?"

"Well, that too, Sir. However, no, I was thinking more about what we just did back there and what lies ahead for us. We did not kill anyone, but we hurt many people in that little town. They will never forgive us."

"Yes, that is undoubtedly true, but in doing so, we shall have helped end this terrible war. However, today we were lucky; no one died; I think we may not be so lucky in the days ahead. Tomorrow the Rebs will be out in force looking for us. We might be fortunate enough to stay beyond their reach for a day or two by using the train, but soon we will have to abandon the train for they shall be waiting for us along the way. We may have to run to avoid a trap here in enemy territory. Moreover, the longer we stay on the train it moves us that much further from our own forces. Our trip back shall be fraught with more danger than what we shall encounter as we move further on into enemy territory. By that time every Reb soldier in the state shall be looking for us."

"They will surely seek revenge and take it out on all of us if they capture anyone of us."

"You're right, Stewart, but I try not to think of the consequence when I do something like this. The mere thought of destroying a man's home and livelihood and the hardships we have burdened his family with is not something I take pleasure in, besides there is a bit of a paradox here for me."

"How so, Captain?"

"I have deprived good men of their property and livelihood; unjustly, some would argue, at the behest of a foreign government. This is not too unlike what the Brits did to my father and grandfather."

"I wouldn't see it that way, Captain. From the little understanding of the British/Irish, conflict that I read about, the English wanted your ancestor's land and took it without just compensation. I believe our situation here in the states is quite different. The Rebs started a war to dismantle our country; I have very little sympathy for any of them."

"I understand Stewart, yet I cannot help but see the irony in all of this; it will not be lost on some.

"Incidentally, why is the train moving at such a slow pace?" Then turning to the engineer, he asked, "Why are we going so slowly, Mr. Williams; surely we could double our pace here?"

"Two reasons, Yank," the engineer responded angrily, "we are pulling twenty-five cars, and we only have two brakemen. We cannot stop on a moment's notice. We routinely operate with five brakemen with this many cars. Besides you should have noticed, the track is in terrible shape. Many of our train and track repair crews left for the army; the only gandy dancers available work the main lines, nearly all that are left out here, for these spur lines are the old darkies. The young ones split when your president announced they were free. You Yankees are really stupid."

"That's the same story I got from one of the brakemen, Captain." Lieutenant Moore offered. "A railroad job in the South, is now an old man's last hoorah; both brakemen are in their sixties or older."

"That is good to know, Steward." James responded, nodding his head. "That will necessitate a change of strategy. We will not be able to outrun a Confederate troop, should they spot us while we are still on board this train. We shall have to be ready to high-tail it out of here on our mounts at a moment's notice."

"Our boys will catch up to you and kill you Yank, no matter what you do." Williams sneered. "They have had lots of practice doing that." He laughed.

"Well, Mr. Williams," James offered, his voice grave, and barely audible over the rumble of the engine. "Our boys are professional soldiers and right now they have seen to it that your General Lee and his troops are trapped up Richmond way and at Petersburg, with no place left to run. Their choice is to surrender or die. Mr. Lincoln would like them to surrender, but General Grant doesn't care much one way or the other, so we are going to see to it that a lot of them meet their maker before we go home to our families."

The old railroad engineer just shook his head; he did not know how to respond to what this Yankee soldier said. From his experience in transporting wounded Confederate soldiers home from the front lines, he was fully aware that what Captain McCaffrey said was true; the South was losing the war and the cost in dead and crippled young Southern men was appalling.

"We are coming up on the bridge, Captain." Lieutenant Moore called out. "It's a big one; looks like a beam bridge, wooden trestle, a hundred or so feet above the river, with a span of two-hundred feet with a single center pier. If we blow the pier the whole thing should come down."

"Good. Do you think you can handle the engine from here on, Lieutenant?"

"No trouble, Captain; it's quite simple to operate."

"Okay, we'll put Mr. Williams and his crew off after we cross over and let Lieutenant Robert's demolition people go to work."

Then turning to Mr. Williams he said, "Mr. Williams, after we take care of your bridge, you and your crew will be free to go. You should be able to make it back to town without a problem."

"We won't have a problem, Yank, but ye will. Our boys will come after ye and I will see ye hang before this weeks over. They'll take care of ye for sure."

"Lieutenant Robert's men made short work of the bridge, Captain." Lieutenant Moore commented as the bridge came crashing down with a loud roar. "Those two days spent in training in the use of the Haupt Torpedo have paid off."

"Yes, the engineers said that a couple of cans of black powder, along with the torpedo attached to a key timber on either side of a center pier will take a bridge down quickly. However, I do not think that most of them will come down that easy. Yet, before we can walk away with some assurance that Reb railroad repair and construction crews will not have the bridge up and operating again within a day or two, we have to follow the engineer's advice and twist those rails. That will be more difficult."

"I watched Mark's troops working with the engineers on that," Lieutenant Moore replied, nodding his head. "That twisting device they have is certainly doing the job for us; Mark has about four teams down there working together. It looks like he has most of the rails from the bridge deck already twisted like a pretzel."

"Good, let's get aboard, Stewart." Captain McCaffrey replied as he watched a half dozen troops scramble up the river embankment from the crumpled remains of the railroad bridge. The soldiers were soon on board, leaving behind several sections of rail no longer useable.

"Let's get this thing rolling, Lieutenant. We need to put some distance between this little bit of handy work of ours, for we are apt to have visitors."

"That should shut this line down for quite awhile, Captain," Lieutenant Moore commented with a smile. "However, I see Mark's people didn't set it ablaze. I thought we were going to set fire to every bridge we took out."

"That was our original intent, Stewart; but as long as we stay with the train, the smoke from the fires will give our position away. Each fire will tell them exactly where we are and where we are going. We cannot have that. They will hear the blast from the torpedoes, but from miles away, the Rebs may have a tough time zeroing in on our location. Nevertheless, after another explosion or two, they'll know we are attacking the railroad and shall be waiting for us down the line."

With two blasts from the train whistle, the signal for the release of brakes, a half-dozen troops on as many cars, fulfilled their temporary assigned duty as brakemen. By the time locomotive lurched ahead, Lieutenant Robert's troops had already climbed aboard.

"We are coming up on another small town, Captain."

"I see that, Lieutenant. How far have we come? I would guess maybe fifteen or twenty miles."

"That would be my guess too, Sir. It has been nearly an hour since we left the bridge. Mr. Williams wasn't lying when he said the roadbed was in bad shape, so I have kept the speed down."

Turning to the trooper firing the boiler, Captain McCaffrey said, "I will take over your duties soldier. Contact Lieutenant Roberts and have he and Sergeant Davis come forward then pass the word that everyone is to remain out of sight."

"Yes, Sir," the trooper responded and quickly made his way over the top of the coal-tender to the lead boxcar.

"You sent for me, Sir?" Lieutenant Roberts reported as he and Sergeant Davis climbed down into the locomotive cab.

"Yes, Mark, we are about to enter another small town; it looks smaller than Crystal Springs. We are close to the Danville/Petersburg main line so it is quite possible that the Rebs could have a contingent of troops garrisoned here. Do not take any unnecessary chances. We shall stop the train a half mile or so short of the depot, that will give you an opportunity to off-load your troop and move to block any escape of the townspeople or Confederate soldiers that may be garrisoned here. Once you are on the ground you will have to move fast. Unless we come under attack, we will give you twenty minutes for your troop to seal off the south end of town, before we move in and block the north and west side of the village. I hope that we can secure it as we did at Crystal Springs without too much trouble. On our map, we have a river crossing coming up about three miles further down the line; it is a suspension bridge with at least two cofferdams. Our boys will need more time in setting their charges, so we'll have to make sure no Confederate military people escape our net."

"We shall take care of it, Captain."

"I know you will, Mark." James replied confidently, with a grim smile and nod of his head. "Sergeant Davis shall handle the engine and give one long blast on the engine whistle when we are in position. Good luck." Without further comment, Lieutenant Roberts climbed back over the coal tender then onto the top of the coupled freight cars.

"Stewart, let Sergeant Davis take over here, you need to get to your troop."

"Right, Sir, I am on my way. Just remember, Sergeant two short whistles blasts, followed by a single longer one, shall let your brakemen know that you want to stop the train. They need sufficient warning as each man needs to set a brake on two cars or this thing will not stop. The engineer's whistle is the key; for even at a very low speed, it will take two or three-hundred yards to bring this monstrous thing to a complete stop."

"Yes, Sir," Sergeant Davis responded.

"We shall move on to the depot in twenty-minutes, Stewart. Lieutenant Robert's troop should be in position by that time. Just remember that whistle shall be the signal for our people to move; then we shall see what the Confederates have in store for us today. Okay?"

"We'll be ready, Captain."

With Sergeant Davis at the controls, the train stopped approximately a half mile short of the depot, where Lieutenant Roberts's troops quickly exited the freight cars dropping into a shallow gully that concealed them from view of the townspeople. Looking ahead through his spyglass James was surprised by the number of town folks he saw gathered at the depot, not learning until much later that Mr. Williams and his train from Crystal Springs, commandeered by his Union forces was already a day late. He could clearly make out the name of the town on the depot, Fairbrook, Virginia. However, the arrival of any train in small town America was a special event; but this one was more than a curiosity for it was a day late in arriving at its destination. The towns folks would want to know why, with many fearing the delay would be war related, for rumors existed in abundance that the dreaded Yankee Army would soon ride roughshod over the entire state.

"Let's move on slowly, Sergeant," James stated succinctly, "It looks like we are going to be greeted by a reception committee and if I am not mistaken, I see a few Confederate soldiers in the crowd." When within approximately five-hundred yards of the depot Sergeant Davis blew the three requisite whistle blasts and engaged the locomotive brakes. The train slowed abruptly, coming to a full stop with the engine cab only a few yards beyond the station where Davis again engaged the whistle in a long earsplitting blast.

Sergeant Davis, following James, jumped from the locomotive cab to the platform below startling a dozen or more civilians gathered there; Lieutenant Moore and nearly fifty of his troops quickly rushed forward surrounding the depot and those gathered nearby. Sergeant Robinson and two of his men quickly entered the depot and disabled the telegraph while others, already mounted spread out across the northern reaches of the village to prevent anyone from fleeing the area. Soon gunfire erupted from different locations throughout the village as Union troops went about their business of destroying the livestock and anyone who fired upon them. At the depot, two Confederate soldiers, one an officer, and the other a sergeant were quickly disarmed and brought into the station where James was questioning the stationmaster.

Turning his attention to the man dressed in the threadbare grey uniform of a Confederate cavalry officer, boots, spurs, leather belt, and an empty holster he quietly asked, "What's your name, Sir?"

"I am Major Gregory Zimmerman, Captain and this is my aide Sergeant Lewis."

"What outfit are you with, Major and what are you doing here?"

"I might have asked you the same question, Captain, but I recognize for the moment that I am in no position to do that. Notwithstanding that, I can assure you, that had there not been a whole slew of civilians on the train depot platform a few moments ago that I undoubtedly would be the one asking the questions. However, such are the fortunes of war. I am a member of a cavalry unit from Mobile, Alabama, in service to the Army of the Confederacy."

"What are you doing here, Major and how many men do you have with you?"

"That truly is a strange question coming from an enemy soldier, Captain. I am defending my country and protecting our citizens from you Yankees; yet you sound more Irish than Yankee." He smiled. "We have a lot of fine young Irishmen in our army. Moreover, I have twenty-five men with me who will fight to the death for me in our effort to drive you people out of the Confederacy. I am sure the gunfire we hear will be my people carrying out my orders to that effect." "I hate to disappoint you, Major," James replied, "but there were only ten of you, now three of them are dead, five wounded and you and your sergeant here are in the custody of my troops. Therefore, Sir I would say you are not doing too well today. However, I am curious Major, what is your unit designation? Are you a member of the Alabama Regulars? That's what one of your men told us."

"Yes, that is correct and I am proud of that fact for we have beaten the Yankee soldiers in every battle."

"Every one, with possibly one exception," James responded. "I was not there, but I understand your people did not do too well at Gettysburg." Zimmerman gave no response. "I just have two more questions Major."

"Yes."

"Are you a West Point graduate?"

"What a strange question to ask, Captain, particularly under these circumstances, but nevertheless, I am only too glad to answer that. Yes, I am a graduate of West Point, class of fifty-eight."

"Then I have to ask, were your men involved in the raids upon our supply trains last year at the Rapidan River crossing?"

"No, but I heard about those, our people were very successful there in closing down that route for some time."

"Why do you ask, Captain?" Zimmerman inquired.

"I was wondering if while at the Academy whether or not the United States Army taught their officers to torture and kill defenseless military prisoners and burn their bodies, or was that something a Confederate officer would learn in your army. Whatever happened, Sir, to the West Point code of Duty, Honor, and Country?"

Zimmerman appeared stunned by the question; then regaining his composure, responded quietly. "I know about the Rapidan River Crossing incident only because I am aware that a Courts Martial board cashiered one of our fellow officers for killing enemy prisoners taken in that raid. His failed leadership led to disastrous consequences for the South. He lost his entire troop and several of his own men testified against him. They said the officer ordered several Yankee soldier prisoners tortured and then he executed them. He burned their bodies to conceal the fact that the men had been tortured."

"What was the man's name, Major?"

"Schmitz, Captain Joseph P. Schmitz."

"Why so interested in that one incident, Captain? Surely, there had to be many cases during this violent period that were of greater concern to the Yankee army than this single incident. It was a heinous crime, an anomaly if you will, committed by a brutal, sadistic and undisciplined officer."

"You may be right, Major, but this was personal to me, and I promised my men that I would find that officer and deal with him directly."

"I see," Zimmerman replied, quietly nodding his head, his mouth pursed, but he said no more.

"Can we wrap this up, gentlemen?" Captain McCaffrey asked as he and Lieutenants Mark Roberts and Stewart Moore gathered together with Sergeants Brad Adams and Gayle Davis on the train station platform. "We're running out of time; have we accomplished what we came here to do, Mark?" He asked Lieutenant Roberts.

"Yes, Sir, except for the Rebs' mounts; we have killed off the livestock and fired all the out buildings including two warehouses full of supplies destined for Lee's troops at

Richmond. We lost two men and another six wounded. Their injuries are serious and we will have to leave them here. We have two women that have volunteered to care for them along with the five Reb wounded. The women offered us the use of their one-room schoolhouse here and are converting it into a temporary aid station."

"What about your troop, Stewart, any casualties?"

"Yes, Sir, two wounded and one trooper, assigned as a brakemen is dead."

"What happened?" James asked, shaking his head.

"He fell between the boxcars while setting the brake. The train ran over him; we did not find him until we started accounting for our people. His injuries were severe; he simply bled to death."

"Oh, Jesus, Stewart, how do I explain that to his family?" James responded, stealing himself to keep from being overcome with remorse."

"I will handle that, Captain, it was John Casey, he was a New York man; we have been together since the war started."

"Thank you, Stewart, Let's get over to that school house and then get the hell out of here."

Upon returning to the train station, James found Lieutenant Roberts waiting. "I take it you have loaded the Reb mounts with ours; is that what you had in mind, Mark?"

"Yes, Sir, we will turn them loose with our spare mounts maybe eight or ten miles from here; that should preclude the Rebs from pursuing us or reporting our whereabouts for at least a day or two."

"Good. Let's get aboard, but first bring that Reb officer out here; I want a word with him."

When Major Zimmerman arrived, accompanied by Sergeant Adams, he addressed James, "Your man here, tells me you wanted to talk to me again, Captain. I am your prisoner, whatever. . . ." He responded, nonchalantly holding both hands out as if expecting the unknown.

"We are leaving Major and my options as what I should do with you are limited. We could take you with us as our prisoner, but I think that would be more trouble than I need right now. Or turn you loose on foot someplace up there in the hill country," James said, pointing off to the West. That would give us a day or two, head start before you contact your command. Or, I can just leave you here; and that is what I propose to do, on one condition."

"And that condition is what, Captain?"

"Your word, Major that you shall see to it that my wounded men are treated as you would expect your men to be treated under similar circumstances."

"You have my word, Captain," Zimmerman responded, quietly, offering his hand. "We shall get all the wounded into a hospital at Danville or Greensboro as soon as we can; from there when your men are ready they will go on to the prison at Andersonville, Georgia."

"Thank you, Sir," James replied, shaking the man's hand as the two men separated.

"Let's get out of here, gentlemen, we have a date with a bridge down the line."

CHAPTER 12

THE BRIDGE

"There it is, Captain," Lieutenant Moore called out over the roar of the train engine. "It's a big one. It looks like when we get across, the track ties into the mainline. That has to be the route from Greensboro, Danville and ties into the Lynchburg and Richmond line. The Reb army will be all over us if they get wind of what we are up to here."

"Keep an eye out for them, Stewart."

"I shall, Sir," he replied as the locomotive slowly moved out onto the bridge. When half way across he signaled his brakemen and just as the last car cleared the end of the bridge the train came to a full stop. Dozens of troops climbed to the top of the boxcars, some assigned by their supervisors as lookouts, but most to get a glimpse of Lieutenant Mark Roberts and his two explosive ordinance teams as they made their way to a spot above the two cofferdams supporting the huge wooden trestle. Robert's men stopped near the top of the two towers rising out of the supporting cofferdams, and then quickly disappeared into the honeycombed recesses of the trestle to plant their explosives.

"Keep your eyes peeled for Johnnie Reb; stay alert, don't forget for a moment that we are operating in his territory." James cautioned his troops as he made his way across the top of the train, repeating the admonition to each group he came across. However, there was no sign of a Confederate Army presence, nor had they seen a Reb soldier since leaving Fairbrook. Crossing onto the top of the last boxcar, he came across Sergeants Bradley Adams and Gayle Davis. While

Adams watched for the reappearance of Lieutenant Roberts and his ten-man explosive specialists to reappear on the bridge, Sergeant Davis continued to scan the horizon for any sign of enemy troop movements.

"See any movement out there, Sergeant," James asked Sergeant Davis.

"No, Sir," the man replied, "but take a look out there toward the top of that tallest ridge," he said, pointing off to the Northwest. "There is something up there, besides bushes and trees. I do not think anyone would build a house up there, but if I were to guess, I would say that is a Reb observation tower. It is the highest point in that entire ridge and if I were a Reb commander worried about his supply lines to the South, I would have someone up there with a spyglass and a signal mirror."

Looking through his spyglass, James responded, "I agree with you, that's what I would do. It certainly looks like the people built it there for some other purpose than just mining or logging activities, certainly not for farming. It is occupied, Sergeant. There is smoke coming from the building; it has to be colder than hell up there. We need to get our people off these boxcars now, and prepare for an attack. Send two men out on the bridge to warn Lieutenant Roberts that we are anticipating a rebel response. We cannot underestimate Reb commanders; surely, they will check on an unscheduled train stopped on their main supply route into Richmond from the South.

"Also, send another man up to the engine to warn Lieutenant Moore; we need to move out onto the main line as soon as our men are on board. When we get there, Lieutenant Robert's men will destroy the switching mechanisms behind us.""Which way, Sir, shall we go north or south on the mainline?" Sergeant Davis asked with a quizzical, yet worried glance at his commanding officer.

"North, Sergeant," James responded without hesitation. "The last I heard Lee was at Richmond. I assume he is still there. Our job is to cut his supply lines; well, we shall accommodate him and do just that. We will head for Lynchburg, but if they attack us today, we will have to abandon the train and move into the hill country. However, I do not want to quit the train just yet; our map shows another bridge crossing of this river about eight or ten miles further north on the mainline. We'll shoot for that as our next objective."

"You heard the Captain," Sergeant Davis said to a nearby trooper.

"Yes, Sergeant," the soldier responded; then quickly made his way to advise Lieutenant Moore, who had since returned to the engineer's cabin.

A few minutes later, the two men's conversation was suddenly interrupted with the first of two loud explosions at the bridge; each followed by a tremendous roar when the trestle and track crashed in a tangled heap into the river below. As the first of two demolition teams made it back on board the train, the second team along with Lieutenant Roberts climbed out from under the bridge and rushed to get off the structure. They reached the riverbank just as the detonation took place on the remaining structure; it shook the area, sending timbers and rails skyward before they too crashed into the river below.

The train got under way as Lieutenant Roberts, the last to board, climbed into the nearest boxcar where James greeted him. "Great work, Mark; you killed two birds with one stone, as they say in Ireland. You blew the bridge and twisted the rails at the same time." The two men smiled and shook hands.

"That should hold the Rebs for awhile, Captain."

"You bet it will, but I have one more job for you, before we get out of here; and we may not have much time. Lieutenant Moore is moving us out on the mainline and I want your people to blow the intersecting switching mechanisms and twist some of this heavier gauge mainline rail. Just enough to slow the Rebs down should they try catch up to us before we get away from here."

"Can do, Captain, we'll get at it as soon as the train stops; ten minutes at most and we can be on our way again. I take it we are heading toward Lynchburg?" He smiled.

"That' where we are going, Mark."

"That's what I told Stewart." He chuckled, "I said I knew you well enough that you would go after the devil himself if necessary to end this war so we can go home."

"What did Stewart say to that, Mark?" James asked with a wry smile.

"He said, 'he wanted to go home too, so let's get it done.'"

Lieutenant Robert's two teams wasted little time in setting charges under the switching mechanisms on the mainline, destroying the crucial railroad devices; then using a rail twister, laid waste to more than a dozen heavy gage rails. Their handy work would effectively close the Danville/Richmond line for two or three weeks, again depending upon the efficiency of Confederate repair crews.

"Let's get underway, Stewart." James said, as he climbed up into the locomotive cab. "Lieutenant Robert's people are back on board."

"I walked the track a ways, Captain; the rail here is the heavier 60 pound T-rail, and although not in excellent shape it is certainly better than that 22 pound U-rail we just came off of."

"So what are you telling me, Stewart? I take it we can travel a little bit faster than we have so far."

"Better than that, Captain, we can more than double our speed, and depending on the terrain, even outrun most cavalry troops."

"That's great, Stewart. Just remember that lookout station back there above the river; keep an eye pealed for troops ahead, or heaven forbid, that we crash head on into a high speed train coming from Richmond."

However, Lieutenant Stewart Moore did not respond. There was no other sound in the locomotive cab other than the roar of the steam engine and wind whistling through the open windows, yet Moore slumped to the steel floor of the cab, blood spurting from a fatal head wound. The second shot fired at James or the young trooper nearby, missed its target; yet there was no doubt it was a bullet aimed at one of them. It ricocheted around the cab of the engine, eventually coming to rest on the floor of the locomotive not far from James McCaffrey's feet.

"Take control of the engine," James yelled at the soldier then grabbed the rope to the train whistle and blew a continuing series of long blasts to alert the battalion. However, it was unnecessary; for looking back along the train, he saw several troopers already firing at enemy soldiers along the right of way. Yet at the speed they were traveling James realized it was undoubtedly futile, even the best cavalry soldier firing from a horse or moving wagon seldom hit what they were shooting at. Then as the train rounded a long curve, he could see several Confederate cavalry troops moving swiftly to catch the train. They were quickly lost to view however, when the train crossed over a bridge above a small river with steep banks on either side.

Continuing for several miles, they entered a steep ravine overgrown with brush and scrub pine on either side of the railroad right of way. "Set your brake," Captain McCaffrey yelled as he grabbed the whistle lanyard and blew three blasts on the train whistle. It took less than a quarter of a mile to bring the train to a complete stop; the novice brakemen did their job well.

"Everyone out, pass the word," he called out to the men in the nearest boxcar. Within minutes, Lieutenant Roberts and two sergeants, one of whom had their Captain's mount in tow arrived at the head of the train. Climbing up into the saddle, he turned to Sergeant Brad Adams, "Sergeant, assume command of Lieutenant Moore's Troop. The Lieutenant is dead."

"Yes, Sir", the man replied without hesitation. Then James issued a series of rapid-fire orders, "Pickets out, quarter mile, double pickets both north and south along the track, watch for Reb troops and trains from the North; also put two troops up on that ridge north of us and keep a watch out for a train. Bring an explosive team forward; I have a job for them." Turning to Lieutenant Roberts, he said, "I want your explosive men to set a contact charge on the front of that engine, Mark, large enough to disable or destroy it and anything along the track we may encounter."

Then turning to Sergeant Davis, he said, "Sergeant you are our new engineer; uncouple the boxcars from the tender and move the engine; we shall burn the train here. We may have an hour, two at most, before the Reb cavalry catches up to us; by then we shall have a little surprise for them. When the explosives are in place, take two men and move the engine north until you are out of sight of this location and wait. If you sight a Reb force, get out and

send the train on its way; let it carry our fight to the Rebs."
"Yes, Sir," Sergeant Davis replied solemnly.

"Lieutenant Roberts, we shall set up an ambush for our Reb friends; dismount and deploy your troops along the ridge above the train, then send a squad north along the right of way with our mounts. That should cover our footprints in the snow. I want the Rebs to think that we rode off in a hurry. Before they get here however, we shall fire the train. That should create the distraction we need; when they stop to examine our handiwork, we attack. Based upon what we saw earlier, I believe we are looking at two or more companies. Let's get it done, gentlemen," he added, his articulation and demeanor firm, his face grim, leaving no one to wonder whether this young officer was qualified to command in the Army of the Potomac.

Although shocked at their captain's startling disclosure of Lieutenant Moore's death, neither Sergeants Adams or Davis, nor Lieutenant Roberts asked any questions about the man. They knew that time would come in due course, but for right now, their survival depended upon their attention to detail, details that may determine whether-or-not they would still be alive at the end of this day.

"Captain, there's the signal from our men on the ridge; if I read them correctly, it's a full troop coming in fast from a mile out."

"I see that, Mark, fire the train."

A few matches tossed onto the straw and hay scattered across the deck of each boxcar and spread earlier into the coal cars ignited easily; the fire developed quickly, spreading within minutes throughout the entire length of the train. Soon a huge black cloud of smoke and flame erupted over the entire length of the train, leading James to comment, "Well, Mark if the Confederate Army didn't know where we were they do now; when this thing is over we've got to skedaddle out of here in a hurry."

"You're right, Captain," Lieutenant Roberts replied. "They will be thicker than flees on a hound dog and out for blood, but if we are lucky here and with the explosive charge maybe after today they will not be too anxious to engage."

"You are dreaming, Mark, they will be out to kill us; and luck won't have anything to do with it. Your men will prevail because of you and Stewart; you trained them, you disciplined them and they truly are professional soldiers. I am proud to be here with them."

"Thanks, Captain, that's good to hear; yes, they will do the job for us."

"Here they come, Mark." James whispered, "Two scouts, let's see what they do. It looks like our ruse is working; the focus of their attention is on the fire. They must believe we have moved on and it looks like they are going to follow our horses' tracks."

"That's the way it looks, Captain, but wait they are splitting up; one is continuing on and the other is turning back to his troop."

"Jesus," Lieutenant Roberts exclaimed quietly, "I hope none of our people get careless."

"They'll hold, Mark; all we need is a few more minutes." Although James tried his best to be convincing, so many troopers in this battalion hated the Reb cavalry he was not sure that hate would not boil over into at least one or two of his men shooting the Confederate scouts. However, the two Rebs soon disappeared from view; the Union soldiers presence, remained undetected.

"Here they come, Mark. God, it looks like a whole company; there are more than a hundred men in the column."

"Your plan is working, Captain, they too are distracted by the fire. They are not even looking for us."

"No, they are not, Mark, but let's wait a bit longer; I want them bunched together up against the train, directly below." Moments later, as the Reb column approached the front of the burning train; James opened fire with his Spencer rifle on the officer leading the column, taking down the man's mount. Within seconds the scrub pine and brush along the ridgeline above the train exploded with rifle fire. The carnage that followed, as James would later describe it to Brigadier General Charles Murray, made him sick; yet he knew he could not stop it until the Reb officers still standing dropped their weapons and surrendered. Unfortunately, the Confederate officer in charge chose to continue to rally his men urging them to take cover and return the Sixteenth Battalion's fusillade. Three or four minutes into the battle, another officer and what appeared to be two enlisted men waved white flags, and called out loudly for their men to cease fire. Although nearly obscured by the haze of heavy smoke from gunfire, James could see the Reb officer who led the column, the man was down and not moving.

"Cease fire, cease fire!" James shouted loudly, having to repeat the order three more times before his men stopped firing. "Let's go down and see what we have, Mark. It looks like the Rebs have had it for today."

Within minutes, Union soldiers rounded up twenty or more uninjured Confederate cavalrymen and relieved them of their rifles, then secured the weapons of the dead and injured.

Sergeant Robinson moved quickly in to take charge, finding most of the Confederate soldiers too stunned to realize the enormity of their loss. He shouted, and then quietly coaxed them to render aid to their comrades.

"Come on men, you have a task ahead of you; take care of your fellow soldiers. There is no reason why any more of you should die. Get in here and bandage these folks; make them as comfortable as you can. Your aid people will not be here for a while. Come on now," he pleaded, "hurry along. We shall help you as much as we can, but you are going to have to do this or some of these men will die."

James watched Sergeant Robinson and marveled at his compassion and leadership expertise, never having witnessed such an event where just minutes before two groups of professional soldiers were trying to kill each other and now one of his men took on the role of savior; a true knight in shining armor.

"We have four dead, Captain and nine wounded; three of the wounded can ride but we will have to leave the others behind." Lieutenant Robert's solemn report on his own losses startled James, for he quickly realized that after nearly four years of warfare the Confederate Army was still a formidable foe. The Sixteenth Battalion's casualties during these last few days were a testimony to that.

"Have you talked to them, Mark?" James asked solemnly.

"Yes, Sir, all of them remember General Murray's talk to us before we left Petersburg. They knew that this could happen and are resigned to the fact they shall be left behind."

"I shall talk to them before we pull out of here. God, I hate this. This far removed from medical assistance and we compound the problem by blowing up the only means of getting them to a hospital."

"What is your count on Confederate casualties, Mark?" James asked, "any idea yet on the dead and wounded?"

"A Reb lieutenant with their troops is taking a count now; we should have it within a few minutes."

"What about their commanding officer, is he still alive?"

"No, he's dead."

"Jesus, I don't know what that man was thinking. He never even looked up on the ridge; he would surely have seen us had he done so. He lost his whole troop, what a horrendous blunder. So many young men gone, for what! My God won't we ever learn!"

"We were lucky, Captain; that could have been us."

"Yes, Mark, but I experienced this once before with Colonel John Bream at the Rapidan River, remember; at that time however, it was our men who were caught in the ambush. The Sixty-Ninth learned a hard lesson that day and I shall never forget it. However, I owe you and men like Jack Kelly and Captain Swartz more than I shall ever be able to repay. You folks have been at this for four years, from Gettysburg to Virginia, while I am such a novice. I could never be a professional soldier like you; I do not have the training nor the education or experience and I know I have been very lucky. However, I have had the advantage of having men like you and Captain Kelly to guide me through this god-awful war. Anyway, get me that count as soon as you can, then see to it that our people are ready to ride. I will talk to the men we have to leave behind."

"Captain, over here, Sir," Sergeant Robinson called out to James when he went in search of his wounded troops. Robinson had moved both the dead and wounded soldiers down off the ridge to level ground and was tending to the needs of the injured men.

"How many Sergeant?" James asked as he approached the wounded troopers, some sitting up, others lying next to four bodies, now partially covered with blankets.

"Four and nine, Sir. Two of them are the Malone twins, one dead and one so severely wounded, he will not ride out of here."

"Oh, Sweet Jesus, not both of them; which one is still alive?" He asked Sergeant Robinson, with Kevin struggling to get up off the ground when he heard James talking to the sergeant.

"I am, Jimmy; it's me, Kevin. It got rough for a while, Dennis took a bullet for me, and then they finished him off. I am sorry, Jimmy. Will you tell the folks? I guess neither one of us will get to see the Western Territories from the back of an army mount now."

"What happened, Sergeant?"

"About twenty Rebs at the end of the column broke and made a run for it and I ordered these boys, including those four lying over there, motioning toward the dead troops, to cut them off. None of the secessionists got away, but my people eventually ran out of ammunition and it turned into a real donnybrook. Your Dennis and Kevin gave a good account of themselves; all of them did. I am sorry I lost them, Captain. There was just too many Rebs and they fought like the devil; but my boys took them all down."

"Don't be sorry, Sergeant, you did what you had to do; if those soldiers escaped our trap, we would have paid a high price down the line. For those that can ride, get them mounted. We are pulling out of here right away."

A few minutes later Captain McCaffrey knelt down beside the badly injured soldiers; he assured each that he would write to their families to inform them that their father, son, or husband was alive and would be coming home soon.

"Do you really think that's true, Jimmy?" Kevin Malone asked, his tone of voice exhibiting a note of skepticism.

"I really do, Kevin," James responded to his cousin, in a loud voice so the wounded lying nearby could hear what he said. "General Grant is preparing for a spring offensive at Petersburg and when that city falls that will be the end of the Confederacy. It puts General Lee's people in a noose and all we have to do is close it up tight. Lee will be dead or in jail within six months."

"Jesus, do you really think so, Captain?" One of the other men lying nearby asked.

"I know that to be true, soldier; otherwise we would not be here. Your job was to make it happen sooner, not later and that's what you did here today."

As evening approached, it was a solemn group of men that rode off from the ambush site where sixty-four dead Confederate soldiers, their bodies now arranged in two tidy rows failed to adequately reflect the carnage and suffering that took place a few hours earlier alongside this burned-out Confederate train. Although separated until now, both physically and philosophically from their adversary, the two blue uniformed clad bodies at the end of each row of dead soldiers was a stark reminder that death was the great equalizer. A surviving Confederate officer made no distinction except agreeing with Captain McCaffrey that his burial detail would inter the four Union troopers' bodies and mark their graves accordingly. The six troops whose injuries precluded any thought of riding on with the Sixteenth, accepted their fate knowing that thanks to the demolition teams' efficiency it could be days before a hospital train would get through from the Carolinas.

The Union soldiers that rode away from this scene of death and destruction were a quiet and somber group. To date the men of the Sixteenth fought valiantly; they destroyed two confederate supply centers and a superior force of Confederate soldiers. Yet, thus far, they would leave behind nine dead and fifteen wounded friends, some of whom had been with them since those terrible days at Gettysburg.

Captain McCaffrey, Lieutenant Roberts, and Sergeant Robinson took the lead as the column began to form along the railroad right of way. Before leaving the area, they ran off the Rebs' mounts, and rekindled the fire in one of the partially burned out boxcars to burn weapons. Taking Lieutenant Roberts and several sergeants aside James ordered Sergeant Robinson to take one man and escort the ambulatory wounded back to Petersburg. "They will slow us down, Sergeant and that could cost us more lives. Cross-country, or as the crows fly we are probably sixty to seventy-five miles Northwest of Petersburg; would that be a close guess?

"Yes, Sir, I think you are right. It will be tough on them, as we will have to travel at night and hole-up somewhere during the daytime; but we should make it in four or possibly five days."

"Good, when you arrive I want you to report to General Murray on our progress," he said. "Tell him what we have accomplished to date and that we shall plot a course for Richmond taking out whatever transportation infrastructure we come across. We still have enough supplies and explosives to continue operating, but from now on, we shall have to utilize hit and run tactics. Even though they know we are here, it should work. To put us out of business the Rebs will have to hunt us down, but I believe we can stay ahead of them.

"Mount up, Gentlemen; let's get the hell out of here. Sergeant Robinson we shall follow the main rail line North, but stay with us until after dark, then break off and head for home. We'll send a troop up onto that ridge tonight and take their observation post out at daybreak."

"What are your plans, Captain?" Lieutenant Roberts asked, reining his mount in alongside James now leading the column of troops north along either side of the railroad right away.

"We shall join up with Sergeant Davis and after dark follow the engine slowly while your men take out that Reb observation post on the ridge above."

"Yes, I have a squad ready to go, Sir. We will hit them early; if we go in on foot, maybe catch them unawares it should work out for us."

"Not we, Mark," James replied, "You have been in the forefront of every engagement that this troop has been involved in. Assign a sergeant; you and I have an entire troop to manage. The loss of Lieutenant Moore changes the equation. Don't forget for a moment that we are in enemy territory and if I go down there is no one else with your knowhow and command experience to carry out our orders and to see that these men get back safely to our own lines."

Reluctantly, Lieutenant Roberts acquiesced, nodding his head, his lips pursed. "Yes, Sir, I understand, Captain, anyone of my sergeants is capable of handling this."

"Good show, Mark. You trained them well; I am sure it will work. We shall move slowly enough that they should be able to rejoin the column by midmorning."

With dusk settling across the countryside, Sergeant Robinson left the column behind and guided the wounded soldiers south along the railroad right of way. On their long trek back to Petersburg, he would bypass the village of Fairbrook. At the same time, Lieutenant Roberts dispatched Sergeant Leon Andrews and five troopers to take out the Confederate outpost on the ridge overlooking the rail line.

The following morning James climbed into the locomotive engine with Sergeant Davis, "Let's move out, Sergeant. Keep it slow, by the time we get around that ridge, Sergeant Andrews should be coming down the other side and will rejoin the column. If by chance we meet a train coming our way, the occupants will not be friendly, so full steam ahead and jump."

"Yes, Sir, Captain; but by that time, Sir we will need both water and fuel. We should run across a fueling station soon; here in Reb country they're located along the right of way about every twenty-five miles or so. We have not loaded-up since we left Crystal Springs."

"We may not have to do that, Sergeant; it all depends on what lies ahead. The map shows another bridge coming up soon; stop on the other side. On the map it looks like a minor tributary, but it will take a while for the demolition teams to set their charges."

It was mid morning when Sergeant Andrew's squad arrived back from the Confederate out post.

"What did you find, Sergeant?" James asked the veteran noncom; "Anyone hurt?"

"No, Sir. It turned out fine; they were primed for trouble and put up a good fight; but there were only three Rebs there. They expended a lot of ammunition, but they could not see us and all we had to do was fire into the building; it was just a weather shelter really, with a small camp stove. None of them survived, the poor bastards."

"Good work, Sergeant, anything else?" His captain asked.

"I picked up this code book and we brought out their signal mirrors and a spyglass; I thought we might find a use for them."

"Great, but you had better get your men fed we will need to move out as soon as Lieutenant Robert's men destroy this bridge." While the two men talked a sharp explosion jolted the area; this was followed by a thunderous roar as the huge train trestle came crashing down onto the rocks lining either side of the river gorge. After settling down their mounts, frightened by the blast, troops in the process of congratulating Lieutenant Roberts and his demolition teams were startled to hear a train whistle. At first some thought it came from the nearby locomotive; yet, when that happened again it became obvious the sound originated from a remote location.

"Mount, mount up," James called out to those nearby with Lieutenant Roberts and his sergeants loudly and urgently repeating the order.

"What are your orders, Sir," Lieutenant Roberts asked, when his captain returned to the cab of the locomotive.

"We shall accomplish what we came here to do, Mark. I will stay with Sergeant Davis until we see what lies ahead. If it is moving south we shall fire up the boiler and send your explosive package on to greet them. If it is moving north, we will follow at a distance unless attacked. If that happens, we will jump and send the engine on with your package."

"Jesus Christ, Captain!" Lieutenant Roberts exclaimed, "There is enough black powder there to kill everyone that comes within a hundred yards. You cannot wait, you have to get out of there right away, or you and Sergeant Davis will not live to see another day."

"I know, Mark. I do not plan to get any closer than I have to; but we will have to assess the situation first. Just bring our mounts along. We'll be fine."

Yet Mark Roberts, knowing Captain James McCaffrey as he did, knew the man would go to any extreme to assure success for his troops in battle. In many ways, he was not unlike his two cousins Dennis and Kevin Malone.

They had gone less than a mile when the other train became visible, coming toward them on the main line at a high speed as evidenced by the clouds of grey and black smoke emanating from its smoke stack.

"Full steam ahead, Sergeant," he yelled, "and get out of here!"

Opening the steam valve all the way, Davis replied, "After you, Sir."

"Get out of here, Sergeant, Jump!"

"Yes, Sir," and the man hit the ground, rolling along the right of way from the momentum into the brush. By the time he got to his feet, Lieutenant Roberts arrived.

"What the hell is the captain doing, Sergeant?" Lieutenant Roberts hollered at the man as both men watched the locomotive rapidly gain momentum on its way to assured destruction. "If he waits too long he'll wind up with a broken leg or worse; if he gets too close to the blast, he's a dead man."

When within half-mile distance, with both trains rapidly closing toward one another, James jumped from the locomotive, rolling off into the brush, his fall cushioned by deep snow. By the time Lieutenant Roberts and Sergeant Davis arrived on their mounts, with their captain's horse in tow, James was on his feet, watching when the two locomotives disappeared in a cloud of dust, smoke, and debris, all visible before the sound of the explosion and its shock wave reached them.

"Let's take a look at our handiwork, Lieutenant," James said, calmly as he climbed up into the saddle. "One column each side of the Reb train," he called out, "be watchful and prepared to shoot should we take fire from anywhere on the train."

The explosive charge accompanied by the violent eruption of the steam boilers resulted in the destruction of both engines and tenders, with severe damage to nearly every car on what they were soon to learn, was a six-car hospital train. The lead car carrying food and water supplies lay on its side, torn apart with its cargo strewn along the right of way. Although scattered about as if by the hand of God five of the six cars remained upright, each appearing to have suffered major structural damage. Riding in closer, with the smoke and dust drifting off in a slight breeze, James thought it strange, almost eerily quiet. Expecting an ambush, he repeated his command for caution, with the warning passed back along the column. Still, there was no sign of a Confederate soldier, then a train crewmember, dressed in the traditional garb of his profession emerged from one of the cars and approached James.

"Good morning, Sir," James replied in clipped tones, greeting the railroad man. "What have we got here; who or what do you have on board?" He demanded rather gruffly.

"Good morning yourself, Yank. What do you think we have here? We have been expecting you, but we did not think you would be cutting us off from the Carolinas. They said you all were in Petersburg. As for what we have; you are welcome to look, we have about four-hundred wounded men aboard. That is we started out from Richmond with four-hundred, a few have died en route, however, if I am not mistaken you just killed several more."

"Do you have an armed escort or security detail traveling with you?" James asked, curious that there was no evidence of an armed group escorting the wounded soldiers.

"We did have, there were three when we departed Richmond." the railroad man replied, "two of them were riding atop the coal tender when you yanks blew the engine to hell and gone. I suppose they're dead now," the man responded shaking his head.

"Where's the third man," James asked.

"The last time I saw that fellow, he was assisting the surgeon in the last car; he's probably afraid to come out now. The chances are he most likely figures you people will kill him as soon as he shows his face."

"What is your name railroad man?"

"I'm Joshua Goodman; I work for the Piedmont Lines as the head brakeman on this run between Greensboro and Richmond. We were taking these young fellows to the hospital in Greensboro when you blew the hell out of our train."

"Mr. Goodman," James, addressing the man kindly asked, "would you go and get that soldier for me, please? Tell him we have no intention of killing him or anyone else, but if we have to go in and get him, he may not be so lucky."

"Yes, Sir Yankee Captain," the man responded and quickly hurried off toward the last car. Goodman returned in a few minutes accompanied by a middle-aged soldier; the man walked with a limp as if injured.

"What's your name, Soldier," James asked him as the man stepped down off the train. He was not armed. "I am Sergeant

Alfonse Bennetti, New Orleans Mounted Lancers, Sir," the man responded politely. "And you, Sir?" He asked.

"Captain James McCaffrey, Commander, New York, Sixteenth Calvary, Sixty-Ninth Division United States Army."

"You are a long ways from home, Captain McCaffrey." The man responded.

"I might say that about you too, Sergeant." James replied, with a slight grin beginning to show on his face.

"No, I was just thinking, Captain that you and your people have placed yourselves in harm's way between our troops in the Carolinas and here in Virginia. There is no way you and your troop will make it out of Virginia; you're completely cut off from your own army."

"Thank you for your advice, Sergeant Bennetti, but we did not come here with the view of returning. We plan on joining General Grant when he accepts General Lee's surrender of all Confederate forces at Richmond."

This last response appeared to demoralize the Reb sergeant; he just shook his head but offered no response.

"Sergeant, please show me what you have on board here," James requested of the man as he climbed down off his mount. "It is not our intention to see that any harm comes to your wounded."

"Yes, Sir," he responded meekly, leading Captain McCaffrey and Lieutenant Roberts aboard the nearest passenger car. "You can see what happened here, many of these young fellows would not have survived even if we had gotten them to the hospital at Greensboro, but it was their only hope until you people came along. Now they have no chance at all."

Rapidly making their way through each of the other passenger cars, James was sickened at what he saw. There were hundreds of sick and wounded Confederate soldiers, cared for by a half dozen medical aid workers and two middle-aged surgeons, one of whom was operating on a wounded man. They also found more than a dozen bodies of dead soldiers, men that had died en route from the battlefields South of Richmond, their corpses now stacked like cordwood at the end of each car.

Exiting the train, James turned to the Confederate sergeant and asked his tone of voice and demeanor solemn. "Can you ride, Sergeant Bennetti?"

"Yes, Sir," the man replied, "are you taking me as a prisoner?" He asked apprehensively.

"No, Sergeant, we are not." Then he called out to a nearby troop, "Bring up one of our spare mounts.

"We have destroyed the bridges between here and Danville, so it will be at least a week before they can move these men to a hospital in the Carolinas. I cannot tell you what to do, but I would like you to ride back to Richmond for medical assistance. The wounded men will need food and water; tell the commanding officer we shall give him two days to come and get them before we blow the bridges between here and Richmond. What happens after that shall be his responsibility. Do you understand, Sergeant?"

"I understand Captain and I thank you for that. I shall do my best to get aide to our injured."

"I am sure of that," James replied as Bennetti mounted. You might pass on another warning to your superiors, Sergeant," he added, "Tell them that General Grant and his army will be along soon."

Sergeant Bennetti made no comment as he spurred his borrowed mount away.

With the Reb sergeant on his way along the railroad right of way, Lieutenant Roberts asked, "What now, Captain? We're going to have to get the hell out of here; the Rebs will be thicker than hair on an old junkyard dog, looking for us."

"That they will, Mark; let's head up into the hills. We will find a spot with good cover and hole-up for a day or two; our men and our mounts need a rest. We'll find a fresh water stream where we can setup a cold camp, wash some of this grime off and get a good night's sleep. God knows' our men deserve it."

As the column moved higher into the Virginia hill country the temperature dropped precipitously; a weather front moving in from the north brought with it a scattering of rain that soon turned to sleet and snow. Although discomforting to all, James felt relieved for their tracks would again be lost to view by those who would hunt down this band of butchers; as they were sure to be called by now, hopefully by those who had witnessed the carnage left in their wake.

Shortly before midnight, Lieutenant Roberts returned to the column accompanied by the two lead scouts and reported finding a clearing ahead, both large enough to setup camp, along with terrain suitable to establish a defensive position should they be attacked. By midnight the storm had moved on and the clearing, now emblazed with light from a full moon shining on a clear field of pure white snow. It appeared to be an ideal setting for a military bivouac; they quickly unloaded the packhorses and half dozen men began preparing a cold meal of hard biscuits and cold smoked beef, courtesy of the Confederate Army warehouse at Crystal Springs. Too exhausted to eat some merely threw their blanket roll down onto one of the large canvases used to cover supplies carried by the packhorses, now laid out on top of the snow; they were asleep within minutes. At least they would get a few hours of rest before being aroused later for picket duty. Others tended to the needs of the mounts, loosening cinches, watering, feeding, and hobbling each to assure that the animal would not stray even if it broke loose of the tethering rope.

"Did you want to talk to the troop, now, Captain?" Lieutenant Roberts asked as the two men prepared to bed down for the night.

"No, Mark, let them eat and get a good night's sleep; Lord knows they've earned it. We'll talk in the morning." Within minutes, both men were sound asleep.

CHAPTER 13

THE SNIPERS

"Good morning, Captain," Lieutenant Roberts called out to James, who had just awakened from a sound sleep. The sun was high above the horizon shining brightly and the weather had warmed considerably from the night before.

"Happy New Year, Sir." Lieutenant Roberts offered with a smile.

"Good morning, Mark. Good Lord, I guess I was so preoccupied that I never even thought about the date. Happy New Year to you too, Mark."

"Thanks, Captain. I hope that this year will be a good year for all of us. If the general gets his way maybe this God-awful war will be over and we can go home."

"I hope you're right, Mark. We could make a run for home now, but General Murray sent us out here to do a job and our job is not finished, so let's gather the troops around and we will talk about it."

In the early morning sunlight, the disheveled group of young men that gathered around Captain James McCaffrey and Lieutenant Mark Roberts for a briefing looked bedraggled and worn. The accumulation of dirt and grime from ten days in the saddle, sloshing through the mud and snow of the State of Virginia left its mark on both their uniforms and bodies. Although each man took great pride in their appearance, the cold camps took a heavy toll on the soldiers' personal hygiene. When several men came down with dysentery, it further exacerbated an already serious problem. James recognized that without adequate food and rest if he continued to demand a high level of performance from his men, some would fail jeopardizing this excursion into enemy territory.

"Good morning, everybody," James greeted his men with a smile as they gathered around he and Lieutenant Roberts. "Lieutenant Roberts reminded me this morning that it is New Year's Day today, so I wish all of you happy New Year."

Several of those standing close to their commanding officer quietly returned the greeting. "Happy New Year to you, Captain," they said.

"I thought it would be appropriate to take some time this morning and talk to you about what lies ahead for us. First of all, if Johnnie Reb leaves us alone for a few hours we'll use this day to rest up and maybe clean up a bit. I think we can chance it and build a fire, at least long enough for us to make coffee and pancakes and heat up some of those smoked ribs we picked up at Crystal Springs. In addition, we can tend to our mounts' needs. When we move out we will take advantage of the river beds to hide our track as best we can, but that may be a little tough on your mount."

"Are we heading back to Petersburg, Captain?" One of the men asked; while two or three others laughed, with one responding, "Are you dreaming?"

"No, not yet; we still have work to do out here. I told the Reb sergeant that we sent off to Richmond that we would give Confederate Command two days to come and get their wounded, and then we planned to take out their bridges on the Richmond, Lynchburg line. Keeping that in mind, I would assume they would be expecting us to do just that. However, when we leave here we shall move south toward Petersburg and then hit the Petersburg, Richmond rail line south of Richmond."

"Jesus, Captain," Sergeant Davis exclaimed. That's right in the middle of Reb territory; they will be all over us."

"You are correct, Sergeant," James responded, firmly, nodding his head in agreement with his sergeant. "But we are in the middle of Reb territory now and from here on there is no safe place for any of us. We must move clandestinely, attacking at night or at daybreak and try to stay one-step ahead of Johnny Rebs' people. Just remember that our people are once again preparing to attack the breastworks at Petersburg; you have been there, you know what that means. We lost over a thousand men in our last attack; General Murray has promised the men who will be leading the next one that we would do whatever was necessary to make sure that does not happen again. Our job is to help keep that promise by interdicting the Reb supply lines and destroying their ability to reinforce Lee's army at Petersburg. So far, you have done a magnificent job towards accomplishing that objective. The Rebs use three rail lines to run supplies and troops into Petersburg. We have taken out one of them, the Danville, Petersburg line; but the Lynchburg, and Richmond to Petersburg routes are still operating. Richmond is the Confederates' key staging area for shipping men and equipment into Petersburg, if we can block that line we can stop General Lee in his tracks.

"Our next target then will be the Richmond, Petersburg rail line and we have a three day march ahead of us before we get there. So rest up today, but be prepared to move out tonight."

"The fires, Sir, is that wise?" Lieutenant Roberts asked, sounding worried, as the men began to move off to gather firewood. "On a day like today the Rebs will be able to see the smoke from miles away."

"Take a good look at your people, Mark. They need to dry-out their boots and change into dry clothing, they also need a hot meal, or we may very well lose some of these men to pneumonia or something worse. We will have to take our chances, but stay alert and ready to move out at a moment's notice."

Shortly after seven o'clock, as the Sixteenth Battalion prepared to move out, with the moon clearly illuminating the snow covered bivouac area, a shot rang out. The sound reverberated across the nearby foothills, followed by a fusillade of rifle fire.

"Mount up, and hold your positions," Captain McCaffrey called out, "pass the word."

The men of the Sixteenth did not have to wait long before the north picket came galloping toward the clearing, bringing his mount to an abrupt halt near James and Lieutenant Roberts.

"Report, Trooper," Lieutenant Roberts' clipped words greeted the young man.

"Trooper Buckley, reporting, Sir. It was a scout, Sir, I shot him." The man responded excitedly; "I don't think he even saw me until I drew down on him; he turned to run and when he went down his horse took off. He was alive, Lieutenant and I went over to check him out, and then I saw the first group of three or four troops coming in at a gallop, shooting. There were a lot more behind them, so I skedaddled out of there as fast as I could."

"How many more, Trooper?" James demanded his voice grim.

"I don't know, Sir, but I would guess more than one hundred, possibly a full troop."

"Thank you, Trooper Buckley, you did a fine job; now take your place in the column we are preparing to move out."

"Yes, Sir."

"You heard that, Mark?" James asked Lieutenant Roberts.

"Yes, Sir," Mark responded.

"Then let's move out, we'll head south then circle back around toward Richmond. The Rebs will expect us to hide out somewhere nearby, yet their cavalry will be tracking us, so we shall follow the rivers and streams wherever we can to conceal our tracks. However, as we discussed before; we may have to fight our way out of here."

Within minutes of the arrival of the trooper, the other perimeter pickets, hearing the rifle fire, following procedure, quickly returned to camp. With no sign of the Confederate troops encountered earlier by the lone picket, and all hands accounted for, James led the column at a fast pace through a brush-covered gulch and away from the bivouac rest stop. He assumed the Reb cavalry troop commander would scout out his enemies base and probably wait for daylight before moving in on the now empty clearing. However, he was also aware that Reb cavalrymen were some of the most skilled and feared soldiers encountered by Union forces. Once they learned their quarry had slipped away in the night, James knew they would be quick to follow and would attack his column without hesitation. He figured they had at least an eight or possibly ten hour head start; enough time to put twenty miles or more between his men and their very capable adversary. They would take full advantage of the moonlight and move as swiftly as the rough terrain allowed, but all of them knew that with the light of a full moon and sound of a rapidly moving cavalry column of nearly eighty men, it could lead to discovery by an unseen enemy.

Coming down out of the foothills, James brought the column to a halt in the middle of a shallow stream to water their mounts and to send out a decoy designed to buy time for his men.

"You know what we need, Mark," he said quietly to Lieutenant Roberts, "two squads upstream a quarter mile or so; make sure they leave a clear trail along the riverbank. We will wait here, and then move downstream when you return."

While waiting the return of Lieutenant Roberts, who led his men upstream, James rode in among the troops, who had dismounted and were now standing along the water's edge watering their mounts. Responding to their queries and concerns, he found, to his great pleasure that nearly all appeared to be in good spirits. Dry clothing, warm food, and a day's rest appeared to have transformed these young men from a band of tired, devitalized individuals into a close-knit body of professional soldiers anxious once again to take on their next assignment. Several expressed their desire to hit the Confederates again, here in the secessionists' own territory.

"What do you think, Captain," one man called out, "will we put the Reb railroad people out of business tomorrow?" While another responded, confidently, "Not tomorrow, Jack, but soon. Right, Captain?" The man asked.

"Not tomorrow, we are still about forty miles or so out, but you can bet that when we hit that main rail line between Richmond and Petersburg a lot of Reb soldiers are going to wish to hell that they had stayed home and taken care of their women folk."

"I would volunteer for that duty, Captain." One man replied, "There has to be a lot widows down there just waiting for me." The men laughed at the trooper's response.

Upon Lieutenant Robert's return to the column, he reigned in his mount next to his captain, clearly satisfied that their decoy would give them a few more hours of unhindered troop movement from any pursuing force. "It looks good, Captain; we left enough track that would indicate we moved on upstream. It might throw them off for awhile."

"Good, Mark, we may need it. Looking at the map it appears that we have about forty more miles to cover before we get to the main rail line. I would like to get there undetected and give the explosive teams the opportunity to set up shop before the Rebs find us; from now on, no matter where we turn, we shall be outnumbered. Your men will not have much time to set off an explosive charge if we are exposed."

The column traveled downstream in the shallow water for more than a mile, then breaking out onto a series of small sandbars James led his men out of the riverbed where the terrain leveled and they soon found themselves in a farmer's pasture. In the distance, they could see a small cottage and several out buildings, but they were far enough away that even in the moonlight, should anyone be awake it would be doubtful they would spot the column as it moved silently across the farmer's field.

Shortly after midnight the men of the lead scouts noticed a faint glow of orange light that began to appear on the eastern horizon; word passed quickly through the column, "Rebs ahead."

"Reb campfires?" Lieutenant Roberts responded.

"That would be my guess, Mark."

"How many miles would you guess, Captain?"

"Twenty, maybe twenty-five; it's hard to say. This time of morning most of them will be asleep, so the fires have probably burned down, unless those are pickets just trying to keep warm. What is it, about three o'clock?"

"Yes, about that, the moon has moved clean across the sky since we broke camp."

"Well Mark we know where we want to go, but we do not need to see what Johnnie Reb is having for breakfast. We shall set an easterly course, bypassing their camp by a mile or two. When we get closer, send a scout out to see how many troops are there and what they are up to."

"The Reb campsite is about two miles northeast of us, Captain," Sergeant Gayle Davis said, reporting in to his captain upon returning from a mid morning scouting of the Confederate base. "It is a small camp, Captain; two or three wooden structures, probably some farmer's former home with the usual out buildings and I counted twenty or so military tents and a remuda of about two-hundred mounts. There are a few wagons and a upwards of half dozen field guns with limbers attached, but no sign of patrols moving in or out of the base. They must feel pretty secure this far from the front lines."

"Thank you, Sergeant. We will give them a wide birth and continue east toward the rail line. My map does not cover this area, but I estimate that we should see some sign of the Richmond, Petersburg line by tomorrow. Let us move out, Mark. We need to find a secure bivouac site until after dark."

By late afternoon, the weather had warmed considerably and the warm sunlight provided an opportunity for those in need, to catch up on their sleep. Yet sleeping on a moving animal was never a "bed of roses," as Sergeant Davis would remind his men. Still, troops who spent many hours in the saddle often felt completely refreshed even after a few minutes of deep sleep while traveling great distances on their mount.

"We best find a campsite soon, Mark. Our people need a rest. It looks like a heavy growth of scrub pine and brush up ahead. It may provide us the cover we need and the terrain is high enough that our sight distances will not be obscured."

"I'll check it out, Captain." Lieutenant Roberts replied, calling for Sergeant Davis to join him, the two men galloped off toward the nearby site. A few minutes later Roberts signaled with his hat for the column to come ahead. The area turned out to be an ideal place with a small mountain stream running through it with plenty of open space in a park like setting of Virginia Pine and evergreen bushes. After attending to their mounts and assigned picket duties, troops wrapped themselves in their blankets and were soon sound asleep in the warmth of the afternoon sunlight.

At sunset, the column was once again on its way toward the Richmond, Petersburg rail line. This night however due to the difficult terrain and heavy growth of pine and scrub brush they made little progress until shortly after midnight when the lead scout returned to the column. "Trooper Collins reporting, Sir" The young man said bringing his mount to a halt near Lieutenant Roberts.

"What is it, Collins?"

"A roadway about one-half mile ahead, Sir; it runs east and west," the trooper reported. "It appears to be heavily used. Lots of supply type wagons and possibly fully loaded limbers and all the indications of a mounted escort have used it recently. I would estimate twenty or more troops came through within the past day, or two days at most."

"Sounds like a secondary supply route for the Rebs," Lieutenant Roberts commented to James.

"I agree with you, Mark. It probably leads to either a supply dump at a rail siding, and or a support facility for troops, or both. So let's take advantage of the roadway, we can pick up our pace a bit. Those lights we saw in the distance earlier this evening are most likely at the main rail line or awful close to it. Send Sergeant Davis along with a Troop to lead the way at a canter; we should wind up fairly close to that camp before daylight."

Shortly before sunup with the moon quickly fading, and a faint glimmer of light beginning to show on the eastern horizon, the two men reined-in their mounts. Ahead the roadway dropped precipitously over the edge of a ridge and led directly down into a Reb campsite.

"Looks like we found trouble, Sergeant," Trooper Collins said quietly.

"I believe you are right, Soldier. Let's watch this for a moment or two."

From their location on the edge of the ridge, the two men had an excellent view of the predawn awakening of a Confederate campsite. After a few moments Davis said, "I think we have found what our Captain was looking for. I shall stay here and keep watch; you skedaddle back to the column and tell the Captain what we have here."

As Trooper Collins approached Captain McCaffrey and his troops, McCaffrey raised his arm bringing the column to a halt, "Pass the word, hold here, and wait," he commanded quietly.

"What is it, Trooper?" James asked.

"It's a large military complex, Captain, larger than anything we have come across since we left Petersburg. Several buildings and hundreds of tents, it's too dark yet to get an accurate assessment of the size; but I would guess it would accommodate a division or even two."

"Let's take a look, Lieutenant," he called out to Mark Roberts and the two men followed Trooper Collins back to Sergeant Davis's location. They found the man now about two-hundred yards off the roadway, sitting on a ridge overlooking the huge valley below.

"Looks like we found what you were seeking, Captain," Sergeant Davis said, smiling. "Not much activity yet, but it looks like they are lighting up the fires in the kitchen for breakfast and I saw a couple of men at the corrals, probably feeding livestock."

"We best move the battalion out of here, Mark right away; will you see to it, please. We shall bypass the camp for now, but find something within a mile or two of here for a secure bivouac. Sergeant Davis and I shall stay here to get a good look at what the Rebs have down there and then we shall join you. It could be that, that hilltop you can see there in the distance may work for you." James pointed to the southwest to a series of low-lying, heavily forested ridges.

"Be careful, Captain, if Sergeant Davis is right the people in that camp may use this roadway today; we are awfully close."

"We shall be careful, Mark."

When Lieutenant Roberts and trooper Collins left the ridge, James and Sergeant Davis sought to find a more secure observation site, which would also provide a better view of the Confederate Army base below. With the Sun starting to clear the horizon, their new location gave them what they needed; a clear view of the entire valley below. At this location, they were surprised to see, what had to be the main north, south rail line between Richmond and Petersburg. There was a train, on the main line and another on a siding nearby.

For the next four hours, using James' spyglass, the two men identified and sketched the key components of the army base. It included a clearly marked headquarters building flying the Confederate flag, with a nearby mess hall and both the officer and enlisted men's tent areas. Beyond this sat several storage type structures, corrals, cannons, limbers, armory, explosive storage bunkers, and haystacks. There were a cluster of tents nearby, apparently the home of fifty or more Negro field hands and servants, both male and female.

Before noon James had what he needed, "I think that will do it Sergeant, now we have to figure how to get out of here without being seen and find the troop."

"I think I know what you have in mind, Captain." Sergeant Davis commented with a slight grin showing his tobacco stained teeth.

"What is it, Sergeant?" James responded, innocently.

"You are going to hit them right here, tonight. We will get two for one, tie up their rail road, and close down this base, at the same time."

"Yes, we'll tie them up for at least a few days. How would you go about it, Sergeant?"

"You know me, Captain, I'd hit the bastards while they're sleeping and run like hell for home, but I don't think that's what General Murray had in mind when he sent us on this little excursion. I mean the running for home part." He laughed quietly.

"You're right on target, Sergeant; we shall hit 'em before sunup tomorrow, but no, we cannot head for home until these people are dead or raise the white flag. However, I haven't seen any indication that, that is in the cards for us; at least not for the immediate future."

Within the hour, James and Sergeant Davis rejoined the column, now bivouacked in a secluded grove of trees five miles south of the Reb military encampment. The men appeared rested and anxious to hear from their commanding officer; with several wagering that because of the presence of such a large number of enemy troops camped in the valley below the captain might choose to cut a wide path around this base and move on. Earlier, they had suggested just such an eventuality to Lieutenant Roberts, telling the Lieutenant "There are too many Rebs Lieutenant. They must outnumber us five to one." "You don't know the captain like I do if you think he will walk away from this fight; you're wrong. He will go after those people wherever they are, until they surrender or die. He's in this to win and so am I." To those who favored bypassing this target, his response was not what they wanted to hear.

"Gather around, gentlemen," James called out quietly to his troops, now waiting anxiously to learn what lay ahead for members of the Sixteenth Battalion. "This afternoon, Lieutenant Roberts and your sergeants shall work out the details for an attack on the Reb campsite at dawn tomorrow. There are many well-armed people down there, too many for us to hope to overcome. However, what I propose to do is to diminish their ability to make war on our men at Petersburg by destroying their ammunition dump, food supplies, and the two trains in the rail yard. Sergeant Davis and I have a detailed map of the base and high priority targets. If we are going to succeed in this, it will depend on how well we coordinate our attack, timing is everything. We must maintain absolute silence and your knife, not your saber should be the weapon of choice to that end. You ordinance men will need time to set your charges in the railroad engines and bunkers; then we shall burn them out and skedaddle. Your sergeant will give each of you specific assignments later today, so get some rest, for tomorrow you shall be very, very busy."

Sergeant Davis described in detail to Lieutenant Roberts and the noncommissioned officers the layout of the camp and the exact location of specific targets. Listening to this discussion, James found himself quietly admiring this staff of professionals; some demanded a second or even a third clarification of the role a particular sergeant and his men would pursue during the raid. When the planning session was over it was obvious to all that to be successful their primary objectives were the explosives' bunkers and the need to get the explosive team in and out quietly, and onto their secondary targets, the destruction of the train engines.

Yet, before they finished, Lieutenant Roberts warned, "It is crucial that we scatter the Confederate mounts; otherwise there will be little chance of escaping a contingent of enemy pursuers this large. When it is over, should any one become separated from your squad, we shall regroup on the ridge overlooking the camp."

"Also, remember," Sergeant Davis, added, "Although there is no indication of remote picket assignments, or guards on the explosive bunkers, that may not apply at night. I say that because even after four years of combat experience, you men are primarily horse soldiers and most of you have not been in a position where your life or someone else's life depended upon your willingness to use a knife to silence a guard. Some may find themselves in those circumstances tomorrow." His fellow sergeants knew of the revulsion experienced by veteran soldiers when first required to end a life with a violent thrust of a knife into the throat of another human being.

Before sunup Lieutenant Roberts and the explosive teams, and one squad of troops assigned to run-off the Rebs' mounts, worked their way around the outer edge of the Confederate campsite to the railroad siding and into the explosive bunkers and corrals located nearby. James, along with Sergeant Davis and four other sergeants with their squads, quietly approached the main entrance to the camp on foot. Finding only one guard at the gate, who was sound asleep and the gate wide open, Sergeant Davis struck the man on the head with the butt of his carbine rendering him unconscious.

Staying clear of the Rebs' housing quarters the men quickly spread throughout the camp starting fires in each of the wooden structures that they believed might contain explosives. When they entered the headquarters building, they found the base commander, a brigadier general, and his deputy both sound asleep. The attacking force took the two men into custody without incident.

Yet, within minutes, a yell came from the enlisted men's housing area, when a Reb hollered, "Our mounts are out, somebody left the damn gate open." Shortly thereafter two enormous explosions occurred from within the locomotive engines that shook the entire campsite. Within seconds of the second explosion, hundreds of rebel troops emerged from their tents, with some firing at Lieutenant Roberts' men, others at shadows or merely from fright. By this time, Captain McCaffrey and his "fire starters" began to arrive back at the main gate in time to meet with the wranglers who brought in their mounts. "Who do you have there, Sergeant? James asked as Davis and two of his men approached with two men still dressed in their underwear and little else.

"This is Brigadier General Horace Sutherland, he says he is the base commander and that poor fellow there is his deputy, Colonel Johnson."

"Good show, Sergeant, we'll take them with us, for now." As they were speaking, a huge explosion rocked the ground around them jolting the entire base and surrounding countryside. The shockwave that followed rolled across the valley floor with the speed of a lightning bolt. Shortly thereafter, a fusillade of musketry erupted from a hundred different locations within the camp itself. Lieutenant Robert's men on the eastern edge of the camp now caught out in the open, bore the brunt of this Reb response. Captain McCaffrey and his men, silhouetted in the light from burning structures as they moved back toward the front gate also came under fire.

"Get the General and his aide aboard our spare horses, Sergeant and watch him," James yelled, then turning his attention to Lieutenant Roberts' plight, called out loudly, "provide cover fire for Lieutenant Roberts' men." However, by now the smoke from more than a dozen structural and haystack fires obscured the view for both Union and Confederate forces, leading James to yell, "Fire low into the smoke and keep firing until we are out of here."

Meeting Lieutenant Roberts's men at the main gate, James called out, "move out at a gallop, we cannot stay here." The column reformed and fled west on the road from which they came, with James dropping back to the rear to get a last look at the burning campsite. Later when they reached the top of the ridge overlooking the campsite, Lieutenant Roberts brought the column to a halt and waited for his captain.

Upon regaining his position at the head of the column, James, said, "Move out quickly, Lieutenant; lead us back to your bivouac area, we cannot stop here." Moving at a fast pace they soon arrived at their former campsite where James ordered, "Captain's conference, pass the word." When his men assembled, he was saddened to find that only seven of his sergeants were available to report in to he and Lieutenant Roberts, and one of those, Sergeant Bruce Taylor suffered severe injuries in the raid.

"Report Sergeant Taylor," James said addressing the injured man, as two troops attended to his wounds.

"Sorry, Captain, I was too close to the explosives bunker when it blew; I was struck by debris. I lost two of my men in the explosion, the rest made it out okay."

"You can be proud of those men, Sergeant; today you saved the lives of dozens of our people at Petersburg and for sure you have shortened this war." Yet as the sergeants, one after another vocalized their reports, it was evident the Sixteenth Battalion had suffered severely in this, their third major encounter with Reb forces since leaving Petersburg. In this short but violent firefight with the Rebs in the rail yards and at the corrals, Lieutenant Roberts lost one sergeant and two troopers. For those who followed Captain McCaffrey into the interior of the camp, Sergeant Albert Miller and four members of his squad met a violent end while attacking a large group of Rebs holed up near the Reb mess tent. However, six others, although wounded, made their way through the heavy smoke to the main gate and escaped capture. In the absence of medical aid, it was now up to their fellow soldiers to save their lives.

After receiving the last report from his sergeants, James addressed the assembled group, "Gentlemen, you accomplished something quite spectacular here today; I would venture to say, no other group of men in the history of warfare can add such a victory to their credit. It is not that I wish to diminish the accomplishments of others, but today, men of the Sixteenth deprived an entire army division the tools necessary to make war against their fellow citizens. You really are New York's finest soldiers and it has been an honor to serve with you. However, now we have to get our injured out of here."

Turning to Sergeant Taylor he said, "I am going to send you home, Sergeant. Do you think you can ride?"

Taylor, responded with a smile, "Yes, Sir I can ride. I would like to stay with you Captain and the men of the Sixteenth for this has been most rewarding for me personally. However, I understand; I will only slow you down."

"Good, I want you to take our Confederate general, with you," James said pointing to General Sutherland held under guard along with his deputy standing nearby, and our wounded troopers. I would estimate we are about fifty miles out; you will have to travel at night, but with luck, you should be in Petersburg in three to four days. Lieutenant Roberts will assign four troops to accompany you. They will have to take care of the wounded men and guard General Sutherland. When you get in, I want you to report directly to General Murray; fill him in on what we found here and what we accomplished to date. However, right now, we have to move out of here; it will not take long for the Rebs to round up enough mounts to come looking for us. We shall leave a trail that their scouts can follow, so stay with us until we ford the nearest river then break for home. Good luck to you, Sergeant."

"Thank you, Sir," the man responded quietly, "Good luck to you too, Sir."

Turning to Sergeant Davis standing nearby, James said, "Cut Colonel Johnson loose, Sergeant. Taylor will have his hands full with one prisoner plus our wounded; let's not burden him with too many problems." Then nodding to his

Lieutenant, Mark Roberts yelled out, “Prepare to mount,” once the wounded men, with the aid of their comrades were in saddle he called out, “Mount, let’s move out.”

The column traveled in silence for several miles before James asked his Lieutenant the first of many questions. “Did your men take down the telegraph line, Mark?”

“Yes, Sir. However, I believe the telegraph office must have been located in the Division Headquarters building. I never found it in the rail yard.”

“Check with Sergeant Davis when you get a chance; Davis and his men took custody of our two prisoners within minutes so it’s doubtful that either one got a message off. Knowing the military, it would be a challenge for men of that rank to be knowledgeable of telegraph operations. What happened with Sergeant Taylor and his two men at the explosives bunker?”

“Damp powder, our fuses did not work, they went back in and used the Rebs’ powder as a fuse. Sergeant Taylor told me he underestimated the time they had to get out; it burned faster than he imagined it would.”

“What about the armory; did we get it?”

“Yes, Sergeant Taylor was setting the fuse in the armory when the bunker went up; he was hit by flying timbers.”

“And your other men, what happened there?”

“They drew down on us as we came out of the corrals; we never got a shot off. There were eight or ten Rebs, still dressed in their underwear; but they blew my guys apart.”

“How many cavalry mounts would you estimate were in the corrals, Mark?”

“Upwards of two-hundred cavalry mounts, the rest were limber or supply wagon types; maybe four-hundred in all. They must have been planning to move out this morning otherwise most of the horses would have been out to pasture. The camp had to be a productive farm at one time, the barn was quite large along with, a half dozen granaries, and fenced pasture adjacent to the corrals."

"Your men did a magnificent job, Mark. You put the railroad out of business and even got to their grain supply and haystacks; they will burn for days. General Sutherland will have a lot of explaining to do to his command when this war is over. Can you imagine trying to explain to President Davis that you lost your entire command because you failed to post pickets or sentries to protect the Confederate assets entrusted to you by your fellow citizens." James laughed at the irony of it all, "Think of it, Mark, five thousand men at war with their neighbors, with only one sentry on duty, and he took time out for a nap."

"We were lucky, Captain."

"Yes, I suppose we were, Mark, but just maybe the Good Lord was on our side today."

The column continued to wind its way south along the shores of a small river until after dark where it turned back toward the Richmond, Petersburg rail line. "Stay with the river bed as long as you can, Sergeant Taylor." James offered, "We shall leave a heavy trail eastward and hopefully the Rebs will come after us. Stay alert, your prisoner will not go willingly; dishonor and humiliation is not something a general officer will want to be burdened with for the rest of his life. He will kill you or some of your men if the opportunity presents itself."

"Thanks, Captain, we shall watch him closely. I shall hog-tie him if we have to." James smiled at the sergeant's response. "Good luck to you and the men of the Sixteenth, Captain. It was a pleasure serving with you."

"Thank you, Sergeant, good luck to you; take care."

Turning east, away from the river, James brought his mount and the column to a halt while they watched Sergeant Taylor and his people move down river, until lost to view.

"That was good advice you passed on to Sergeant Taylor, Captain. I watched Sutherland closely and I think he may be a mean, conniving son of a bitch. He is apt to kill somebody to get loose; he knows he screwed up and the Reb commanders will hold him responsible. His own people will hold him in contempt."

"That's my assessment of him also, Mark. That's why I sent four troops along with Sergeant Taylor; he will probably try something, but you tell me our Sergeant Taylor is a tough nut."

"I think he will bring that Reb General in tied over a saddle if need be." Lieutenant Roberts responded with a quiet chuckle. "Taylor would do that."

The men of the Sixteenth rode on in silence for four hours, all the while climbing slowly into the foothills of Central Virginia. Coming across a small stream, James, addressing Lieutenant Roberts said, "Let's rest here for a spell, Mark. Have the men eat and care for their mounts. "How is our grain holding out?" He asked.

"We are just about out, Sir, maybe enough for one more day, we'll have to raid some farmer's granary soon or put our mounts out to pasture. There aren't any farms up this high, however lots of new grass showing up with the snow melting; we will be okay for awhile."

"Good, when we get up on the top of this hill, if we have a clear view of the surrounding area, we'll set up camp and have our people rest for awhile. What about our explosive supplies; what have we got left?"

"Only two tins of black powder, but we still have a couple of dozen Ketchum grenades, and one Haupt's torpedo, that's it. However, it's enough to bring down any one of the smaller railroad trestles, but nothing large."

"What about food, Mark?"

"We are in good shape there, Captain; we've lost so many troops that we now have enough supplies to last the rest of us for four or five days." Lieutenant Roberts responded with a clear note of sorrow in his voice.

"You and I shall have a lot of letters to write, Mark when we get back to Petersburg."

"Yes, we certainly shall, Sir."

"Tomorrow I will need your help, Mark. I must bring our reports up to date. I am sorry to say this, but I cannot remember all of their names. I remember their faces, or at least I think I do and their rank, but for the life of me, I cannot remember all of their names. The names are there on my duty roster, but God help me, except for Lieutenant Moore and couple of others, I'm drawing a complete blank."

"You are no different than the rest of us, Captain, you're worn out; and your men are on the verge of collapse. Neither you, nor the rest of us have had a hot meal or bath, or a bed to sleep in for nearly three weeks; when is it going to end?" Mark Roberts asked rather pointedly, for he too was feeling the strain of this patrol with their most recent escape from the clutches of the Confederates' Angel of Death.

"I guess it will end, Mark when we have accomplished our objective and I cannot tell you now when that is going to happen. The Rebs are still killing our people and they will continue to do so until we stop them. General Murray said our job was to interdict, harass, and destroy the Confederate

Army's ability to wage war against their fellow Americans. The Rebs are still on a killing spree, so when that ends, I guess we can go home."

It was a beautiful spring morning when James awoke from a sound sleep. The sun was shining brightly its rays warming everything it touched including his feet for he had taken his boots off before going to sleep to dry his stockings. Even though the ground he slept on was hard, he felt completely rested with the sun and warm air bringing a sense of comfort to his entire body. While getting into his boots, Sergeant Davis came by and handed him a cup of hot coffee.

"Good morning, Captain," he offered cheerily, "I took it upon myself to approve of the campfire, Sir. I told the men to warm up the rest of those smoked ribs, and stir-up a plate or two of biscuits; we have some great cooks in this outfit of ours, Captain." He chuckled.

"No sign of confederate activity, Gayle?"

"No, Sir, nothing. We have a three-hundred and sixty degree view from this hill top and no sign of a Reb patrol, but just in case our pickets are out about a mile and I gave one of them your spy glass and he is over there on top of that nearest peak." Davis offered as if to assure his commanding officer the battalion would be safe from a surprise attack should the Rebs move in on their bivouac area. "He has the mirrors that we took off the Rebs last week, just in case."

"That's great, Gayle," James responded. "Has everybody eaten?"

"Everybody but you and the lieutenant, Captain. Lieutenant Roberts is still asleep; he was pretty well worn out; so I let him be."

"Great, let me wash some of this crud off and I'll join you. Where is that stream?"

"Right down there, Captain." Sergeant Davis said pointing to a small mountain creek running through the clearing.

Later, when James approached the small fire, he found all five of his remaining sergeants there enjoying a last cup of coffee and a hot biscuit. Although they had already eaten they purposely came back to the campfire to find out what lie ahead for them.

"What are your plans for us today, Captain?" Sergeant Mike Addison, never one to shy away from questioning an officer, asked.

"Nothing today, Sergeant. We need to get our people and livestock fed and rested; tomorrow we head back toward the Richmond, Petersburg rail line. I want to take another crack at the secessionists' supply line. We have a few explosives left; Lieutenant Roberts thinks we have enough to take out a small to medium sized trestle. I have a map for this immediate area and it looks like we are about twenty miles out from the James River. We will head for that, there is a small mining town between here and there so we might pick up a few supplies. If the mine is operational they'll have dynamite and we need grain for our mounts, so that will be our first stop."

"Eat up, Sir, and I'll get you some more coffee," Sergeant Davis offered, handing a tin plate of biscuits and beans, with a couple of smoked ribs on it to his captain.

"What do we do then, Captain?" Sergeant Addison continued to pursue the questioning and James was glad he did. He wanted his men to know what lie ahead for them and to assess their eagerness to take on another superior force of determined Confederate soldiers. By now the Rebs not only knew a Union Cavalry unit was operating in their territory, but that they had successfully pulled off four raids and taken down several railroad bridges and in the process, killed more than one hundred Confederate soldiers.

"We keep doing what we came out here to do, Sergeant," James offered, quietly. "The only thing that has changed is that our enemy now knows who we are, why we are here, what our intended targets will be and our approximate strength. He will be able to surmise the rest. He knows that they have killed several of our men. He also knows that they will have to kill us to stop us, and that is what they shall most assuredly try to do. Therefore, we have to change our tactics a bit. We will continue to focus on the Richmond-Pittsburg rail sector, but as we are short on explosives, we will focus on tearing up and twisting their rails at several locations. When they send in repair crews, our snipers will take them out."

"Do we take out both the train crews and the security folks, Captain; Reb troops are sure to be with them?" Sergeant Addison asked.

"We shall do what is necessary to interdict supplies destined for their people at Petersburg, Sergeant," James responded firmly, leaving no doubt in anyone's mind that their captain intended to carry out General Murray's orders to the letter.

As darkness settled across the Virginia hills, the Sixteenth was again underway, still heading east toward the Richmond, Petersburg rail corridor.

"What do you think the Reb response will be, Captain, when we show up there tomorrow morning?" Lieutenant Roberts inquired solemnly as the two men traveled side by side in the moonlight. "If I were the Reb commander, Mark, I would have pickets out all along this section of the Richmond, Pittsburg rail corridor, with snipers and heavily armed cavalry troops nearby. I think they will do whatever is necessary to protect their only viable link between these two cities."

"I tend to agree with you, Captain, so what shall we do?" Lieutenant Roberts asked solicitously.

"Scout them out thoroughly, Mark. Once we take sight of the rail line, we hold up the column and send in our scouts, on foot if necessary, taking full advantage of this heavy growth of underbrush. We take out their scouts, and then position our snipers to take out any additional troops that may happen along. This should give our teams the opportunity needed to take out two or more sections of rail, possibly a half mile apart. If a larger force shows up before we get our men out, we shall have to commit the column for back up. If their responding force looks like it would not prove to be vulnerable to ours, we shall have to make a run for it; but that contingency plan is no different than what we planned for before we undertook this assignment."

"There is our first target of the day, Mark," James said handing his spyglass off to Lieutenant Roberts and pointing to a small cluster of buildings in the distance. "It looks like a coal mine operation on the edge of town; perhaps that will be our source for a supply of dynamite."

"There are a couple of farms between here and the mine, Captain," Mark Roberts exclaimed while using the spyglass, "and if I am not mistaken, there is a locomotive with a couple of coal cars and it's moving from the town out toward the mine. If we move in now, Captain we can rip up the rail behind them and cutoff their access back to the village; then dismantle the locomotive at our leisure."

"Okay, Mark, there is no sign of Confederate troops so let's get it done. Take two squads and take out the track; I will send Sergeant Davis with his men to visit those two farms, we need to replenish our grain supplies and burn anything that the Rebs can use. Afterwards, we shall meet at the mine and then move on into the village."

Within the hour, Lieutenant Roberts' men successfully ripped out a half dozen lengths of rail and destroyed each by twisting them like the proverbial pretzel, and then quietly moved off toward the coalmine. In the meantime, the train crew began to take on the necessary water to refill the coal tender's tanks. Yet before completing this task, troopers from the Sixteenth moved in and surrounded the locomotive surprising the three-man crew.

"Jesus, Yank! Where the hell did ye come from?" The startled train engineer said to Captain McCaffrey, as James and Lieutenant Roberts climbed into the steam engine directly from their mounts while two troopers dropped down from the coal tender into the cab.

"Good morning, Sir," James said, smiling, responding to the surprised man's greeting. He was a heavy set, middle-aged individual dressed in the typical grey coveralls, blue hat, with a red kerchief tied around his neck, not unlike the railroad men encountered earlier at Crystal Springs and Fairwood incidents.

"Mr. Lincoln sent us, Sir; we came for your train and I would like you and your crew here to get as far away from here as quickly as you can as we are going to blow it apart."

"Well it is not my train, young fella," the man offered, soberly, it belongs to the Piedmont Richmond Railroad Company; but it has been a good train. Is it really necessary to do that?"

"I'm afraid it is old timer," James replied, quietly, "all three of you best be moving, we do not have much time."

"I can believe that, Yank," another member of the crew offered, sarcastically. "When our boys get here, they'll cut you and your gang to pieces."

"You better take the captain's advice, Sir," Lieutenant Roberts replied curtly to the man. "If you stay here, you die."

"Come on Charlie," the engineer called out to his crewman as he stepped off the train, "get off the engine, these fellows look like they mean business."

"Did you find the dynamite, Mark?" James inquired as he watched the three train crewmembers walking back down the track toward the village.

"Yes, Sir, more than we need; they are loading it out now on our pack animals and the charges are set to go in the mine shaft when you give the okay."

"Are all the miners out?"

"Yes, Sir, they're heading across the fields for home; they know what we have in mind."

"Good, your men know what has to be done here; make sure they get far enough away, there is a lot of heavy metal in this old engine."

"They will, Captain."

Moving across the fields toward the village of Easton James brought the column to a halt with everyone turning to watch the two-man demolition teams' handy work on the Piedmont, Richmond train. As they watched, the two men quickly rejoined the man with their horses, mounted and all three rode away from the train to rejoin the column.

"It should blow right about now, Sir," Trooper Al O'Brien said reporting to his Lieutenant. The explosion that followed literally tore the train engine apart with huge sections of the engine, shards of metal, wood, and chunks of coal scattered in every direction for a quarter mile or more. A second explosion, more seen than heard shook the ground around them and a huge black and grey cloud of smoke and coal dust poured from the mine entrance, completely engulfing the train engine and cable towers.

"Jesus, O'Brien," Mark Roberts exclaimed, "how much dynamite did you use?'

"Every stick that we could not carry away, Sir, we put a whole case in the fire box with a half dozen grenades and about five boxes in the mine shaft. It will take them at least a year to get the mine back in operation."

"Great job, gentlemen, congratulations, but let's get out of here and see what the townsfolk have to offer us before their troops show up."

When they entered the Village of Easton, Virginia, two groups of townspeople greeted this enemy in the blue uniform carrying the American flag. One was a morosely looking gathering of white citizens who stood in front of the coal company's combination grocery and dry goods store. While across the street, a small group of Negros appeared more receptive to their uninvited guests, with a few of the children even coming forward to greet the troops. At first glance upon observing the citizens of Easton, Virginia James thought of his former home village of Mala in County Cork. There whenever the High Sheriff of Cork County or a group of the Royal Constabulary came in mass to evict a member of the McCaffrey or Malone Clan from their ancestral lands, the families gathered in the village quietly. Most of the men and several women came armed with a hidden knife, sword, or gun. James wondered if that might not be the case here today.

Although the war had taken its toll on these working families, the evidence of a long lasting and debilitating poverty was everywhere. The children, both black and white were barefoot, wearing patched and sewn hand-me-down clothing, while their mothers' wore long drab looking dresses that showed wear and repeated stitching by someone skilled with needle and thread.

The town itself was most uninviting, a typical company town where each home was nearly identical to its neighbor, indistinguishable one from another except for an occasional different display of a garden or empty flower bed or clothes line or out house. None of the buildings showed any evidence of being painted and the housing for negro servants or slaves was indistinguishable from their white property owner's except the buildings were smaller and grouped closer together at some distance from their white neighbors.

"Do you have a mayor or spokesperson for your village?" James called out to the crowd in front of the store, where a middle-aged man dressed as if he just came out a coal mine stepped forward. "I am Sam Owens, the mayor of this town, Yank;" he responded angrily. "What is it that you want of us?"

"We came to destroy your mine and the railroad so that it and you can no longer provide supplies to the Confederate troops at Richmond and Petersburg. That is our mission and our sole purpose is to help end this terrible war. When we have accomplished that, we shall move on. We will take only what we need from the company store, and leave you in peace."

As James was talking to Mayor Owens a shot rang out, followed by a woman's scream, then another screamed, "You shot my daughter."

"He's on the roof, Lieutenant," one of the troopers called out.

"Sergeant Davis, your squad, go get him."

Spurring their mounts into action, Sergeant Davis's men surrounded the coal company's supply store with two troopers quickly climbing onto the roof. Within minutes, the shooter was in custody, and now stood before Mayor Sam Owens and Captain McCaffrey, his face bloodied, but otherwise uninjured.

"That was a stupid move, John," the mayor commented disgustingly to the shooter whom the mayor obviously knew. "He's a coal miner, Captain, what are you going to do with him?"

"It's not what I am going to do with him, Mayor; he shot one of your citizens, he is your problem. If he had killed one of my men, he would be a dead man by now." Then turning to Lieutenant Roberts he asked, "Did we get what we came after, Mark?"

"Yes, Sir. We are all loaded up and ready to move out."

"Very good, mount 'em up; let's get out of here." Then once again acknowledging the Mayor, James touched the brim of his hat and said, "Good bye, Mayor Owens." The man did not respond.

With the Sixteenth, again heading off into the nearby hills, nearly an hour would pass before Lieutenant Roberts asked the inevitable question, "Why didn't we burn them out, Captain. I thought after that coal miner took his shot that would be the least we would do; after all he was shooting at you."

"I know he was shooting at me, Mark, but how do we justify burning someone's home when the people that live in that town probably don't even own their own homes. If we had burned the company store, some of those folks would starve. You saw what I saw; the people are poor as church mice. In all probability, the only thing they own is the clothing on their backs. God help them, they are innocent prisoners locked into a corrupt culture no less detrimental to their wellbeing than that of their black slaves. They are captive to an unjust system of servitude in a society no less corrupt than that of Ireland. It is shameful, for they have nothing to look forward to except a lifetime of pitiful ignorance and wretched poverty. Maybe this war will change some of that."

"Smoke ahead, Captain," Sergeant Davis riding near the front of the column, called out as a puff of smoke was seen high up on the hillside coming from a grove of trees about a half mile ahead,. "Holy Christ!" he exclaimed. "There's a sniper in the tree. One of our scouts is down." No sooner had Sergeant Davis warned of the danger than the rifle shot echoed across the hills, soon to be followed by a second round fired from a nearby location with its telltale emission of smoke drifting out from the hidden gunman's position. At the base of the hill, the column's two forward scouts, their bodies' twisting grotesquely in their saddles tumbled to the ground, their mounts galloping off.

Bringing the column to a sudden stop, James yelled, "Lieutenant Roberts, two squads out, cut 'em off."

"Lieutenant Roberts was quick to respond, "First and Second squad, move out, circle around the backside of the hill and cut those people off."

"We'll get 'em, Lieutenant," Sergeant Davis called out as he, Sergeant William Callow, and their men spurred their mounts to circle the hill where the hidden gunmen had taken down the two forward scouts.

"Dismount the troops, Lieutenant; the column shall continue on foot. Keep their mount between them and the hillside above, we shall proceed cautiously."

"Yes, Sir. Dismount! You heard the captain." Lieutenant Roberts called out, "Stay alert, we do not know how many Rebs we are up against."

With a wave of his arm, James led the remainder of the column forward watching for any further sign of the Reb snipers or other troops concealed in the thick brush and scrub pine covering the hillside above. As the column approached, it quickly became obvious that both men were dead. They suffered a single catastrophic gunshot wound from a large caliber weapon.

"We know where the snipers were holed up, Mark, but they are probably long gone now; send a detail up to that location and see what they can find."

"Right, Sir, they undoubtedly saw our men breaking off to move around behind the hill and skedaddled out of here."

Shortly after the departure of the three troopers detailed to check out the location where the Reb snipers lay in wait for the Union column, several volleys of gunfire erupted in the distance.

"Looks like our troops caught up with the Rebs, Sir." Lieutenant Roberts commented.

"I hope you are right, Mark; unless they ran into a Confederate patrol. Be prepared to ride; scouts out, one half mile maximum." Within minutes of posting, the forward scout signaled the return of Sergeants Davis and Callow and their troops. When the two squads came within sight of the men in the column, an audible groan came from those waiting the return of their fellow soldiers. Two mounts carried the lifeless bodies of trooper David Deak and Sergeant William Callow. As they approached, James called out, to Sergeant Davis, "Report Sergeant."

"Yes, Sir, Captain. They did not get very far; we cut them off before they even got down off the other side of the hill. It was quite steep and that slowed their decent. There were four, two snipers and two cavalrymen. With their sniper rifles, they shot Sergeant Callow and Trooper Deak before we even got within the range of our weapons. They out-gunned us but where they made their mistake was trying to outrun us, and not taking the time to reload their heavy weapons. We killed all four of them before they made it off the hill. If they had stayed put, they had good cover and we would never have been able to get close enough to engage. I am sorry, Captain, neither Sergeant Callow nor I took into account the capability of those guns. We brought out their heavy weapons along with about one-hundred rounds of ammunition; they are top of the line British made .45 caliber Whitworth sniper rifles. I don't think the Union has anything like them."

"We will talk about this some more, Sergeant, but right now let's get our men buried and move out of here. The Rebs know we are behind their lines; they would know where their snipers and the two cavalrymen were. There's apt to be a patrol out here looking for them at any time."

It was a somber group of Union cavalrymen that Captain James McCaffrey lead away from an unnamed hillside in Central Virginia on a bright but cold day in January 1865 for they left behind four fellow soldiers in shallow graves; friends to some, comrades to all. The only remaining physical evidence that Sergeant William Callow and the three dead Troopers lived to see Central Virginia were their names hurriedly carved onto boards taken from a box of dynamite and placed above their graves, plus a written record entered into Captain James McCaffrey's logbook. Their captain listed all four men as "Killed in action, Central Virginia, January 1865." Captain James McCaffrey however, was not even sure of the exact date.

"Did you take a good look at the guns, Mark?" James asked of Lieutenant Roberts.

"Yes, Sir, I did; they are that prized .45 caliber British Whitworth sniper rifle alright, that the Confederate Army is so proud of. We have seen a few of them before. The blockade-runners were alleged to have brought in thousands for the Rebs from Britain, but apparently only a few hundred, or possible a thousand or so got through. They have a killing history against our people at nearly 1,500 yards. Captain Kelly had one at the range, but no ammunition; it was very similar to these two."

"Did Kelly train anyone of our mounted troops here as snipers?"

"No, I don't believe so; a lot of cavalry troops trained at the range when Captain Kelly was the duty officer, but no, none of the horse soldiers received sniper training that I know of. What do you have in mind, Captain?"

"Well, Mark, in the last month we have inflicted a considerable amount of damage to the Confederate railroad system; if I were a Reb general I would be assigning a lot of my resources to not only finding us to kill us, but also to protecting whatever remaining railroad bridges they have. Reb troops will be protecting those bridges on the supply lines west and south of Richmond. If they have these rifles we will not even be able to get close enough for your demolition teams to operate. However, if we could train a couple of our men on the use of these two long guns we could inflict some serious damage of our own to their bridge security teams; that would allow us to destroy the bridges or at least hold them at bay while your men set their charges. What do you think?"

"I think it's a hell'u've good idea; let's find a remote location and train our men to do just that. I have a couple troops in mind. They seldom miss a target."

CHAPTER 14

TRAPPED

Lieutenant Mark Roberts saw to it that the two guns recovered by Sergeant Davis's men would enhance his troops' firepower. He selected four men to practice dry firing and the rapid reloading of the two .45 caliber British Whitworth heavy sniper rifles. Just three days ago on a hillside in Central Virginia, these two weapons took the lives of Sergeant William Callow and three troopers.

"Are your men ready, Lieutenant?" Captain McCaffrey asked Roberts as the Sixteenth prepared to break camp shortly after sunup.

"Yes, Sir, we have set up targets at 1000 and 1,500 paces and our two primary shooters will fire five rounds each at each target; allowing for a maximum one minute for reloading we should be able to move out within a twenty minute time frame, start to finish."

"That's good, Mark, I would guess that we'll have an hour at most, for once the firing begins with those heavy weapons every Reb officer within five miles of here will be asking their staff to check it out. We'll have to get out of here in a hurry."

"How far is it to the bridge on the Appomattox, Captain?" Lieutenant Roberts asked regarding their earlier discussion of the next target for his explosive teams.

"Maybe twenty-five miles, or so; the main rail line between Danville and Richmond crosses the river about midway between two small villages. We still have a good day's ride to the river. If we can avoid contact with the Rebs today, we ought to see the river by early evening. Once there we will have to move north along the western shore for a mile or two before we reach the bridge. There will be good cover all along the shoreline so we'll be able to move in within sniper range and should be able to take out any troops that may be posted there."

"If it is the typical truss bridge, Captain we will need at least thirty minutes to set our explosives. The support timbers on any of these main rail line bridges will be quite substantial, built to last if you will. However, none of us have experience handling dynamite so just to be on the safe side we will use a larger explosive charge than we normally do."

"Whatever you think is necessary, Mark, I have no knowledge of the business use of dynamite. You do what you have to."

"We cannot afford to make a mistake, Captain. Too many of our men paid a high price to get us here, so we want to make sure that when we ride away that bridge is sitting at the bottom of the river."

"I realize that; our troops will hold the Rebs at bay until your men have completed their job." James responded grimly. "We shall use their guns against them if necessary. Only the Good Lord knows how many Union troops have been taken down with those two rifles."

"Looking at our two make-shift targets this morning, Captain all ten rounds fired at 1,000 yards were right on, but the boys did not do well at the 1,500 yard distance. Only three strikes out of ten shots fired; not something you would want to bet on, but their reloading times were acceptable."

"No, you're right, Mark, but then that was the first and only time either man had an opportunity to fire those weapons. I think they shall do quite well."

"I hope so, Captain; when I am out there on that bridge, I want someone I can rely on to cover my backside."

"You are not going out there on this one, Mark; you will have to delegate that job to Sergeant McAllister. We cannot afford to lose you."

"Jesus, Captain," Mark Roberts protested, shocked that his men would pursue the destruction of one of the largest bridges on the Danville/Richmond rail line, without him. "I trained those men, Captain, we are a team; we work as a team and we have brought down a half dozen Reb bridges since taking on this assignment. Why would you pull me off now?"

"The reason is simple, Mark. Look around and tell me what you see; since we left the fort at Petersburg we have lost more than half of our sergeants and nearly one third of our troopers. Granted we have accomplished a good bit more than the Army had asked of us. However, you and I have a responsibility to these men and to the country, for after we have carried out General Murray's orders we must see to it that they are brought back safely to our own lines. If I do not survive, that burden falls on your shoulders."

"Oh Christ, Captain, I understand that, but this is the main line, if they fail here, we may not get another chance to shut down one of the Confederate's primary north/south supply routes, and more of our people will die at Petersburg."

"I am aware of that, but they won't fail; I am as sure of that as I am that the sun will come up tomorrow morning. You trained these men, they shall do what you taught them to do, and do it right."

The compliment from his Captain did little to decrease Mark Robert's discomfort with his bosses' order; it did not set well with him that he would not be with his troops when they sent a prized target crashing down into the Appomattox River. "I hope you are right, Captain." He offered quietly.

"I know I am, Mark, besides if our timing is right we may be able kill two birds with one stone, as they say, that is if we could take out a train along with the bridge. You and I shall be busy coordinating our attack if that opportunity arises. If successful, it would be a major setback for the Confederate Army. Think about it mark, a trainload of confederate supplies or military ordinance at the bottom of the Appomattox River."

"That sounds good, Captain; let's get it done."

It was early evening when the column reached the hills overlooking the Appomattox River, after two days of heavy rain the river was running high, and fast; they heard the rush of the water before the men caught sight of the river itself.

"With this rain and early spring run-off I would hate to try to ford that tonight." Lieutenant Roberts commented. "It would be risky even in daylight."

"I agree with you, Mark, but if it stays up it could work to our advantage, particularly if we are on opposite sides of the river from the Confederate Army, it may give us a chance to set our charges before we're discovered. No matter what we do however, we cannot forget for a minute that we are operating in enemy territory. Pickets out, both up and downstream, two men to a post, sabers ready. We must assume that the bridge will be guarded; we do not need a gunshot in the middle of the night to forewarn the Rebs of our presence."

"Yes, Sir, but you better get some sleep, Captain; you were up most of the night."

"I will after we get a bite to eat, then I want to take a look at that bridge. The clouds have moved off to the west and it looks like we will have a near full moon so we should be able to get fairly close to it on foot. I will take Sergeant McAllister with me; if we are not back by dawn you may want to reconsider your target."

It was nearly midnight before Captain McCaffrey and Sergeant John McAllister got near enough to examine and sketch the Appomattox River railroad bridge. There was no sign of an enemy troop presence and the bright moonlight enabled McAllister to draw a rough draft of the structure.

"It's huge, Captain," he commented, quietly. "It will take every bit of dynamite we have to bring it down, but I need to get in there and take a look at one of the cofferdams. With the size of that thing, we will have to concentrate on one or two key timbers on the near side. If we get this right, the weight of the structure will bring the whole damn thing down. What a shame," he added, shaking his head.

Somewhat confounded by McAllister's comment James responded, "I think I know why you may feel that way Sergeant, but just in case, what am I missing here?"

"Before the war, Captain, I was involved with heavy construction, I know what it must have taken to build this bridge, probably one-hundred or so men worked ten or twelve hour days, six days a week for more than a year. They built a beautiful structure, and to me it is beautiful. Yet you and I are looking forward to lighting a match that will bring this whole thing crashing down into the river. What a waste."

"You are so right, Sergeant, but unfortunately we do not have the luxury or the time to worry about that. Whether we like it or not, the trains that continue to roll over that bridge are bringing death to hundreds, if not thousands of our men.

For that reason, I doubt that a time will come in my life when I shall regret killing as many people as we have since joining the Union Army. After all, you and I have helped keep this country from destroying itself. Such is war."

"You are good at what you do, Captain," Sergeant McAllister responded grimly, "and God has given me the skills to do what I do best; unfortunately, between us we'll get it done."

Captain McCaffrey waited on the riverbank above the bridge watching as Sergeant McAllister climbed down and out onto the nearest cofferdam; from there he gained access to the base of the structure and soon disappeared from view. While waiting the sergeant's return James marveled at just how fortunate he was to be working with such a genuinely remarkable young man; he was not much older than James, and a veteran of three years with four major battles to his credit including Gettysburg and Bull Run. Yet, there certainly was no pretentiousness about Sergeant McAllister, or for that matter, any of the men assigned to his command. All were of a mind to defeat the Confederate Army, reunite their country, and go home to their families. Few of them were professional soldiers, the one notable exception was Lieutenant Roberts a true career soldier, also a veteran of Gettysburg, but even he had become disillusioned by the destruction that this war brought to the American people, Union and Confederate alike. James knew that Roberts, like the Malone twins planned to stay with the army after the war was over; however the twins wanted to use their enlistment as a vehicle to explore the wonders of their new world. Unfortunately, the Sixteenth's last major confrontation with the Reb horse soldiers changed all of that.

The unmistakable whistle of a train engine in the distance quite suddenly interrupted his musings; Sergeant McAllister, hearing the whistle dropped down off a support beam onto the cofferdam and quickly made his way back up the riverbank to rejoin his captain.

"You heard it too, Sergeant?" James asked, then not waiting for the answer, continued, "which way, north or south?"

"I thought it came from the north, Captain, but it was hard to tell under the bridge, I could be mistaken."

"I think you are right; that's what I thought. If we are correct, it could be another load of Reb wounded en route to the hospital at Greensboro or Raleigh. God, I don't want to get involved with another one of those; let's wait it out and see what happens."

Within the hour, three whistle blasts from a train engine echoed across the hills as the southbound train slowly came into view approaching the bridge. With a number of lanterns burning brightly in each of its several cars, it appeared to be a fully loaded hospital train. It came to an abrupt stop just short of the bridge. From their vantage point on the riverbank, a full moon provided Captain McCaffrey and Sergeant McAllister with an excellent view of the train until a low fog began to move in across the river that obscured much of the area around the bridge. Still there was enough moonlight that when the train moved on they saw something that surprised them; a large contingent of heavily armed Confederate soldiers were now deployed along the railroad right of way and they were moving toward the bridge.

It was nearly daylight by the time Captain McCaffrey and Sergeant McAllister made it back to their campsite. Although well hidden within heavy brush along the riverbank, the location was less than a mile downstream from the bridge with its newly arrived contingent of Confederate soldiers.

Lieutenant Roberts and his sergeants were waiting anxiously to hear what the two men had to say. Captain McCaffrey was the first one to speak, and in a quiet, but firm voice warned, "We are less than a mile from the bridge and it is protected by three or possibly four squads of heavily armed Reb soldiers, so the first order of business is absolute quiet and no smoking. We cannot move farther downstream in the daylight or we run the risk of detection. Moreover, if someone up on that bridge gets a whiff of tobacco smoke, we will have Rebs all over us. Sergeant McAllister shall brief you on what we found."

Over the next hour, Sergeant McAllister briefed Lieutenant Roberts and Sergeants Davis, Brian Murphy, and Tommy Sanders on what he and their captain saw during the all-night vigil at the Appomattox River Bridge. When finished he took his explosive teams aside, went over his sketch of the bridge structure with them discussing in detail the specific beams, and iron trusses where the charges were to be placed. Because of the bridge's size, McAllister said they would concentrate on destroying only one corner of the structure, but that it would be necessary to destroy both the overhead and roadway trusses at that location.

"I believe that, if we destroy the viability of two or three support beams above one of the four coffer dams that hold this span in place, it is of such a size that the weight of the bridge alone will be our ally and the entire structure will come down."

When he finished, Captain McCaffrey called out quietly for the troops to gather around, and then in detail outlined their responsibilities. "Gentlemen, we shall move out quietly before daylight tomorrow. We will tether our mounts in a large thicket of scrub pine and brush located about two-hundred yards this side of the bridge and go in on foot. Lieutenant Roberts and Sergeants Davis and Murphy will lead their assault teams against the west side of the bridge and Sergeant Sanders and I shall attack from the east side. Your primary objective tomorrow will be to protect Sergeant McAllister's two explosive teams while they move onto the bridge to set their explosives. Our sniper teams shall set up about one-hundred yards out, one upstream and the other downstream from the bridge. Their objective shall be to concentrate their fire on anyone who can be an immediate threat to McAllister's troops.

"We shall begin the attack at daylight following my lead. If it looks like our explosives people can access the bridge structure without being detected, we shall allow that to progress; but if discovered we shall attack immediately. Should a Reb train come upon us such as occurred last night we stay and fight until Sergeant McAllister's men have completed their task. The sergeant believes he can accomplish that in one-half hour.

"So Gentlemen that is our target for tomorrow; when that is over we have some good news to look forward to; we shall head for home. We have carried out General Murray's orders, and then some, besides it is going on two months since we have had a decent hot meal or a comfortable bed to sleep in. We have done our duty as best we could; you men have performed miraculously. However, pray that we do not have to fight our way out of here; we have a long ride ahead of us after tomorrow."

After eating, James and Sergeant McAllister joined a half dozen troopers just in off of their nightly picket duty assignment now curled up in the brush in their blankets. Some of them were already asleep. Dead tired, James quickly dosed off in the warm sunlight filtering through the canopy of Virginia Pine and scrub brush. He awoke with a start to find Lieutenant Roberts with a firm grip on his shoulder shaking him lightly and was startled to find that he had slept throughout much of the day, for the sun was now low on the Western horizon.

"What is it, Mark, trouble?" he inquired of his lieutenant.

"It could be, Captain, another train came through about two hours ago, we heard the whistle, but I did not want to wake you until our pickets from the forward observation post reported. It only stopped for a few minutes, but our men saw a contingent of cavalry troops off loading. Sergeant Murphy and I went up to see what they are doing. There appears to be a full troop of forty men or more. They setup camp a half mile beyond the bridge, but they have not attempted to cross the river. I thought it strange that they did not stay on the train and offload on this side, but I suppose they figured they had a readymade camp with their infantry already in place. I would not expect them to cross tonight. The river is still running high, but it has dropped a great deal since yesterday. If the rain holds off, that will all change by tomorrow morning."

"Let's get the sergeants together, Mark, we may have to modify our plan of attack a bit."

When the four sergeants along with Lieutenant Roberts gathered around their captain, James was pleased to hear that they had already considered how the sudden arrival of the additional Confederate troops would affect their plan of attack and waited anxiously to discuss this with him. They wanted the attack to proceed, but with some modifications suggesting a nighttime attack instead of waiting for dawn. James and Lieutenant Roberts however, had seen too many nighttime attacks fail when the attacking force became so disoriented they ended up firing on their own people or just simply got lost. After some further discussions, the sergeants agreed with their captain that the attack would proceed at dawn as planned, but they would reposition the two sniper teams. James directed that the four men take up positions at the top of the bluff overlooking the bridge where they could concentrate their firepower on both the bridge and the Confederate cavalry should they arrive before Sergeant McAllister's men completed their mission.

By four o'clock in the morning the men of the Sixteenth Cavalry were in position, the two explosive teams quickly placed their explosive charges at the site of key support columns within the superstructure of the bridge. As Sergeant McAllister explained earlier to Captain McCaffrey that as he had not handled dynamite before, to assure that the span collapsed completely he would scale one of the uppermost truss supporting beams where he would place additional explosive charges. However, once the operation got underway it took longer than McAllister estimated. With daylight fast approaching, he had yet to complete the task when a Reb soldier spotted him and fired his musket, the ball ricochet off a nearby iron girder. Other Confederate soldiers soon arrived and began firing at the Union sergeant now fully exposed high up on an upper truss busily tying-off fuses. McAllister continued working, and then yelled at his team underneath the bridge, "Light her up and get out of there and get everyone off the bridge." With this signal to light off their charge, he dropped onto the railroad track, calmly removing the cigar he held tightly clinched between his teeth and touched it to the end of the fuse leading to a dozen sticks of dynamite strapped to the top truss.

"Get the hell out of there, Sergeant," one of his men called out from the riverbank over the roar of Confederate musketry and Union Spencer rifle fire. McAllister made a hurried retreat working his way up the riverbank to where both assault teams were heavily engaged in firefights, one on either side of the railroad right of way firing down on two dozen or more Reb troops. From his vantage point on the riverbank overlooking the end of the bridge, James heard the loud crack of the Whitworth sniper fire before he saw their target. The two snipers had zeroed in on a hoard of rebel cavalrymen fast approaching the far end of the bridge.

Soon an ear shattering blast from the first detonation on the uppermost truss hurled huge pieces of cast iron beams and wooden timbers flying skyward. James waited two or three minutes, for the second explosion in what seemed like hours yet nothing happened. Looking over to where Sergeant McAllister had gathered his team he saw the man break cover and rush back out onto the bridge, with his men yelling at him to come back. "It will go, Sergeant," one man called out to him, "Come back, for Christ's sake, you'll get killed." McAllister, ignoring the warnings continued on, quickly climbing over the near railing of the bridge where he dropped down onto the cofferdam. Moments later, he was lost to view as a dirty black cloud of smoke and flying debris erupted from underneath the bridge. The explosive blast hurled more beams and timber support girders in every direction, it was followed by a shockwave which so startled the two warring factions that for a moment or two, no one fired a shot. After the explosion there was no sign of Sergeant McAllister, he simply disappeared in the wreckage and rubble erupting from the huge blast that destroyed the support structure of the bridge above the cofferdam.

The loud crack of the Whitworth rifle and Confederate musketry quickly redirected everybody's attention to a more immediate problem. Reb cavalrymen rushing forward to support their infantry units on the bridge, split into two attack groups, one group dismounted upon arrival at far end of the bridge. The other, a contingent of approximately twenty troops moved north along the riverbank apparently looking for a safe place to ford the river.

Captain McCaffrey yelled, "Snipers concentrate your fire on the mounted troops." As he watched, two of the lead riders tumbled from their mounts. His snipers were helping to even the odds. Turning to Trooper Robin Leads, a Signal Corps trooper pressed into service as the battalion bugler he said, "Stand by," with Leads readying his bugle for all to hear over the roar of gunfire emanating from both sides of the river.

Turning to Lieutenant Roberts he said, "We cannot afford to get trapped between these two groups, Lieutenant, when mounted be prepared for a hasty retreat. Keep our snipers in place until our last man is ready to ride."

"Execute!"

With Trooper Leads' loud blare of the bugle sounding retreat, the men of the Sixteenth pulled back from the riverbank and quickly mounted. While waiting for the others to mount the two Union sniper teams continued to fire at the fast moving Confederate cavalrymen, yet by now most were well beyond the range of even the best of riflemen. Shortly thereafter Captain McCaffrey and Lieutenant Roberts accompanying the sniper teams quickly rejoined the column.

However, before leading the column out and away from the river, James and his troops, hearing the terrible screeching and twisting of metal and breaking timbers turned to take a last look back at the bridge. Unfortunately, it was still standing, yet as they watched, as Sergeant McAllister had predicted, the weight of the structure was such that the damage inflicted by the two dynamite charges was enough to send it crashing down into the Appomattox River.

"Look, some of the Rebs are trapped on the bridge." One of the troops yelled. "They're going down with it."

"Move out," James called out in a loud voice. Although he saw a half dozen or more Confederate soldiers vainly clinging to the structure as it disappeared from view, he had no desire to further witness the inevitable demise of so many young men.

Without speaking Captain McCaffrey and Lieutenant Roberts led the column at a fast pace through a lightly forested area then out into open country before slowing their mounts to a walk. Moving in close to his captain Lieutenant Roberts commented quietly, "I had my doubts, Captain, but the sergeant knew what he was talking about."

"Yes he did, he was a good man, Mark; we shall miss him."

"Yes, he was," Mark Roberts, replied solemnly.

For the next few minutes as they walked leading their mounts, James was buried in thought about Sergeant McAllister and the terrible loss the Rebs suffered at the bridge over the Appomattox River. Then, shaking his head he put it aside knowing they were still in great danger. "Let's move out, Lieutenant; let's put some distance between us and those Confederate boys before they find a convenient place to ford that river."

The men of the Sixteenth rode hard for nearly eight hours before James raising his hand brought the column to a stop near a small creek at the base of a heavily wooded hillside. He called out, "Dismount, rest your animals," then turning to Lieutenant Roberts said, "Mark hold the column here while

Sergeant Davis and I explore this area. We need to rest our mounts and we need higher ground; I do not want to run into any of our Reb friends unexpectedly." When the sergeant reigned in at the head of the column, James asked, "Do we still have those Reb signaling mirrors, Sergeant?"

"Yes, Sir, Captain."

"Good, bring them along; you and I shall take a hike up to the top of this hill. Stay alert, Mark. I doubt those folks from the bridge are still following us in force; it is more likely that they are licking their wounds. Our boys beat them up pretty badly; however, if I were that Reb commander I would have a couple of scouts following our tracks. Eventually they will come after us in force."

Leaving the column behind, the two men crossed the small stream and began an arduous climb through a heavy growth of brush and scrub pine up the steep hillside reaching the crest in less than an hour. Finding it nearly devoid of vegetation, the higher elevation provided a commanding view in every direction. "This is what we need, Sergeant; signal Lieutenant Roberts to come ahead."

Within the hour Lieutenant Roberts led the men of the Sixteenth Battalion over the crest of the hill and out onto the small plateau where James and Sergeant Davis awaited their arrival. "Pickets out, Mark, but I would keep them close by; watch for a lone intruder, probably one of their trackers or a couple of scouts. We shall be able to see the approach of any sizable force from quite a distance. Cold camp, have the men get some rest, but before that, let's get a count of our ammunition and food supplies."

"Yes, Sir, we are running on short rations now, and not a lot of ammunition; some of our men fired nearly everything they had at the bridge."

"Yes, I saw that, but they did one hell'u've job; they taught the Rebs quite a lesson, one they won't forget as long as they live. If any of their infantry lived through that firestorm or did not die when the bridge went down I would be surprised."

"Our snipers also took out about a dozen or so cavalrymen, Captain so they won't be rushing in on us anytime soon; but when they do come, God help us, for it will be a large number and they will be seeking revenge."

"I think you're right, they'll probably outnumber us ten to one."

"How much farther do you estimate, Captain? "I would have to guess; looking at these old railroad maps I would say probably twenty-five miles or so. I am sure many things have changed since we left camp in December. General Grant was to bring in heavy reinforcements to end the siege at Petersburg; by the time we get there, it may be all over. We may even run into our own patrols before too long."

"I hope it's over, Captain, I'm not looking forward to going back on the line; too many good men have died at that godforsaken place."

"I agree with you." James replied, quietly.

It was nearly daylight when the first of several rifle shots aroused the camp; James woke with a start to discover Sergeant Brian Murphy rushing toward him and Lieutenant Roberts who had been sleeping nearby. "What is it, Sergeant?" He asked.

"Not sure, yet Sir," he responded as two pickets rushed down to the camp from their late night ridgeline picket duty assignment.

"Report," the sergeant called out to the two troopers as Lieutenant Roberts, Sergeants Brian Murphy, Gayle Davis and Tommy Sanders quickly assembled nearby to hear what the two men had to say.

"Four Rebs, Sergeant, they dismounted at the bottom of the hill and came up on foot; we killed two of them, but the other two got away. Sorry about that, Sergeant," the young man said.

Interjecting himself into the conversation, James said, "You don't have to be sorry, Trooper, you men did just fine," then turning to Lieutenant Roberts, said, "Lieutenant, prepare to move out, but first assign a sergeant to the ridge. We will not have much time, but perhaps he can get a look at what the Rebs are sending after us and from what direction they are coming. Also, have these two retrieve whatever ammunition and firearms the Rebs were carrying. We may need it; we do not have enough ammunition for a sustained engagement with Johnnie Reb."

The morning sun was high above the horizon when Sergeant Davis came galloping down off the ridgeline and reentered the camp. Without taking the time to dismount, he reported directly to Captain McCaffrey and Lieutenant Roberts, standing nearby.

"Two columns of Confederate cavalry en route, Captain, one coming in from West and the other from the North; they're riding hard and raising a lot of dust. I estimate a full troop, up to fifty men in each column; we probably have an hour to an hour and a half at most."

"Let's mount up, gentlemen and move out," James called out, South by East, it's time to go home."

For the next two days, the men of the Sixteenth Cavalry Battalion traveled mostly at night to avoid death or capture. The excursion into enemy territory had proved to be deadly for many of their fellow soldiers. Sixty percent of the original one-hundred and ten men that left Petersburg nearly two months ago, were no longer with them. Most of their ammunition and food supplies were gone, including the grain salvaged for their mounts.

Their captain and his veteran troops were well aware of the enmity they had generated within the Confederacy because of their unprecedented successes in attacking Reb transportation and supply lines. Each member of the Sixteenth also realized the Rebs had branded them as pariahs and if taken prisoner they knew they probably would not survive the war. However, of equal concern to their commander was the physical and mental wellbeing of his troops. Sleeping on the ground in a cold camp, without hot food, or a bath, shave, haircut, or change of clothing for nearly two months had taken a heavy toll in both appearance and the physical condition of every man. His men were exhausted, as was their commander and at least three of them were in need of medical attention as evidenced by a high fever and a persistent cough. Yet, surprisingly, beyond the usual grousing common among veteran troopers, no one complained; they were proud to be a member of such a battalion with its unprecedented record of accomplishments. Their captain's immediate worry however, was of their shortage of food and ammunition; James thought it could be their undoing. He knew they had to keep on the run for they could not win in a firefight with a well-armed Confederate force.

On the morning of the fourth day since leaving the Appomattox River battle, James thought a rainstorm might be heading their way. Shortly after six o'clock in the morning, the ominous sound of thunder rolled across the Virginia hills, yet there was hardly a cloud in the sky. Bringing the column to a halt and listening for a moment or two it quickly became evident that a massive artillery barrage was underway within miles of their present location.

"It's ours! One of the troopers called out, while others joyfully chimed in; "The Rebs will be running for cover."

Another exclaimed, "I hope they blow those bastards all the way back to Mississippi or wherever the hell they came from down there."

Turning to Lieutenant Roberts, James asked, "What do you think, Mark, how far, fifteen, twenty miles or more?"

"Twenty to twenty-five, Captain, that sound will carry quite a distance on a clear morning like this. However, if you listen closely the Rebs are shooting back. Those loud flat booming noises have to be our 24-pound howitzers; but you can hear the sharp crack of the Reb 18 pounder canister shot. No one who has been on the receiving end of that pretty piece of mayhem will ever forget that sound."

With his sergeants now gathered around him, James called out, "Let's find some hill with heavy brush cover, being this close to Petersburg there will be both Union and Reb patrol groups out scouting and probing the other side's defenses. It could be our people, but remember we are still behind enemy lines, so it is more likely that Confederate troops will be prowling around this area."

Within the hour, Sergeant Sanders led the column up a steep slope, leading out onto a small plateau the size of an Irish rugby field. Although covered with heavy brush and scrub pine it provided sight locations in which to view the countryside in all directions.

"Set out our pickets, Gentlemen; we shall stay here until after dark. If our luck holds, we may run across our troops by early morning. Get some rest."

Once the sergeants left to tend to their duties, James took Lieutenant Roberts aside to express his misgivings about this unexpected turn of events.

"I do not like this, Mark, the barrage has lasted now for more than two hours, and no sign of a let up, that has all the earmarks of an attempt to break through the Rebs defensive positions. We are apt to see steady stream of Confederate troop reinforcements from all over western Virginia passing through here; we must get out of here tonight. I would feel better about it if we were not so short of ammunition."

"Maybe we'll luck out, Captain," Lieutenant Roberts replied, "I feel confident we can remain hidden until after dark and then slip through the Confederate lines undetected and make our way home."

"I hope and pray that you are right, Mark, but I have a bad feeling about this."

No sooner had he uttered these words when a trooper on watch quietly called out, "Reb patrol coming in from the south; twenty or more cavalry troops, about two miles out."

"Let's take a look, Mark," James said in reply to the trooper's sighting and the two men hurried to the sentry's post on the south end of the plateau.

"Right there, Captain, Just to the right of that tall stand of timber," the lookout reported. "It looks like twenty or so troops and they are moving fast. If they stay on course they will end up right below us."

"What do you recommend, Mark? Shall we run or stay hidden and wait them out?"

"We cannot run, Captain, they are coming from the direction we want to go; we can't go back or we are apt to come up against the two groups that chased us here in the first place. I suggest we prepare an ambush for those boys, and hope we do not have to execute; they might pass us by if we keep quiet and maintain our cover."

"I agree with you completely, Mark. Form the men up into two lines, one on either side of our lookout's position with the sniper teams on the outer end of each formation. However, we must maintain absolute silence and hopefully they shall pass us by; if they do not, let them come in close while we still possess the advantage of surprise."

"Will do, Captain." Mark Roberts replied, his voice grim.

Within minutes the men of Sixteenth Battalion, or what was left of them, now concealed in outcroppings of rocks or fallen timber that lay across the south end of the plateau were ready. Captain McCaffrey and Lieutenant Roberts moved from man to man in quiet support, encouraging the men to maintain their silence and to hold their fire. The men readily accepted such orders for they understood the serious predicament in which they now found themselves. They were behind enemy lines and short of ammunition.

Watching from a concealed position, James now in the middle of his deployed troops quietly muttered to himself, "What the devil are you doing, Mister? You do not want to die here today." For unexpectedly the Confederate troop commander brought his column to a halt at the base of the hillside. However, what James hoped for never happened. The Reb commander motioned for the column to follow and started up the hillside. Yet, as they moved closer, James got a glimpse of what he hoped might benefit his beleaguered force;

at the end of the Reb column were twelve or fifteen heavily loaded pack mules. James surprised those around him when he rushed over to the two sniper teams located near Lieutenant Roberts.

"If this goes down your first target will be the pack mules; they may be critical to our survival, but hold your fire until I see what this Reb commander has in mind." He did not have to wait long, the Confederate soldiers continued up the hillside on a course that could lead to their sudden death.

"I am going to take a chance here, Mark," he said quietly; "I will offer them an opportunity to surrender. I do not feel right about cutting them down without a chance. We still have an edge on them if we keep our people concealed."

"Jesus, Captain, you're taking a hell'u've risk, they will cut you down; they know that we have destroyed nearly two dozen bridges, burned their buildings and supplies and humiliated their forces. You won't have a prayer."

"Maybe not, Mark, but I've got to try. If I don't survive, make sure our people take down their officers and kill those mules; that may be your life-line out of here."

The Confederate officer leading the column, accompanied by a junior officer were within fifty yards of Captain McCaffrey's hidden force when James stepped out from behind a huge boulder and called out to the two. "Gentlemen, I am James McCaffrey, captain New York's Sixteenth Battalion, United States Army. Please hold up your column," he offered politely, then walked out to meet the two officers. The Reb column with some considerable confusion came to an immediate halt.

"What is it you want, Captain? You realize that you are within the confines of the Confederate States of American and an enemy combatant; I can order you shot here and now. If I am not mistaken, you are the Yankee commander who has been operating illegally in our territory for the past two months and there is a price on your head. What is it that you seek today, your death?" The junior officer laughed at his commander's remarks and then interjecting himself into this conversation asked, "Let me kill this son of a bitch, Colonel; he needs killing now."

"I seek your surrender, Sir," James replied, calmly. "There is no need for anyone to die here today. You see, Sir you and your entire troop are surrounded by my men, and they are prepared to shoot should you not surrender."

Once again, the junior officer interjecting himself into what thus far was a tense but civil discussion between the Reb Colonel and Captain McCaffrey; he yelled, "Kill him now!"

"No," the colonel responded angrily, "calm down, Major or remove yourself from my presence."

"You must realize, Captain that you are in no position to be making such a demand upon a Confederate officer, particularly since you and your men are not only trespassers you are completely cut off from your command."

"He is bluffing, Colonel," the younger officer responded, yelling an obscenity directed at James.

"I believe Major Hanson is correct, Captain, I am not easily fooled. You, Sir are under arrest and you shall surrender your sword to my men or you shall be shot here and now."

"One moment please if you will, Colonel for I can assure you that there is no need for any of us to die here today." Then calling out to Mark Roberts, he said, "Mr. Roberts will you demonstrate to the colonel and his men that we are not bluffing."

Within seconds of the captain's last words, the loud report from one of the sniper's Whitworth heavy rifles echoed across the hillside as the Union trooper killed one of the pack mules, the animal dropping in its tracks.

"Why you Yankee son of a bitch," the Confederate major screamed as he drew his saber and spurred his mount toward Captain McCaffrey. However, these were the man's last words. Lieutenant Roberts never convinced that the desire of his commanding officer to treat their enemy humanly was a wise thing to do, was ready. He cried out, "Open fire, take 'em down!"

When the first shots rang out, the Confederate major with a shocked look of hate and pain on his face, lurched backward out of his saddle and died before he hit the ground. His colonel suffered a similar fate with a fatal wound to his chest; he tumbled off his mount, landing just feet away from his adversary. He lived only long enough to utter the words, "I thought you were bluffing." Yet James had no time to consider the man's last words; for Lieutenant Roberts and Sergeant Murphy grabbed him and rushed him back under cover. Quite suddenly, the cacophonic roar of gunfire and shriek of ricocheting bullets permeated the atmosphere

"You'll get yourself killed yet, Captain;" Lieutenant Roberts yelled, then with a grim smile, added "If you do that again, I shall have to explain to General Murray why the hell we stayed out here in this damn wilderness for two whole months." "I shall try not to let that happen, Mark." He replied, embarrassed that by his efforts to save the lives of several Confederate soldiers, he endangered the lives of two of his own. As quick as it started, the battle ended. "Cease fire!" Sergeant Davis called out; "I think they are all down, Lieutenant, either dead or wounded." "What about our people, Sergeant?" James asked as the troops slowly came down the hillside to examine the results of this coldblooded violent act of war.

"Not a scratch, Captain," Sergeant Davis replied, "We were lucky."

"I would not agree with you, Sergeant, luck had nothing to do with this battle. You folks trained your men and used your professional competence to plan an action that will help the Union end this terrible bloody conflict. Maybe we can talk about it later, but for now we must move fast." Turning to Lieutenant Roberts, he issued a series of explicit orders, "Mark, take a look at their wounded and see if any of the walking wounded can take care of their own people. Also, get their guns and ammunition and see what supplies we can salvage from their pack animals. Many of their mounts look like they may be in better shape than ours; our priorities are pickets in place to watch for intruders, ammunition, food and the ability to stay ahead of the Reb Army until we meet up with our own people."

"Right, Sir, we'll get it done."

Within the hour, Lieutenant Roberts and his four sergeants had completed their assignments and now gathered around their captain ready to move out.

"Report, what do we have Mark?"

"Seven enemy troops dead, twenty-three wounded and three men unscathed; I think we just scared the hell out of them and they gave up. Eight or ten of the wounded are ambulatory, but half dozen of them probably will not make it through the night. The three prisoners and a few of the walking wounded are capable of caring for their own. We on the other hand fared much better; one trooper with a slight wound to the neck.

"As far as Reb supplies are concerned I guess we were lucky to have come up against our Reb Colonel. He name was Simon Foster and his troop carried an abundance of food, ammunition and ten 18-pounder cannon, dismantled and strapped to the mules along with a large quantity of shells. We also picked up four more Whitworth heavy sniper rifles and nearly a dozen of our own Spencer guns with plenty of ammunition; they have been a busy group of veteran soldiers. I am just surprised as hell that they walked into our trap. One of the wounded officers told me the colonel was highly regarded by cavalry troopers and was always out in front with his men; a sad ending for a brave man."

"I have to agree with you, Mark. Let's mount up and get out of here before some of Colonel Foster's colleagues catch up to us."

As Captain McCaffrey's men prepared to mount a picket shouted, "Enemy troops, two columns inbound from the north, four to five miles out, coming in fast."

James gave the order to mount and once in the saddle, he and Lieutenant Roberts moved quickly up the hillside. "Where are they, trooper?" Mark Roberts ask as they stopped at the lookout post.

"Due north, Sir, just below the horizon in that clearing; two columns, I would estimate over one-hundred men and they are moving at a quick pace."

"I see them, Mark; take a look," he said, handing his spyglass to Roberts. "That has to be the same group that came after us three days ago. They are a persistent bunch, I'll give them that, but there are too many of them, we will have to run." Yet before he got back to the clearing, another picket called out, "Large column of enemy troops moving in from the south, both cavalry and infantry, moving slowly."

Upon hearing this, Lieutenant Roberts and his four sergeants anxiously turned to their captain hoping but not expecting that the man would come up with a miracle. They now faced an overwhelming number of enemy troops and there appeared to be no way to escape the inevitable, surrender or die.

"Back to the plateau," James ordered, "take those pack mules with the Reb cannon and set 'em up; we are going to buy some time, time enough for General Grant's troops to come to our rescue. That group of Confederate troops coming our way should be moving toward the front lines to support their troops at Petersburg; but they are not. They appear to be in full retreat; that is good news, it means that if we can hold out until our people show up we shall prevail. However, what we have to do right now is prepare a surprise for the two columns coming in from the north. That is our number one priority; get our snipers in position and everyone under cover. Also, Mark, bring one of those wounded Reb officers up here."

When the Confederate officer arrived, under guard James introduced himself to the injured man.

"I am Captain James McCaffrey, New York, Sixteenth Battalion, Sir; what is your name and rank?" he asked, offering his hand, whereupon the man saluted, shook his captor's hand and then replied, "I am Lieutenant Lionel Sanford, Sir, Virginia Cavalry, Army of the Confederate States of America."

"Can you ride, Lieutenant?" James asked the man dressed in his blood soaked Confederate uniform from a bandaged head wound.

"I certainly can, Captain, if necessary."

"I assure you, Lieutenant, it is quite necessary. Look to the north through my glass and you shall see two columns of your fellow Confederate troops coming our way. They have been tracking my troop for the last three days; when they come within range a lot of good men may die unnecessarily."

"I see them; but it seems to me that you have a problem, Captain." The lieutenant responded quite straightforwardly. "They appear to be superior to you in number and I presume in firepower."

"That's quite possible Lieutenant, however please look to the south, and tell me what you see."

After a minute or two of scanning the horizon, he turned back to Captain McCaffrey and said, "It looks like my men and I are about to be rescued, Captain," he replied smiling. "You and your men are now between the devil and the deep blue sea, as they say here in the South. You're trapped behind enemy lines; you and your men have no place to go."

"I would not come to the same conclusion, Lieutenant and you may wish to reexamine what you saw; for it appears to me that your army is in full retreat from Petersburg. If you look closely, those supply wagons are filled to capacity with wounded men; that is not the image one would expect to see from an army about to do battle with a small group of Union cavalrymen."

Nervously, the man reached for James's spyglass, "May I, Sir," he said then taking his time reexamined the Confederate troops slowly approaching the plateau from the South. Handing the glass back to his captor, he responded, "I have to agree with you, Captain, it certainly appears to be the case. Yet you still face a serious challenge from our cavalrymen coming in from the North, from what I see they out number you three or four to one. Your men will be destroyed; you should consider surrendering to me, your men would be treated fairly by our forces."

"Good try, Lieutenant," James responded with a grin, "if they come at us like your colonel did, most of those men will be dead before this day is over. You know that to be a fact; we have the advantage; we hold the high ground with plenty ordinance and supplies, including your eight pounders. We can sit up here on this hilltop and await the arrival of our people from Petersburg, for there is little doubt in my mind that General Grant will have broken through your defenses at Petersburg and the Confederate Army is in full retreat."

"If that is the case, why bring me up here; you appear to have the upper hand," he responded obviously shaken by what he saw, then he added, "at least for now."

"The reason is simple, Lieutenant, this war shall be over in a matter of a few days or a week or two at most and you and I have an opportunity here and now to stop the killing. If we can do that, we may be able to save the lives of several of your own soldiers. My men tell me that some of your wounded shall die before this day is over unless they receive medical attention immediately."

"Unfortunately, that is true, Captain; what do you propose?" he asked, solemnly.

"I suggest that you ride out to meet those that have been pursuing us these past three days and intervene on behalf of your wounded. Tell them what we have here and that my plan is to defend this hilltop until Union Army reinforcements arrive here from Petersburg. You have experienced firsthand the cold-blooded capabilities of my troops and I assure you that we shall be no less hard-hearted toward your colleagues should they attack. If the commander is amenable to stop or delay his attack on our forces, we shall hold our fire until all of the wounded have been cared for and removed from the field of battle. If he is agreeable to this, I suggest that he dispatch a rider to bring any medical aide teams that may be with those retreating from Petersburg."

"That's a fair bargain, Captain; I shall do my best to forestall any immediate assault they may have planned."

"Thank you, Lieutenant, good luck." Then turning to Sergeant Davis, he added, "Let's get Lieutenant Sanford on a mount, Sergeant."

"What do you think, Mark? I should have consulted with you and the sergeants on this, but we were running out of time. I would like to save those wounded men if we can and at the same time give us some breathing space. They're about a mile out now and it looks like they've stopped; they have probably spotted us by now." "No, I think you did the right thing, Captain; I am sympathetic to the needs of the wounded, but frankly, I was more worried that we would not have time enough to assemble the Reb guns. Those eight pounders in our hands should scare the hell out of any Reb commander. As it is, the guns are ready and our troops are in place; they will give a good account of themselves."

"I am sure they shall, Mark."

"He's coming back, Captain," Sergeant Gayle Davis cried out from his location on the north ridge of the plateau. "He's accompanied by a Reb officer and there are two riders going around the base of the hill. They are moving fast, it looks like they may be heading out to contact the Petersburg force."

"Let them come through, but maintain your cover."

The two, Lieutenant Sanford and another Confederate officer came over the ridgeline and headed directly for Captain McCaffrey and Lieutenant Roberts, now mounted and waiting in the center of a small clearing on top of the hill.

Lieutenant Sanford was the first to speak. "This is Major Donald Atkinson, Captain; he is commander of the Tenth Calvary Regiment, Georgia Volunteers."

"Good morning, Major, I am sure Lieutenant Sanford has told you of my concern for the many Confederate wounded and the conditions I set forth with him for their wellbeing. Unless fired upon we shall take no hostile action against your men while the wounded are cared for. If that is agreeable with you, I see no reason to delay this endeavor any further."

"I fully agree, Captain," the man replied, grimly.

"Good day to you, Sir" James replied politely. "It is sad that we had to meet under these difficult circumstances, but I am sure you'll agree with me that if we can save the life of even one of Lieutenant Stanford's men it shall be worth our time."

"Yes, I concur, Captain" the man responded without any outward sign that he truly appreciated the consideration extended by this enemy soldier to his fellow soldiers.

"Sergeant Davis shall escort you and Lieutenant Sanford through our lines to the injured men."

"Thank you, and good day to you, Sir," the man replied grim-faced.

After the three men departed, James turned to Lieutenant Roberts and asked, "What do you think, Mark, is he going to give us trouble?"

"You know what I think, Captain; it's the same thing you're thinking, he's a coldblooded son of a bitch and can't wait to get back here to kill all of us."

"Yes, that's what I think, Mark. If I were to guess, they will hit us with everything they have at dawn tomorrow. We have two choices as I see it; we stay and fight or we run. If we stay very few of us will make it out of here alive; if we run, some of us may make it back to our own lines. However, there are a hell'u've a lot of enemy soldiers between here and Petersburg."

"So what do you plan to do, Captain, fight or run?"

"That's not my decision, Mark; the troops must decide this one for themselves. We have carried out General Murray's orders and accomplished more than I ever imagined was possible. Therefore, I shall abide by their decision. They are tired, along with you and I; all of us, I believe just want to go home and forget about this terrible war. However, that is not in the cards for us right now; but the decision to fight or run may be the last chance our men shall have to determine their own future. Let's bring them all in and discuss it while the Rebs are busy taking care of their wounded."

While the troops were gathering around Captain McCaffrey, Sergeant Murphy stepped forward, "I should tell you, Captain that I talked to one of their wounded, a sergeant from Mississippi. He said their colonel, his name was Adam Holden, expected our forces to break through at Petersburg and should that happen Colonel Holden was ordered to establish a secondary position to slow the Union advance. That's why they zeroed in on this hilltop and why they were so well equipped; at this elevation retreating troops from Petersburg would be in a superb position to ambush Grant's forces."

"Well it could have been troublesome for our folks, but I think they were grasping at straws; once our people breach those breastwork defenses at Petersburg there will be no stopping Grant. He will be relentless and push right on into Richmond; nothing will stop him."

"I think I agree with you, Captain," Sergeant Murphy added soberly.

After a briefing by Lieutenant Roberts on the agreement reached between Captain McCaffrey and the Reb commander, the survivors of the Sixteenth Battalion, now gathered around their officers and sergeants where James quickly laid out three possible options that he believed were open for them to pursue.

"Thanks to the Confederate Army we now have an ample supply of ammunition, weapons, and supplies that can sustain us for another three to five days. We can stay and fight, and we have the advantage of the high ground and good cover. The Rebs outnumber us probably five to one, however, when their retreating army arrives, that number may increase tenfold. Our second option is to run, but whichever way we turn we are still behind enemy lines. Some of you will undoubtedly make it through to safety, particularly if we pull out tonight, ride hard, and hide in the daytime. A third option may be the toughest--surrender. It is something you must consider, for I truly belief this war shall be over within a matter of weeks if not days. You have seen the poor condition of the Reb soldier, but he is a tough, tenacious son of a gun. The only time they were well equipped was when they were fortunate enough to acquire Union Army supplies or when they get their hands on British weapons. Therefore, I personally believe that between General Grant's spring offensive and the Rebs deteriorating ability to supply their troops, they shall just quit and go home.

"However, this is not my decision; you must decide here and now, what you want to do, for these Rebs will come after us as soon as that Rep Major takes care of those wounded men lying out there on that hillside."

"What do you recommend, Captain?" Sergeant Tommy Sanders asked, with a worried look on his face. "I certainly do not wish to surrender; after what we have done, they will surely hang some of us, probably starting with you, Sir. They are as mad as hell, and I don't blame them, but that's war."

"I am not going to make a recommendation, Sergeant until you folks have had a chance to discuss this and have made up your mind about what you want to do."

"Well I know what I would recommend, Captain, I say we fight the bastards. I am not going to run and hide from a fight and I certainly do not want to become a prisoner; I do not trust 'em. We all know what happened last year at the James River crossing."

Captain McCaffrey and Lieutenant Roberts stood mute listening for nearly a half hour as one after another trooper expressed his views, asked their sergeants or fellow troopers a question or offered a recommendation. However, all of them leaned toward Sergeant Tommy Sanders' viewpoint. They wished for an end to this bloody mess; but if it was necessary to kill more enemy soldiers to accomplish that objective, they wanted to get on with it and end it here.

"What about it, Captain?" Lieutenant Roberts asked, interrupting the troopers' discussions. "It looks like we fight. Running or surrender is not an option."

"You men have made me proud to be a member of the Sixteenth Battalion," James responded quietly. "It has been an honor to serve with you these last three months, and you have made it much easier to make this decision. Fight, it will be and it begins now." With their captain's very animated expression and obvious show of enthusiastic support for his troops' decision several lighthearted comments were exchanged between a number of those present with one trooper calling out, "Let's finish these Reb bastards off and go home."

CHAPTER 15

THE LAST BATTLE

"Mark, do we have the Reb cannon assembled and ready to use?" Captain McCaffrey asked of Lieutenant Roberts.

"Yes, Sir, all ten, they are loaded with grapeshot. Those guns would have killed many of General Grant's people when he breaks through the Reb defensives at Petersburg and moves on Richmond. They would come right by here."

"You're right, Mark, but now they are in our hands, let's use them to set up our own little surprise for Major Atkinson and his boys."

"What do you have in mind, Captain?"

"The Reb Major will undoubtedly want another look at our defenses before he returns to his troops; so we shall give him a quick peek. Let's set up a mock scene that indicates we are preparing a defensive position to protect our force from the Rebs pulling back from Petersburg. However, we also want to leave the impression that we are not professional soldiers. If you look at our hair, beards and uniforms we are one sorry looking bunch; no one would mistake us for professional soldiers and right now, that is what I want the Rebs to think.

"We do not have much time; I want you to reposition most of those guns. Set up one or two of them pointed at the Rebs south of us. You will need time to do that; to give you that time I will take two men and we will go down and offer whatever assistance Lieutenant Sanford may need in caring for his wounded. When we return we will again escort our Reb major back through our defensive positions on the way to his own people. In the process we shall allow him a quick glimpse of what we are up to here."

"That's pretty risky, Captain," Lieutenant Roberts cautioned.

"Yes, I realize that, but I want him to return to his troops thinking that we are preparing to repulse an attack from the Rebs moving on us from the South. Those people are in no position to attack anyone. If I am not mistaken, there has to be three or four hundred wounded Confederate troops in that column. They are escorted by no more than two or three dozen soldiers and most of those, if not all are the walking wounded. The rest of the column is composed of mostly Negro medical aide people and muleskinners. We shall not have to worry about them. Our Reb Major here will be our biggest problem. He is chaffing at the bit to kill us all. He appears to be a veteran of many battles and if I were he, I would plan on coming after us at daybreak tomorrow. He may even risk a nighttime attack in order to take out the people that killed so many of his fellow soldiers. He also knows that we destroyed their rail system here in Virginia, and burned their supplies. He is not a very happy soldier."

"I agree with you, Captain," Roberts responded. "I think of all the Reb soldiers that we have come up against this man may be the most difficult one we have dealt with; he is probably a West Point graduate. He appears to be heads and shoulders above the average Reb officer. Ever since entering our lines, even while you were talking to him, he was continually scanning the deployment of our men. I think he is a dangerous son of a bitch."

"I do too, Mark; so let's get our newly acquired guns deployed leaving only one or two to cover the North Ridge with the rest of them either partially disassembled, or set to repulse an expected assault from the Reb column coming in from the South. Give me an hour or two at most and then I shall bring him back through our lines and send him on his way. Do whatever else you can think of to ally his suspicions about our readiness. Those are experienced cavalry troops down there, but they can only come at us from the North or South; the East and West ridges are too steep for a mount. You know horse soldiers better than I do, but I don't think they will dismount and climb up here."

"That would be my guess too, Captain. They might send a scout or two around the hill, but one of our snipers at either end of the ridge could take them out."

"Then let's get at it, Mark. You know what we have to do. I will go down and check on our Major to see how the Rebs are progressing with their wounded. They have enough mounts to take all of them off the ridge; they should be able to join up with the Confederate column coming in from the south."

"I take it you're a West Point man, Major." James said to Major Atkinson as the two men watched the Confederate wounded being d south.

"Is it that obvious, Captain?" The Confederate officer responded casting a quizzical glance at Captain McCaffrey.

"Well you certainly are a trained professional soldier, Sir. I assumed that was the case."

"Yes, I was a member of the United States Cavalry, West Point Class of Fifty-Eight until my country turned against my people." He responded quietly. "And you, Captain, you are not even an American; Irish, I take it you're probably a newly arrived immigrant from 'The Old Sod,' as they call it here." He laughed bitterly. "What did my former government promise you if you took up arms against my fellow Americans?"

"My brothers and I were not really given a choice, Major; if we had not joined the American Army we would have been conscripted. However, even that would have been a gift considering the Brits ran us out of our own country. Nevertheless, I have no regrets; this war will be over soon and the President has promised all who serve shall be eligible to acquire, and eventually own a piece of this great country. We are very fortunate, for had we stayed in Ireland we would be forever beholding to the Queen and her henchmen."

"Well, you believe what you want, Captain, but Lincoln's promise that anyone who takes up arms against the Confederacy shall be honored by all Americans is false. General Lee shall see to it that that promise will never materialize for your boys. Before another year passes The Confederacy will defeat him and his hired mercenaries; from then on, The South shall be free to manage our own affairs."

"Then I guess we shall just have to leave it at that, Major, for from my perspective, the South has lost the war, and you may agree with me if you look through my glass and examine your troops coming in from the south. Look closely at the column." James said, handing his spyglass off to the Confederate officer. "Those are your wounded warriors retreating from Petersburg; it appears to me Major that General Grant has broken through the siege at Petersburg and your army is, or shall soon be in full retreat. There will be no stopping him now, he will roll over any troop that stands in his way and capture Richmond, and your General Lee before the month is over."

Taking his adversary's glass, the man stood frozen in place, examining in the distance the huge column of wounded Confederate soldiers moving slowly toward Richmond.

After a few minutes, James commented quietly, "It is time Major, my men and I shall see you back to your troops. After what we have witnessed here today I would hope that you would agree with me that there is no reason why any more men, Blue or Grey should die today on this hilltop here in Virginia."

"I shall consider what you are suggesting; nevertheless, we are still at war with the North, Captain. Your commanders sent you and your men into Virginia to destroy the Army of the Confederacy and our way of life; and I must agree that you have had some success in those endeavors. However, we are not a defeated people. We shall fight to the bitter end if necessary for what we believe."

The four men mounted and rode in silence back to the top of this small hill in Virginia; as they broke out onto the summit James noted the Confederate officer's quick, yet subtle scrutiny of the positioning and readiness of his Union troopers and their guns. In a quick review, James found that Lieutenant Roberts had staged a quite plausible scenario of a very few, clearly undisciplined group of Union cavalry soldiers in unkempt and ragged uniforms. The filthy uniforms, long hair, beards, and obvious lack of personal hygiene were not something that a West Point graduate would expect to find in a professional soldier. This unwholesome combination and apparent haphazard deployment of Union soldiers was exactly the impression Lieutenant Roberts and Captain McCaffrey had hoped would happen.

For all practical purposes, the Union Army Regiment he was looking at was an untrained and undisciplined lot. From all appearances, they knew little or nothing of the care, maintenance, and operation of the Confederate Army's sixteen-pound cannon seized from Reb troops. Only three appeared to be operational and in position, one at the North ridge of the Union encampment and two along the Southern ridge. Seven others, with limbers still attached appeared abandoned in a small grove of trees and brush at the Western edge of the plateau. Nearby six or eight Union soldiers, wrapped in their blankets, lay on the ground and appeared to be sound asleep while a sergeant and two troopers played cards onboard one of the ammunition limbers.

Without comment, Major Atkinson, and Captain McCaffrey accompanied by the trooper escort rode their mounts through the Union campsite to the North slope leading down toward the Confederate troop encampment.

"I hope that you take into consideration what we spoke of this morning, Major," James offered quietly. "I firmly believe this war shall be over within a month or two at most; and as officers we have an obligation to bring it to an end as soon as possible and in doing so, save as many of our people as we can."

"I do not disagree with you entirely, Captain, but we shall see how this plays out. Nevertheless, I do thank you for your compassion toward our wounded. Because of your kindness, some of them shall make it out of here alive." Then without further comment and only a wave of his riding crop, the man made his way down the North end of this small hill en route to rejoin his troops in the distance.

By the time James returned to the top of the plateau, Lieutenant Robert's men had already redeployed the Reb cannon and everyman was busy setting up secure defensive positions near the North and South ridges. Roberts positioned six of the eighteen-pounders, loaded with grapeshot to the Northern ridge, concealing them behind a camouflage of cut brush and tree limbs. Along the South ridge, should the Rebs circle the hill and mount an assault from that direction they moved two of the eighteen-pounders to cover that approach. Then planning for the prospect of being overrun by Reb cavalry, he positioned the now empty limbers with the two remaining guns and their ammunition in a circle at the center of the clearing, in effect providing a small, yet somewhat secure 'last stand' enclosure.

"You are way ahead of me, Mark; you have obviously gone through this before. I would never have thought of this last stand business. How do you see this playing out?"

"As you know, Captain, I am not a West Point man, but I was fortunate in that my commanding officer at Gettysburg was and he taught us this type of defensive posturing. It worked for us there. Unfortunately he was killed in the battle that followed, but he was a great tactician and a fine man; he saved our hides on more than one occasion."

"So this is our last stand, here behind these limbers, is that how this works?"

"More or less, Captain, but we have more to do. Cavalrymen are a lazy group; they do not like to walk anywhere so they will come at us fast. The mere sight of a hundred or more mounted soldiers coming toward you at a full gallop is a frightening thing to behold and some men will run for cover. Yet the mount is often smarter than the soldier on his back. The horse will not charge into or over a physical barrier unless the animal is competent that it can go over or through the barrier without getting hurt. They will shy away from the wheels on these limbers, and if we bring all those mules inside this wagon-wheel barrier and kill them inside this circle, that will be our shield.

"An enemy soldier, lying on the ground with a rifle, behind a wagon wheel and a dead animal as large as one of these mules can be a formidable challenge for a foot soldier; but a cavalryman's odds of surviving such an attack are next to none unless they completely overrun us. This will help to even the odds. For hundreds of years armies around the world have used their wagons, mules, or oxen to help them survive, and when the battle was over, they wind up eating the animal's carcass.

"I figure there are upwards of 100 hundred Reb cavalrymen down there that will come charging up that hill tomorrow morning at daybreak. If that happens we may be able to take out twenty-five to thirty percent of them with the Reb guns loaded with grapeshot. However, after that we will have to pull back here; the limbers and our dead mules will be our 'Ace in the Hole.'"

"And our snipers, Lieutenant, where do you plan on placing those folks?"

"I thought I would leave that up to you, Sir," Lieutenant Roberts responded with a wry grin. "However, since you are asking, I would position two men at the East and West end of this ridge and a couple of teams on the South ridge, just in case."

"Just in case of what, Lieutenant? What do you expect?"

"Well, you know me, Captain," he responded, smiling, "I am regular army and one thing I learned early on in my career was that if something can go wrong, it usually happens when you least expect it. That Reb Major is no dummy; he knows that we know more about the Confederacy's strengths and weaknesses than anyone else in Mr. Lincoln's Army. We have been operating in Reb territory for nearly three months now and our people have intimate knowledge about the capabilities of the Confederate Army and of their willingness to continue to wage war against their fellow citizens. Therefore, that man will not want any of our people to get back to our own lines.

"In addition, if you will pardon me for saying so, he thinks you are just another green Irishman, probably a farmer's kid, a long way from home and out of your element. He will push you hard. He will try to surprise you and probably attack at dawn, hoping to catch this bunch of Yankee soldiers sleeping. Do not forget, if he trained at West Point, after dark he will be sending a recon party out to encircle us to make sure none of us leave here alive. He probably believes that by noon tomorrow we shall either be dead or a prisoner of the Confederate Army."

It was near dawn before the sniper teams on the Eastern ridge reported hearing what they believed was the movement of troops below the ridge; the noise indicated there were several mounts involved. When Lieutenant Roberts asked the question, how many? The teams were not sure, but as the noise continued for several minutes they thought there had to be at least a dozen mounts involved.

"What do you think, Captain?" Lieutenant Roberts asked as the two soldiers walked back across the small clearing toward their men on the South side of this small plateau.

"Well, Sergeant Davis and I scouted the entire Western edge of this plateau when we first came here and it is not only steep, it is heavily wooded; if I were that Reb commander I would not choose to send mounted troops up that route. They would make one hell'u've a racket coming through that brush. So let's pull our snipers in from that post and reassign them here along with five more troopers."

"That will short us on our battery at the North ridge."

"I know that, Mark, but I do not see an alternative, do you?"

"No Sir, I do not. Maybe a couple of them should be our boys with the Reb sniper rifles. They may be able to pick off some of the Rebs before they get within range of our picket line."

"Good thought, Mark; I want to go back and recheck our gun crews on the North ridge. If we are going to survive Major Atkinson's move on us from the North, our men will have to remain hidden until the Rebs are within firing range. If I were to guess what he might do, it would be to dismount about half a mile out and approach the ridge on foot. When they got within two-hundred yards or so, I would expect them to mount quietly and charge us at a full gallop. If I am right, we should be able to get two rounds off; particularly if our snipers hold their fire until after our first volley, then I want our snipers to open up on the Reb troops at the rear of the column. That should create enough confusion to allow us that extra minute we shall need to reload our Reb cannon. If this breeze continues, it's bound to clear some of the smoke away so the target should remain visible."

"A word of caution, if I may Captain."

"Certainly, Mark. Do you have a problem with what I am suggesting?"

"No, but you and I both talked to that Reb officer and I think we know him for what he is. He is a trained professional; he is a cold fish and has been around for a long time. I would expect that he will have a troop or two held in reserve in case his initial attack fails. I would suggest that we be ready for the unexpected; possibly an attack from the East or the West if his first assault fails."

"I will have to think about that, Mark. However, with our limited number of men I am not sure that even if we knew how the Rebs were coming after us we would have the answer to that problem. We will just have to see how this all unfolds. I want you to take charge here and of our snipers on the East Ridge. If we are forced to retreat you will hear the ruckus and you will know it is time to pull your men in, but you will have to move fast."

"Will do, Captain, good luck."

"God speed, Mark; I think our people shall do just fine."

James next sat down with Sergeant Gayle Davis and the two unassigned snipers to discuss what their role would be in the defense of this small bit of land in Central Virginia. Although usually well concealed, the smoke from a snipers' weapon often gave away their position; when that happened, retaliatory vengence from enemy troops was often swift and deadly.

"Sergeant Davis will position you fellows on the opposite ends of this ridge; once in position, I want you two to hold your fire until the Rebs charge our men. I would expect them to come in quietly on foot leading their mounts until they are right close to our boys on the ridge; then mount and charge up the hill. The only place a mount can come through this heavy brush and onto the ridge is where our guns are located, however knowing the Rebs as we do, I would expect them to hold a full troop in reserve at the base of the hill. That is where I want you to concentrate your fire. I was there yesterday with the Reb commander; it is probably a distance of six- to eight-hundred yards, but if you cannot take down a rider at that distance, kill his horse. If the Rebs come after you, pull back and join us behind those limbers and the Rebs' dead mules."

"Any questions?" He asked, addressing the two men quietly. "If not, good luck," he added, knowing these two young American soldiers would need more than luck to survive this latest assignment. When the men left, James, taking advantage of the moonlight walked over to examine the area around the dismantled limbers and dead animals now laid out in a circle in the center of this small hilltop clearing. The stench of death emanating from the animals, something he first encountered at the Rapidan River crossing those many months ago, brought back that terrible fear of the unknown that every combat soldier encounters. The smell was not yet pervasive, but he knew that were his men forced to use the dead animals as shields for long, it could wreak havoc upon their abilities to function as a viable fighting force.

Fortunately, Lieutenant Roberts had seen to it that a quantity of food, water, and ammunition was safely stored away in two of the limber boxes nearby, one on each end of the enclosure. Roberts had thought of everything, yet James was aware of that which could seal their fate on this hilltop in Confederate territory. Should the Rebs overrun them and seize their mounts, now tethered in the brush nearby there would be no escape.

"There is movement down there, Captain," Sergeant Davis commented quietly. "It looks like you read that Reb Major's mind; he is coming in as quiet as he can but the sound of a shod hoof on a rock is a dead giveaway. A few more of those and he will convince himself that it is time to mount and charge in here. He will be swinging that big bright saber his fellow West Point graduates probably gave him when he joined the 'Cause.' I just hope one of us gets to shoot that bastard before he gets too close."

"It's nearly daylight, Sergeant, pass the word hold your fire; wait for my command. I want them in close, it is our only chance."

"You heard the Captain," Sergeant Davis said. "Pass the word. Hold your fire; we want the secessionists right up here under your nose. So hold until the Captain gives the order; he wants to smell those bastards before we kill 'em. Hold your fire," he repeated, quietly. Within a moment or two, Union troops all along the ridgeline heard the Confederate commander's order shouted out to men. "At a gallop, attack! Attack!"

As James predicted, the Reb commander had brought his troops forward on foot to the base of this small hill arriving at daybreak where upon command, they quickly mounted and charged up the hillside. They came in two waves of twenty or more each stretching across the narrow slop leading to the top of the hill. Walking back and forth behind the concealed cannon, James called out for all to hear, "Hold your fire, hold your fire, and let them come in." When the lead riders came within two-hundred yards, he yelled, "Stand by," and again, "Stand by." Then at a distance of approximately one-hundred yards, he yelled, "Fire." The result was sudden death and/or catastrophic injury for more than forty Reb cavalrymen and several of their mounts scattered across the hillside. The harsh squealing of injured horses and the moaning of dying men soon followed.

"Reload," James called out to his n, having to repeat the order twice as the men appeared awestruck at the death and destruction they had just unleashed upon their opponent. Sergeant Davis intervening quickly grabbed hold of several of his men redirecting their attention to the needs of the group. The need was urgent for Reb cavalrymen were reforming for what appeared to be another cavalry assault upon the entrenched Union troops. However, by now the Reb Commander having lost nearly a quarter of his men in this single attack, apparently thought better of sending what was left of his troops in a second assault against the guns arrayed s the ridge above. Yet the battle was far from over; the guns of the Union snipers positioned on either end of the North ridge continued to ring-out across the hillside forcing Reb troops at the base of the hill to seek cover. In addition, a staccato of rifle and cannon fire continued the south ridge.

A short time later, as the firing on both sides of this narrow plateau ended, James rushed across the narrow field to the south ridge.

"What is it, Mark?" He shouted as he approached his lieutenant now checking on the welfare of his men deployed along the edges of this small.

"They are all down, Captain. Holy Christ, I cannot imagine what they were thinking of; about twenty of them rode up here as if they expected all of us to be asleep. It was like shooting fish in a barrel. We fired grapeshot from both cannons then took down the rest of them with our rifles. Only two of them got away; I called a ceasefire on our people. I thought it best that those two take the word back to their command that this was not an open route into our fortification."

"Good work, Mark. Our plan worked out fine, for now. However, I would expect that Major Atkinson is not finished with us. He held the majority of his troops in reserve so they will be coming back at us before this day is over. Hold your position here until we see what he is up to."

" your fire," Sergeant Davis called out from the North ridge. "Hold your fire," he repeated. "White flag, Captain; four men coming up the hill, Sir. It looks like they want to retrieve their wounded."

"Keep your men undercover, Sergeant. I don't want them to see just how few men we have up here, for they will be back."

When the Reb troops appeared to be satisfied their opponent would not fire on them they called out for stretcher-bearers; three two-man teams quickly responded. Over the next hour, they attended to the wounded then carried seven men off the battlefield disappearing from view into the heavy brush at the base of the hill.

"At least the Major's a humane son of a bitch, Captain," Sergeant Davis commented quietly. "He takes care of his own."

"I hope that is what he had in mind, Sergeant and it wasn't to get a head count on the number of people we really have here. We shall wait and see what he does with those poor bastards on the south slope. If he thinks for a moment that he has succeeded I am sure he will mount another attack right here, right about now."

"Riders coming up from the South," Lieutenant Roberts called out, where two men, one holding a white flag slowly approached the South ridge. When the Reb soldiers reached the first of their fallen comrades below the South ridge, they dismounted and began checking the fifteen or more bodies scattered across the hillside. They found one man alive tended to his wounds, and then hoisted him aboard one of the mounts. One of the soldiers mounted behind him, and then holding the wounded man upright, the three Rebs left the battlefield.

With an unexpected stillness, settling over the two battlefields even Captain McCaffrey's two snipers withheld their fire; there were no longer any Confederate soldiers within the Union soldiers' killing range.

"What do you think, Mark? Will they be back?" James asked his lieutenant.

"You can bet on that, Captain; will have to kill that Reb Major before any of his men retreat," Lieutenant Roberts responded quietly. "I think he trained those cavalry boys; they aren't about to leave this part of Virginia until they get even. They got their ass kicked by our people this morning. So, my guess is they will be back with a vengeance."

"I have to agree with you, Mark; we not only took out about one-third of Major Atkinson's force today, but we injured their pride. Yet if I were to guess, they will not come at us while mounted. I think they will wait until after dark then try to infiltrate our position and move on us with sabers and fixed bayonets."

"That would be my guess, also, Captain, because they out number us by at least three to one. If that happens the odds are in their favor."

"Then let's even the odds a little in our favor."

"What do you suggest, Sir?" Lieutenant Roberts asked somewhat incredulously.

"You have already started to build our defensive position, Mark; I want you to send our men out and recover the rifles, and water canteens the Reb cavalrymen left behind when they retreated this morning. We shall need those guns and water; then I want you to move everything we have inside our fort."

"Our fort, I don't understand Captain, you're not suggesting those dead mules and a few wagon wheels are a fort?"

"That's exactly what I am suggesting, Lieutenant." James responded with a wry grin. "In many respects, men are like animals, Mark. If they can avoid it, they will not step down on a wagon wheel lying flat on the ground for fear of entangling a foot. They will either step around it, or move it out of the way. With both limbers and gun c, we have forty wagon wheels at our disposal. roll them back to our dead mule redoubt and dismantle them. The wheels and the dead mules shall be the walls of our fort. Atkinson's men will have to come through or over them to get to our people."

"Sweet Jesus, Captain," Lieutenant Roberts responded. "Do you really believe it will work?"

"I know it will work. I trust our people, so let us get it done. Between us, we shall beat that Reb Major son of a bitch. We shall kill him, or send him and regiment home to their mothers."

Within the hour, the wheels from the gun carriages, and limbers ringed the "Dead Mule Fort," as one of the men so aptly named this improvised fortification. No one doubted but that the enemy's mounts would shy away from this makeshift barrier. Yet, Captain McCaffrey knew he needed to convince the men that the barrier would hamper the swift advance of enemy infantry long enough for the defenders to prevail.

"Thanks to the Rebs we now have plenty of ammunition, spare guns, and food, so join me please gentlemen," James said, "we need to reassure our men that we can hold on here until Grants' men come to our rescue. The Rebs appear to be in full retreat mode from Petersburg and all we have to do is hold here until we see those uniforms down there in the valley turn from grey to blue."

Accompanied by Lieutenant Roberts, Sergeants Gayle Davis, Brad Adams, Leon Andrews, Mike Addison, Brian Murphy, and Tommy Sanders they quickly contacted their men outside the perimeter of this improvised fort. However, as they made their rounds they were surprised to learn that there was no sign of Major Atkinson's men. Nor had the pickets seen any Rebs since they retreated into the heavy brush in the valley below.

"The foliage is too heavy, Captain. We have not seen hide, nor hair of the Rebs since they skedaddled out of here," one of the troopers offered. "But they are still down there. Every once in awhile we can see a small dust cloud apparently raised by horses on the move, but the brush is too thick. The only thing we can tell you for sure is that they are still there. They have not left the area; to do so they would have to come out in the open in that clearing, so they are still with us."

Later that afternoon, Captain McCaffrey called for another meeting with Lieutenant Roberts and his sergeants. "Let's kick this around a bit, Gentlemen," he said. "If there is no sign of a Reb troop movement by dark, let's reposition our men inside our makeshift fort; I think Reb will come at us again after dark. I would expect two things to happen. First, I think the Reb commander will attack in the middle of the night and secondly, knowing that man, if I were he, I would come at us on foot this time, sabers, and bayonets at the ready. Tell me where I am wrong, Gentlemen." James added quietly, "all of you fellows have had more experience in this than I have. What about it, Mark?"

"I agree with you, Captain," Lieutenant Roberts responded very straightforwardly. "However, I would still keep two men posted on the Westside of this hill. In addition, the Rebs know that from up here we cannot see a troop movement should they come at us from the east because of the heavy growth of brush and timber along the entire face of the hill. However, to play it safe, I would still leave two men there on post."

"And you, Sergeant Davis, what would you do?"

"I agree with the Lieutenant, Sir, besides the Reb commander has nearly a battalion of troops at his disposal and they could finish us off if they come at us in force from two different directions. Then if they put a half dozen battery of cannon on this godforsaken hilltop, they could hold off a whole army for days. I do not expect that to happen, but we should be in a position to warn our people that are moving on Richmond just what to expect. Maybe, traveling at night a couple of our men could get a message through to our troops."

"I don't disagree with you Sergeant. What about you, Sergeant Adams, what would you do?" James asked, addressing this veteran army man with nearly three years field experience, including two of the failed assaults upon the breastworks at Petersburg.

"I agree with Sergeant Davis, Sir." Sergeant Adams responded quietly. "Just think of what we have accomplished up here with less than a full troop. I believe that we can hold this Reb major off; it is obvious that he does not want to commit his entire force, because of that old army saying, 'He who fights and runs away, may live to fight another day.' Major Atkinson knows that eventually he is going to come up against General Grant and the Army of the Potomac and he certainly does not want his people all killed off by a Union cavalry force one-quarter the size of his before that grand day arrives. I think he is a contemptuous son of a bitch and looks upon us as a fly in his breakfast oatmeal, so to speak."

"I think we are all in agreement with you on that, Sergeant." James responded smiling. "What about you, Sergeant Andrews. How do you feel about this?"

"You know me, Captain," he smiled, "I am a farmer at heart and I have a farm and a family at home that I am anxious to see, the sooner the better. I agree with everything you fellows are suggesting; let's hope they come tonight and we finish these bastards off tonight."

His captain smiled at the man's response for in his free time, family and farm were all that Sergeant Andrews ever talked about. Yet every man there knew that the Sergeant was one of the most experienced and reliable soldiers in the regiment. He never complained and he looked after his men and tried to do what was in the best interest of his country.

"And you, Sergeant Addison, do you think we can survive this, or is there something the rest of us may have overlooked?"

"No, Captain, you are doing fine and I agree with what I have heard and seen here today; let's take this arrogant, traitorous West Point bastard down when he comes at us tonight. He will come; you can see it in his eyes and by his attitude toward not only you, Captain, but toward all of us. I believe he is completely contemptuous of all of us and after his embarrassing defeat this morning, and that is what it was, he will come after us to kill us. In his present mental state he will make more mistakes, we need to take advantage of that kind of enemy combatant whenever he makes those mistakes. However, I am sure even he knows his continuing presence here is a huge mistake.

"When you think about it, we are no threat to the Confederacy; we are tired, we are short of food, ammunition, water and most of all manpower. What do we have here? This morning, I counted thirty-two tired, hungry, and worn out soldiers that are no longer a major threat to the Confederacy. If he were thinking rationally, he would know that by what he saw here yesterday. He should be gathering up his troop and riding south to help his fellow soldiers that are retreating from Petersburg. With that new British rifle they have, he could leave a dozen riflemen behind and ride off into the sunset, so to speak to help that poor bunch of bastards that the Confederacy has left hanging out to dry in Petersburg. Ten or twelve men with that British weapon could pin us down on this damn hill until hell freezes over.

"However, this Rebel Major is not thinking rationally; he wants to kill us because we embarrassed him and his command. We must watch him closely, because he will make a mistake and we can be the better for it."

While Sergeant Addison was talking, James was watching the man's contemporaries as they nodded their heads in complete agreement with their fellow trooper's comments. When the man finished talking, he sat down on an ammunition box, brought out his pipe, calmly filled it with tobacco from a pouch, and lit it. His captain had to suppress a smile, for he knew everything the man said was true; James thought just how lucky he was to have such men in his command.

Then turning to Sergeants Brian Murphy and Tommy Sanders he said, "Sergeant Murphy, you and I and Sergeant Sanders discussed this earlier, and I take it you still agree with everything these men have said here."

"Yes, Sir, I believe we are." Murphy responded, quietly, while Sergeant Sanders merely nodded affirmatively.

"You both have been very vocal on your support of what we are doing and I appreciate that. We can hold on here and rejoin our units when General Grant's people come through. With the Rebs retreating in the numbers that we see, we should be out of here in a few days or a week at most. If we are all in agreement, then gentlemen," James added, "let's get back to work and prepare a little late night reception party for our Confederate friends."

As expected, shortly before daylight Major Atkinson's men arrived on foot at the Northern ridge of the Union entrenchment. They came in quietly and although not heard were clearly visible to the alert defenders on this cloud clear moonlit night. There appeared to be at least two troops of nearly thirty or forty men each. When they came over the ridge they paused, apparently surprised that the cannon that tore so many of their fellow troopers apart just two days earlier, were gone. Still they continued on, moving quietly toward the Union troops concealed behind their makeshift fortification of limbers, wagon wheels, and dead animals. By this time, the stench from the dead mules permeated the air around them and apparently became an immediate distraction for the Reb soldiers, for they paused again, now less than one hundred yards out from the Union's improvised fort. The distraction worked in favor of the Union soldiers.

"Fire, fire at will," Captain McCaffrey called out loudly; even before his last words were spoken his men unleashed a hail of musket balls that tore into the Reb troops arrayed across this small glade. Many of the rebel troopers in the front ranks fell mortally wounded from this withering barrage of musket fire. Yet it soon became obvious that the Rebs had learned a bitter lesson in their first violent engagement with these Union veterans. Most of the attacking force dropped to the ground and took cover, but the cries and moans from the wounded and dying indicated the Rebs suffered a severe loss of troops in this second attempt to take out these Union soldiers inside their makeshift fort.

However, before Captain McCaffrey realized that the assault upon his men from the North was merely a diversion, Major Atkinson led a charge of nearly fifty cavalrymen racing in from the South. Unseen by Union troopers the Confederate cavalry had circled the Western approach of the hill and when the battle began quickly dashed across the south face of this small hill. Yet, Atkinson, with all his military training and vast experience made two tactical errors. First, he was not aware of, or ignored the possibility that his enemy had recovered dozens of rifles and thousands of rounds of ammunition lost or abandoned by his Confederate troops in their first attack upon these Federal soldiers. The man led his troops in a wild charge against these same Union troops, who were now armed with two, and in some cases, three loaded rifles all of whom were well prepared to use them. In addition, the Reb Major apparently never expected, nor was he prepared for the reaction of his troopers' mounts when they encountered the downed wagon-wheel fortification.

When the lead horses suddenly stopped short or turned unexpectedly to avoid a downed wagon wheel the Reb soldier aboard was unprepared and unable to fire his weapon. This sudden and unexpected consternation and confusion of the attacking force worked to the advantage of the Union soldiers.

"Fire your weapons," Captain McCaffrey called out, while he and Lieutenant Roberts moved swiftly from man to man, continuing to encourage each of them. The soldiers, with rifle propped up over a dead animal took deadly aim at the mounted troops coming at them from the south. Their first volley took down more than a score of Confederate troops and two or three others close by who suddenly found themselves unseated from their horse from the violent reaction of their mount to a downed wagon wheel.

Seven days later as General Grant's main forces, accompanied by Brigadier General Charles Murray, moved into the area, Colonel Dan Jackson of the New York Volunteers Battalion rode in fast from the North accompanied by an aide.

"What is it, Colonel?" General Murray asked of the cavalry officer. The two men saluted the general, and then Colonel Jackson reported. "I believe we have found your men, General, or what's left of them; about three miles out. You can see the top of that small hill there in the distance. There are only about a dozen or so still alive, all wounded. My people found them this morning, their commanding officer, is Captain McCaffrey and he is alive, but in poor shape. I sent a rider for our ambulance corps people; it looks like your people gave a good account of themselves."

Within the hour, Colonel Jackson led General Murray and a small

contingent of staff officers up the south approach to the top of what one Union cavalry officer later named Cemetery Ridge. There were dead bodies everywhere, both man and animal and no way to escape the stench of decaying flesh.

"My God, Colonel! What happened here? General Murray exclaimed.

"From what I understand, General, the Sixteenth was coming home. As you know they have been out here for nearly three months, but the Rebs cut them off before they could get back to our lines. Trapped back here, they built themselves what one of their own called "Dead Mule Fort." You will see where he got the name when we get in there; there was no brick or mortar, but there were lots of dead mules and wagon wheels. It looks like it worked, because they killed nearly two-hundred Rebs here. It looks like a slaughter house up there."

Colonel Jackson led General Murray and their staffs onto and across the top of the small hill where the Union's Sixteenth Battalion fought and held off a superior force of Confederate militia for more than ten days. No one spoke until one of General Murray's staff members upon reaching the center of the clearing on top of this small hill, blurted out. "Jesus Christ, this is terrible."

Dismounting, General Murray walked over to one of Colonel Jackson's ambulance attendants busily bandaging a wounded trooper, then on to another.

"Are there only two of you here to assist these wounded?" He asked the second man, who from his uniform markings indicated he was army cook.

"Yes, Sir, General; we rode on ahead, it will take some time to get our wagons in. The Ambulance Corps was about ten miles out when Colonel Jackson's men came for us. We just brought what we could carry, but our ambulances should be here within an hour or two. As you could see, Sir, in the retreat, the Rebs cut trees and moved a lot of rock to block General Grant's Army."

"I understand, Son." General Murray responded quietly. "Do what you can."

"Where will I find Captain McCaffrey?" He asked of the man.

"Over there, Sir, on the ridge. He is badly injured, but I think he will make it if we can get him out of here and to a doctor within a day or two. He said he did not want to die here with these damn mules." The man smiled.

"Hello Captain." General Murray said quietly when he came across James lying alongside several other wounded men, including half a dozen Confederate soldiers.

"Hello, General, it is nice to see you again; I am sorry I cannot get up. One of those Reb officers lying over there got me pretty good with his saber."

"Where did he get you, James?" General Murray asked solicitously.

"He came up behind me, Sir while I was dealing with one of his men. I think I killed the Reb soldier, but the officer was good, he sliced me across the back and when I turned around, he tried to gut me. He damn near succeeded too. That young medical aide man said my men told him they tied these bandages around me tight enough to stop the bleeding and saved my life, General; but I have lost track of time, I think it happened yesterday."

"Actually James, I understand that was about three days ago, but we will get you out of here today. You just hold on."

"What about my men, Sir. How many survived? Our Reb boys came after us every day; they were a persistent bunch. I will give them that. However, I think we killed most of their officers and sergeants, but I really don't know how many of our people survived, do you know, Sir?" James asked.

"No, I am afraid I do not know the answer to that, but I shall get that information and come back. You rest now; we will get some transportation in here shortly and move you and your men to the railhead at Petersburg."

Before General Murray finished speaking, thanks to the laudanum administered by the army cook, Captain James McCaffrey, Commander of the U. S. Army's Sixtieth Cavalry Battalion had drifted off to sleep.

"Wake up, Jimmy," the familiar feminine voice said, yet when he awoke, he was not sure but what he had been dreaming. He did however recognize his nurse and then standing next to her, he saw Colleen Haggerty dressed in the formal attire of an army nurse. "Hello Jimmy," she said quietly, while smiling broadly. "How do you feel?"

James did not reply to her question, he merely reached out to her, grabbed her hand, and pulled her close.

Three days later James and Coleen Haggerty were enjoying lunch in the atrium of the Army hospital in Washington, D.C. he in a wheelchair and she sitting beside him, dressed in the attire of a nurses' uniform.

"Did you hear the good news Jimmy? The war is over. Yesterday, General Grant accepted Lee's surrender at the Appomattox Court House in Virginia. That's not far from where you were wounded."

"What is the date today, Colleen?"

"April 10, 1865, Jimmy, why do you ask?"

"All those years, Colleen, all those lives lost and you and I separated, for these past two years; and my brother Michael lost an arm and Joseph, a prisoner of the Reb Army. God help us, what a waste."

"Well it won't be long now, Jimmy until we are all back together; Michael is coming into town next week, and he is going to bring the boys with him. That will be Thomas and Daniel's first train ride; a trip they shall never forget. Maybe by that time we will have heard from Joseph; our wounded and our men captured by the Rebs have priority going home on whatever trains that are available."

"I am anxious to talk to Michael, Colleen; he wrote last year saying he had already filled out the paperwork necessary to file for homestead rights for all five of us. Each one will have to file a formal application, but if it goes through we could have our own farm by this time next year."

"Where will we be living, Jimmy if we are accepted?"

"I don't know, in the Northwest someplace, I guess; Michael said we should shoot for someplace in Southern Minnesota, or in the Dakotas. He says it is rather remote and wild, but there is a lot of good farmland in that part of the country."

It was midmorning when Nurse Ann Anderson returned to her patient's room at the army hospital in Washington. Smiling as usual, she came rushing in and exclaimed excitedly, "You have a visitor this morning, Captain. He tells me you two know each other." Then turning to the guest, exclaimed. Here is your man, General. I will bring you gentlemen some coffee."

"Thank you, Nurse," General Murray replied, then turning to James, greeted his subordinate officer with a warm handshake and a few kind words. "You look much better today than when I last saw you, James. What was it your man called that place, Dead Mule Fort; is that right?" He smiled.

"Yes Sir, a God-awful name for a horrendous place."

"Yes it truly was a horrible place, in all my years in the army I have never seen such a sight, nearly two hundred men, and boys gone." The man said shaking his head. "What a terrible waste. The burial details worked up there for nearly two weeks; someday Congress will probably recognize it as a National cemetery. However, James that is not why I came here; first the good news, I talked to your doctors and they tell me you have recovered to the point that they can release you next week. The Army, will of course see to it that you are on a train headed for New York when that happens.

"In addition, I am here to offer you a commission in the Regular Army if you would re-up, as our boys call it, for four more years. The Army is expanding its operations in the territories in the West and we have a need for young, capable officers to lead the way. These are exciting times for this young country of ours, James, but for those seeking free land the vastness of the West is such that as our people move into the territories they are demanding, and rightly so, that the Army assure their safety."

"That is quite an honor, Sir." James responded quietly. However, he was surprised, yet pleased that the American Army would make such an offer to someone of his background. He was not only poorly educated and ill trained, but a foreign national, one who had spent time in prison for assaulting a member of the Queen's militia.

"The Army does not need your answer today. However, I believe that you could have a great future in the United States Army, Captain. I say that after talking to Lieutenant Roberts and your two surviving sergeants, Adams and Davis and some of your men. Your exemplary service to this country during these terrible times puts you in a class of service personnel that has and will continue, I believe bring great credit to our country. That is why I recommended you to my superiors."

"I am humbled by your kind words, General." James responded quietly. "I certainly shall consider the Army's offer and I thank you for what you have done for me. I suppose I am still a farm kid at heart, but I shall consider the offer and discuss it with my family and let you know."

"Good." General Murray responded, apparently satisfied that his subordinate would respond favorably to the Army's offer. "However, I have both good and bad news to pass onto you. First, several of your wounded men from the Sixteenth taken prisoner by the Rebs, have been located and are homeward bound as we speak, or are now recovering from their wounds in a local hospital. I have their names here." He said, handing a copy of his report to James. "I understand from Lieutenant Roberts that one of these young fellows is a close relative of yours, Trooper Kevin Malone. As you will note on that report he is one of those released from Mower hospital in Philadelphia and is on his way home to New York.

"However, I am sorry, I did not mention this earlier because it has not been confirmed, yet, but we have unverified reports that your younger brother Joseph died in a Confederate prisoner of war camp known as Andersonville, in the State of Georgia. Our people are in the prison now investigating the deaths of hundreds of Union soldiers that died there. We have arrested the prison commandant; but it may be months before we are able to identify the remains of all our people buried there."

"Oh, no Sweet Jesus, what did they die from, General?" James asked, shaking his head.

"We do not know the answer to that question; I am sure that some may have died from their wounds or disease, but the early indications are that many may have died from malnutrition and some may have been murdered. The Army is investigating the circumstances and we should have an answer on that before the end of the month. The prison warden was a Confederate Army Major by the name of Heinrich Wirz, and he and his entire staff are in Army custody. I believe we should have more information on this before the end of the month. "I am sorry, Captain to be the one to tell you this, but keep in mind all of the dead have not been identified, but the early reports from Georgia indicate the death toll from that prison alone is beyond comprehension."

It was a beautiful warm day in July 1866 when James and Michael McCaffrey met the westbound train from New York as it pulled into the railroad station in Winona, Minnesota. On board were over two-hundred passengers including more than one-hundred and fifty former members of the United States Army on their way to Saint Paul and Minneapolis. Most of the military men, recently released from hospitals in New York City still wore their blue uniform, but the war was over; their wounds were healing and it was time to go home. Within the group, were two young brothers Thomas and Daniel McCaffrey, and Mrs. James Robert (Colleen) McCaffrey along with James and Colleen's two-year-old son, John. Trooper Kevin Malone also accompanied the younger members of the McCaffrey family from New York. The following morning the McCaffrey/Malone party of seven, the state's latest immigrants, boarded a buckboard, and wagon and struck out for their newly acquired homesteads on Irish Ridge Road near the village of Rushford, in Houston County, Minnesota. The two younger boys joined their cousin Kevin in the wagon that carried household goods, farm equipment, and lumber for their new homes.

CPSIA information can be obtained at www.ICGtesting.com
Printed in the USA
BVOW080623011212
306978BV00001B/32/P

9 781627 092555